For Your glory, Lord

ACKNOWLEDGMENTS

I LOVE TEAM SPORTS—football, basketball, hockey—because they illustrate that it takes every player working their position with their A game to produce a win. Writing a novel is no different, and the more books I write, the more it becomes clear to me that producing a powerful story takes a team of people.

I am deeply grateful to the following "teammates" who brought their A game to this story:

David Warren, who knows exactly the right questions to ask me as I build my plot. I expect his books to line my own shelves someday!

Noah Warren, who is always willing to listen, brainstorm, and give me great ideas. Another storycrafter in the family!

Peter Warren, who taught me that letting go of your superstar is a good thing, even if it's painful. You make me proud of the man you've become.

Sarah Warren, who helps others find their dreams, supports mine, and lifts her voice to inspire us all. Thank you for being exactly you.

Andrew Warren, for sharing the journey with me. It had to be you.

Rachel Hauck, for helping me craft every scene, every moment, every sentence. You are my secret weapon. (Okay, not so secret anymore!)

Elaine Clampitt (aka P. J. Ryley), who knows her hockey. Thank you for fielding my endless hockey questions and tapping into your network of coaches and family to find me exactly the scenarios that would work. All mistakes are mine alone—but I am grateful for your knowledge, patience, and insights! I can't wait to read *your* hockey books!

Alena Tauriainen, dear friend and amazing writer. Thank you for giving me God's words for the unseen. You are a treasure to me.

A special shout-out to Diane Stoddard and her amazing book club friends for their brainstorming. Thank you for "Jace"!

Karen Watson, for her enthusiasm and dedication to this series. Thank you for investing in these stories.

Stephanie Broene, for her ideas and insights that make every book stronger.

Sarah Mason, for making me sound good. You work magic with every mess I send you.

The readers of the Christiansen series, especially the SMW Fiction launch team. Thank you for praying, encouraging, and sharing my books with such enthusiasm. I'm blessed by your generous support.

Steve Laube. Amazing agent. Pastor at heart. Dear friend. The Calm One. Thank you.

Jesus—of course—who shows me that I can trust Him with every single book to untangle it and reveal new truths that set me free. Thank You for fresh grace and for teaching me to delight in You too.

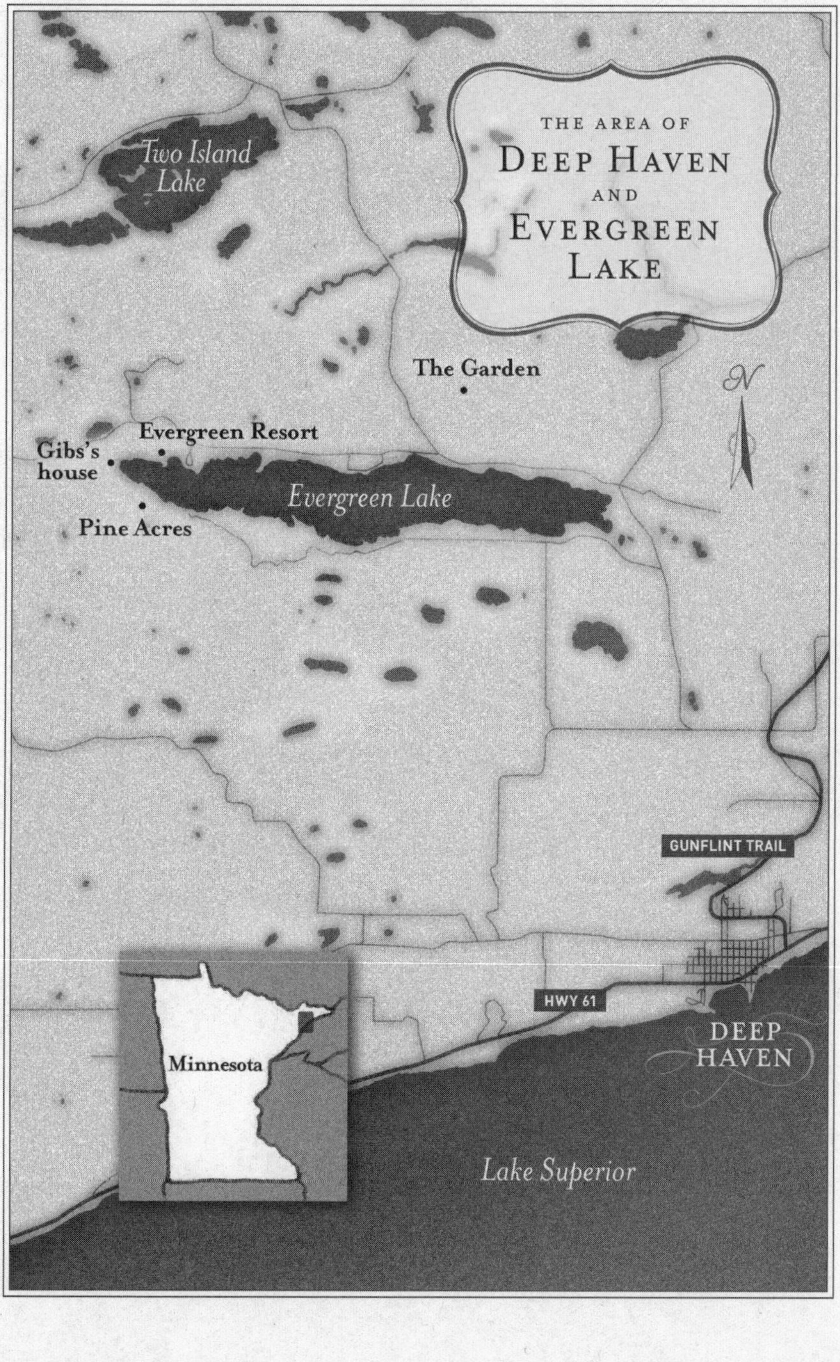

THE AREA OF
DEEP HAVEN
AND
EVERGREEN LAKE

Two Island Lake

The Garden

Evergreen Resort

Gibs's house

Evergreen Lake

Pine Acres

N

GUNFLINT TRAIL

Minnesota

HWY 61

DEEP HAVEN

Lake Superior

My dearest Eden,

I suppose, someday, after I have passed, you will dig through my journals and happen upon this letter. I pray that it finds you as amazed at the life God has gifted to you as I was when I discovered a daughter in my arms.

In truth, Eden, I thought you would be a son. In fact, I feared having a daughter because I didn't know how to parent a little girl. Not yet, having only Darek for experience. I quickly discovered not only that you were not Darek, but that having a daughter would become one of my greatest delights. I saw myself in your curiosity, and when, at the tender age of two, you climbed onto my lap holding a book and said, "Read to me, Mommy," I knew you would be special.

While Darek stretched my faith, you, Daughter, taught me to enjoy the journey. I relished the moments when you would wrap your arms around my neck, meet my eyes, and tell me a story. "Mommy, wait until you hear what happened to me today." Whether it was the discovery of a bird's nest in the yard or one of your siblings (probably Casper) digging themselves into trouble, you knew how to rivet me to your every word.

You've always been a storyteller, Eden, but more than that, you can look at someone and find the good in them, something to believe in. And if you can't see it, you simply create it. You give your heart wholly to the ones you love, are fiercely loyal, and don't know how to let them fail. More, you blame yourself when they disappoint you.

This may be your biggest challenge. Because I fear that for all your ability to see the potential in others, you're blind to it in yourself. You see your value only in what you bring to your siblings, your friends, your world, instead of believing in the remarkable woman you are, in the person God created.

For some reason, you believe you are a failure. Only you believe this. And only you can change that belief.

As a child, you would spend your free time buried in a book, hiding in other worlds, other lives. I believe you are still hiding. That it feels easier, perhaps, to believe you aren't as amazing as your siblings. But you don't have to change the world to earn the applause of heaven.

My prayer for you is that you would believe God has a good story for you, too. Because only then will you truly hear the voice of God, telling you what He told me years ago when He put you in my arms:

"I will take delight in her. I will rejoice over her with joyful songs" (Zephaniah 3:17).

I pray you hear the delight of your Savior, Daughter, as we have been delighted with you.

Always,
Your mother

CHAPTER I

EDEN CHRISTIANSEN'S CAREER, her love life—even her car battery, for that matter—were frozen stiffer than the late-January cold snap encasing the city of Minneapolis. Icy black snow edged the curbs, and the pavement glistened with salty grit. Breath hung between every conversation.

The blue-mercury windchill blew through the thin-paned windows of Stub and Herbs, a restaurant located a couple blocks from the offices of her old haunt, the *Minnesota Daily* newspaper.

Back then, Eden would wander over for a burger after a week of reporting and find her cohorts gathered around a fresh issue of the paper, newsprint on their fingers, arguing over the editorials and who had landed stories above the fold.

Back then, it was only a matter of time before she found the perfect story to earn herself a real byline. Back then, her career was hot. Her future was hot.

Maybe even *she* was hot.

Now, in a white down parka, a lime-green woolen cap, and a pair of sensible black UGGs, she looked like she might be dressed for dogsledding through the streets of Minneapolis.

No wonder her date's attention fell upon the gaggle of under-dressed college girls who pushed through the frosted doors, young and hopeful as they thumbed the screens of their iPhones. They walked up to the long wooden bar and waved to friends seated at a nearby table. Overhead, a flat-screen TV spilled out the news; another showed ESPN highlights.

She should have tried harder to put a little flame into dinner with Russell. What if his out-of-the-blue invitation was the real thing and had nothing at all to do with her brother Owen's recent trade from the Minnesota Wild to the new Blue Ox NHL franchise in St. Paul?

"I really like the blue cheese burger," Eden said, perusing the menu.

Now Russell's attention was on the ESPN coverage of the NHL stats.

Shoot. She closed the menu.

Who was she kidding? This wasn't a real date. She could see right through Russell Hays. Until last week, the mortician had spoken to her three times a week as if she were his personal secretary rather than the obits clerk. Then Owen Christiansen became the new superstar face of the Blue Ox, and out of nowhere, Russell had sent her an e-mail. Not the classiest way to ask for a date, but he'd followed it up with a Starbucks-coffee-and-malted-milk-ball gift basket.

And he wasn't exactly hard on the eyes. Funeral directors should be short, squirrelly men with comb-overs and bad polyester suits. But Russell didn't fit that description either.

Tonight he looked like a man who actually meant his words: *I know we haven't really gotten to know each other over the past four years, but would you like to have dinner?* He wore a pedestrian red sweater, but with his brown eyes and short, curly blond hair, he could be a sort of L.L.Bean model. He wasn't a big man—probably slimmer than she and just as tall—but he had wide shoulders, and he'd held the door open for her and crooked his elbow out as if she needed help trekking to the restaurant over the icy parking lot despite her sturdy UGGs.

The thought counted.

However, the sparks stopped there. They'd shared a sum total of four sentences since sitting down, and now—

"Last week's snowstorm sure kept us busy," Russell said over the top of his own menu.

Really? They were going to talk shop?

Fine. She'd play along. At least it would take her mind off the trouble Owen might be finding tonight.

Oh, she'd promised herself she wouldn't think about Owen. Behind the wheel of his new Dodge Charger. Not an expensive car, but Owen's first, and it had gone straight to his 3.1-million-dollar-contract brain.

"My parents said that it would be a banner year for them if they were finished rebuilding their resort," Eden offered.

Russell closed the menu, and his gaze caught on a couple college jocks who sauntered in and took seats on the black leather stools at the bar. One wore a U of MN sweatshirt. Hockey players. Eden could tell by their long hair brushing their collars, the hint of beard, the swagger. Minnesota grew hockey players like pine trees—big, strong, and everywhere.

Russell turned his attention back to her. "Rebuilding?"

"Our resort on Evergreen Lake burned last summer during the wildfires."

"I'm so sorry." He fiddled with his watch, a Rolex, gold with a blue face. It looked similar to one that Owen wore, but his had been a Blue Ox signing gift.

"It's okay. My brother Darek is heading up the rebuild. It's going to be spectacular: a sauna, a playground, Wi-Fi, and brand-new cabins—all state-of-the-art."

"Sounds spectacular indeed." Russell leaned back in the chair, gave her a smile. It touched his eyes. "I didn't know you were from northern Minnesota."

He said it as if he meant it. As if he hadn't scanned the player pages online and picked out every tidbit of information about Owen. Eden cupped her coffee mug, warming her hands. "I went to the University of Minnesota, and I live here, but I go home as often as I can."

Which, for the last four years, hadn't been often, with Owen's junior hockey schedule and then his development years with the Wild's AHL franchise. He'd finally seen real ice time last year, and she'd acted as the Christiansen family emissary to his games. That, and maybe more, she could admit.

The door opened and another coed strutted in, bringing the chill with her, looking smart and successful, a messenger bag over her shoulder, a golden future ahead of her. Eden glanced at her and then to Russell, expecting his gaze to be on the brunette.

Nope. He was smiling at her. "I've been wanting to ask you out since that first day you answered the phone at the obits desk."

He had?

"I'm sorry it's taken so long." He had nice teeth, a warm smile. So he wasn't a big guy—she liked guys who seemed approachable. Human.

Maybe he wasn't here trying to score tickets to a Blue Ox game. Eden shrugged her parka off her shoulders.

"When Charlotte mentioned she had hired an obits clerk, I guess I thought it would be some temp girl—"

"I'm a reporter."

Oh, why had she corrected him? She wanted to snatch it back. In truth, Eden was more a classified sales representative selling line ads, not a reporter. And she was starting to think she never would be, after four years at the obits desk. When she'd taken the job at the *Star Trib*, she'd thought it might be a jumping-off place to opportunities in metro or even features.

But it was just a matter of time. The right story. Someday, she would land on the front page with her own byline, be just as amazing as her siblings.

"Of course. Reporter." Russell looked uncomfortable now, shifting in his chair. His gaze drifted up to the television over the bar. The news was on—the sports report. No hockey game tonight or she would have had other plans.

"I wrote a couple pieces for the remembrance section last year."

"I remember," he said. "Your editor was in Hawaii."

Yes. Which meant Eden had gotten her big opportunity to follow her gut on a couple of the notices that came across her desk. One led to a two-column article on a World War II veteran. The other on a librarian who'd founded a tiny mobile library.

So it wasn't riveting, life-changing news. *Your articles belong in*

Ladies' Home Journal, *not on the front page.* The metro editor's words still stung a year later.

"I remember that piece you did on Mr. McFarland," Russell went on. "The family had it framed at their father's funeral."

"I just took your information and rewrote it. It's not really reporting. But I won't be in obits forever. You'll see."

In her pocket, Eden's phone vibrated. She fished it out in time to see Owen's number moved to missed calls. She noted two previous ones and frowned.

"Everything okay?"

She nodded but put the phone on the table. "Owen's at a private birthday bash for one of the Blue Ox players tonight. I'm not sure why he's calling me."

"Do you need to go?"

"Of course not. He's a big boy."

"Whose birthday is it?"

"Jace Jacobsen, the team captain." Also known as the team troublemaker and Owen's idol. She had a secret hunch that Owen's eagerness to join the Blue Ox had something to do with skating with his childhood hero.

She considered Russell for a moment. "I got an invitation . . . I guess we can go if you want."

He stared at her for a second; then a half smile hitched up his face. "No . . ."

She didn't mean to let out an audible sigh, but there it was, and along with it died more of her suspicions that he might be just like every other man she'd dated in the past year.

Truth was, she could wear a bag over her face, shuffle around in burlap, and she'd still have a lineup of dates. But a real relationship with a man who might like her? Listen to her? Really see her, instead of walking by her in a crowd? Choose her over hockey? Right. One mention of Owen and she knew what her date wanted: box seats.

But maybe Russell was different.

"Unless you want to go," he finished.

She forced a smile. Shook her head.

"You know, you should try to get a job as a sports reporter. With your connections, you could get exclusives with the Blue Ox."

"Yeah, our sports guy would like that. What—I'm going to walk into the locker room after the game, interview the players as they peel off their gear? No thanks."

A frown touched his eyes.

"Sorry." Maybe it wasn't all Owen's fault she couldn't get beyond date number one. She simply walked into every relationship with her dukes up. No wonder she spent most nights alone, reading or writing in her journal.

Her phone vibrated again. She glanced at it, then at Russell.

"Take it," he said.

Eden answered. Heard music, then yelling. "Hello?"

Nothing. She raised her voice. "Owen?"

More music, then, "Eden, is this you?"

She could barely make out the voice. "Yeah!" Oops, she was yelling on her side.

"It's Kalen. I . . . I shouldn't be calling, but I think you need to get over here."

Kalen Boomer, the Blue Ox goalie. As young and talented as Owen, and the other blond, blue-eyed star of the team. "What? Why do you have Owen's phone?"

"He's had a little too much to drink."

What kind of prank were they pulling on her? "Very funny, Kalen. Ha-ha." She was pulling the phone away to hang up when she heard it.

Singing. A warped version of Elvis, loud and boisterous and . . . Oh no. She put the phone to her ear. "Seriously?"

"He won't listen to us. Maybe if you come down here, you can get him home."

"I'll be right there." She pressed End.

"What's the matter?" Russell said.

She shook her head, still staring at her phone. For three years Owen had managed to keep his nose clean, show up early for practice, and become a stellar rookie player. Now, two months into his new contract, she almost didn't recognize her kid brother. It seemed that Owen's fame had rushed straight to his naive, small-town head.

"Can I drive you somewhere?" Russell had leaned forward, his kind brown eyes full of concern.

She took a breath. "Would you mind driving me to Sammy's Bar and Grill in St. Paul?"

"Sure." He reached for his leather jacket.

Eden led the way out to the parking lot, the wind not touching the anger heating her cheeks. What if Owen got in trouble or drove drunk? His name would appear on the front pages—or at least the police reports—and destroy everything he'd worked for.

Russell opened the door for her, and she climbed into his Nissan Pathfinder, hitting the seat heater button as he got in and started the car. "Thank you."

"It's no problem."

"It's that stupid Jace Jacobsen," Eden said, staring out the window. "He's a bad influence on Owen. Almost since Owen could lace up his skates, he's wanted to be like J-Hammer."

"And why not? The guy is a beast on the ice," Russell said, turning onto the highway. "And he didn't get his reputation for nothing. In his rookie season, he got in a fight with a legend and flattened him. And when he joined the Blue Ox three years ago, he launched the franchise. There's a reason he's the captain—he totally intimidates the other team, and with him on the ice, players know to back off. Last season alone he had 310 penalty minutes. You should be glad he's there to protect Owen from dirty hits."

"Are you a Blue Ox fan?"

"I live in Minnesota," Russell said. "I also root for the Wild, the Vikings, the Timberwolves, the Gophers, the Bulldogs, and the Twins."

"Right," she said. "Of course. I'm probably overreacting about Owen."

"J-Hammer's rep isn't just on the ice, and we all know it. He's dated more supermodels than a man has a right to, and last year, he made *Hockey Today*'s twenty-five most eligible bachelors."

If you liked scars and the dark expression of a man who lived for violence. At least he had all his teeth. Still, she wasn't impressed by the so-called team captain, and the last thing she wanted was Owen turning out like J-Hammer Jacobsen.

Except what was she going to do? Drag Owen home by his ear? He wasn't ten; he didn't need her babysitting him.

Or did he?

They cut off the highway, toward downtown St. Paul, and Russell drove like he knew the way. Sammy's was a sports bar located on University, near the arena where the Blue Ox played and practiced. As Russell parked his car, she spotted Owen's Charger in the lot across the street.

"Thanks, Russell," she said as she climbed out.

"Do you need any help?" he asked, and she tested his words for sincerity. Not that he didn't want to help her, but maybe . . . Oh, see, she read into everything.

He was a nice guy. And she'd blown this entire date. "I'm just going to get him and drive him home. We'll be fine."

Russell didn't protest, only nodded. "Sorry about this."

"You're sorry? I'm the one who is sorry. I'll make it up to you. Maybe get us a couple tickets to a game."

He shrugged. "Can I call you again?"

"Yes, please."

The cold swirled around her legs and up the back of her jacket as she stood there letting a perfectly good date drive away. She swallowed, regret like a boulder in her throat. This was a bad idea—the last person Owen would want to see was his big sister.

It didn't matter. Apparently tonight someone had to watch his back, and that's what sisters did. Eden turned up her collar and marched across the street.

Sammy's Bar and Grill hosted one of the largest collections of hockey paraphernalia in Minnesota. The pub had been an old shipping warehouse, its grand windows now lit up with neon beer signs. Inside the brick-and-mortar interior, promo posters, signed pictures, goalie equipment, and framed team sweaters plastered the walls. Flat screens hung from the ceiling and were tucked into every nook, televising games from around the nation.

The owner, Sam Newton, had played eight seasons as a Minnesota Wild defenseman before being sidelined by a hip injury. Now he lived out the action from behind the long oak bar.

As Eden entered, the sweaty heat and raucous noise flooded over her. The odors of too much cologne, fried foods, and chaos tightened her stomach. Bodies pushed against each other, and she heard the chanting even as she stood at the entrance and looked over the crowd.

"Fight! Fight!"

Perfect. She plowed through the onlookers, ignoring the protests, dreading what she heard—the familiar sounds of men hitting each other, laughing, huffing as they tumbled onto the floor.

She reached the edge of the brawl and there he was. Owen, power forward for the St. Paul Blue Ox, with a button ripped off his shirt, his long hair over his face, his nose bleeding, writhing as right wing Maxwell Sharpe caught him in a headlock.

"Tap out!" Max yelled.

Oh no. Eden watched as Owen flipped him over, broke free, and found his feet, his eyes too bright.

"Eden!" Kalen caught her arm. "We have to get him out of here." He wore a black Blue Ox T-shirt, a plastic lei around his neck. And he had cut his hair into what looked like a Mohawk. Nice.

"Where are his keys?"

"Jace took them. He's at the bar. I'll get Owen's coat."

She turned and found the hulking form of Jace "J-Hammer" Jacobsen sitting at the bar.

Someone, probably the Blue Ox PR department, had tamed the beast, at least for tonight, dressing him up like a gentleman in a pair of black wool pants and a silver dress shirt with the sleeves rolled up over his strong, sculpted forearms. Up close, she could admit that—for others—he possessed a raw-edged, almost-dangerous allure that might have the ability to steal a girl's breath. Maybe *Hockey Today* magazine hadn't been completely wrong about putting him in its lineup. His dark, curly hair fell in tangles behind his ears, as if groomed by a fierce wind, and he'd close-trimmed his dark beard. His fitted dress shirt only accentuated all his cut muscle and brawn, but she knew he had the finesse of a skater, smooth and liquid on blades. And his eyes—blue as ice—yes, they could look right through a gal, send a shiver through her.

But Eden was immune to Mr. J-Trouble and his apparently lethal smile. Because she wasn't a rink bunny, wasn't a crazed fan. Wasn't dazzled by the star power of one of hockey's top enforcers. She was family, thank you, here for one reason only.

Owen.

Yes, Eden was made of ice, and Trouble hadn't a prayer of thawing her anger. She marched up to Jace. "Nice birthday bash. If Owen gets in trouble and kicked back down to the AHL, it's on you."

"Hey!" Jace turned, looking backhanded.

But she didn't plan on listening to his lame excuses. "You're the team captain. Who else is supposed to watch Owen's back?"

He rebounded fast. "Are you kidding me? You're not his mother or his trainer. He's just blowing off steam. Trust me. Your brother can watch his own back."

"Really? This is watching his own back?" She gestured at Owen, who had grabbed an eager girl, begun to slow dance. If that's what she could call it. "Who gave him alcohol, anyway?"

"Seriously?"

"He's underage. He doesn't turn twenty-one for three months." Jace raised a brow at that.

"Yeah, that's right. And if he makes the papers—"

But Jace's eyes tracked past her, to the door.

Eden followed his gaze. And the terrible roaring of anger inside stopped on the burly image of Ramsey Butler, Blue Ox manager, sliding into a booth.

Kalen appeared with Owen's coat. "You distract Butler, Eden, and we'll get Owen out the back."

She gaped at him. "*Distract* him? How?"

Jace slid off the stool, towering nearly a foot over her. "Flirt with him or something."

Flirt—oh, for crying out loud. "Fine. Get Owen to his car, but don't let him drive." She shrugged out of her coat and draped it over the chair. Flirt. Right . . . But what choice did she have? As long as this was the one and only time. Besides, truth was, she would do anything to protect Owen's future.

She looked like a mortician in her black pants and white blouse, but maybe Butler wouldn't notice. She still had game, right? After all, tonight she'd had a date.

Maybe she was hotter than she thought. Eden put a little sashay into her walk, feeling stupid, but making her way to the booth. "Hello there, Mr. Butler. Nice to see you tonight."

In his midforties, Butler had his own reputation to manage—the kind that traded players midseason and fired those who embarrassed the newborn franchise. Eden managed not to look behind her as she stood at the booth, blocking his view of Owen. She added a smile, propped a hand on her hip. Tried to look . . . flirty.

He looked up from where he perused the menu. "I'll take an appetizer basket of curly fries and a Guinness on tap."

She stilled. "Huh?"

"And what are your specials?"

So much for flirting. She glanced at the chalkboard over the bar. "Uh, fish-and-chips and a cheddar bratwurst?"

"I'll just have the bacon cheeseburger."

"Good choice. How do you want that done?" Now she glanced

back and saw Kalen with his arm over Owen, directing him through the kitchen entrance.

"Rare. And bring out some of Sam's special mayo sauce."

"You got it."

She quick-walked to the bar, grabbed her parka, and stepped out into the frigid cold.

Jace stood over Owen, barring him from opening his car door. Owen put up a meager fight, then let Kalen maneuver him to the passenger seat and buckle him in.

Eden shook her head and held out her hand. Jace set the keys in it.

She closed her hand around them. "I know I should say thanks, but frankly, you should do better. You're some *captain*. Is this how you take care of your players? Or maybe this is what you want— for them to all turn out like *you*." Then she opened the door and climbed in, ignoring Jace's glare. "Owen, what were you—?"

Owen turned to her, wearing a green expression. And then his double-mushroom-and-Swiss cheeseburger, curly fries, and about a fifth of whiskey mixed with the sweet syrup of Coke landed on her lap.

"Thanks for coming to get me, Sis."

The Blue Ox should never have named him captain when they signed him. Not with his reputation, and not with his career sinking into a slow, deep freeze.

Jace sat at the end of the bar in a darkened corner near the kitchen, counting the seconds on his Rolex, waiting until the last of the rink bunnies threw in the towel and headed home.

Alone.

They sat at the far end of the bar, a trio of danger—blonde, redhead, brunette. He knew the blonde, the one wearing a white jacket with fur at the neck, unzipped enough to show exactly what he might be turning down. Haylee. She worked for the local ESPN outfit and seemed to possess a sort of hockey radar that put her at every private Blue Ox shindig. She cut a glance his direction and he looked away.

No thank you. The society page could find other fodder for gossip—especially with the flock of good-looking rookies in search of some new fans.

Not only that, but he'd given up any hope of a real relationship with a woman, the kind who might see past the headlines, the limelight, to the truth inside.

No woman wanted to stick around for that.

Hockey players were trouble. He'd started to believe that his rookie year, and Owen Christiansen fed every stereotype. Still, Owen could handle himself despite tonight's debacle. He almost felt sorry for the kid after facing his sister in the parking lot.

Eden Christiansen. He'd heard her name a few times in the locker room, seen her hovering after practice. Pretty, with her blonde hair. Not tall, a little curvy. Okay, so he'd noticed her more than once, entertained the thought of talking to her. However, after today, he'd keep his distance from Owen's personal bodyguard and overprotective representative of the Christiansen clan.

Except she had probably saved them all from a scandalous front-page appearance.

Still, he hadn't deserved the parting shot. He'd stared into those green eyes, ripe with fury, and for a second he'd felt punched, right in his solar plexus. He didn't have a hope of defending himself against the likes of Eden Christiansen. Not with her opinion of him already cemented.

At the end of the bar, Haylee slid off her stool and started toward him, her hands tucked into her pockets, her hips swaying.

His head hammered right behind his eyes, his pulse beating in his throat. Oh, this wouldn't be pretty.

"Take this. I'll get rid of Haylee." Sam set a coffee cup in front of him, rich with the smell of leaves and twigs. "It's Holy Tea. Good for migraines. Try it." He slid a couple of tablets across the counter too, then rounded the bar, intercepting Haylee. He wasn't a big guy like Jace, but everyone loved Sam Newton. It probably had something to do with his nine-year-old princess, Maddy, who had surely inherited her father's smile. But the girlie grace had been all Mia.

Jace had half expected Maddy to appear tonight for his party, but that wouldn't be appropriate for a little girl. Besides, with the frigid cold, she needed to be safe at home, tucked into bed.

Jace watched out of the corner of his eye as his best friend worked his magic and herded Haylee and her girlfriends out the door.

A different night, a different birthday, and Jace could easily imagine a much more exciting ending to this bash. Exciting, but not necessarily satisfying.

And wasn't that, really, the epitaph of his entire career? His entire life? Exciting, but not satisfying.

He swallowed the pain relievers and sipped them down with the tea. It tasted like tree bark, but he expected that.

Sam came back around the bar, began to clean up the napkins and dirty glasses. "You should be at home with a cold compress."

Jace nested his face in his hands, rubbing at the tension around his temples. "And miss all this fun?"

"Right. I know this was the last thing you wanted to do." Sam received a tray of glasses and other debris from Nellie. "You can punch out, Nell. Thanks for staying."

In her early forties, Nellie wore her years around her eyes. The rest of her looked about twenty-five and still reliving the eighties, in her tight black T-shirt and painted-on jeans, her bottle-red hair piled onto her head. She untied her apron and walked by Jace, squeezing his shoulder. "Happy birthday, J."

Bar glasses clinked together as Sam loaded the dishwasher. He moved the tables back into place from Owen's tussle, then grabbed a rag off the counter to wipe tabletops before putting up the chairs.

"We both know this party had nothing to do with me. Nothing. It was simply a PR gimmick to stir ticket sales. And a subtle reminder that the only thing I am to them is a name. As long as I drop my gloves and can hit harder than the other guy, I'm still an asset."

"Wow, I thought this was a birthday party, not a pity party," Sam said.

Jace winced. So maybe Sam had a point. He had a life many men would envy. Things could be worse—he could have Sam's problems.

"Sorry. I hate all these PR appearances. I'm a hockey player, or at least, I was. Until everyone started worrying about my head."

"Apparently it's not as hard as we all thought."

Jace laughed, then looked up at Sam when he didn't. Oh. He'd thought the man was kidding.

"It's not a laughing matter, Jace. One more concussion and your career is over. Maybe even your life. It's not worth it. You should have taken this opportunity to announce your retirement."

Jace stared at Sam. "I don't have anything else."

"That's not true."

"Really?" The migraine more than anger made his voice sharp. "I've been playing hockey since I was six. Professionally since I turned eighteen. It's all I have, especially after—"

"Jace." Sam's voice quieted. "I'm just saying that you're only thirty-two. And you're at the end of your contract. You need to face the truth that the Blue Ox might not renew it."

Thanks, Sam.

"Life isn't over, friend. At your age, I was getting married. Starting a family."

And look how that turned out. But Jace didn't say it.

"I know. Sorry. It's just this headache." In fact, Jace might be bleeding from his ears, the pain nearly able to send him to his knees. He needed to climb into bed with that cold pack Sam suggested. "I don't think your Holy Tea is working."

"Get outta here. I can handle this."

"No. You need to get home to Maddy."

"Maddy's sleeping upstairs."

He frowned at Sam.

Sam lifted a shoulder. "The police finally arrived with the eviction notice. I cleaned up the apartment over the bar—it's actually really nice."

Nice? Jace had sacked out upstairs a few times, back in the day, and *nice* seemed a stretch, with the rusty toilet and tub, the stench of the sewer bleeding through the sink, giving the tiny apartment the odor of vagrancy. Sam probably slept on the dilapidated pull-out in the tiny living room. He couldn't even imagine Maddy's four-poster bed crammed into the dingy bedroom.

"Dude, when did this happen? Where was I?"

"I didn't tell you, Jace. You've helped so much, and I'm grateful for it. But the truth is, I gotta figure this out on my own." His eyes tracked past Jace. "What are you doing up?"

Jace's gaze followed Sam's and landed on Maddy, hidden in the shadows just inside the hallway to the bathrooms. She emerged, her golden-brown hair falling from two haphazard braids, one of the flannel sleeves of her purple nightgown pulled over her hand, the lacy edge of the cuff gnawed into a frazzled mess. She held her other hand behind her back.

"I wanted to wish Uncle J. a happy birthday," Maddy said softly.

As Sam took a deep, shuddering breath, Jace could nearly read his mind, cataloging the odors, the bacteria, the chill seeping through the room.

In two long strides, Jace scooped her up, her body the size of a six-year-old's, at best. "Thank you, sweetie." He noticed her bare feet and imagined they might be ice cubes as he set her on the counter. He picked up his jacket and draped it around her.

Sam came around the bar. "Maddy—"

"I made you a card." She produced the card from behind her back, a piece of green construction paper folded in half. On the front, she'd written, *Happy Birth*—

Jace took the card and opened it. Inside, it said, *Day!* On the opposite page, she'd drawn a hockey player: black skates, an over-size blue jersey, a black helmet, stick, and puck. Brown hair curled out from the player's helmet. "Is this me?"

"Uh-huh."

"Are you sure? This guy is better-lookin' than me."

She giggled.

"That's true." Sam looked over his shoulder. "C'mon, Maddy, you need to go back to bed." He reached for his daughter, and she went into his arms.

"My stomach hurts."

"Again?" He pushed her hair away from her face, gave her a kiss on the forehead.

Jace frowned at him, but Sam shook his head, dismissing the question in his eyes.

"Thanks for the card, Maddy," Jace said, playing along. He kissed Maddy on the cheek. "You go back to bed, and I'll make sure you get some rink-side tickets soon."

"Really?"

Sam glared at Jace. "Maybe."

Well, maybe Sam was right. A professional hockey game might not be the right environment for a nine-year-old girl. Especially one on antirejection meds.

And seeing him up close, fists flying as he slammed his opponent into the glass, might be the last thing her delicate heart needed.

"I'd better get her back to bed." Sam handed Jace his coat.

"I'll close up."

"No—"

"Sam," Jace said quietly, using one of Sam's signature voices.

Sam drew in a breath, and in it, Jace saw a glimpse of the worry, the fear, the stress. "Thanks."

"Happy birthday, Uncle Jace." Maddy slid her arms around her daddy's neck, laying her head on his shoulder.

"Thanks, kid."

Jace finished putting up the chairs, then swept and mopped, his migraine subsiding a little in the quiet activity. He finally shut off the lights and locked the door, stepping out into the frigid night.

Happy birthday.

He trekked through a puddle of streetlights into the blackness of the parking lot, hitting his key fob to unlock the doors of his Nissan GT-R. He let the seat warm for a moment before pulling out onto the deserted, icy streets toward his loft in the Lowry Building.

He parked in the heated underground garage and used his key to access the penthouse level.

Maybe the tea had worked—the pain had died to a small, tight knot at the front of his head. Still, after toeing off his shoes in the entryway and shrugging free of his leather jacket, he headed down the dark cherrywood floor to the kitchen, where he dug around in his freezer for a gel pack, then set it on the black granite countertop while he unearthed a kitchen towel.

Wrapping the pack in the towel, he wandered toward the window of his rooftop terrace, now laden with snow, and traced where the impending sunrise had just begun to turn the night to silver. It cast a pallor over his white leather furniture and turned his glass kitchen table into a shiny skating rink.

The place smelled of white oleander, evidence that his housekeeping team had come and gone. He'd have clean sheets and towels in the master, the place freshly dusted, his sinkful of dishes sanitized and neatly replaced. And a stack of dinners waiting in his Sub-Zero freezer.

Dinners for one. Not that he didn't like to cook, but Graham, his agent, insisted that he have something easy when he came home from practice to keep his mind on the game, away from worry.

But really, what else did he have to worry about?

The thought found tentacles, wrapped around his heart. Why hadn't Sam told him he'd finally lost the house? And what about Maddy's upset stomach? Could be something she ate. Or . . .

Jace pressed the cold pack to his forehead. Closed his eyes. Hated the thought of sleep, despite his fatigue.

If Owen gets in trouble and kicked back down to the AHL, it's on you.

He winced, not sure how Eden Christiansen and her venom had found their way back into his head. He could still picture her standing there, dressed like a snowman in her white parka, that long blonde hair spilling out of her hat, green eyes simmering with fury. Her words had sparked something inside, and for a second, he'd been angry enough to tell her off.

But what could he say? Because she was right. Owen *was* headed for trouble. And if he didn't stop it, or try, the kid would turn out just like his hero, Jace Jacobsen.

And Jace didn't wish that tragedy on anyone.

He turned away from the window, climbed the stairs to his bedroom, and flopped down on top of the covers, the cold pack draped over his forehead, his eyes.

Maybe, just tonight, God would let him drift into dark, dreamless oblivion and forget, for a few hours, the man he'd somehow become.

CHAPTER 2

THIRTY-SEVEN MINUTES late for work. Eden tried not to look at the time as she punched in and shed her parka in the employee entrance of the Minneapolis *Star Tribune*. She kept her scarf wound around her neck and pressed her hands against her cold cheeks, hoping to warm them after the biting wind on the walk from the bus stop.

She hadn't had time to wait for the auto service to arrive and jump her old Taurus. And she couldn't take the Charger, not with Owen's dinner still all over the seats and floor mats.

Next time she dragged her inebriated brother out of some hole-in-the-wall, she would make sure he landed on the sofa instead of shuffling into her bedroom and flopping onto her double bed before dropping out cold for the night. She'd have to call him later and make sure he woke up. This morning, he'd been a rock, rolled up in her comforter, and hadn't moved despite her attempts to wake him.

He'd knocked her alarm off the nightstand—if it weren't for her internal clock, she might be snoozing away the morning in her one-bedroom walk-up.

The sky had done nothing to encourage her out of bed, with the gray blanket of frozen doom overhead. Minneapolis in January had all the charm of a mausoleum. Maybe she should head home for the weekend, soak in some of her sister Grace's cooking, trek out into the woods on her snowshoes with Amelia and capture some pictures. Go over the plans for the rebuild with Darek.

But Owen had a game. And she had season tickets. And someone had to be there to root for him, even if lately he seemed to be doing everything to push her away.

She hated being late and ducked her head a little as she walked into the reception area of the obits/classifieds department. Frannie looked up from the desk. She wore her dark hair tucked into a white knit beret. "There's a delivery on your desk," she said, smiling.

"Please let it be coffee," Eden said, knowing, in fact, it could only be a stack of mail-in death notice orders.

"It's better than coffee."

Really?

Eden conceded to a jump in her spirit as she walked down the hall, past the rows of classified-ad takers, back to the obits department. Maybe it was a note from Hal in metro saying he'd read her latest article submission. Or even a note from her editor, Charlotte, asking her to follow up on the two leads that came in yesterday for articles on the remembrance page. Certainly the world would like to know more about Stanley R. Barker, the butcher from south

Minneapolis who made award-winning wild-rice sausage. He'd earned a Purple Heart in Vietnam, had a side job as a magician, and raised champion mastiffs. Eden's brief, quiet investigation had unearthed a story about how he'd served as a volunteer fireman and had pulled three people from a burning house back in the early eighties.

A true hero and one worth illuminating.

She passed by Charlotte's office, but the door was closed, and unfortunately the editor didn't stick her head out to shout Eden's brilliance down the hallway.

Okay, that might be asking too much.

She noticed that Kendra wasn't at her cubicle, although a Caribou Coffee cup sat open by her keyboard, her bag on the floor by her rolling chair.

Eden entered her own cubicle, and her breath caught.

No, not a telephone message from Hal. Or even a scribbled note from Charlotte.

Flowers. Roses—giant red buds and tiny sweetheart buds in white—dressed up in paper, a red ribbon wrapped around the vase, which sat in the middle of her desk on a stack of envelopes and other assorted messages.

"Wow, someone is keeping secrets."

Kendra came up behind her, a lime-green sweater wrapped around her, her auburn hair curly and long down her back. She wore a pair of gray dress pants and a white blouse all pulled together with a bright-pink scarf.

For a second, standing next to Miss Sunshine, Eden felt like a mortician, especially dressed in her black blazer, dark-blue dress pants, a neat but boring white blouse, and black boots, whitened by a spray of drying street salt.

She *looked* like she worked in obits.

Kendra should be writing for the social media department, maybe updating the *Trib*'s Facebook page. She'd started only six months earlier, fresh out of St. Thomas, and already had two remembrance articles with her byline. Eden had no doubt some eager editor would snatch her up before the June interns arrived.

"Who are they from?"

"I have no idea." Eden let her bag slip to the floor, unwound her scarf, and then searched the flowers for an envelope. She found only the plastic stem that should hold the florist card. "Do you see a card? It seems to be missing."

Kendra looked around her. "Nope. Maybe it's a secret admirer."

"I doubt that."

"Did you have a hot date last night?" Kendra had walked into the cubicle and pressed her nose against one of the roses. "Oh, that is a day brightener."

Indeed. Something warm and sweet started in Eden's chest, fanned out into her arms. "Not really. I had a date, but I sort of wrecked it. Owen . . ." She shook her head. "He got *drunk*."

Kendra raised an eyebrow. "Whoa. The golden boy's not quite so golden, huh?"

"It's just a fluke. He's . . . well . . ."

"A hockey player? A rich, handsome, young one, at that?"

"Trust me, this isn't Owen. He's not that kind of player. But I had to cut my date short. Russell drove me to pick him up—"

"*Russell?* Not Russell Hays. From Hays Funeral Services?"

The way she said it, Eden wanted to deny it, but—"Kendra, he's a nice guy. Really nice. And he cleans up well. He was a perfect gentleman." She glanced at the flowers. "Maybe there's potential there."

"If you stop babysitting Owen."

"Listen, I know you think I hover too much, but he's only twenty, and he has a real chance to shine with the Blue Ox. I don't want him to blow it, not after all his work to get here."

She moved the flowers to the side of her desk. Touched the petals. They had to be from Russell, right? "Did I miss the coffee cart?"

"I don't know. I was in Charlotte's office." Kendra returned to her side of the cubicle. "I can't believe it, but she assigned me another story."

"Oh?" Eden picked up the pile of mail-in notices, then reached for her earphones to begin listening to her voice mail messages.

"It's about some sausage maker in Minneapolis who had an award-winning recipe or something. It's sort of a boring story, but at least it's a byline, right?"

Eden stilled. *Breathe.* Just breathe. In. Out. Let it go. "Right." But she glanced at Charlotte's office, her jaw tight. The door was closed.

She could be a team player, right?

Pulling up her chair, she opened her company e-mail, downloading the few obits that had come in, rewording them, and sending them back for proofing.

Breathe.

Then she opened the mail-in forms and entered them, printed confirmations, and sent them with the checks down to accounting.

In. Out. Breathe.

She heard Kendra on the other side in a telephone conversation, probably talking to Gretchen Barker, Stanley's effusive daughter.

Just let it go.

No. She got up, glanced at the flowers, and then headed for Charlotte's door.

It now hung ajar. Eden stood outside, ready to knock as soon as Charlotte finished her call. The woman caught her gaze and held up a finger for Eden to wait.

She'd spent her entire life waiting in the hallway, it seemed, watching other people step into the limelight. And it wasn't that she needed a spotlight, but when, exactly, might it be her turn to become someone who did something amazing?

Frannie intercepted her as she waited. "Eden—I'm so sorry. I found this in the lobby. I think it's from your flowers." She handed her a florist card.

Charlotte hung up the phone. "Eden?"

"Thanks, Frannie," Eden said and pocketed the card. She stepped into Charlotte's office, debated closing the door, and then gently pushed it shut.

Charlotte raised a penciled eyebrow, her computer glasses perched on her nose, her hair freshly darkened, a white silk scarf draped around her shoulders. "Yes?"

Eden swallowed hard, then tempered her tone even as the words emerged from the angry place inside. "Help me understand why you gave the remembrance piece to Kendra instead of me."

Charlotte leaned back in her chair, pushed the glasses up on her head, narrowed her eyes. Then she glanced at the clock. "I went looking for you at 8:16 this morning. Waited until 8:32. Does that answer your question?"

Oh.

"I'm sorry I was late, Charlotte. My car—"

"It's your career, Eden. No one is going to hand it to you. You have to earn it."

Heat crept into Eden's face. "Right. Thank you."

28

Charlotte nodded and replaced her glasses, her attention already on the computer screen.

Eden backed out of the office, wanting to go home, climb into bed, and start her day over.

However . . . She pulled out the florist card and opened the envelope.

Dear Kendra,
Is it too early to ask you to be my valentine?

Love, Nick

Eden froze. Felt a fist closing over her chest.

Yes, it's too early, Nick.

She walked back to her desk, picked up the flowers, and silently brought them to Kendra. Kendra looked up, a frown on her face even as she continued her conversation. Eden handed her the card, not meeting her eyes, and returned to her desk.

Mercifully Kendra said nothing, even after she hung up.

Eden grabbed her phone and dialed Owen. He should be awake by now.

No answer—her call went to voice mail.

Fine.

She managed to avoid Kendra until lunch, when the woman tracked her down in the cafeteria.

"What are you working on?" Kendra slid her orange tray onto the table. It held milk, an apple, and a plastic-wrapped turkey sandwich.

Eden set her pen in the crease of her notebook and shut it. "Trying to choke down this salad." Her phone lay on the table. She hit redial.

Kendra eyed the notebook, then gave her a wry smile. "Sorry about the flowers."

"Forget it."

"You should call him anyway."

"Who?"

"Russell Hays. See if he wants to go out again."

Eden hit End on her phone. "Shoot. He's still not answering."

"Who?"

"Owen. He was in pretty bad shape last night. And he's got practice at two o'clock." She reached for her bag.

"Holy cats, Eden. Seriously—you're obsessed."

"I'm not obsessed. He's my brother."

"He takes up all the available space in your life. And you let him. What happens if he's traded again? Or injured?"

"Don't say that."

"I'm not trying to jinx the ice, but you have to be honest with yourself."

"I'm his big sister."

"Right. Not his trainer. Not his coach, not his mother." She shook her head. "You gotta show a little tough love here."

"I can't let him destroy everything he's worked so hard for."

"What *you've* worked so hard for."

Kendra's words stopped her. Then, "Listen, I'm all caught up, and if anything comes in, call me. I'll be back in an hour or so." Eden picked up her plate to dump it.

"Don't forget your notebook."

Eden shoved it into her bag. The last thing she'd let anyone see were her journal entries about the lives she'd encountered in obits. She didn't know why chronicling the extra information that didn't make it into the obituary column mattered, but the details—like a man's coin collection or dedication to bird-watching—intrigued her. Everyone had a story. And inside everyone was a hero—you just had to dig for it.

Eden hung her bag over her shoulder and headed to the employee entrance, grabbing her jacket and punching out.

She texted Owen while standing in the frozen bus shelter. He didn't answer.

Maybe he did take up too much room in her life right now. But that's what family did for each other. And she refused to let him fail.

She boarded the bus, hand on her phone, but it never vibrated the entire eight stops to her apartment.

Her heart sank at the sight of the Charger outside her building.

Upstairs, the odor of burnt toast filtered out into the hallway, and frustration formed on her lips as she unlocked her door and pushed her way inside. "Owen! You're supposed to be at practice!"

A layer of smoke hovered against the ceiling, the smoke alarm dangling from its electric leads. Crumbs littered her white Formica counter, and as she walked farther into the apartment, the foul odor of old gym socks flooded over her.

What?

"Owen!" She headed straight for the bedroom but found it empty, her bedspread a mess where he'd rolled up in it like a burrito.

She tapped on the bathroom door, but it eased open into darkness.

The smell seemed to emanate from her living room, so she returned.

Then stood there in a sort of stupefied silence looking at the white bundle of laundry the size of a Volkswagen Bug sitting on her coffee table. She approached it, nose curled, and hooked one finger into the drawn-closed hole.

Oh! Owen's clothes, everything that his team trainer didn't wash, apparently. His private workout gear, disgusting socks, sweaty Under Armour, and she didn't want to guess what else was crammed into the bag.

And next to it, on the sofa, in Owen's handwriting:

I had this laundry in my car, but it was starting to get stinky.
Can you wash it, and since you have my keys, get the seats
and mats cleaned too? I'll pick up my ride tomorrow after
practice. Thanks, Sis.

Eden picked up the note. Crumpled it in her hand.
Threw it across the room.

It hit the sliding-glass door, where, outside, the sky had begun to turn a dark gray.

To Jace Jacobsen, skating over a sheet of freshly layered ice felt akin to flying. The arena air freezing his skin and drying his eyes as he flew scraped away the last vestiges of the migraine that had chased him into the morning, even after two cups of full-brew caffeine.

He loved the early hours before practice, when the rink belonged to him. He supposed the habit started in grade school, when he hiked over to the ice shed behind the school to kill hours before evening practice. He'd had nowhere else to go, really, and it gave him time to hone his skating, sharpen his slap shots.

Now he took the ice and stretched out in long glides, skating the length twice, then around again at top speed, the wind in his ears. He grabbed a bucket of pucks, dropped one, and gave it a slap, chasing it toward the net.

He could hear the announcer playing in his mind and reveled in it. *Jacobsen with the breakaway. He's flying down the ice, tucks it in between the pads—scores!*

The puck shot into the net, and Jace rounded the back of it, hands up. Then he fished the puck out and repeated the play on the other end.

He skated a few quick lines, back and forth, working on his stick handling; then he emptied the bucket of pucks on the ice at the blue line.

One by one, he took shots on goal. The sound echoed like rifle fire against the expanse of the arena. He imagined fans, two tiers high, screaming, and smiled.

He made eight goals before he missed, then managed six more.

The Wild had first drafted him because of his blue-line slap shot. Somehow, that fact had faded when he started dropping his gloves. And then his legend took over, and he'd stopped playing hockey and started playing for ticket sales. The Blue Ox picked him up because he made a top-notch enforcer, and he sold seats.

The pucks swam around the net, waiting for him to retrieve them, and he grabbed the bucket.

But not before glancing up at the stands. More out of an old habit than anything—he didn't really expect to see her. After all, she'd been gone for two years now. But for a second, he imagined he saw her there, in her fan gear, wearing a self-knit cap, her cheeks red from the cold. Grinning. And cheering. Always cheering, even when he missed his shots or got ejected from a game.

Mom. His biggest fan. The only person who'd stuck around in his life, through the good, bad, and ugly.

Jace swallowed away the loneliness that could creep up his throat as he gathered the pucks, one by one, shooting the last out to the blue line.

When he skated back, he spied movement near the penalty box. Silly him, his heart skipped, as if fooling him, and then settled when he recognized Graham, his agent.

Only a couple years older than Jace, Graham had signed him when Jace didn't know better, a punk still in high school, playing in the juniors, dreaming he would be a star. He guessed that Graham had shaped him into one, although he could admit, looking back, that he'd become more infamous than famous.

To cement his image off the ice, Graham had practically thrown women at him that first year, helped him purchase his first sports car. Arranged for a handful of magazine shoots.

Sometimes he wondered just what he might have been without Graham's nudging. Without his urging to make a name for himself on the ice, regardless of the cost.

Only, wasn't this what he always wanted?

Jace didn't know anymore. It just felt like, when he looked in the mirror, he'd envisioned a different man looking back. But maybe this was all he'd ever be—and that should be enough. Plenty of guys would give everything they had to have his golden life.

No, he wouldn't complain.

"Hey, Graham," he said, skating close, spraying ice as he stopped. "Did they come back with a new contract?" He tried to keep the worry from his voice, but he was no fool. With two concussions last year that had kept him sidelined for sixteen games and a handful of migraines that took out a dozen more this year, it was enough for the franchise to take another look at his numbers.

He was still an asset, still the one guy who knew how to play old-style, rough-and-bloody hockey. And he still had chops—had managed thirty-two assists and fourteen goals last year. That should count for something.

Graham always looked dressed for the boardroom, today in a silver silk suit, baby-blue shirt, black tie, shiny shoes, his hair gelled north of his forehead. "Yeah, they gave me some numbers." He wasn't smiling.

In fact, his gaze darted past Jace as if he didn't want to talk about it.

"Give it to me, straight up."

Graham took a breath. "Have you talked to CEP? They've got some great ideas for guys heading into ret—"

"I'm not talking to the career enhancement guys. I'm not done yet, Graham. I still have plenty of hockey in me."

"Fine. They offered $1.2 million in a one-year, two-way contract." Graham met Jace's eyes then, his own steely black.

"Two-way? You've got to be kidding me."

"I suspect they want to keep their options open."

A two-way contract meant less money if the Blue Ox decided to send him down to the AHL. Not that they would, him being a veteran, but they had the option. In fact, they could tie him up playing games with kindergartners if they wanted and reduce his pay to pennies while they did it. A one-way contract at least secured his income, wherever they played him.

"Shred Warner just nabbed $10 mil one-way, and he's only a year younger than me."

"And at the top of his game, Jace. He's a top scorer. And he didn't spend most of last season on the injured reserve list. Most of all, he doesn't go out on the ice with a giant target on his back, almost a dare for the younger enforcers to take a swing at."

"Are you saying I can't hold my own?"

Graham held up a hand. "Nobody's saying you aren't still the best enforcer out there. But you come with risks. Liabilities. The franchise doesn't want to put all their eggs in the J-Hammer basket only to have you go down with the next hard hit."

"It would take more than one hard hit—"

"Not according to Doc. He says you're about at your limit. And don't tell me you don't know it. When was the last time you ended a game without a headache rolling in?"

Jace looked away, tapped his stick on the ice. "This is all I got, Graham."

"That's not true."

Now Jace met his gaze with his own steely eyes. "Really? Because we tried, remember? I can't read the teleprompter fast enough to announce, and I'm not necessarily the pretty face they want for endorsements."

"What about that opportunity to coach?"

"The guy wanted me to teach kids how to fight. Not even I want to do that. If anything, I want to teach real hockey. *Play* real hockey." He sighed, running a hand through his hair. "What if I didn't take the offer? What if I finished the contract and threw my hat into the ring as a free agent?"

Graham checked his watch. "You'd have to make sure you weren't hurt, not even once."

"And if I wasn't? If I ended the year injury free?"

He had Graham's attention now. "The Blue Ox might pay more for you if they feared losing you."

"Now you're talking."

"But you'll have to be at the top of your game. And I mean best play of your life."

"Are you kiddin' me? I can still outskate any of those rookies."

Graham raised an eyebrow. "Like him?"

Jace turned and spied Owen Christiansen stepping onto the ice. He should have guessed the kid would be in early, warming up.

He reminded Jace of himself in that way also.

Owen warmed up like Jace, skating around the oval, then diving in for a sprint. Jace watched him in silence, studying his glide, the way he dug into the ice.

"Yeah, I can outskate even Owen Christiansen."

"Show me," Graham said.

Really? Fine.

Jace skated to center ice, singled out a puck. "Owen!"

The kid skated closer. He looked like he'd done hard time face-down on a mattress, the lines still embedded in his growl. He wore cracked red eyes, his beard scraggly.

Jace smiled, something of a dare in it, and met Owen's eyes. Then he glanced down at the puck. "Can you get past me?"

Whatever Owen had sucked down last night, it vanished in a second. He snaked out his stick to hook the puck, but Jace saw it coming and checked him away, flicking the puck between Owen's legs. Owen caught up fast—a second before Jace slapped the puck into the goal, Owen checked him hard, and he flew into the boards behind the net. By the time he'd turned around, Owen had the puck, scooping it out of the crease and into the open.

Jace took off, breathing hard, and charged Owen into the far end of the ice. They slammed together against the glass. Jace was first to find the puck and danced away with it. Owen reached his stick in, trying to trip him up, but Jace stepped over it, then stopped hard, and the kid skated right past him.

Jace shot toward the goal as Owen regrouped. He faked again, left, then right, and it just seemed too easy, with Owen scrambling to catch up. He was nearly parallel to the goal. One flick of his wrist and—

Owen came right at him and, in a move he hadn't expected, slammed his elbow into Jace's chin.

The blow turned Jace's vision gray, just long enough to lose the puck.

And in that second, Owen found it.

Jace stifled a word and lit out after him, but Owen had put on the gas, and Jace couldn't catch up. He finally reached out to spear him, but Owen was too fast; with a flick, he sent the puck into the net.

He raised his stick and glided backward around the goal, pointing at Jace, grinning. "Got ya, old man."

Jace leaned over, catching his breath, his stick across his knees. "I didn't know you knew how to fight dirty, kid."

"I learned from the master." Owen laughed and skated away. And then, as Jace straightened, he saw Owen approach Graham.

The kid dropped his gloves, glad-handing the agent like they might be cousins.

So that's why Graham had shown up. For Owen. Probably to check up on his superstar.

Jace watched, sweat trickling down his back, across his chest. His jaw ached where Owen had elbowed him. And in the front of his head, a tiny knot began to form.

Without looking back, Jace skated off the ice. He dumped his stick, slipped on his guards, and walked up the ramp to the locker room.

Inside, his teammates were lacing their skates, some of them still dressing. He sat down on the bench in front of his locker and leaned his head back, closing his eyes.

"You okay, Hammer?" Kalen, their new goaltender, stood over him. He'd recently decided to shave his hair into a Mohawk, as if that might get them into the Stanley Cup play-offs.

"You look ridiculous. No hockey player with any self-respect has a Mohawk."

Kalen grinned. "See you on the ice."

Jace closed his eyes again, listening to the rest of his team empty into practice. Then, finally, quiet. Blessed quiet.

He should just take the team's offer and be done. Or find a new career. Sell insurance, maybe, for dopes like him who thought they were invincible.

CHAPTER 3

The January chill had warmed to a miserable drizzle, the air foggy with melting snow, as Eden left her apartment.

Please let this night end better than the day began.

Two days of not talking to Owen had worked her into a full boil this morning. *"You need to grow up and take some responsibility!"* Of course her words, echoing across her tiny apartment, had lacked any oomph thanks to the piles of clean, folded laundry on the kitchen table.

"I am grown up! I have my own car and my own apartment." Owen shoved the folded laundry into his bag. "I don't need your hovering, Eden."

His black eye had turned to green around the edges, and he'd looked fierce, even triumphant, the look he got on game day or after a good practice.

41

"Being a grown-up is more than paying your bills. It's about making wise choices and having healthy relationships. Neither of which apply to you."

"I have plenty of healthy relationships. Trust me." He flung the bag over his shoulder and winked.

She wanted to smack him. "You make me sick. Is this how you want to make a name for yourself? You're turning out just like every other hotshot hockey player. Think about how this affects your family. Mom and Dad, and everything they raised you to be. What about your beliefs? I thought you called yourself a Christian! Either change your name or change your ways."

He picked up his keys. "Fine. I'll change my name." He walked out the door.

She stood there, her heart clogging her throat. "Owen—"

But he didn't turn around.

Have a good game. She'd wanted to say that—wanted to stop, rewind, and enact their pregame ritual, the one where she prayed for his safety and then told him to make at least one goal.

Instead, she'd stood at the window and watched him drive away. And been late for work, again.

She couldn't keep doing this—she knew it. Which was why tonight would be different. Tonight, she'd simply be a fan, out on a date with a nice guy.

Perfect.

Russell was climbing out of his car as she stepped out of the brownstone. "I was going to come up and get you." He wore a ski hat with long tassels and an oversize black parka. Perfect attire for a hockey game.

"I'm early." She slid into the passenger side. He had turned on her seat heater—thoughtful. "Thanks for driving. My battery seems to have given up the ghost. I've jump-started it three times with AAA and even tried plugging it in, but it's dead. Lately I've had to take the bus to work."

"Want me to take a look at it?"

"You're a mechanic as well as a funeral director?"

He shrugged. "I dabble in lots of things." Once he'd pulled away from the curb, he said, "I'm glad you called me. I meant to call but things got busy at work."

She reached into her pocket, her hand around the tickets, just checking that she had remembered them. "I felt bad about the way things ended. You were so nice to drive me to get Owen, and . . . well, I wanted to make up for it."

"Not necessary, but thanks. This will be fun. I've always wanted to see a Blue Ox game."

He smiled but didn't look at her, and it only confirmed what she hoped. She was out with a regular guy. Not one addicted to sports or winning. Not one using her to get close to her brother or the hockey team. Just a nice, even boring guy—clean-cut, responsible, and so what if he ran a funeral parlor? Someone had to, right?

Maybe this was the beginning of normal for her, too. A life without worrying about practices and injuries and equipment and games. A life without hovering over Owen.

She looked out the window at the passing cityscape, the fluorescent lights soggy in the rain. Russell had turned on his windshield wipers. Their rhythmic thumping matched her heartbeat.

"Who are they playing tonight?"

See, a hockey enthusiast would know this. "The Denver Blades."

"Where are our seats?"

"In the family-and-friends section. It's on the glass, near the goal."

He nodded. "Nice."

"We're sort of like a club—we all know each other."

"And I'm the newest member."

Member? She looked at him. He hadn't shaved, and the slightest layer of stubble gave him a hockey player look. Not that she wanted a hockey player type. She wanted a man for his heart, his head, not his ability to outmuscle another person. "Yes."

"So I'd better be on my best behavior."

He had white teeth, a nice smile. She'd noticed that last time as well.

"I am sure you'll be fine."

They pulled into the parking garage, and she directed him to the private lot, next to the players' cars. She didn't look for Owen's, but it caught her eye anyway.

The arena smelled like an NHL game—the vendors serving up popcorn, nachos, and hot dogs. Fans roamed the corridors wearing everything from their Blue Ox hockey sweater replicas to foam hats of pucks and tasseled Mohawk snow hats. A few crazies sported faces painted blue and white.

She'd never been a nutso hockey fan. In fact, sometimes she wished Owen had picked basketball. Or badminton. The violence in hockey could turn her stomach—she'd seen too many games with blood on the ice. But this was Minnesota. Even football took a backseat to hockey.

And she was here for Owen, not the sport.

She found the section and led Russell down to their seats, third row up from the glass. "Will this work?"

Russell was standing in the aisle, taking in the arena. The expanse of it could still steal her breath, with the chilly tingle in the air, the sense of something dangerous and bold about to explode on center ice. Flags from the other NHL teams hung from the ceiling, posters of the players lined the upper deck, and like a chandelier, a four-sided Jumbotron played scenes of fans filing in, holding beer cups and hot dog boats. Classic rock—Queen, Zeppelin, Metallica—played from the massive speakers, stirring the bated excitement of the fans.

"This is going to be a wild game," Eden said as she flipped her seat down.

Russell sat beside her, and she noticed how his hands gripped his knees, almost jumpy.

"Have you ever been to an NHL game before?"

He shook his head, grinning, his eyes shiny.

Cute.

She greeted the family in front of her—the parents of Kalen Boomer—and Brendon Sharpe, brother of Max Sharpe, a wing like Owen. They all glanced at Russell and smiled.

Cora Sutten sat down next to Eden, wearing a replica of her son's Blue Ox sweater. Cora reminded Eden so much of her mother. Ingrid would love to attend more of Owen's games. But she had a resort to rebuild, and frankly, she'd spent a decade in her SUV shuttling him to games. Seeing him play on television was a sort of victory.

"I see you brought a friend," Cora said quietly.

Eden smiled. "Yes. A *friend*." But that news would get around. Hence why she usually gave her extra ticket away—bringing a date to a Blue Ox game might be akin to going steady.

The team skated out under thunderous applause and began to warm up. Owen circled by her numerous times but didn't glance her way. She sort of expected that, but it tied a knot in her stomach. Fine. She would still pray he had a safe game.

They stood for the national anthem, and she noticed Russell didn't remove his hat. He did, however, place his hand over his heart, so maybe that made up for it. Still, it wasn't that chilly in the arena.

When they sat, Eden turned her attention to the ice as the announcer introduced the forward line, then the defensemen.

She didn't see Russell unzip his jacket, or she might have stopped him. Might have gotten up right then and climbed over him, abandoning him in the stands. Or maybe scrounged up the courage to tell him to leave.

At the very least, she would have had a moment to prepare before turning to him and seeing—

No. Oh *no*.

She thought she even let out a little scream, but in the roar of the crowd as Jace Jacobsen and Owen Christiansen took the ice, no one but herself could hear it.

Still, any second the camera would turn her direction, zero in on her crazy bare-chested date, painted in two-toned blue and white over his entire upper body. He must have spray-painted himself because even—and she averted her eyes—his chest hairs were a bright blue.

She shot a glance at Cora, who looked back at, then past, Eden. She wore an appropriate expression as she met Eden's eyes again. Eden shook her head quickly, like, *Please tell me this isn't happening.*

Cora took her mittened hand and squeezed. "Go Blue Ox!"

Right.

Next to her, Russell was flexing what little body mass he had, shouting at the Denver players as they circled the ice. And then, whooping it up, he took off his hat and waved it in the air like a lasso. He flung it at the glass, nearly hitting someone in the front row. The big guy with a beer and a Blue Ox jersey looked back at her, then at Russell, and frowned.

She didn't want to look. But like a train wreck, she couldn't help it.

Blue hair. Russell caught her eyes and smiled big. "This is awesome!"

Oh. She wanted to dissolve into the floor, but really, what could she do? Trapped in the middle of her row, she'd have to climb over him and make an even bigger spectacle.

Brendon Sharpe gave her a sympathetic smile from the row below. That's right; he'd brought a crazy fan to the game once—his date had dyed her ponytails blue and worn a too-low Blue Ox fan shirt, one that made the Thomas family shuffle their grandchildren out of viewing range.

Like Brendon, Eden would never live this down.

At least the Blue Ox scored early on a power play and went into the second period one up over the Blades.

"Would you like a hot dog?" Russell asked.

She shook her head, praying he'd leave for the vendors, but instead he stood up like an idiot and waved his hands above his head.

Oh, please, let the arena cave in right now.

The team returned for the second period, and she shot a glance at the box, saw Owen leaning on his stick, itching to get in. He'd been more aggressive tonight, already doing time for charging. He climbed over the wall to change lines, coming out hard and fast, scooping up the puck and racing down the ice.

One of the Blades clipped him, and he went head over end, landing hard. The crowd erupted in fury, cheering when Jace slammed the Denver player to the ice in retribution. He skated away, though, instead of following with a punch, and the crowd seemed deflated.

Owen got up hot, and it turned him reckless. He spent two precious minutes in the penalty box for slashing.

Eden had never seen him play so dirty. By the end of the game, he'd spent more time in the box than Jace, who'd managed to emerge from the game without a punch thrown.

Russell seemed angry. "Not even a fight. Who goes to a hockey game and doesn't get to see one fight?"

She'd give him a fight if he wanted one. "Please put your jacket on," she said, picking it up from where it had fallen to the floor. "You must be cold."

"No. I'm hot." He grinned at her. What, did she miss something? Like a shot to the head from a wild puck? Where was nice, pedestrian Russell? The mortician?

"Yeah. Right. Let's go."

"I thought we were going to see Owen." Russell took his jacket and flung it over his shoulder.

She did want to see Owen—just to talk to him. Smooth things out. But—"Put your jacket on first."

He frowned at her but slipped it on, even if he didn't zip it.

"See you at the next game," Cora said.

Eden nodded, still wanting to die on the spot.

They followed the crowd out, and Russell did an impressive job of staying on her tail, despite her attempts to distance herself. She flashed her pass to the security guard and took the players' tunnel outside, the cool air sloughing off the frustration of the game.

She would just apologize to Owen, make things okay between them. It was probably her fault he'd spent so much time burning off penalties tonight.

She watched her breath coil in the air, hoping she could talk her brother into giving her a ride home.

"So when's the next game?" Russell was leaning against the wall, his shoulders hunched, his jacket still unzipped. She hoped he was freezing.

"There is no next game. At least not for us."

"What?" He came off the wall. "Why? I thought we had a good time."

She looked away.

"Listen, you want to go out for dinner or something first? We can do that. I get it—it's not all about hockey. But we have a good thing going, and I think it could be something special."

She just stared at him. "I didn't think you were so into hockey. I dropped hint after hint—even invited you to the Blue Ox party."

"I don't care about a party—I wouldn't fit in anyway. But a game . . . Besides, I thought you were a fan."

"I'm not a fan. I'm family. And I'm certainly not going to dye my hair."

"Where's your sense of adventure? Fun?"

"This is not fun for me. You embarrassed me."

"Sorry." He had advanced toward her and now stepped up, almost too close. "Just because I got a little enthusiastic about the game—"

"A little? You *painted* your body!"

"I could paint yours if you want." He said it softly, with a strange quirk to his mouth.

Eden nearly raised her hand to slap him. "Get away from me."

"Eden, you're too uptight." He reached out to touch her, but she jerked away. His eyes darkened. "What's your problem? I thought you were like me—looking for a little fun. I'm around dead bodies all day—and so are you. Don't you want to loosen up?"

"I don't get that loose."

"C'mon, don't be that way—"

"What's going on here?"

She jumped at the voice echoing from the darkness of the tunnel. Not Owen, but she recognized it and wasn't sure she should call it relief that rushed through her when Jace Jacobsen appeared from the shadows. He had showered, his hair still damp and combed back, curly behind his ears. He wore a long wool coat over dress pants, a silver tie at his neck.

Not looking in the least like trouble.

"J-Hammer. Wow," Russell said. "So what happened tonight? You going soft?"

Jace frowned as if not sure what to make of Russell. Well, her either.

"I mean, you practically ran away from at least three fights. What's wrong with you?"

She saw Jace's fist tighten on the workout bag he held. "We won, didn't we?"

"No thanks to you."

Eden looked at Russell. "I think you should go now."

"You're right." He reached out to grab her hand.

She pulled it back. "Not with me."

"You came with me, honey. You're coming home with me." He reached for her hand again and this time caught it.

"Let go of her." Jace hadn't moved, but his voice did. Lower, warning. The growl of something dangerous.

"Stay out of this, Jacobsen. She's *my* girl."

Eden recoiled in a sort of silent horror. "No—I'm—"

"Whoever you are, I can promise you that you won't like how this ends. Let her go." Jace had advanced now, stood beside her.

Russell looked at him, his mouth tightening, then back to Eden. "You going to let this bully push you around?"

"Which one?"

"Fine. Find your own way home." Russell released her hand and glared at Jace. "*Now* you choose to pick a fight." He shook his head and walked toward his car.

Eden hadn't realized she was holding her breath until she saw his brake lights flash and he pulled out.

"You're shaking. Are you okay?" Jace hadn't moved. Just stood there beside her as Russell stalked away. And he smelled annoyingly good—something fresh and a little spicy against the dank cement of the tunnel.

"Thank you. I don't know what happened. Last date, he was a perfectly nice guy. This time . . ."

"Hockey can do that to a person. Turn them into something they're not."

"Or maybe it's his true nature." She noticed that Jace looked tired tonight, not unlike that night at Sammy's. "For what it's worth, it's nice to go to a game without a fight."

"Your brother nearly picked three."

She shivered and pulled her jacket around her. "I know. I'm going to talk to him about that—I don't know what his problem is."

"Hmm . . ."

"What's that mean?"

He lifted a shoulder, glanced past her. "If you're waiting for him, Owen lit out right after the game."

"He's gone?" Shoot.

"Uh, I hate to point this out, but do you need a ride?"

She looked up at Jace, standing there in the tunnel, the lights of the parking lot turning his face dusky, shadowy, hard-edged. "I . . . I can call a cab."

"Don't be stubborn. I have a car; I can drop you."

"I live in Minneapolis. It's not close."

He started walking past her.

"Really, you'll drive me home?"

For a moment when Jace turned, he resembled a sort of Highland warrior, his shoulders wide, his beard darkening his face, his blue eyes clouded and mysterious. "No, I'm going to drive you to Canada and dump the body."

She stilled.

"Of course I'll drive you home. It's the least I can do after scaring off your date."

She smiled but then doused it as she caught up to him. "You did scare him off. Thank you for that."

"It's what I do," he said quietly.

Jace didn't know why he was in such a surly mood. Tonight should have been a sort of victory for him—no fights, no significant penalty time, and one assist. And except for a few jeers as he left the ice and a mild chewing out from his coach for letting Owen take his own hits, Jace managed to emerge uninjured. Best of all, he wasn't leaving the game with a roaring headache. A twinge of pain in the front of his head, but that was nothing.

It was just that . . . something itched under his skin. Unfinished business, maybe, and it scared him.

For a second there, he'd almost wanted Eden's date to make a move. Just so he could exhale, release the pressure from the game.

It might be wise to stop by Sam's, get some of that Holy Tea, talk it out of his system before he did something stupid.

Like offer Owen's bossy sister a ride home. It wasn't as if they'd become friends—the woman hated him, and he knew that. But he couldn't exactly leave her standing in the cold, could he?

Maybe. Because she acted like she'd rather be walking home, the way she huddled on her side of the car, her hand around the door handle as if he might skid out into traffic, off the bridge into the Mississippi.

Thanks, but he'd learned his lesson about driving like a maniac in a serious machine. He kept it under the speed limit and between the lines.

"You shouldn't be so uptight. The roads aren't that bad."

She glanced at him, and it occurred to him that she might not be worried about the roads.

Really, you'll drive me home? He began to take her words apart, wondering exactly what she meant. He'd joked with her, but . . . "You didn't think I'd . . . well, that you weren't safe in my car with me, did you?"

Her eyes grew wider.

"Maybe I should call you a cab," he said, shaking his head.

"Sorry. It's just . . ."

"It's okay." He sighed. "I get it. Too many headlines."

Her voice came too fast. "Your life is your life, Jace. And I never believed the accusations, even before that girl dropped them."

"I don't want to talk about it." How he hated the press—the way they pried, reported half-truths and dismantled lives. "And I was cleared, by the way."

"I know."

"I wasn't even there—"

"I *know*."

"But you still don't want to be alone with me."

She drew in a long breath, and he wanted to floor the gas, get her home as soon as possible.

And never see Owen's judgmental sister again.

Because if she knew about the scandal that had muddied his name, then she probably knew the rest. Knew about his mother, knew about the accident. Yeah, there could be plenty of judging from Eden Christiansen.

Which made him even more surly. "For what it's worth, Owen is going to be a great hockey player. He doesn't need quite so much mothering."

Her mouth fell open before she said, "I'm not trying to be his mother. But for your information, all this fame and money has gone straight to his head, and he's not himself lately. He's going to destroy his career—"

"And turn out just like me."

She said nothing.

"You were thinking it. And you're not wrong. I do see shades of me in Owen."

"Then talk to him. You're the team captain. You're supposed to be watching the younger guys."

"They're grown men."

"He's a kid."

"He's *not* a kid. And you need to let him live his own life."

"Stop talking to me. Just drive."

She was right—Minneapolis *was* out of the way.

Eden folded her arms, looked away from him, out her window. "You know, I never set out to be his babysitter. I don't even want the job. But the fact is, my parents were busy running our resort, and when he joined the junior league, it made sense that I helped out, making sure his equipment was in good shape, driving him to practice, checking in on his injuries. He's basically lived with me for the last three years. This new contract with the Blue Ox is a huge change for him."

Jace well remembered the stress of his year in the junior league—pressure to always be at the top of his game, of scouts watching. He supposed that, without his mother to watch his back, he might have crumbled.

"I'll never forget when the Wild signed him. I felt like *I'd* gotten that contract, watching him at the press conference, seeing his smile. He worked for it, you know."

"As did you."

She glanced at him. "It just felt like what you do when you're in a family. Be there to cheer for each other. But yeah, his victory was my victory."

Hmm. He'd seen that sentiment too often in his mother's eyes. Loved it, really.

Her voice softened. "I try not to play favorites—I have two other brothers—but Owen . . ." She drew in a breath. "When he was ten, he was injured at an away game. I had driven him to the game, so we were there alone. A kid skated across his hand during warm-ups and nearly took off his finger. Scary stuff. We sat at the hospital in Duluth for two hours before my parents could get there. He climbed into my lap—even though he was ten—and held on, poor kid. I don't know—being needed like that . . . I just, you know. Love him."

Jace said nothing but felt her words like an ache in his chest.

She sighed. "It's not about the hockey. It's about Owen. I'd be his biggest fan even if he played Ping-Pong."

He smiled at that. "But then he couldn't check."

"Seriously. What burr got under his breezers tonight? A charging violation, clipping, slashing, elbowing—"

"He knows what he's doing."

"That's not Owen. He's never been a dirty player. It was always about technique and finesse for him."

"The NHL changes you. I used to be all about finesse too."

She glanced at him, quick, as if surprised.

He tried not to be offended. "I came into the league with a slap shot that made goalies duck. And then, in my first NHL game, I mixed it up with one of the league's legends. After that, I had a rep. They stopped seeing my slap shot and started seeing my . . . Well, anyway, the pros are all about the show."

"But . . . you're so good at it."

He knew that wasn't a compliment.

"Although I'm not sure your fans were too happy without a fight tonight."

He glanced at her, feeling weirdly like he owed her some sort of explanation. "So was I dreaming, or did your boyfriend paint his body?"

A frown creased her face for a second. "I'd call it more of a nightmare, but yes. And he's not my boyfriend."

He wasn't sure why, but that information stirred something inside him. "Really?"

"Yeah. I know him from work. And that's the last time I go out with him."

"You're not looking for a rabid Blue Ox fan?" He meant it as a joke but wanted to wince when the words emerged like he might care or something.

"Hardly. I want someone tame. Pedestrian. Kind. Not a guy

who has to be in the limelight to feel good about himself." She shook her head. "I want someone unremarkable, like me."

"I wouldn't say you're unremarkable."

She looked at him. "You'd pick me out of a crowd? You wouldn't walk right by me?"

"Of course not. You're pretty enough."

Her face fell. Oh, way to go, charmer. He used to be a guy with moves, with the right words on his lips. In fact, he used to be a guy who didn't even have to try.

Apologizing would only make it worse, but he heard the word tumble out anyway. "Sorry."

Her tone suggested she was trying not to be hurt. "For what? Being honest? Listen, you and I run in different circles. And I'm happy with that."

Happy with staying far away from him. He couldn't pretend that didn't punch him in the chest a little, despite the fact that extended time with the woman might make him want to hit something too.

However, Jace *might* indeed pick her out of a crowd. Might be knocked off his stride by those green eyes, the spray of freckles, and ask her to share a cup of coffee with him. Maybe dinner.

Yeah, he would notice her. But she wouldn't even look twice at a guy like him. He wasn't pedestrian. And the limelight had kept him alive for too many years. Most of all, no one would ever call J-Hammer tame.

No, she'd never want to be with a guy like him—in fact, if he read her right, she couldn't stand him.

This night couldn't get any better.

They were nearing the bridge to Minneapolis, the cityscape rising to meet them, the IDS tower shimmering against the wet night.

"You're going to have to tell me where to go."

"Get off at Eleventh Street, then go south on Portland. I live on Franklin, west of Portland."

His gaze drifted to the University of Minnesota buildings as they crossed the bridge. He'd never attended college, but then again, his test scores would have made any admissions counselor laugh him all the way to tech school.

If it weren't for hockey, he might be working the iron ore mines or maybe selling insurance door-to-door, just like dear old dead-beat Dad. Not that a guy couldn't make a decent life out of working the iron range—plenty of his high school buddies turned it into a livelihood and figured out how to live without hockey.

He just couldn't see it for himself.

"I attended there. Lived in those multicolored buildings," Eden said casually.

"Cedar Square West?"

"Yep. Walked to school every day. Worked at the *Minnesota Daily*."

He stilled. "The newspaper?"

"I went to the school of journalism."

Jace tried to keep his voice even. "Eden, what do you do for a living?"

"I'm . . . a reporter."

Of course she was. Probably a sports reporter, trying to get the latest on his contract deal. Or his health. No wonder she'd gone digging about his performance—or lack thereof—tonight.

He turned onto Portland, the slush kicking up onto his car. He turned his wipers on higher.

"Take a right here."

"On Franklin. I remember." He didn't mean the chip in his

voice. But her declaration had him wondering how much of this night would appear online or in the paper or . . . well, how much would come back to haunt him.

His hands tightened on the steering wheel.

"I live just ahead, in the brownstone on the right."

Jace pulled up under a streetlight.

She paused, her hand on the door. "Thanks, Jace. I appreciate the ride home. But this doesn't change the fact that I think you need to step in and help Owen find his way." Then she looked at him fully, and shoot, she did have pretty eyes—green, with gold-flecked irises, the kind that could mesmerize a guy, make him drop his guard, let her discover more than he wanted.

Reporter eyes.

She softened her voice, going in for the sucker punch. "Couldn't we be on the same team? Maybe work together to keep him out of trouble?"

He wasn't that stupid. The last thing he needed was to be netted into some "save Owen" quest with this woman.

This overprotective, judgy newspaperwoman.

"You might be his babysitter, honey. But I'm not," he said, his voice curt.

"Fine." She opened the door.

"Try to stay away from creeps like your date," he said, wanting to make it a little better, despite himself.

"Yeah. Good idea." Then she slammed the door.

Jace watched her storm through the building's arched entryway and disappear inside.

He drove by Sammy's on his way home and noticed the lights were still on. Maybe Sam had a minute, just to help him shake away the lingering frustration. The door was locked, so he went around and used his key to open the back entrance. "Sam?"

The bar kitchen still smelled of barbecue wings, french fries, and the tangy residue of beer on tap. He flicked on a light as he walked through, then stood in the door of the empty bar. The chairs were still down, evidence that Sam hadn't closed too long ago. And three glasses puddled water on the bar.

Jace walked down the hall, past the bathrooms, then opened the door to the upstairs apartment. Okay, it was late, and Sam was probably sleeping, but Jace spotted light trickling from under the door, and Sam understood the need to blow off steam after a game.

At the top of the stairs, he knocked. "Sam?"

"In here!"

The voice that responded sounded tight, almost panicked. Jace stopped long enough to find the source and headed to the bathroom.

Sam sat on the floor, Maddy cuddled in his lap, dressed in her nightgown, her body trembling and sweaty, her hair clipped back, as if hastily. Her breathing emerged labored.

Jace's heart lodged like a fist in his chest as he looked at Sam.

His friend had aged a year since he'd seen him three days ago, his eyes red, bagged by circles of sleeplessness. He still wore his waist apron and a black T-shirt with the words *Sammy's Bar and Grill* across the chest.

"What's going on?" Jace said as he came into the room. It did look better than he'd imagined earlier—the bathroom having received the scrubbing of a lifetime, a new blue shower curtain, some fresh bath linens. But it still resembled a widower's bachelor pad, desperate and pitiful.

"I'm sick." Maddy raised her head. "And my back hurts. And I can't breathe very well."

Sam gave him a grim look. Swallowed.

Oh no.

Then Maddy fixed Jace with those sweet brown eyes. "Did you win?"

Jace crouched in front of them. "Yes, sweetie, we won."

She smiled, just a little. "I knew it."

Jace reached out for her. "You get her bag and her medicines. I'll put her in the car."

Sam nodded and released her into Jace's arms.

Then, just for a second, his best friend lowered his head into his hands. Jace turned them both away before Maddy could see her daddy cry.

CHAPTER 4

How COULD HE be here again? Sam leaned forward in a bright-orange chair of the transplant center at the University of Minnesota children's hospital and scrubbed his hands down his face. "I don't think I can do this . . ."

The hospital resembled a children's day care, with pictures of cartoon characters painted on the walls, friendly orange stripes directing traffic, colorful furniture, and large flat-screen TVs affixed to the walls.

But all the decorations couldn't hide the truth. Children came here to die, and no amount of SpongeBob SquarePants or Dora the Explorer could distract from the families girded in masks and protective gear, living on the edge of tragedy.

Sam had walked by rooms with parents sleeping on the long padded couches along the windows as tubes and wires and oxygen kept their tykes alive in the beds. He couldn't bear it and escaped to the end of the hall.

"This is my fault."

"This is not your fault." Jace turned from where he stood at the window overlooking the parking lot. The sunrise bled across the University of Minnesota campus. It had taken five hours to get Maddy admitted, evaluated, stabilized, tested, and into a restless slumber. The doctor had scheduled her for a biopsy first thing in the morning.

And now the waiting began.

What would he have done without Jace keeping him calm, driving them to the ER, then staying with Sam to help him stutter out Maddy's history?

Yes, she had a transplant three years ago.

No, she'd had no signs of rejection, but yes, okay, he'd missed her appointment three months ago and hadn't yet rescheduled. But he could be termed a near fanatic about her medicine. How could she have missed her antirejection meds?

Still, with the move and her being sick, maybe he'd messed up.

"I just thought that her stomachaches had to do with losing the house and moving in over the bar. Maddy was always a finicky eater and—" Sam shook his head. "I should have figured it out. She's retaining fluid, and she's been so tired. She falls asleep during her schoolwork and often at dinner."

"She doesn't sleep—she's up waiting for you to get off work." Jace leaned against the opposite wall.

"No, see, that's what I told myself. But anyone with a brain would have added it up. And if I hadn't missed her appointment . . ." He looked at Jace. "This is my fault. If she's in full rejection . . . well, it's not like they're going to give her another heart."

Jace pushed himself off the wall. "Why not? She's nine years old—"

"You know that it's not about age. It's about viability. And . . . the brutal truth is I don't have the financial resources to care for another heart. They look at that too—your ability to manage the aftercare. They could even send a social worker around and decide that her home life isn't compatible with proper post-transplant care." He looked down the hall, listening in case Maddy had woken and needed him. He should get back in there, but he just couldn't stand by her bed, count her breaths, watch the IV drip methylprednisolone into her veins in some desperate attempt to stop her frail body from rejecting her heart. He couldn't see her sink into the cotton blankets without hating someone.

Like himself.

Or God.

Sam shook his head before he let the thought take root. No. If he didn't have God, he'd have no one. Still, sometimes he wanted to ask, whose side was God on, anyway?

"You don't need to worry about money, Sam—"

"Stop, Jace. I know you mean well, but we both know that you can't keep funding her medical expenses. I am an idiot for not getting enough insurance—we can agree on that—but she's not your responsibility."

Jace's eyes narrowed, just for a second, as if he'd been punched, but he took a breath, nodded. "Right. Sure."

"Don't take it that way, dude. I'm sorry. It's just . . . I'm so angry, you know? I just want to hit something."

"You have every reason to be angry. If it makes you feel better, you can hit me."

Sam managed a short grin. "Thanks, but you're already sporting a bit of a shiner there, J. I'm sorry I missed the game. Please tell me you got a few licks in."

"Sorry to disappoint you—and the rest of the St. Paul Blue Ox fans, apparently—but I managed to have a fight-free night. The shiner is from a teammate."

"Really?"

When Jace lifted a shoulder, Sam suspected more behind his answer, but Jace said nothing, and Sam didn't chase it.

"I could go for some coffee."

"On it." Jace settled a hand on Sam's shoulder, squeezed. "I'm going to stop by the chapel, too."

Sam nodded. Yes, please.

He listened to Jace's steps and closed his eyes.

He couldn't pray. Not yet. Because if he went into the little hospital chapel and lay prostrate before the altar, cried and begged and hoped like last time, it meant that he believed Maddy might really die. He couldn't let his brain—his heart—go there.

He clasped his hands in his lap. *I'm sorry, Mia. I'm sorry I didn't take better care of our daughter.*

Sam tightened his jaw, looked toward Maddy's dark room, and wished, not for the first time, that God had taken him instead of Mia and left his daughter the mother she so desperately needed.

Eden didn't care what Jace Jacobsen thought of her. She really didn't care. Certainly not enough to let his annoying voice chase her through the night, tie her sheets into knots.

You're pretty enough.

Fine, Jace's words had hurt, just a little. But that was crazy, right? Because she couldn't stand the guy.

And clearly the feeling was mutual.

She rolled over in her bed toward the window. The sun had already turned her room to gray, an orange glow just tipping above the horizon. Not that she could see past the building behind her to catch any hint of a glorious sunrise, but at least she could justify peeling herself out of bed. Sucking down four cups of coffee while she read the obits.

Most importantly, at least she'd be on time for work.

A chill lingered in her flat, the thin panes rattling against a nasty wind; January must have turned frigid again, which meant today would be littered with black ice and car accidents.

She'd have to brace herself for a call from Russell.

Eden grabbed her parka, still flung over her kitchen chair, and wrapped herself in it as she heated water for coffee.

Listen, you and I run in different circles. And I'm happy with that.

And she was. Gloriously happy. Over the moon with joy.

She pulled out a box of granola, shook some into a bowl.

Hopefully she'd never have to be in the same room with J-Hammer Jacobsen again.

Or the same car.

Or the same airspace.

Oh, the man took up way too much room in her head. And she kept smelling his cologne, like it had embedded in her pores . . . or her jacket.

She shucked it off and hung it up near the door, going into her bedroom to retrieve a sweater.

On the way, she picked up her phone from the bedside table. Owen had dialed her three times before she'd finally shut it off somewhere around 5 a.m. She turned it on now, noticed the missed calls, ignored them, and set her phone on the counter while she added milk to her granola, then poured coffee grounds into the French press. A gift from Owen for her birthday.

Owen is going to be a great hockey player. He doesn't need quite so much mothering.

Whatever. Clearly she couldn't count on Jace to help her keep Owen out of trouble. And to think, for about two miles there, he'd seemed a real . . . Well, *gentleman* might be going too far, but friendly. A womanizer, maybe, but not the guy who'd lured a girl to his room and attacked her during a party. Eden still remembered the headlines and the press conference when he revealed his alibi—sitting at his dying mother's bedside. The reporters hadn't exactly let the poor woman die in obscurity after that. They'd dug into her past, and even Eden felt sorry for Jace then.

It seemed that shortly thereafter, Jace had driven his car into an icy lake.

He might not have deserved the public examination of his life—or the wild accusations—but he'd certainly sealed his reputation in the years before that. And even Jace agreed that Owen reminded him of himself.

Still . . . *You might be his babysitter, honey. But I'm not.*

Jerk.

She poured the hot water into the French press, stirred it, then set the top on to let it steep.

Her phone rang, and she nearly ignored it until she saw her mother's face on the screen. "Mom. Hi."

"Oh, good, you're up."

Eden could imagine her mother, Ingrid Christiansen, sitting in her leather chair in the lodge living room, overlooking Evergreen

Lake. In this chill, it would be frozen over, with snowmobile tracks crisscrossing the snow-laden surface and fishing houses clumped in the center. Her father might have cleared a patch of ice for Darek and his son, Tiger, to slap a few shots around. The six-year-old was another hockey star in the making, for another generation. Maybe Darek would teach Ivy, his girlfriend, how to skate. Eden held out hope that the two would get engaged soon.

"I know it's early, honey, but I haven't talked to you all week, and I thought I might catch you before work."

Eden went to her front door to retrieve the paper. "I'm sorry. It's been a busy week. Did you see Owen's game last night?"

"Yes, of course. So how's work?"

"It was terrible, Mom. He was out of control, playing angry. It reminded me of the section finals against Duluth East when he was a junior. Slashing, charging."

"Did you go with anyone?"

"I . . . uh . . . Sort of." She grabbed her cereal and went to the kitchen table. "A guy I know through work. It was awful. He turned out to be a crazy fan—even dyed his hair blue."

"Oh, my."

"I know. And then, after the game, I went to wait for Owen, but he took off right away—didn't even wait for me."

"Your date left you at the game?"

"No, Mom, *Owen*. He left after the game. With some friends or something. Didn't even stick around to talk to me."

"It's beautiful up here. We just got a fresh snowfall. We'd love to see you—why don't you escape this weekend and come up?"

"Aw, I'd love to, but Owen has a game Friday night, and I think he'll be too tired."

"Eden, I'm not talking about Owen—I want *you* to come up and visit. Without Owen."

Without Owen? "He needs me to be at his game—"

"Owen is a big boy. He'll be just fine."

Uh, no, he wouldn't. Wasn't. It tipped her lips to tell her mother exactly how not fine Owen was, but then what? She couldn't bear to add Owen to her list of failures. Job, romance . . . No, Owen and his stellar career were all she had left.

She refused to let him fail.

"I don't know—"

"Eden. We appreciate you keeping an eye on your brother, but you're not responsible for him. You have your own amazing life. Now, tell me, how can I pray for you this week?"

Her own amazing life? Right. She set the paper on the table, pulling out the sports section. Of course, Owen's picture had made the front page, above the fold. He wore a grimace as he slapped in his second goal.

"I don't know, Mom. For my car to start?"

"Oh, honey, just buy a new battery. Or better, a new car."

"I gotta go."

She heard a sigh on the other end of the line. "I believe in you, Eden. Even if you don't believe in yourself."

What was that supposed to mean? "Thanks, Mom. I'll tell Owen you said hi."

She hung up and stared out her sliding-glass window to where the sunrise now burned over the top of the buildings. Snow covered her rusty terrace furniture. Inside, her spider plant had long surrendered to winter, dormant and sad, and an old floral sheet covered a hole in her garage sale sofa.

The telltale signs of an amazing life.

She opened to the obits and scanned Kendra's remembrance article. She'd written a nice piece about Stanley R. Barker, unearthing the story of his rescue of two small children and their mother from a burning building.

An unsung hero. See, that's what obits were about—discovering what made people special. Remarkable.

Yeah, and when she died, her obit would read . . . *sister of Owen Christiansen.*

She closed the paper.

Maybe her mother—and Jace—had a point. Maybe she did put too much of her identity in Owen's successes. Feared too much his failures.

Fine. Today she'd ignore Owen and his crabby attitude. Let him fail, just a little.

It wasn't like his career was in immediate danger. According to the sports reporter, last night, despite his penalties, he'd had one of the best games of his life.

And if she walked away, he'd wake up and realize that he missed her. That he needed her.

She was in the shower when her phone rang. She thought she heard it again as she dried her hair.

It rang a third time as she was brushing her teeth. Owen's face appeared on the screen. Again.

See, he missed her already. She spit and answered. "Owen, this better be you, live, in the flesh, and not you rolling over in your sleep, fully clothed—"

"Is this Eden?" A man's voice—vaguely familiar, but she couldn't place it.

She shut off the water, grabbed a towel. "Who is this?"

"Max Sharpe. I play right wing—"

"Yeah. I know who you are. Why do you have Owen's phone? Did he leave it somewhere?"

It was the hesitation on the other end that made her sink down on the edge of the tub. "What's happened?"

"Owen's been injured."

She closed her eyes.

"We were . . . we were playing a game of pickup hockey—"

"What? In the middle of the night?"

"A couple hours ago. It was a pond game—me and some of the other guys and Owen. We met up with some of the Denver players, and things got heated, so we decided to take it on the ice—and, well, we were kind of drunk."

"Of course you were." Oops, she probably didn't need to say that, but—"Just tell me what happened, Max."

"Things got wild and he got nailed in the eye by the end of a stick."

That was it? He'd been backhanded before, ended up with a black eye. "Okay."

"Yeah, it's pretty bad."

"So put an ice pack on it." Maybe this was when she would teach him a lesson, make him fend for himself. "Listen, I'm going to be late for work—"

"We're at the hospital, Eden. University of Minnesota. They think he might lose his eye."

It seemed the room swam then, a complete circle. She slid off the tub and onto the floor.

Lose his eye.

"Are you there?" Max said.

"Yes," she said, her voice shaking. "Stay put. I'll be there as soon as I can."

"He was asking for you."

Finally.

In truth, Jace had just wanted to run. No amount of pretty paint or high-tech gadgetry could erase the odors and tastes of a transplant wing.

Too much desperation saturated the hallways, slithering under his skin even as he found his way to the chapel.

He sat on a pew before the altar, fighting to find words through his own tangle of anger.

Jace agreed with Sam. He, too, wanted to punch something or maybe lace on his skates and fly over an open pond, take as many shots on goal as he could until his entire body ached.

Anything to erase the feel of Maddy's delicate, failing body in his arms.

God, it's just not fair.

It was as far as he got before he gave up and headed out to the elevators.

He needed some air, and Sam deserved something better than cafeteria coffee. He thought he remembered a real coffee shop down the street.

January had revived with a vengeance in the hours since they arrived at the hospital, the day bright and crisp as the early morning sun lifted above the skyline. His frustration emerged in a puff of breath as he took off in a run down the sidewalk.

His lungs burned, and he liked it.

He had to clear the smell, the memories, from his nostrils.

The sight of his mother tucked into a bed, not unlike Maddy, disappearing before his eyes, waiting . . . waiting . . .

Sybil Jacobsen had died slowly, in agony, suffocating.

He stood at the light with a crowd of pedestrians, jogging in place like an idiot in his dress pants and shoes. He refused to look around at a father and son who'd edged toward him. The boy—he looked about twelve—glanced at him, then again.

Yes, hello, it's me.

Only, maybe they wouldn't recognize him without a blue-and-white sweater, a helmet, a stick in his hand—

"Good game last night, Mr. Hammer."

He didn't correct the kid, just smiled. "Thanks."

The light changed and he quick-walked across the slick street. His dress shoes did nothing to assist him as he slipped on the ice, and for a second he regretted his impulsiveness.

Especially when the wind kicked up and scraped at his ears.

But he ducked his head and found the coffee shop, adding himself to the line. He tried to remember Sam's order—a macchiato? And a moose-size black coffee for himself. Taking out his phone, he thumbed through the *Star Trib*'s online news, reading the headlines. The sports section had posted pictures of Owen—one with his hands high in triumph, another with his fists in a Denver Blades player's sweater, his face in a grimace. *Boy wonder sidelined by penalties, still pulls out victory.*

Yeah, Owen had a stellar, J-Hammer-style game. And if he didn't straighten himself out, he'd land a rep that might change his career. Soon that pretty-boy face would sport its own crooked nose, maybe some loose teeth. Jace had four not his own.

Couldn't we be on the same team? Maybe work together to keep him out of trouble?

Eden's voice chipped at him, and he ignored it as he stepped up to the counter and ordered, adding a muffin and a yogurt. Probably Sam wouldn't eat anything else the rest of the day.

Poor Sam. Jace couldn't imagine living through it all again—the despair, the hope, the coiled tension every time the phone rang, praying it would be a donor organ.

The helplessness could drive a man crazy. Still, Sam had always possessed the ability to pick up the pieces of his life when it seemed the darkest. Like when he'd climbed out of the devastation of losing his hockey career, met Mia, fallen in love, had Maddy.

He'd found a way to keep going after losing Mia, too, rising to the challenge of being both mother and father to Maddy. Sam's daughter gave him focus.

She gave Jace focus too. Since the day she wrapped her chubby fingers around his, Jace had fallen hard for his best friend's kid.

He moved over to wait for his order and did a quick Google search of his name.

No new blogs or weird news reports. So maybe Eden wasn't out to exploit their ride home for the world's scrutiny.

Perhaps his guilt just gnawed at him. He shouldn't have been quite so cold toward her. After all, she was right—maybe he did have a responsibility to Owen and the other younger players. He hadn't exactly acted like the team captain lately, so focused on his injuries and the demise of his career.

Maybe he *should* have a sit-down-and-come-to-Jesus meeting with Owen.

The barista handed him the drinks, and he took them with his bag of food over to a table, propping his loot on it while he scanned his phone for Owen's number. No time like the present to roust the kid out of bed, help him see the light. He thought he'd downloaded the team roster onto his phone, but apparently not.

He found Max's number, however, and dialed it. He'd seen the guy leaving with Owen, and even if he was snoozing, it would do the other troublemaker good to join them in that little sit-down.

Already Jace could feel the helplessness sloughing off, the steam subsiding. He'd get in Owen's face, make him see exactly where he was headed with a vivid and ugly cautionary tale.

If this ended up being Jace's last year in the league, he would leave with a legacy of something more than his reputation.

Max answered, quicker and more alert than Jace expected. "Hello?"

"Max. It's J. I know it's early, but I—"

"J., listen, I'm so sorry. It was stupid, I know it, and—"

Max was breathing hard, too hard, what sounded like panic in his voice.

"Calm down. What are you talking about?"

He heard Max exhale, could almost imagine the guy rubbing his hand across his forehead.

"Where are you?"

"I'm in the waiting room. At the university hospital. It's Owen—he was in a fight."

Of course he was. And now he probably had stitches and orders to sit out the next game. Or two.

"Perfect. That's just awesome." Jace nested the phone against his shoulder, picking up the coffees and the bag. "When will he be all stitched up?"

Silence.

"Max?" Jace paused a second before he pushed out the door.

"Uh . . . he's in surgery, J. Like, it's bad. I think you need to get over here."

Jace stepped back inside, out of the cold, as another patron entered. He set the coffees on the garbage can. Surgery? "How bad?"

Max sighed again, a tremble in it, and the sound reminded Jace of the morning his mother had slipped away. Reminded him of sitting beside her bed as his world crumbled.

"I'll be right there."

CHAPTER 5

EDEN CLUTCHED THE COLLAR of her parka to her neck and hunched against the cold, hating that the bus had seemed to inch along today. She'd thought about getting out and running but doubted she'd get much speed in this wind. Now it streaked down her back and turned her body to ice.

His teammates were overreacting. So like hockey players to reach for the dramatic and overblow the incident. After all, with all the injuries Owen had already survived, a little black eye wouldn't take him out of the game. He was only twenty years old; his entire spectacular career stretched before him.

Wrong. They were simply freaked out and wrong.

And even if he had suffered a painful injury, well, she'd nurse him back to the game. How many times had she soaked up his blood from split lips or iced his knees or fetched Gatorade to keep him hydrated? And ER visits to stitch up stick wounds were routine.

They'd get through this. He wasn't going to *lose his eye.*

Eden pushed inside the ER and stood for a moment in the entry under the heaters that fought to ward off the chill. She pulled off her gloves, then pressed her hands to her cheeks as she walked to the nurses' station. Glancing around, she didn't see Max or any of the other Blue Ox players.

"Did Owen Christiansen pass through here earlier?"

The nurse looked up at Eden wearing a half-tolerant smile. "Who?"

"Owen Christiansen—a hockey player. Might have had a black eye?"

"And you are?"

"His sister." Eden pulled out her wallet, showed her license.

"I . . . uh . . . Yeah, I think so. Let's see." The nurse sat down at the desk. "He plays for the Blue Ox—"

"Yes."

"He's in surgery. You can go up to the surgical waiting room, and the doctor will find you."

Surgery? So maybe Max hadn't just been freaking out. She drew in a long breath and found the elevators.

The university hospital had an academic feel about it. As she got into the elevator and pushed 3, following the directions to the surgical floor, it gave her a moment's pause that they'd brought Owen here.

A handful of players sat in the lounge. Some snoozing on the sofas; others, like Max, wearing shock, their faces pale. Max sported a freshly opened lip.

He got up as she entered. Smoothed his hands on his jeans. They were shaking. It made Eden shake a little too.

"What's going on?" She lifted her bag off her shoulder, set it on one of the vinyl couches. She'd already called in sick, but she didn't see the need to worry her parents until—and unless—she had news.

"He went into surgery over an hour ago. They called in a specialist—"

Eden held up her hand. "Tell me everything."

Max glanced at one of his buddies—she recognized Kalen, who pushed himself up into a sitting position. His Mohawk now resembled a bad toothbrush.

"It was my fault," Kalen said. "I guess I started it. We were slapping around the puck, and I threw one of the Denver players into the snow. He came back at me, and we ended up on the ice, throwing fists."

Max added, "I tried to get in there, but Owen jumped in for Kalen, and I followed, still holding my stick, and then we're not sure what happened . . ." He looked away. "All at once, he was on the ground, screaming. There was blood all over the ice—the cops came. They took him to Hennepin County Medical Center, and then the doc there sent him here. We met the surgeon in the ER, and we've been here ever since."

Eden sank down onto the couch. "And no one thought to call me?"

"What are you talking about? We called you constantly."

Right. "Sorry. I thought it was Owen, pocket dialing me." She pressed her hands against her roiling stomach.

"Do you need a drink?"

She looked at Max, made a face.

"I meant coffee."

"Oh. Uh . . . no. I just want to wait for the doctor."

"They called about fifteen minutes ago, said he was out of surgery. He should be here any—Jace, man, I'm so glad you're here."

Eden glanced up as Jace Jacobsen came into the room, looking like a man who'd walked through fire. His cheeks red from the cold, his hair blown back from his face. He carried a coffee in his whitened hand and wore what looked like the same clothes from last night.

Of course. She didn't presume to think that J-Hammer would have gone straight home.

He frowned, then surveyed the room before returning his gaze to Max. "Update me."

After a glance at Eden, Max gave Jace a similar rundown on the night's events.

Jace listened, his expression grim. Finally he asked, "So where are the Blades players now?"

As if he might round up a posse and finish the fight? She should have expected as much.

"It doesn't matter," she said, standing. "Owen is all that matters."

"Of course," he said, glancing at Max. "Where's Doc?"

"He was here—I think he went to talk to Coach."

Jace said nothing, just took a sip of his coffee.

Eden wanted to strangle him. She knew—she just *knew*—that Owen would get himself in trouble. He had it written all over him last night.

She should have tracked her brother down instead of letting Jace drive her home.

Eden turned away before she said something she might regret, although at this moment, she didn't know what that might be.

She had to do something, however. She walked to the coffee

table, began to pick up the debris of candy wrappers and Coke cans, and dumped them in the garbage. Then she went to the coffee station, found the pot empty, and filled it, brewing a fresh batch.

The clock ticked out the seconds in the room.

She watched the coffee brew, straightened the sugars. The surgeon would fix it, whatever it was, and Owen would be fine. Just fine.

Behind her, someone had turned on the news.

She closed her eyes. *Please, Lord, don't let him lose his eye.* God wouldn't take away the one thing that Owen longed for . . .

"Is there an Eden Christiansen here?"

She turned at the voice and saw a doctor in blue scrubs, his feet capped in cotton covers, his scrub hat still partially covering gray hair. Behind him, a female nurse waited, carrying a chart.

"I'm Eden."

"Dr. Harrison. I'm the ophthalmologist on staff. Can we talk privately for a moment?"

She looked at Jace, at his team, all leaning in. "I need to call my parents. But . . . tell me. How bad is it?"

The doctor pinched his mouth into a thin line. "The blow crushed parts of his orbit, or the socket that holds his eye. It lacerated the eye, which we repaired, but he has quite a bit of papilledema, or swelling of his optical disk. It was a blow to the head, too, so we're watching his intracranial pressure. We're concerned with his raised levels of cerebrospinal fluid pressure, so we'll be moving him to ICU to keep a watch."

A head injury. Eden had the sense of the room tilting, of Dr. Harrison swimming in front of her. But she couldn't fall apart.

Not when Owen needed her.

"Will he lose his eye?" Jace asked quietly.

The doctor looked at Jace, then back to Eden. "It's too early to know the extent of the damage. But you should call your parents." He pressed a hand to her arm.

"We're going to get through this," she said softly. "He's going to be just fine."

No one answered her.

"I'm scared, Daddy."

Maddy lay in her bed, and even Sam, a nonprofessional, a parent who wanted to camp long and hard in denial, could admit that his daughter appeared worse. At death's door. Her feet, hands, and face were plumped up with fluid, she ran a low-grade fever, and she couldn't go off oxygen without her breathing becoming labored. A muted cartoon played on the TV on the wall, but behind her, another screen monitored her heartbeat, her oxygen levels. He tried not to let it trap him as he watched the stats.

"It's just a biopsy, honey."

But it was still general anesthesia, still his baby wheeled away, out of his arms. Still needles and pain and more fear, held back by the faintest press of hope.

He rubbed her forehead, his hand cool against her skin. "They need to test your heart and see how it is."

"But it hurts."

"I know."

Jace had sent over balloons from the gift shop, as well as a bear the size of a buffalo, but Maddy hardly had the energy to thank him when he'd stopped by with coffee and breakfast. Then the phlebotomist came to draw blood, and Maddy had dissolved into hysterics.

Sam wasn't sure what had happened to his brave, strong daughter, but he didn't blame her. He wanted to let out a feral cry as well.

Jace had mentioned some kind of emergency with the team, and Sam could hardly expect him to hang around the hospital all day.

No, that was *his* job.

He wouldn't even think about the bar and grill. Nell could manage for a day or two, but not a month or two . . . or eight like last time.

He would go under, and then they'd lose even the restaurant. That would look stellar in the transplant viability report.

Please, God, don't let Maddy need another heart.

The nurse came in wearing a uniform with bears on it. Around her neck dangled a pink stethoscope with Dora the Explorer clipped to it. "Good morning, Miss Maddy. My name is Britta, and I'll be taking you down to surgery."

"No!" Maddy turned to Sam and grabbed his arm. "Please, Daddy, don't make me, please—"

His chest threatened to implode. "Maddy. It's okay. You can do this."

"Tell me the story again. Please."

The story. He took her hand, soft and fragile in his. "Your mommy knew, from the day you were born, how strong you were. She would lay you down to sleep, and you'd get so angry."

"I would cry."

"Yes. And your little face would get red and your back would arch and she'd say, 'My little girl is a warrior.'" He cupped her face with his hand, ran his thumb down her soft, wet cheek. "You had eyes as big as saucers, and your hair stood on end, but you were the cutest thing your mommy and I had ever seen. I just knew that angels sang over you. One day you were in your walker and we'd forgotten to close the gate, and before your mommy knew it, you headed toward the stairs. She dove to catch you, but down you went, tumbling head over tail in your walker—"

"Like a bouncy ball."

"Right, like a bouncy ball." He moved aside as the orderlies wheeled in a surgical gurney. They picked up Maddy and transferred her over.

She shot Sam a panicked look. He kept his voice even. "The crazy, miraculous thing was, you bounced from the bottom step into the air, right through the middle of the doorframe without touching it, and then . . . you landed right-side up, holding on to the sides of your walker like you'd just gone on a roller-coaster ride."

"And I didn't even cry." Her lip trembled through her smile.

They moved out of the room. "You didn't even cry. And your mom said, 'My little girl is brave.'"

Bless her tiny, frail heart, Maddy put on her brave face. She managed a shaky smile, her eyes filling. "I'll be right back," she said, remembering.

"Yes. And I'll be right here," he responded, smoothing back her hair and kissing her forehead.

"'Kay," Maddy said, but her eyes grew wider as they wheeled her down the hall. She tightened her hold on Sam's hand. "Sing to me, Daddy?"

"Yeah, baby." He licked his lips, his voice shaking. "Uh . . . 'Jesus loves me . . . this . . . I know . . .'"

Shoot, he could do better. He took another breath. "'For the Bible tells me . . . so . . .'"

Maddy's lips moved with his, her brown eyes so big they might swallow him whole. Just a few more feet . . .

And then she'd be gone. His voice died.

"'Little ones to Him belong.'" Maddy's voice picked up the song. "'They are weak, but He is strong.'"

Oh, God, thank You for my strong, brave daughter. "'Yes, Jesus loves me . . .'"

Yes, Jesus loves me. Please.

They finished the song together as they stopped by the doors to the surgical suite. "'The Bible tells me so.'"

Then they wheeled Maddy through the surgical doors, leaving him alone in the hallway, his heartbeat so loud in his chest, he could hear nothing else.

Not even the song.

"Sam, how are you holding up?"

Jace sat in a chair across the hall from Owen's hospital room, cell phone to his ear. They'd posted a guard and cordoned off the area from local press, but he'd still had to run interference when the hospital transferred Owen out of ICU.

He didn't know what impulse compelled him to stick around all day—save for the two hours he escaped to his condo for a shower and a change of clothing. Maybe he couldn't dodge the sense that Eden might need him.

Probably just hopeful thinking.

No, not hopeful. Just a sense of responsibility or guilt. Because he also couldn't get past the look in his teammates' eyes when he walked into the waiting room. As if he were the father of a bunch of juvenile delinquents.

He'd aged a couple decades right before his own eyes.

Still, maybe he should have picked up on the chatter in the

locker room last night after the game when they suggested finishing what they started on the ice. He'd been tired and just glad to escape without a headache.

Jace had finally sent Max and the guys home to shower and sleep and get ready for practice.

He, however, decided to stay and keep an eye on Eden, who'd sat in the ICU waiting room all morning, downing cup after cup of coffee but otherwise stiff and unmoving, as if willing her brother to wake up. Maybe it had worked because around noon he'd woken briefly, and the team doc, Dr. Wilson, had set up a press conference for later today. Jace had no doubt the PR department would prepare a hazy, nonspecific statement about the night's events.

Who knew but there might be suspensions in Owen's—and Max's and Kalen's—near futures.

"I'm okay, Jace," Sam said. "Maddy's back from her biopsy and feeling pretty punky."

"When do you get the results?"

"Later today." His voice was muffled as if he was holding his hand over the phone. "But I think we're in trouble. She's bloated with the fluids, and her temperature is up."

"I'm sorry, Sam."

"What's going on with you?"

"Owen Christiansen took a hit to the head last night while mixing it up after the game. He's out of ICU, but he's got some damage to his eye." He glanced at Eden, now sitting in Owen's room by his bedside. Vigilant as he slept. Jace should get her something to eat.

"Wow, that's rough."

"Yeah—hey, I think his family's here. I'll talk to you later. Call me if something changes."

Jace clicked off as a troupe of Christiansens tromped down the hall, led by Graham. He spoke to the guard, who let them pass.

Jace recognized members of the family from the few times Owen had brought them to games, but he'd never really seen the entire tribe together. Owen's father—Jace couldn't remember his name—recognized him and came at him with a handshake. A big man, he wore a skullcap and a canvas work jacket and looked like a man used to handling everything life threw at him. He gave Jace a grim smile. "Jace Jacobsen. I recognize you. Thanks for being here."

"Good to see you again, sir."

"John."

"Right."

"And you remember my wife—" He turned, but the blonde woman had already walked past him, into the room, and Jace watched as Eden wrapped her in a hug. "Ingrid."

"Yes." Jace gave him a nod, and John followed his wife into the room. Behind him shuffled in a couple girls—a redhead and a blonde like Eden—and then a brother, a taller version of Owen, except with dark-brown hair.

He stopped at the door. "Aw—you're J-Hammer." He stuck out his hand. "Casper. I'm Owen's brother." He glanced behind him. "We had to endure the radio news the entire way down. What don't we know?"

"Call me Jace, and I don't know—just that it was an accident."

"Casper!" Eden had suddenly come to life and run out of the room. She didn't look at Jace as she wrapped her brother in a hug. "I'm so glad you're here."

Casper kissed the top of her head. "Hang in there, Sis."

She nodded, but Jace saw the fatigue on her face, her forced smile. He hung back as the doctor came down the hall and entered the room.

Probably it was a good time to exit. Maybe find some grub. He'd stick around for the press conference and then head over to practice.

Jace walked past the cop, then down to the elevators. He was thumbing through the tweets with Owen's hashtag when he saw Eden walk by.

She reached up as if to wipe away a tear. He glanced down the hall—the door to Owen's room remained closed.

Where was she going? He didn't mean to pry, but something about it felt abrupt—enough that he followed her. At a distance, casually looking at his phone.

She had turned down a corridor and stopped, slipping into a crouch and burying her face in her hands.

And he got it. After sitting all day, stoically holding together Team Christiansen, she had to run away to crumble. Sort of like his own escape two years ago.

He didn't want her to accidentally end up in a lake, nearly drowning, freezing from hypothermia.

Which was why he put his phone away and walked toward her.

She must have heard him because she looked up, her eyes red. "Eden—"

"Just . . ." She held up her hand as if to keep him away.

"What did the doctor say?"

She stood, tugged at her sweater. "Uh . . ." She brushed her hair away from her face, hands trembling. Then she glanced behind him. "Not here."

Right. Media. He glanced around, saw an empty room, the curtain drawn through the center. "In here."

She followed him into the room, let him shut the door. Blew

out a long breath. "It's horrible. He's got some serious damage to his eye. The doctor says that even if they save it, they're not sure if he'll regain his peripheral vision."

Jace leaned against the edge of the empty bed.

"It's just not fair. He's worked his entire life for this. Since he was four—*four*. He was so cute, his little hockey stick almost as tall as he was. He'd go out on the lake the second Dad cleared the ice and spend all Saturday skating." She ran her fingers under her eyes. "Funny thing is, Casper was the one who seemed to be our superstar hockey player. It wasn't until Owen made the team in eighth grade that he really started stepping into his own spotlight. It was like he realized that he didn't have to be in Casper's shadow anymore and that he had his own mad skills."

She shook her head. "He got a nineteen on his ACT. He barely passed high school. The kid has ADHD and is borderline dyslexic. What's he going to do if he can't play hockey? Sell cars? Work with Darek on the resort? Not that that's a bad idea, but . . ."

Jace said nothing. Especially since he had this awkward urge to reach out and fold her into an embrace. Weird, since less than twenty-four hours earlier he'd just wanted her out of his car, out of his life.

And in the silence, maybe she remembered their long, painful ride home too, because suddenly she frowned at him. "What are you still doing here? What, now you start deciding to act like a captain?"

Whoa—

"Really, Jace, couldn't you have shown up last night—?"

"I was busy last night."

"Yeah, doing what?"

He didn't want to be snarky, but she had this . . . this way about her. "Well, after I drove you home, I had to take my best friend to the hospital because his daughter is rejecting her heart transplant."

That silenced her, and the whitened pallor of her expression made him feel like a jerk. But the truth was, he'd already asked himself what might have happened if he'd tracked down Owen and the guys instead of showing up at Sam's.

He didn't want to go there.

"I'm sorry," she said softly.

"Yeah, well, I *do* feel sick about this. I like Owen, and I understand a little about what it might be like to lose everything."

"He's not going to lose everything. He just can't—"

"What are you two doing in here?"

Jace jumped at the voice of a nurse entering the room. An older woman, she wore turquoise pants and a well-filled-out scrub top patterned with tiny hockey players. For a second, he had the feeling of being in the wrong team's locker room. "We're just talking—"

"Arguing. We can hear you all the way down the hall." She flung back the curtain, and he froze at the sight of a young man lying in the bed. Maybe about Owen's age, a breathing tube down his throat, his body hooked to machines.

"I'm so sorry." This from Eden, who looked as horrified as he felt. "We didn't see him."

The nurse waved her words away as she checked the monitor. "Maybe he heard you and it will touch something inside."

"How long has he been like this?" Eden stood at the end of the bed, concern in her expression.

"About a week. He came in hypothermic, with a head trauma, and hasn't woken up."

"Oh, his poor family."

"No family. He's a John Doe."

"A John Doe?" Eden said. "You don't know who he is?"

"Nope. He's all alone." She pulled the curtain across. "Come on now, out."

Jace followed Eden out, seeing how white she'd gone. Even he felt a sting in the back of his throat at the nurse's words.

"Come with me." He wanted to reach out to her, take her hand, but he didn't want to upset their fragile peace.

Thankfully she followed him, and he returned to the elevator.

"Where are we going?"

"This cafeteria has amazing tapioca pudding."

"Pudding?"

She stood to his shoulder, and close like this, he could smell something pretty and floral, maybe her shampoo. Her blonde hair curled over her shoulders like ribbon, and for a moment, his gaze landed on her full lips, and he felt a latent, almost-forgotten stirring inside.

What? No. Not for Eden Christiansen. He shook it away. Still, he knew what it felt like to sit at someone's bedside, hoping. "Listen . . . yeah, I'm still here, and I've hung around in the hallway all day, watching you stare at Owen, wishing this hadn't happened. I know that look—I've been there. And I've found the one and only cure is . . . tapioca pudding."

She raised an eyebrow, even if she didn't smile.

Not that he expected it. But he wasn't the kind of guy to give up, and for some reason he couldn't quite place, he wanted to see her smile.

"I'm frustrated too. And the last thing I want to do is go to a press conference. Or practice, for that matter. So indulge me. Let me buy you some pudding."

She considered him a long moment. "This doesn't mean we're friends, J-Hammer."

"Never. I promise. Just tapioca, that's it."

"Fine. If you insist. Feed me."

He finally got that smile.

CHAPTER 6

"So, PUDDING WITH JACE JACOBSEN?" Casper held his iPad, moving the letters on the screen in the game Words with Friends. "What's next, crumpets with Max Sharpe?" He handed Eden the iPad, grinning. "*Lightest*, for thirty-two."

Their mother looked up from where she sat by the window, knitting. "Well done, Casper." She wore a long black sweater, a dark-green scarf looped around her neck, her blonde hair pulled back in a headband. But the stress of the last twenty-four hours was etched into her face despite her attempts at a smile.

"I do know how to spell, Mom," Casper said. He had crashed last night at Owen's place, and it seemed he had pilfered from Owen's closet, wearing a pair of black jeans and a gray pullover that Eden had freshly laundered. She had a feeling Casper had also taken the Charger out for a spin because the keys had gone missing from Owen's coat pocket. Apparently Max had driven the car to the hospital after the accident.

Amelia looked up from her Mac. She'd taken over access to Owen's Facebook page and Twitter account, updating the world on his condition.

John sat next to Owen's bed, holding the remote, glancing now and again at sleeping Owen. He'd turned the TV to a church service this morning, and Eden experienced a surreal sense of the old days, when they'd file into a pew together.

Only her big brother, Darek, was missing. He'd called last night and today, however, checking in. Both times, her mother had disappeared into the hallway to talk. Speaking the words aloud just might destroy the fragile bubble of hope—or maybe denial—the Christiansen family had erected around Owen, his room, his fans, and even his agent, Graham.

Owen's career might be over.

And then what?

Not only that, but Eden couldn't shrug off the sense that, somehow, they blamed her. After all, she lived in the Cities; she went to Owen's games. They depended on her to help him keep his head on his shoulders.

She could barely look at her parents and risk seeing the disappointment in their eyes.

"I knew I shouldn't have told anyone." Eden shot Grace a frown, then went back to studying the screen. "Jace just bought me pudding. Don't get carried away."

"Pudding. Now that's a sure sign of love." Grace sat on a chair, paging through a culinary magazine she'd picked up in the hospital gift shop.

Eden rearranged her letters. "He was just trying to take my mind off . . ." She glanced at Owen. He'd slept most of yesterday and today, the anesthesia from the surgery sapping him.

However, last night's heartbreaking moment when he'd awoken with no memory of the accident could still wring her out. She'd stepped away from the bed and let her parents take the reins of telling him the details and keeping him calm.

Yes, Owen had needed his dad for that news.

Eden had taken Grace and Amelia home with her. This morning, Grace had scoured her pitiful refrigerator and crafted a miracle with eggs, some onions, mushrooms, a can of tomatoes, and spinach leaves. She brought the frittata and some fresh muffins back to the room for breakfast.

"I like Jace. And the fact that he was here, waiting with you, seems very gentlemanly." Ingrid gave Eden a smile.

"He wasn't waiting with me, Mom." Eden moved an *s* above the word *lightest* and added *hun* across the top. Clicked Submit. She handed the iPad back to Casper. "He was just hanging around. I'm not even sure why. Probably guilt."

"Seventy-two points? Hey, not fair." Casper turned his voice whiny. "Mom, Eden is using her brains to bully me again."

Ingrid rolled her eyes.

"Why would he feel guilty?" Amelia asked.

"Because he sets a bad example for the players. He's the team captain, but he's also the team troublemaker."

Grace grinned at her. "I wouldn't mind that kind of trouble in my life."

"Grace!" Eden said.

"I'm just sayin'—just because a guy is famous doesn't make him trouble. Look at Owen."

Yeah, look at Owen. Had they not listened to the story of how he got hurt?

Eden glanced at the television screen. Her father had flipped to the NHL channel, catching a replay of Friday's Blue Ox game. She wanted to suggest he change channels, maybe find something a little less painful. Like the Disney Channel.

But her gaze glued to the screen, watching the action. *The NHL changes you.* Jace's voice, in her head, from the drive home—what, only two nights ago? It seemed like an eternity. But yes, hockey had changed Owen.

Maybe forever.

Eden felt as if she were holding her breath. Because if it was all over . . .

Well, her parents would return to Deep Haven with Grace and Amelia. Casper would return to his classes at the University of Minnesota, Duluth. And Darek and Ivy . . .

"When is Darek going to pop the question?" Eden asked, keeping her voice even. She'd seen the change in her big brother this Christmas—he'd become the Darek she remembered from high school, only better. This Darek had a smile, a new freedom in his laughter. This Darek seemed healed.

Her father said, "I think he's waiting until after Jensen and Claire's wedding on Valentine's Day."

"Really? Valentine's Day?"

"I think it's romantic," Amelia said.

"They're both in it—Darek is best man, and Ivy is a bridesmaid. I don't think Darek wants to steal Jensen's thunder," Ingrid added.

Or upset the tenuous peace they'd found after years of blaming each other for a tragic accident that cost Darek his wife.

See, one brother had found his way back from tragedy; this brother could also. The thought seemed to linger in the room because Ingrid set her knitting down, got up, and stood over Owen's bed. She touched his leg. "He'll be fine. He has his faith."

Eden refrained from shaking her head, but Owen's last words to her rang in the back of her mind. *I'll change my name.*

She stood. "I'm going to get some coffee."

"I'll go with you." Her mother reached for her purse and hung it over her shoulder. "My treat."

"I can buy my own coffee, Mom," Eden said as they walked out of the room.

Ingrid looped her arm through Eden's. "I know."

They walked in silence down the hall to the elevator. Ingrid sighed, then said, "This isn't your fault, honey."

The words, so sudden, so quiet, bit at Eden. She swallowed the thickness swelling her throat and got onto the open elevator.

Ingrid stepped in beside her. Thankfully a doctor joined them, and Eden blinked back the moisture before she dissolved into some sort of emotional mess.

Despite her mother's words, Eden knew the truth.

They rode down to the second floor and got off, the scent of coffee guiding them to a tiny shop tucked near the second-floor lobby. Leather chairs grouped in circles invited conversation. A bookshelf at the entrance displayed newspapers from around the area. Inside, the sound of milk being foamed, the murmur of patrons, suggested life beyond a hospital room.

Eden picked up a bulging Sunday paper from the stand and stuck it under her arm.

"Did you get a letter from Ruth Hamilton's family? They loved the article you wrote about Ruth for the Deep Haven paper."

"I got it, Mom, but I don't know why it was such a big deal. Everyone knew Ruth—she was a Deep Haven saint."

"But you captured her personality and reminded us why she was so special. It made me cry."

Eden shook her head and stepped up to the counter. "A vanilla latte, nonfat, for me and—" She turned to her mother.

Ingrid was frowning at the board. "I think I want a macchiato. Medium."

Ingrid reached for her purse, but Eden had already found her card. "We have to wait over here." Eden moved to a tiny round table and set the paper on it. Ingrid slid into a chair opposite her.

"I always knew you'd be a great storyteller, Eden. I used to spy on you when you set up your Barbies and created epic adventures for them. You had so much creativity."

"Tell that to the paper. Tell it to Hal." Eden found the obits section and pulled it from the Sunday paper. Set it on the table to read the remembrance articles.

Kendra had a byline above the fold, in a story about one of the first Navy SEALs, who'd passed away on Friday in the VA hospital.

The call had probably come in on Saturday morning, while Eden sat vigil by Owen's bedside. She would have been working the desk.

"What's the matter, sweetie?"

She looked up to see her mother frowning. "Nothing. I'm sorry I'm so crabby. I'm just tired."

"Eden." Ingrid leaned forward to touch her arm. "Tell me what's going on."

Eden shook her head, a boulder on her chest. "It's just . . . I feel stuck, Mom. I sit in a cubicle all day and take phone calls about dead people. And then I write a little paragraph about them— usually dictated by the funeral home. If I do find something interesting, it gets handed off to Kendra. And then I come home, and there's Owen's laundry all over the room, with a note about how he owes me one—"

"Owen made you do his laundry?"

"Oh, you have no idea what Owen makes me do." She closed her eyes, refusing the urge to tell her about his recent bar fight. "Don't tell me that you haven't figured this out, Mom. I mean, look at our family. Darek is a hotshot firefighter, and Grace can create gourmet meals out of nothing. Amelia will be an award-winning photographer someday, and Casper is going to discover a lost treasure. And Owen . . . Well, look at me. I'm the cheerleader. I'm the one who sits in the stands and waves the foam finger. I'm just the bystander. In their lives. In *my* life."

Her words syruped through her, sticky and hot. Yes, she'd become a spectator in her own life. Watching from the outside.

In fact, even pudding with Jace seemed like something that happened to someone else. For a snapshot of time, sitting opposite him in a corner booth in the cafeteria, laughing as he dipped mozzarella sticks into his tapioca, she'd forgotten who she was. Who *he* was.

And if *he'd* remembered, even for a moment, he wouldn't have invited her, the girl he *might* notice, out for anything.

Yet for the space of twenty minutes, he'd seemed to be a regular, even goofy guy. They'd played a game, trying to create a story about each person in the room. Crazy, lighthearted fun.

Until it ended abruptly, without explanation. Just like that, he'd turned cold, led them back to the elevator, and she'd found her own way back to reality: the silent, worried huddle of her family outside Owen's room.

Yes, whatever happened in the cafeteria with Jace Jacobsen had vanished when they both remembered exactly who they were. Or weren't.

Across from her, Ingrid had gone silent. She took Eden's hand. "Out of everyone in our family, Eden, you alone have the ability to make people see their potential. I don't know why you can't see your own."

Eden stared at their hands, not sure what to say.

"A latte and a macchiato?"

Ingrid got up and retrieved their drinks. Eden met her at the counter, took her latte, and doctored it with some sweetener.

Ingrid stood by the table as if waiting to finish their conversation, but Eden didn't want to hear the words she knew her mother wanted to say. *Eden, God has a good plan for your life.*

It certainly didn't feel that way. In fact, sometimes she wondered if God noticed her at all.

Eden brushed past her mother, heading back to the room.

They heard the yelling as soon as the elevator doors opened to Owen's floor. It carried down the corridor, and a nurse rushed toward the star power forward's room as Eden and Ingrid hurried after her.

"Turn it off! Turn it off, Dad! I don't want to see it—I can't see it!"

Oh no. Eden stood in the doorway, frozen at the sight of Owen throwing whatever he could get his hands on. Already he'd shoved the telephone off the bedside stand. John grabbed him by one arm, Casper by the other. Amelia sat white-faced as she clutched her computer to her chest. Grace crouched by the window, picking up what looked like the debris of her delicious muffins.

"Let me go!"

The nurse moved to his bedside. "Sir, please calm down."

"We'll calm him down." This from John, whose voice seemed to act as a cord they might all cling to. "Owen, that's enough."

"Get away from me, Dad. Don't touch me." Owen yanked free of his father's grip, took a swing at Casper.

Casper dodged it, his expression darkening. "Owen—*c'mon*—"

"It's off!" Amelia said. "We turned it off!"

Owen covered his face with his hands, touching the bandage across his eye. And then, as everyone watched in horrified silence, he began to weep.

Their fragile bubble shattered.

He wasn't going to be okay. In fact, none of them were.

"Owen," Ingrid said, going into the room.

Casper backed away, then ran a hand over his forehead, turning to look out the window.

Amelia started to cry, hands pressed to her mouth.

Grace continued to clean up the muffins.

And Eden stood at the threshold of the room. She couldn't watch Owen's life crumble. She turned away from the door, walking down the hallway, her heart in her throat, her eyes hot.

Just breathe.

She turned at the elevators, then again down the next corridor, and found herself at the room with the John Doe patient. She slipped inside. Sunlight streamed in through the open curtains with so much hope that it seemed almost sacrilegious.

Doe still lay hooked to oxygen, his levels monitored on a screen behind him. Alone. No flowers, plants, or balloons wishing him well. No freshly baked brownies, no family clustered around him, talking, playing games.

It made Owen's room seem like a party. Until, of course, reality broke in.

Eden sat on the chair next to his bed. Doe seemed young—maybe in his early twenties. A college student. He wore a bandage around his shaved head. What had the nurse said—something about hypothermia along with head trauma? He had the lean body of an athlete, though—strong shoulders, sinewy arms, reminding her of Owen. And good-looking, with high cheekbones, a square jaw, a growth of golden-brown whiskers.

"So," Eden said quietly, "how did you get hurt? And why don't they know who you are?"

She looked behind her in case anyone might be listening. But no nurse barged in to discover her, so she got up and closed the door. She just needed a moment or two alone. Someplace where no one would find her so she could collect her thoughts, figure out how to put the pieces back together.

Her voice fell to a whisper. "I'm sorry this happened to you. And I'm sorry your family isn't here."

He didn't move. Not like she expected him to, but what did they say about coma patients hearing people around them? Maybe he needed some company. She looked at his hands. His fingernails were clean, filed. Like he took care of himself.

She sipped her coffee. Considered the chaos happening down the hallway. Then she picked up the remote and aimed it at the television. "Let's watch some hockey."

"Get it together, Max!" Jace skated over to the team box and opened his mouth for the trainer to spray in water. It hit him in the teeth and dribbled down his chin, catching in his beard.

Behind him, Max chased down the pass he'd missed, scooping up the puck and bringing it back to the blue line to run the play again.

Everyone seemed on edge, missing passes, playing sloppy.

So maybe Coach had good reason for Sunday's hastily called practice.

Jace wiped his chin with his jersey. He could read the stress in Max's expression—and not just from the fact that Coach had moved the forward up to the first line to play Owen's empty wing position, but also from the news today that Owen might be out for the season.

And the murmuring suggested a career-ending injury.

Poor Eden. Funny, that thought hit him more than the demise of Owen's career. Since yesterday, she'd lingered in Jace's head.

She'd let him buy her tapioca pudding. Let him play funny food tricks to coax another smile from her. And then she'd started playing a game with him.

"Who's that man over there?" she'd asked, pointing at an elderly gentleman dressed in a brown polyester suit and a blue tie, carrying a spray of pink carnations.

He'd frowned, not sure what she meant.

"I think he's a retired English lit professor and he's here because his wife of sixty years is recovering from hip surgery. They used to go dancing on Thursday nights, and he knows she'll never dance again. So he bought her a bouquet of carnations to remind her that he still loves her."

She took a spoonful of her pudding while Jace considered the man.

"And he is secretly relieved that he never has to dance again," he said.

"Jace!"

He lifted a shoulder. "Just being honest." He nodded toward a woman in a lab jacket, her dark hair piled up on her head, glasses low on her nose as she read her iPad and nursed a bowl of soup. "And her?"

Eden had turned to study her, and he took his opportunity to trace the outline of her face, take in the way her blonde hair fell around her shoulders. He'd like to run a strand between his fingers.

He let the thought linger, sinking into her game as she answered.

"She's a doctor. Maybe even . . . Hmmm. I think she must work with children because she's wearing a pink stethoscope. She's reading the file of one of her newest patients, someone she is worried about from the way she keeps frowning. I think she's probably married to the hospital."

"No husband?"

"I can't see a ring, but she has a sort of no-nonsense aura around her. I'll bet she was once terribly in love but had her heart broken." She scooped another spoonful of pudding, giving him an impish smile. "Now she wants nothing to do with men."

"Ouch."

"Yeah, well, we scare easily."

"Really?" He hoped not because he didn't want to send her running. "And you can see her aura?"

"It's a gift I have. I see the truth in people."

He wanted to ask her about his aura, not sure she was kidding, except right about then he remembered.

Of course she knew so much about people. She spent hours writing about them. Dissecting their lives.

He couldn't bear to see what she'd do to his. And though she hadn't mentioned an article, blog, or even Facebook posting . . . well, she probably wouldn't be able to help herself.

Which was why he'd packed up their food, dumped it in the garbage, and ended their little escape. He'd put her on the elevator back to her brother's tragedy and hightailed it over to Maddy's room.

He'd found her sleeping, Sam curled up on the sofa, so he'd headed home.

Where he sat in darkness and wished that he didn't have such an overactive protective gene. But that's what happened when you grew up without a father, only you to protect your mother.

That protective gene was what made him a good enforcer, too.

Although not today. Today he wanted to check his right wing into the boards, maybe grab him by the jersey and tell him to snap out of it. They had a game on Tuesday, one without Owen Christiansen.

Someone had to make the goals.

"Set it up again!" Coach Duggin stood in the box, his arms folded across his pullover, looking peeved at the lack of chemistry between his players. Max seemed so rattled that it might just be easier for Jace to make the shot from the blue line.

Maybe . . .

They ran the play four more times before Max anticipated the pass, before he flicked it in between the goaltender's skates.

Coach left them standing there, sweaty and frustrated, as he called practice. Just for fun, Jace slapped in four shots, then headed for the showers. He stood there as the water sluiced off him, aware of the uneasy quiet in the locker room. So they felt it too—the gaping hole left by their star forward.

Would Jace leave a gaping hole if *he* were injured? Taken out of the sport?

He changed into a T-shirt and shorts, then headed to the therapy room for ice. His knee had stiffened like a board after practice.

Graham found him seated on a table, the trainer wrapping

Jace's knee with ice and saran wrap. He stood at the door, arms crossed over his fancy suit.

"What?"

Graham waited until the trainer finished, then came in and leaned against the opposite table. He looked at his shoes, back at Jace. "Management isn't happy about your decision not to take the offer."

"Of course not, but I need to talk to you about that."

"No, see, they know what you're doing. And they don't like it."

"What are you talking about? They should be happy I'm not injured—"

"Did you even read Saturday's papers? They said the game lacked spark. That if it weren't for Owen Christiansen, fans would be attending a peewee game."

"Oh, for—"

Graham held up his hands. "Listen, at the end of the day, it's about ticket sales. And if you have another game like the last one—"

"I had a *great* game. One assist, five shots on goal."

"You had a safe game. But safe isn't going to get you far at this level. And with Owen out, the pressure is on. You've got to show them something if you want anyone to pick you up after the season."

Jace frowned. "So in order to keep my job, I have to get in a fight without getting injured?"

"At least play with an edge. Give the fans what they want."

Jace adjusted the pack on his knee. Sighed. "I've decided to take the offer."

Graham had turned silent. Again, looking at his shoes.

"Don't tell me—"

"They withdrew the offer when I turned it down."

Of course they did.

"You heard the doc—if I fight and get hurt, if I get another concussion, it could all be over for me."

Graham met his eyes. "I know."

No. This couldn't be happening. Not now.

"Hey, Jace." Max walked into the room, wearing track pants and a T-shirt, his hair slicked back. He handed Jace a cold soda. "I'm going to get it, you know."

Jace nodded, but Max wasn't done. "Can I talk to you?"

Graham moved toward the door but paused beside Max. "And when you're done, I'll be waiting for you in the hallway."

Max's eyes brightened, a little too much perhaps.

Jace shook his head. "'Sup?"

Max couldn't look at him. "I've been thinking about it all day, ever since . . . Well, I think I'm the one who busted Owen's eye. I remember jerking my stick back, ready to level it at a Blades player, and Owen was right there, behind me. It happened so fast—the fight, the yelling—but when I slow it down . . . I hit him. I remember it."

Jace took a sip of his Coke. Considered Max, who looked as if he'd just confessed to sleeping with the principal's daughter. The soda burned his throat as he swallowed it down. "Let it go, Max. It was an accident."

"But—"

"He'll never forgive you if he finds out. Trust me . . . let it go."

Max's mouth tightened. Then he nodded. "Thanks, Cap."

He walked out into the hall, and Jace heard Graham greet him.

Jace set the soda on the table beside him, then leaned back, propping his arm over his head. The faintest throb of pain speared his brain.

Poor kid. He knew what it felt like to live with guilt, even over accidents.

Eden drifted back into his thoughts, the way she'd looked at him when he'd put her on the elevator. Confused. Even hurt.

If he could overlook the reporter in her, maybe they might actually . . .

No. He didn't need anyone else in his life. He had Sam. And Maddy. And hockey.

Well, he had Sam and Maddy.

Jace got up and grabbed one of the crutches by the table, pulled it to himself, and limped out of the room, down the hall. Max and Graham had vanished—probably to plan Max's stellar career, if he could ever figure out how to catch Jace's passes. He made it to his locker, opened it, and grabbed his coat.

Jace could sulk and consider the destruction of his career, his life, just as easily at home.

He worked on the jacket and was reaching for his duffel when his phone vibrated in his pocket. Pulling it out, he found a text message. He'd missed a slew of them but opened only the last.

From Sam.

Maddy's heart is failing. She's going back into surgery.

FORGET HIS OATH not to pray, not to get on his face and beg, because right here, right now, that's all Sam had. Just God and desperation.

Sam sat in the front pew of the tiny chapel, hardly able to breathe, a noose around his chest, his face in his hands.

He wanted to weep, but even that he couldn't manage. Just a low moan of pain. *Please, God.*

Why would God spare him, a rough-around-the-edges ex–hockey player, and take Mia? Kind, wise, beautiful Mia, who knew how to braid Maddy's hair and sing her to sleep and believe in happy endings.

Maybe that was the problem—he had stopped believing in happy endings years ago. Now he just believed in holding on.

Surviving.

Take me, God. If You have to take someone, take me. It didn't sound like the right theology, and he knew it. God didn't bargain, didn't play favorites. Sam's head told him all this, but his heart couldn't quite grasp it.

Why were some children born with perfectly healthy hearts and his priceless daughter born with one destined to betray her?

At the very least, he didn't understand why God stood by and let her suffer.

Sam pressed the heels of his hands into his eyes, hating the spiral of thoughts, the way fear could suffocate him. They'd given him a beeper like they might in a restaurant—*Sir, your table is ready. Your child is ready. Your verdict awaits.* Maybe they knew that desperate parents couldn't hang around in the waiting room, hollow gazes not meeting each other, afraid to acknowledge the grief.

He couldn't bear it.

If Sam could tear out his heart and give it to Maddy, he would. Had even thought it through—how he might convince some doctor to carve into his chest, give life to his little girl. But before he could do it, the unthinkable had happened to some other undeserving family. Their child had died, and because of it, Sam's daughter had lived, and it cost him nothing.

Sure, the medical expenses, even with his insurance, had cost him his home—their home—the one Mia had created for them, with Maddy's pink room, the canopy bed, what seemed like thousands of Beanie Babies that Mia had collected over the years. But Sam would sleep in a cardboard box under a bridge if it meant Maddy might have a safe, normal childhood.

Or even have a childhood at all.

He couldn't go through this again. Sam sank to his knees before the altar in the clean, bright hospital chapel, closing his eyes.

Sam?

He heard her voice like a whisper in the back of his heart and let Mia walk in, let her sit down beside him.

In his memory, he took her hand. Smooth and soft as he ran his thumb over it. *I miss you.*

I miss you too. Her voice could still catch his heart in his throat. And even though he knew she couldn't possibly be here, he let himself talk.

"I'm so sorry. I know I probably messed up. I should have done better, I know."

Hang on, Sam.

The image changed to Mia sinking into her hospital bed, her skin pasty, white, the veins in her beautiful hands bruised. *Hang on, Sam.*

And then she'd slipped away.

"You should have been the one to hang on, Mia." His voice echoed in the tiny chapel, and he opened his eyes to see if he'd shaken anyone.

He'd surely shaken himself, the anger right on the edge of his tone.

But maybe he didn't care. "You should have hung on. Waited for a donor. Maddy needs a mother. She needs someone to do her hair and sing her songs and hold her hand. Because I can't do this. Not anymore."

You're not alone.

Not her voice, maybe. It bore a deeper resonance that sank into his bones.

He covered his mouth before he let sobs leak out. *Oh, God, please help me hold on.*

The beeper went off—loud and abrupt, nearly sending him through his skin. Sam picked it up.

Then he took off running.

To Jace, Sam looked like he'd succumbed to a three-day bender, an odor emanating from him that called up images of the man passing out behind a Dumpster. His hair stood nearly on end; his beard had grown in reddish and gnarly; his shirt still bore the stains of Maddy's illness—

But now was not the time to tell Sam that he might be mistaken for a derelict. Not when he was seated on the couch in Maddy's room, his daughter still on the surgical table, on life support, while the doctor explained to Sam the details of the artificial heart he wanted to use to save her life.

Temporarily.

The device hailed from Germany. Or maybe Jace just thought so because he'd caught "Berlin" in the conversation. He was trying to make sense of the terminology, trying to listen so he could explain it to Sam later if he had to.

Not that Sam didn't know everything about post–heart transplant options. The man had spent years scouring the Internet, reading books, monitoring Maddy's diet, trying to keep her on schedule with her meds. He was a fanatic about her hygiene, and the fact that he'd lost his house and moved above the bar, the fact that somehow in that mix Maddy had missed some of her anti-rejection meds, seemed a cruel tragedy.

Sam didn't deserve this. Maddy didn't deserve this. But life wasn't fair—Jace had learned that long, long ago. If it were, he would have never made it to the pros. He would be working in some bar or mine or paper mill in International Falls.

At the twilight of his career, and especially in light of Sam's journey, Jace might want to remember that.

The nurse handed Sam some papers, and he signed them with the look of a man headed for Folsom prison.

Then the doc took off to connect Maddy's heart to tubes and wire and the desperate hope that it might keep her alive until . . .

Until hope died?

Sam sat back, his hand on his chest as if he couldn't breathe.

"Dude. I'm so sorry." Jace sat on the end of the green sofa. "Tell me what to do."

Sam lifted a shoulder, his eyes empty. "All we can do is wait."

Wait. Jace could taste the helplessness like acid in his throat, and he stood. "I'm going to get you some clothes." He paused. "Unless you need me to stay."

But Sam didn't even look up.

"I have my cell phone. And I'll be back as soon as I can."

"It'll be a few hours at best."

Sam sounded exhausted. As Jace watched, he got up, went over to Maddy's bed, and climbed in, pulling her pillow to his chest.

Yes, perhaps Sam didn't need him here. And "Hang in there" sounded . . . Well, he just couldn't say enough for what his friend needed.

"Call me if . . . I'll be here the minute you need me."

Sam nodded, nothing of comprehension in his eyes.

Jace walked down the hall and dug his thumb into the elevator button, his stomach a knot.

It wasn't supposed to be this way. Not for little girls. Especially not for little girls who'd already lost their mothers.

He took the elevator to the main level, then out to the parking garage. He'd run by Sam's, find him some clothes, pick up dinner, and be back before Maddy got out of surgery.

And yet he found himself pulling into the medical center parking lot. As if his GPS had its own mind.

He'd just do a quick run in and check on Owen.

Jace took the elevator to Owen's floor. He still wore his shorts, although he'd discarded the ice pack. He got a few looks as he traipsed past the nurses' station.

Jace spied the conversation knot from down the hall, the cluster of family members outside the room. He recognized John and Casper, the two sisters, Eden's mom.

No Eden.

They stood in a worried huddle, talking in low tones. Casper spotted him, and for a moment, the conversation stilled.

Oops. "Hey," Jace said. "I came to check on Owen."

Something in John's face gave him pause. Then the way Ingrid pressed her fingers to her mouth, turned away.

"They had to give him a sedative," Casper said. "He's . . . upset."

"Yeah, well, wouldn't you be upset if the doctor told you that you might never play hockey again?" the younger, redheaded sister said.

Jace had heard it already, but to listen to the pain in Owen's sister's voice made his insides tighten.

He just stood there while the family shifted on their feet. Finally, "So . . . where's Eden?" He wasn't sure why that felt important at the moment, but the fact that she hadn't joined her family seemed weird.

Not that he was concerned.

Okay, maybe a little.

"She took off," Casper said. "As soon as Owen started losing it, she left."

"Casper, he didn't lose it."

"What would you call that, Mom?" the redhead said.

"He's just upset."

"We're all upset," John said quietly. He looked at Jace. "She's probably around here somewhere. She always turns up."

He nodded. "I'll track her down."

Casper raised an eyebrow, but Jace walked away. He was just trying to be . . . a friend. Maybe she needed that right now, and it didn't mean they'd become best pals or anything.

What if she'd taken the same runaway route as last time? Jace returned to the elevator and retraced his steps. Stood in the hallway.

The cheers and what sounded like the play-by-play of a hockey game slipped out from under the door of a nearby room.

The room with the coma patient. He hadn't woken, had he? Jace pushed open the door and stuck his head in.

Eden sat with her feet up on the patient's bed, drinking coffee, watching one of Jace's shots on goal. A miss, and the crowd moaned.

"That shouldn't come as a great surprise to you. I missed it before, too." He stepped into the room, and she looked at him, her face slacking as she withdrew her feet from the bed.

"I was just—"

"Hiding. I know. I saw your family outside Owen's room."

"How is he?"

He grimaced. "They had to sedate him."

She swallowed, ran her thumb around the rim of her cup. "He was throwing things."

"I'm sure this isn't easy for him."

"I feel so helpless, you know?"

He sat on the opposite, empty bed. "I *do* know. My friend's kid—Sam's daughter, Maddy—her heart stopped today. They are putting in an artificial heart right now, some mechanical device that will keep her alive until they find her another heart."

"Oh, I'm sorry, Jace." The compassion in her pretty green eyes rushed through him.

"Yeah. He's had it rough. We played together when I was a rookie. He took me under his wing, became sort of a big brother to me. He was a great player—until he was injured and sidelined. Had a tough couple years after that. Then he met Mia. She was a waitress at one of his hangouts, but also a fitness geek, and she gave him a new outlook on his life. When they married, I know he thought they'd live happily ever after."

"What happened?"

"Mia developed an enlarged heart during pregnancy and was put on the transplant list. She never got her heart and died when Maddy was three."

Eden's eyes widened. "I'm so sorry."

"Yeah. But he had Maddy and that helped. Until Maddy developed the same condition."

"Which is why she had the heart transplant."

He nodded. "But the medical expenses made him lose his home, and now . . . who knows if they can find her another heart."

"That's awful."

He drew in a breath. Looked at John Doe. "So you're making new friends?" He tried a smile.

She answered it. "He's a bit tight-lipped, but we're getting along. I like a man who doesn't interrupt me." But a sadness touched her eyes, and her voice changed. "I feel sorry for him. No family. How is he supposed to get well without family?"

Good question. Where would Jace have been without Maddy and Sam to help him heal after he lost his mother?

"I'm sure he has family."

"But wouldn't that be awful—to not know your son or brother was injured?"

Jace walked over to the young man. Clean-cut, despite his growth of whiskers. Jace had never been this guy, but he might have wanted to be.

Or maybe he had been exactly this man, trapped, broken. John Doe needed someone to rescue him just as badly as Jace had that night in the water.

Eden brought him back from the memory. "I keep thinking about who he might be and how sometimes people come out of a coma if they hear a familiar voice." She lifted a shoulder as if already shrugging off the idea. "I was thinking I might try to find his family."

Her words slid like fire through his bones. "You want to find out who he is?"

She made a sort of face then. "I know. It's a long shot, but I feel sad for him—"

"I'll help." He wasn't sure where those words emerged from, but as soon as he said them, something shifted inside him.

Yes. He could find this kid's family, and maybe everything in his life, in his world, wouldn't feel so dark.

Eden looked stunned. "What?"

"I mean, I know you're the reporter, but . . . could I help somehow?"

She set down her cup of coffee. "Uh . . . I don't know—"

"Listen. I get that you don't like me very much. But maybe we can work together on this. I'm just . . ." He shook his head. "I'm sick of being helpless. Of watching the people I care about suffer." Or his career die. "I don't know—it might help to do *something*. Anything. Even help this stranger find his family."

"Uh . . ." She blew out a breath. "Just so you know, I'm not . . . I mean . . ." She made another strange face. "I'm not a great reporter."

He frowned. "I'm sure you are. And it's a great story."

Something flickered in her eyes. Her expression stirred a tingle in him, a curiosity. "It *is* a good story, isn't it? It's a great—even front-page—story. The kind of story I've waited for."

He couldn't help but notice the way her countenance changed as she got up, stood over John Doe.

"He looks like a college student, and maybe an athlete? We could check at the local colleges . . ."

"Or maybe he's just a kid who was in the wrong place at the wrong time?"

"Right. It could be that he's not even from here. Maybe he's from Chicago, and he came to town to hang out with friends. Or he flew in to finally meet this girl he connected with online, and she is still waiting—"

"In the snow."

She glanced at him. "Pining, actually. Knowing he's the right guy, finally, but not sure why he hasn't shown up. Why he's left her in the darkness and cold . . ."

"Wow. Now I don't know if we should help him, after he abandoned her like that."

Eden raised an eyebrow, but he smiled, winked.

"Let's give him a chance. It wasn't his fault. He was on his way to buy flowers when he was jumped," Eden said.

"You're right. For Marilou."

"Marilou?"

"The girl who is pining."

"Right. Marilou." He won another smile, something warm, igniting dangerous, unexpected feelings of anticipation.

So he could admit that the prospect of spending time with her didn't make him want to run. Didn't mean he shouldn't be on his guard. The first hint that she was picking apart his life or bossing him around or telling him what a terrible role model he'd become, he would walk.

Even if she might be right. "So, for Marilou?" he said.

She picked up her coffee. Considered Doe. "Okay. Yes. You can help me. Let's find John Doe."

I get that you don't like me very much. . . .

Jace's words tugged at Eden all morning.

Mostly because she *did* like him, despite herself. Just a little.

For Marilou. Eden had to smile at that. She loved the game of imagining a person's life, but to find him playing along . . . She might be in trouble here. Had she completely forgotten his reputation?

She could blame her fatigue. Her fragile emotional state. And Jace's devastating smile. It slid up his face, stopped at an unexpected dimple, and possessed the power to chase words from her brain.

It would help if he weren't so handsome, with all those chocolate curls, wide shoulders, a warrior's physique.

It only confused her—and her good sense. One second he was shutting down their conversation and steering her back to the elevator; then he was plugging his cell number into her phone and offering to help her land a story.

A great story. Yes, this story would certainly make Hal sit up and take notice.

And maybe, if she found Doe's family, they could wake him up. She might even save a life.

Still, what game was Jace playing? Because certainly famed Jace Jacobsen wasn't serious about donating his time to help her find a kid that society forgot.

Although, for a long moment there, Eden had believed him. Especially when he helped her search Doe's room for his belongings. She'd found them in a big white bag in the closet, and then, with Jace standing guard by the door, she sorted through his grimy red ski jacket, flannel shirt, faded jeans.

She'd unearthed only a flimsy, faded receipt for a sandwich, with the restaurant name partially torn off the top.

Before she had a chance to invoke any investigative powers, the nurse came in, gave them an annoyed look, and shooed them away.

And Jace vanished. Poof! Gone. Like she'd dreamed the entire escapade.

But the sandwich receipt sat like contraband in her pocket, burning Eden as she worked at her desk in obits.

She'd *stolen* it. From a coma patient. She'd rifled through his disgusting, soiled clothing. Three times she'd washed her hands in Owen's room, hanging around while her parents ordered pizza.

The dinner felt like a feeble attempt by her family to inflate another flimsy bubble of hope around Owen, as though his outburst hadn't sent a tremor of fear through all of them. But they didn't know Owen like she did.

He wasn't destined to take this well.

Eden took out the receipt. Smoothed it on her desk. She could make out the time and date and part of a name. *Frog*—?

Maybe this *was* a bad idea. Impulsive, and really, how was she going to find this kid's family if the police couldn't even do it?

Except what if it were Owen in that bed, all alone?

It is *a good story, isn't it?*

She glanced at Charlotte's closed office door. Took a breath. Got up. She put the receipt back in her pocket, then headed to Charlotte's office. Pausing outside the door, Eden ran her thumb over the edge of the receipt.

No, it's a great story.

She knocked.

"Enter." Charlotte looked up as Eden eased the door open. "Oh yes, hello, Eden." She wore a gray cashmere sweater today, a fedora on her head as if she were some *Vogue* editor. "How's your brother?"

Eden brushed her hands across her wool pants. "He's . . . not great, actually."

"I'm so sorry to hear that. I saw the news reports. It sounds like he might be out for a few games."

"We hope he'll be back soon." Yesterday her father had talked with reporters from KARE 11 on the phone after the family devised a party line. *We hope he'll be back soon. Go Blue Ox.*

"Do you need a few days off? I know you and your brother are close." Charlotte smiled, but her gaze had already tracked back to her computer.

"No . . . I mean, thank you, but I'm here because I have a story lead."

Charlotte pulled off her glasses. "Oh?"

"Yes. While I was at the hospital, I happened upon a John Doe. He's in a coma, and they can't find his family. I was hoping that maybe I could track them down."

Charlotte just sighed.

"What?"

"He's not deceased, is he?"

"He's in a coma."

"Is he likely to die?"

"Well . . . I hope not. I'm trying to find his family so he might hear their voices and wake up."

"Then he's not a fit for obits, is he?"

Oh. "But what if . . . ? Why do we always have to wait until they're dead?"

Charlotte raised an eyebrow. "Because we're the obituary department?"

But—and she wasn't sure why she wasted her desperation on Charlotte—"I don't want to write about the deceased the rest of my life."

Charlotte put her glasses back on. "You don't have to. But you are writing obits *now*. And the last time I looked, you had a tidy pile of them to compose. I would say that you might want to focus on keeping the job you currently have."

Eden stood there, her heart a stone.

"You're dismissed, Eden."

She took a breath, and the words just spilled out. "Aren't you tired of always writing about death?"

Charlotte looked up at her, frowned. "But, Eden, I don't write about death. I write about life."

Right.

Eden headed back to her desk, where a stack of mail-in forms awaited her attention, not to mention the online submissions.

She took out the receipt, stared at it a long moment, then crumpled it in her fist.

She wasn't a reporter, and she never should have lied to Jace. Truth was, she hadn't a hope of tracking down this kid's family. The entire thing was a stupid, impossible idea.

"How was your weekend?" Kendra popped over the side of the cubicle. "And your date with Russell?"

So much had happened since then, she'd nearly forgotten. "Tragic. He showed up for the game with his body painted."

Kendra's jaw dropped. "No."

"Yes. And dyed his hair blue."

"No!"

"Oh yes. It was . . . quite the game."

"I'm sorry. And, oh, by the way, I heard about your brother. How is he?"

"We're supposed to tell the news that he is fine, but . . . it's pretty bad. His orbit is broken, and he has a severe cut in his eye."

Kendra made a face. "Wow. That is awful. So they're thinking he'll be out for the season?"

She couldn't say *forever*, so she nodded.

"Bummer. How'd it happen?"

"He can't remember. It was a fight, of course. Owen trying to prove something."

To be tough. Maybe even impress someone, like his team captain.

"What do you have there?" Kendra pointed to the crumpled paper in Eden's hand.

"A receipt. I was trying to figure out where it was from."

"Why?"

Eden flicked her thumb on the paper. "While I was at the hospital, I happened upon this guy . . . he's in a coma. And he's a John Doe."

"How sad."

"Yeah. I was sort of thinking I might try to . . . I don't know—" She shook her head.

"Find out who he is? I love it!" Kendra came around the cubicle. "That's a fabulous idea. And so cool. So . . . is that his?"

"I picked it out of his pocket."

"Oh, you're bad."

"Yeah—"

"No, silly. Bad is good." She took the receipt. "The name is ripped off it."

"I know. But it sort of looks like *Frog*—maybe *Frogtown*. It's an area in St. Paul, about five miles from downtown, across the river. There's a White Castle around there, and Owen sometimes likes to stop after practice."

"You've got to be kidding."

"Hey—don't dis the Castle." Eden studied the print. "I'm going to do some googling at lunch and see if I can find a deli. Maybe after work I'll go down there, see if anyone can help me figure out who he is."

"You're not going by yourself, are you? I've heard of that area . . . it's not the safest. You need a big, strong man. Maybe even one who wears paint." Kendra waggled her eyebrows.

"I'm not calling Russell. Ever."

"Okay, fine. How about your family? Don't you have a couple brothers?"

"No. I don't want . . ." Yeah, that's what she needed—Casper the treasure hunter taking over her search. Or worse, mocking her.

"What about rounding up someone from your brother's tribe of pals?"

"You mean hockey players?"

"Well, I'm not talking about the swim team, for pete's sake.

You know the entire team. Certainly you could drum up one big, muscly—"

"Okay, that's enough. No. I mean, sure . . . maybe I have someone I could call."

Oh, shoot, why did she say that? Because Jace hadn't been serious about helping her, and now Kendra looked at her, all expectant eyes.

"Who?"

"Nobody. It's silly." Eden made to throw the receipt away, but Kendra caught it.

"I mean it—either you find someone, or I'll call Russell. Maybe he'll bring his paint."

"Oh, for—fine." Eden picked up her cell phone. She scrolled down to Jace's name. Let her thumb hover a moment before she sent the call through.

This was a mistake.

Her heart began to beat again when he didn't answer. "Voice mail," she said to Kendra and pulled the phone away.

Kendra pushed it back to her ear. "You leave a message or I'm looking up Hays Funeral Services."

Fine. She took a breath at the beep. "Uh, Jace. Hi. I . . . This is Eden. And . . . I . . ." Oh, she couldn't—really, how desperate was she? "I'm sorry. Forget it."

She pressed End.

Kendra stared at her. "Jace? Jace *Jacobsen*? That's who you called?"

She nodded. "He's a friend—I mean, he's *Owen's* friend, not mine. But we know each other."

"No wonder you don't want to call Russell." Kendra shook

her head. "Mmm-hmmm. Not when you have Mr. J-I-am-hot-Hammer on the line."

"What? No. Listen—he's not my kind of guy. He's too . . . he's too big for my world. He's got swarms of women and fans and . . . really, I don't like him. And he doesn't like me. Trust me."

"Well, he does have a reputation." Kendra made a face. "It doesn't matter how good-looking a guy is. I remember reading about that scandal—"

"Oh no, Kendra. He was innocent; he wasn't involved in that at all. He's actually . . . Well, I think he isn't all the media makes him out to be."

"Really?" Kendra drew the word out long and sweetly.

Why couldn't she keep her mouth shut? She didn't have to defend him. . . .

Okay, she did. Just a little. Because he'd fed her tapioca pudding.

Kendra leaned on the desk. "If he's not a scoundrel, then why aren't you interested in him?"

"I didn't say he wasn't trouble. But aside from the fact that he's not interested in *me*, which I think should be glaringly obvious, *I'm* not interested. I want someone normal."

"Like Russell?"

"No. Like a guy who would rather read to children than read about himself on the front page."

"Okay. No tall-dark-and-handsome, front-page athlete. Got it. And anyone on skates—right out."

"Kendra, please. We're worlds apart. And the fact is, he probably doesn't even remember volunteering—"

Eden's phone vibrated. Kendra scooped it up. "It's him!" She shoved it at Eden. "Answer it!"

Oh, brother. She took the phone. "Hello?"

"Hello, Eden? I'm sorry I missed your call. Did you find something on that guy? John Doe?"

He did remember.

"I found that receipt—"

"In his pants pocket. So did you figure out where it might be from?"

"Maybe. But I don't want to bother you."

"Where is it?"

"Okay. Well, do you know where Frogtown is?"

A pause, then, "Yes. Listen, I'm at the hospital, sort of tucked into some things. How about if I swing by after work—"

"Oh no. You're with your friend Sam, aren't you?"

Another pause. "Yes."

"How's his daughter?"

He sighed, and she chased it quickly with "I'm sorry, Jace; just forget it. I can go—"

"No. That's out of the question."

"Really. You don't have to do this. I know you were just kidding."

Kendra gestured her confusion, but Eden waved her away.

"Why would you say that?"

"Because . . ." Now she sounded like a desperate fan hoping for his attention. She found her voice, the one she used on Owen. "Listen, I don't need you to protect me. I can do this on my own."

His voice turned cold. "You're not going to Frogtown by yourself. I said I wanted to help, and I meant it. I'll pick you up at your house after work." He hung up.

Eden stared at the phone.

"So—is it a date?"

"I don't know what it is, but it's most definitely not a date. I think I just made him mad."

Kendra smiled. "Mad means he cares."

"No. Mad means he feels trapped and is already regretting agreeing to this. This is going to be a disaster."

CHAPTER 8

JACE COULDN'T PINPOINT why Eden's words irked him.

You don't have to do this. I know you were just kidding.

Says who?

He pocketed his phone. The call felt like the final shadow on his already-dismal day. First he'd worked out, doing some power cleans that only made him have to ice his knee again. Then he'd showered and hightailed it to the hospital, where he had to watch Maddy try not to cry over the tubes protruding from her chest.

He wanted to cry. She was a brave thing, offering him a wan smile when he walked into her room, but she had to be sore from surgery and aching from the places where tubes entered her body, straight into her heart to keep it pumping.

Now Maddy was sitting on the bed, tethered to the machine,

drawing a picture of a dog—probably the one Sam kept promising—her tongue parked between her teeth as she filled in the black perimeter of the dog's body.

Sam had finally fallen asleep on the couch, and no one had the desire to wake him. At least he'd showered, shaved, and looked less like the walking dead.

Jace sat down next to the bed, picking up the book he'd set on the table. "Where was I?"

"The frog was talking the princess into kissing him," Maddy said. She didn't look up.

"Do you think she should?" Jace asked as he flipped to the right page of *The Farthest-Away Mountain*.

"Of course she should! He's the prince—she just doesn't know it."

He'd found it in her stack of books when he packed Sam a bag of clothes. It looked worn, well-read. But Maddy hadn't seemed bored.

Just tired. She'd fallen asleep twice, and he'd seen her start to yawn already, her body shutting down from all the energy expended on lunch and coloring.

Maddy yawned again. "Look at my picture, Uncle Jace." She held it up and he took it.

"You're a real artist, Maddy." He taped the picture to her cupboard.

"Someday I'm going to have a dog," she said, leaning back, her eyes closing. He tucked the covers under her chin. Returned to the chair beside her bed and watched her fade into sleep.

He couldn't bear it. Maddy, above everyone else, deserved God's favor.

He tried not to equate it with God's love, but it felt that way. Maybe God simply liked some people better than others.

And he completely understood why God might not like him.

Jace waited until Maddy's breathing evened out into deep slumber, sat with her awhile, then drew the drapes and tiptoed out, heading to the parking garage.

He sat in his GT-R, letting it warm, debating. *I don't need you to protect me.* Obviously Eden still didn't see him as someone she could trust. She still saw the headlines, the photos, the guy he'd been.

Maybe he should forget the entire thing like she suggested.

However, he found himself driving to Minneapolis, toward Portland Avenue to pick up Eden. Because he'd given his word. And Jace Jacobsen wasn't a quitter.

He pulled up to her brownstone and texted her. While he waited, he turned up the country station. "'Take you for a ride on my big green tractor . . . ,'" he sang, drumming his fingers on the steering wheel, trying not to look anxious.

Yeah. Right. He put his hands in his lap.

Eden tapped on the window, then opened the door. "Hi."

"Hey." He kept it cool, friendly.

She got in, wearing her usual uniform—the white parka, knit hat, black boots. She looked at him with a hint of wariness in her eyes, and he had a momentary flashback of her grabbing the door handle as he drove. "Thanks for picking me up."

"You're welcome." He put the car into drive. "And for the record, I signed on for this, so next time you want to do the thinking for me, don't."

She stilled and he pulled away from the curb, letting the tension settle between them. *Way to go, Jace. Bully her into liking you.* He heard the indictment in his head but couldn't shake off his anger.

Or the nagging question of why her rejection irked him so much.

"I'm sorry," she said quietly. And now he felt like a jerk. "I just know you're busy, and . . . it's not like we're really going to find his family."

He pulled onto the highway. "What? Of course we are. I'm like a dog with a bone, honey. When I want something, I get it." That didn't come out quite right either. "I mean, with your crackerjack investigative skills, how can we go wrong?"

She gave him a weird expression, and he knew he was trying too hard.

Better to keep his mouth shut, maybe. But being around her made him say crazy things as if he couldn't help but want her attention.

"I figure we can stop into the Frogtown Meats and Deli and see if they know of anyone matching John Doe's description," she said.

"That sounds like a good idea."

She glanced at him and he caught a smile. "Thanks."

"How's your brother?"

"They took off the bandages for a while today to test his sight. It's improving apparently. Blurry, but we're hoping . . . How's the team doing without him? Are you ready for tomorrow's game?"

"Max's trying to fill in his spot, but Owen and I had a sort of chemistry. Max and I are still finding ours."

"So what will you do?"

"I don't know. Hope for the best. Maybe make a few more shots on goal instead of feeding the puck to Max."

"You should. You've got a deadly slap shot."

He glanced at her. He knew that, but, wow, she knew it too? "Thanks. Maybe I will."

They got off on Dale and headed up to University Avenue, driving by three-story apartment buildings that had seen better days and the ghosts of demolished homes, others small and sandwiched together on tiny plots of land, cordoned off by chain-link fencing.

"I don't like this part of town," Eden said. "It feels so run-down. Dangerous, even."

"Over half of this is rental housing, and over 60 percent of the residents are immigrants. About half are single mothers. Lots of gang activity, but I also read an article about a movement of Christians hoping to give the area a face-lift. They've renamed it Godtown."

He didn't add that he'd worked on a Habitat for Humanity crew last summer in this area. Some things he did for himself, and he didn't need the public prying into his life.

Or Eden, the reporter.

"It certainly needs the help." She held on to her seat belt.

"Well, don't judge by what you see. The folks in this area of town are just as kind as those in the Summit Hill area. Maybe even more so. They don't like the violence any more than anyone else."

She nodded. "I printed out a map to the deli. It's off University, on Rice Street."

He turned onto Rice, and they parked in an on-street space across from a small store. It had its own lot, a few cars parked under the streetlights.

A bell jangled as they entered. A Filipino man whom Jace would guess to be around fifty looked over his shoulder from where he stood behind the counter, slicing roast beef. "Hello?"

"Hi." Eden stepped up to him. "We're looking for someone who may have been here a week ago." She pulled out the receipt and set it on the counter. "Is this from your shop?"

The man glanced at Eden, then at Jace, his face closed. "No," he said quickly.

"Sir, we're not the police," Jace said quietly. "We're just looking for a friend. He disappeared last week, and we are trying to retrace his steps. He was wearing a red ski jacket and bought a sandwich." He reached around Eden and pushed the receipt the man's direction. "Will this jog your memory?"

A twenty sat on top of the receipt.

The man picked it up along with the receipt. Glanced at Jace. Considered him with too much fear in his eyes.

"Please?"

"I don't know him," he said.

Eden sighed.

"But someone left their car in my lot all week. I'm getting ready to have it towed."

Eden looked at Jace. "What if that was him? I did some homework and found a police report filed a week ago Sunday morning after a 911 call about a man found in a park, about two blocks from here."

"Thank you," Jace said and took the receipt.

The man pocketed the money.

Outside, they found the car—an old, rusty Jetta encased in snow and ice. It looked forgotten, or at least like it had sat in the lot for a week. He found a stick and scraped away the snow hiding the license plate number. "Can you look this up through your resources at the paper?"

"I think so. It'll take a day or two, but maybe we can get a name and an address." And then he saw the first hint of warmth in her eyes since she'd gotten in the car.

It reached right in and stirred that easy feeling that made him want to lean into her smile. Tell her things that he probably shouldn't.

To name it, it felt a little like friendship. Or maybe teamwork, the kind he had with his players.

It caused stupid things to spill out of his mouth. Like an offer for dinner.

"Are you hungry?" He caught her elbow before they crossed the street. A car splashed by.

"What, tapioca again?" With her standing against the darkness, her green eyes illuminated by a streetlight, a faint smile touching her lips, he just about gave in to the urge to bend down and ever so slightly brush his lips against hers, capture her face in his hands, rub his thumbs over the curve of her jaw—

Because, yeah, that would make her trust him.

He took a breath, found his voice. "How about a J-Hammer special over at Sam's place?"

"The bar is open?"

"Nell's running it. But I have kitchen privileges."

He unlocked his car but went around to open the door for her. She gave him a tiny frown, but he didn't care. He closed the door behind her and got in on the driver's side.

"So what's in this J-Hammer special?"

"Anything you want."

"Oh." She tucked her gloved hands between her knees, and he turned up the heat, still warm from the ride over. "How about a grilled cheese sandwich?"

"Yep, that's my specialty."

Eden wanted to argue with Jace. His specialty seemed to be making her feel like he cared. Like he truly wanted to spend time with her on this wild-goose chase. Because really, what were the chances that they'd actually found the car of Mr. John Doe?

Still, as she sat in Jace's sports coupe, heading to Sammy's, Eden felt like she'd made a discovery.

Jace made her feel safe. Strange, since three days ago she might have jumped from his speeding car. But standing together in the deli, and his touch on her elbow as they crossed the street, spoke to her in a way she couldn't quite identify.

As if suddenly she could breathe. Or relax.

She glanced at him, at the way he drove, one hand on the wheel, the other on the gearshift, like a man in charge, moving with the traffic like he did on the ice—quick but fluid. Sure of himself.

Comfortable in his own skin. But not demanding. He'd let her pick the station after she'd made a comment about country music.

Not that she didn't like country, but she couldn't believe it when she suggested the Sinatra station and he had it preprogrammed. He even hummed along, his voice deep and thrumming through her.

Maybe she'd misjudged him, just a little.

Or a lot.

They pulled up outside Sammy's, and she noticed the lot was sparsely populated. "It's a Monday night, no game. There's probably not a lot of action," Jace said.

He waited for her before they crossed the lot, then opened the bar door, ushering her in. The smell of fried foods, the slaps and cheers of games playing on the hockey channel, greeted her. Her gaze went to the place where she'd picked Owen off the floor less than a week ago. They'd put the chairs and tables back, cleaned up the fight. As if it had never occurred.

She wondered how fast it might take for Owen to be forgotten.

A few patrons looked up as they entered; a couple nudged their friends and pointed.

She hadn't thought about that—being seen with Jace. She was so used to being in Owen's shadow that she hadn't thought what it might be like to share the limelight. Especially with a man like Jace Jacobsen. Although, frankly, he could easily eclipse all the light in the room.

But having dinner with Jace wasn't exactly showing up on the front pages as his latest squeeze.

Right?

The thought nearly made her turn around, but Jace stood behind her, inadvertently barring her escape.

And he was probably right. Who would notice *her*?

Jace led her to the end of the bar, took off his jacket, and hung it on the back of a chair. "Do you want to wait here or join me in the kitchen?"

"Kitchen, please."

"Hey, Nell. Watch our coats, will you? And can you get Eden something to drink?" He looked at her.

"Um. A Sprite?"

"Two, please," Jace said, surprising her again.

He led her into the kitchen, all stainless steel and redolent with the comfort-food smell of onions, garlic, and french fries.

"This is Emilio. He's Sam's head cook," Jace said. A good-looking Hispanic man in his midthirties raised a spatula in greeting. Two burgers sizzled on the grill; next to them a pile of onions and mushrooms simmered in butter.

Maybe she should have ordered a burger.

"And over there, that's Toua, our line cook." The Hmong man seemed about Owen's age, maybe a little older. He wore a stained apron, and his eyes watered from chopping onions, but he smiled at her through his tears.

"I'm just going to whip up a couple sandwiches, if that's okay?" Jace said.

"No problem, Mr. Jacobsen," Emilio said.

Eden nearly asked if this was a regular occurrence, but, well, she didn't really want to know the answer. Tonight, she would be special.

She watched as Jace fixed two sandwiches.

"Are you sure you don't want ham on it? Or roast beef?"

"Nope. Just the cheese. I'm into comfort food."

"As you wish." He winked at her but turned away fast to add a slice of roast beef to his. Then he slapped them on the grill.

"If you ever retire from hockey, you could make your living as a short-order cook," she said.

He glanced at her but didn't join her smile.

What? Did she say something—?

"I envy Sam a little. I'd love to have a place like this, where friends gather after work, people come to watch the games. It's a real community place."

He scooped up the sandwiches, plated them, then added a handful of homemade chips and a pickle spear from a jar on the counter to each.

"Okay?" he asked, any vestige of the previous chill vanished.

Maybe she'd dreamed it.

"Perfect," she said and took her plate back to the bar.

He joined her there, and Nell delivered their Sprites. Overhead, an Edmonton-versus-Calgary game played. Jace glanced up at it now and again as he squirted ketchup on his plate.

She cut her sandwich, bit into the first half. "This is delicious."

"Garlic butter on the outside. It's Sam's special recipe."

"You and Sam are pretty good friends for him to share his secrets."

He smiled. "Yeah, well, he knows mine, so it's only fair. He picked me up and stayed with me through some pretty bad crashes."

Oh? She wanted to follow that up, but his attention reverted to the game.

"Yes!"

Eden looked up at the screen. "Did someone score?"

"Calgary. I have a pal who plays for them. We were in the juniors together."

She reached for the ketchup. "When did you start playing hockey?"

"I was six years old. My mom enrolled me in an after-school program because she worked and needed free babysitting."

"Wow. I bet she didn't realize she was creating a monster."

Something flickered in his eyes, and she wanted to take it back, rephrase.

"I didn't mean monster—"

"No, that's okay. I know that's how some people see me."

"Not your fans."

"Some of them. But they like it."

"And you?"

He chuckled, but it seemed to have nothing to do with humor. "I was never much of a fighter. Never liked to mix it up at school. I liked to play hard, though, and fighting was part of hockey, especially ten years ago." He took a breath. "It didn't help that I ended Boo Tanner's career the first game of my rookie season."

She stopped eating. "What?"

"You didn't know that?"

"No, why would I?"

His eyes narrowed for a second; then he picked up a chip. "I was jacked up for the game. It was my first time out, and I really wanted to show the Wild what I could do. So I went after one of the legendary enforcers—just so the team could see I could take a hit and be a go-to guy."

"I'm not a fan of the fighting."

"It's controversial, no doubt. But it's about intimidation and strategy. When there's a fight, there are penalties, which means that one or both teams have less guys on the ice and we can get the power-play units out during penalty minutes."

"Owen was on that unit last year."

He put down the chip and took a sip of soda. Didn't look at her. "But I think the biggest reason we still have the fights is because the fans like them."

She'd seen that, felt that—the adrenaline that rippled through the audience during a throw-the-gloves-off brawl.

"I have a pretty strong right hook. And when I hit him, Boo went down so hard that he knocked his helmet off and hit his head. He suffered brain damage." Jace paused. "I was the Wild's new tough guy. But Boo never took the ice again. He's in a wheelchair today."

Oh.

He stared at his plate with a long breath. As she watched him, what looked like pain—maybe even shame—flickered across his face.

She could almost see the reel playing in his head as he relived it, and she heard his words rebounding back to her.

The NHL changes you.

"I'm sorry," Eden said. He didn't move, so she put her hand on his arm. "I misjudged you."

He frowned. Then, surprisingly, shook his head. "Actually, no, you didn't. And that's the worst part. When I'm out there, on the ice, fighting, it feels . . . sometimes it feels good."

She blinked, trying to understand his words.

"It just feels so good to let that adrenaline take hold. To hear the roar of the crowd. I . . . like it. Or I did."

He met her eyes as if searching for something. Judgment, maybe.

"Do you still like it?" she said softly.

"It doesn't matter. It is what it is."

Jace turned his gaze to the television. "I'd like to get back to the days when I loved to play hockey just for the sake of hockey."

"Are you thinking of retiring?"

She read the answer in the way he watched the game, saying nothing.

"What would you do?"

For a long moment, he seemed to ignore her. Then, "Owen says he comes from a small town on the north shore."

Hmm. "Deep Haven. Population 1,300."

"Where everyone knows your name."

She laughed, probably putting more effort into it than necessary. "Yeah. Maybe. But in a way it feels like home."

"Like family?"

"I wouldn't go that far. But yeah, the entire town shows up at the VFW to watch Owen's games. So there's a lot of small-town love."

"I grew up in International Falls. Played on a dozen different teams until I landed on the Wild. I signed with the Blue Ox three years ago when they launched the franchise. It felt like a good idea at the time."

There it was again. The sense that this might be the end of an era.

He took a sip of his soda.

"I have to admit, I expected you to order a beer."

"I don't drink. Gave it up after . . . after the accident." He raised an eyebrow. "Not what you expected, huh?"

She shrugged. "And yet your favorite hangout is a bar."

"And grill." He lifted his sandwich.

"But my guess is that you don't come here for the food, do you?"

When he turned to her, he wore a smile and something in his eyes that made her chest warm. "Nope."

So the man wanted family. Or a place to belong.

Maybe someone to belong to.

Where had that thought come from? She focused on her sandwich. "Mmm, this is good." For cryin' in the sink, she sounded like an idiot.

"Do you miss it?" Jace asked.

"What?"

"Your small town. Or is your exciting life as a journalist enough to keep you busy?"

She wasn't sure if he was mocking her or not. "I miss it. A lot. But I can't go home." Not yet. Not when she still had so much to accomplish. Or prove.

Whatever.

"Why? Don't they have a newspaper in Deep Haven?" He finished off his sandwich.

"Not one that will hire me. We have two reporters, and they've been there since the dawn of time. I'm not likely to find a position there. And, well . . . Owen needs me here. Especially now."

He said nothing.

She looked up at the screen, suddenly thankful for the cheers of the crowd.

Finally she said, "Someday. When the time is right, I'd love to move back home, write articles for the local weekly, maybe raise a family."

"With someone normal and boring."

She felt his eyes, his attention, on her. "Yes." But her voice emerged small.

He smiled, turning toward her, hooking his foot on her chair. "How boring does this guy need to be?"

He said it slowly, and the act of him capturing her stool, even tugging it a little his direction, sparked something so unfamiliar in her that Eden had to catch her breath.

Her mouth dried and she set down her sandwich, wiped her lips. Found casual words, even if they came out a bit shaky. "Extremely. The kind of guy who loves mowing his lawn on a Saturday afternoon. And walking the dog. And isn't afraid to read a book and—"

"Makes boring grilled cheese sandwiches for dinner?"

Oh, he had amazing eyes. Blue with gold around the irises, and they reached right out and tugged her in. His hair lay in tousles behind his ears, and she had the crazy, wild impulse to reach out and twirl her fingers around one of those dark, luscious curls.

So maybe she wasn't complete ice around him.

Especially when he balanced one arm on the bar, the other on the back of her chair, leaning into their conversation. Yes, dressed in a white button-down shirt and dark-blue jeans, he made pedestrian look downright dangerous. Then the smell of his cologne twined around her, the same one that still embedded her jacket.

"Um."

"Or maybe cereal. I pour a mean bowl of cereal."

Cereal? His lopsided, devastating smile must have created a sort of cozy, hypnotic effect on her. Slowed time, dimmed noise, and suddenly only they remained, caught in this quiet, safe place where Jace Jacobsen made her feel as if she were the only girl in the room.

I like Lucky Charms. The words tipped her lips just as a woman ran up and threw her arms around Jace.

"Hammer! Baby!" Thin and sexy, she wore a bright-red shirt that she probably had to paint on, her blonde hair long and curly. Her French-manicured hands caught his face for a quick kiss on the cheek. "I didn't get to give you a birthday kiss." She looked like she might actually climb onto his lap and deliver a more thorough version at that moment.

And right then, the cocoon dissolved.

Jace's hand slipped from the back of Eden's chair even as he turned to the woman. "Haylee."

Eden could have guessed. The woman looked like a Haylee. All curves and too much hope that someone might take her picture and slap it onto Facebook with J-Hammer's tag.

What was Eden doing here? With Jace Jacobsen? Clearly she'd lost her mind.

She looked around, saw a few patrons watching the commotion. One man had his phone out, pointing it their direction.

Oh no. She couldn't be Jace's next hot thing. A momentary glimmer in his life for the tabloids to inspect.

Besides, she wasn't that kind of girl, a rink bunny. In fact, she felt sorry for those girls, needing someone like Jace to make them feel good about themselves.

"I gotta go." Eden slid off the stool. "Thanks for the sandwich."

"Eden—"

But Haylee had her arms around his neck, and that's the last Eden saw before she grabbed her coat and pushed through the crowd. *Oh, please don't let anyone be loading a Twitpic.*

Jacobsen's new girl. #whathappenedtohammerslovelife

J-Hammer goes slumming. #hammerslovelifeslump

Eden pushed out into the cold, fumbling for her phone. Cab, she needed a cab.

"Eden!" Jace had followed her out, his jacket in his fist.

"Jace—no, you can stay. I'm good. It looks like you had something—"

"Stop, please." He shrugged on his jacket as he ran to catch up with her. "Haylee is just a friend."

"Yeah. Of course." Eden forced a smile. "I'm just going to go home."

He stuck his hands in his pockets, his lips a tight line. "I'm sorry if she made you uncomfortable."

"No. Don't be silly. Hey, I'm cool. If you want to stay here with her—"

"I don't want to stay here with her." His blue eyes turned dark, stormy.

And there it was, the legendary J-Hammer temper. She bristled and backed away.

He grimaced as if in pain. "Sorry."

"I'll call a cab."

"I'll take you home." He started across the street, then came back to her when she didn't follow. "What?"

"I just . . . Thanks for dinner, but I think maybe this was a mistake. I know you mean well, but we're . . . we're very different people. I think it would be best if I try to find John Doe on my own."

His mouth opened slightly. "Fine. Whatever. Let's go."

Yeah. Whatever.

She climbed into the car and held on to the side bracket as Jace drove her home in silence.

CHAPTER 9

"We need to go over what happens next, Sam."

Sam stood outside Maddy's room, exhaustion sinking into his bones, his hand braced on the doorframe to keep everything from spinning out of control.

Stay calm. Hang on.

He didn't know Miss Priestly, but he recognized the clinical tone of the transplant coordinator, the pursed lips of disappointment. She was young, unmarried, wore a black turtleneck that matched her dark hair swept up in a bun.

She reminded him of Mia. Except for the fact that she held his daughter's heart in her hands.

"Now that she's stabilized on the Berlin Heart machine, we need to talk through how this happened and how to proceed.

Follow me." She turned, and like a dog on a leash—why not; she had all the power—he followed her down the hallway to a small office.

She motioned for him to sit on one of the lime-green chairs, and no amount of cheery orange cartoons or dancing children on the walls could soften her next words.

"Surely you were warned that something like this could happen if you didn't take care of her."

Sam sat down, stung. "I . . . I don't know what happened."

"It says here you missed an appointment—"

"She was doing so well, and . . . I know. It's just so expensive."

Her face twitched, and she looked away, down at her iPad. "Sorry. Of course I'm compassionate to the costs. This is terrifying for both of you, I know. . . . But the truth is, I have to ask some hard questions. Because this is Maddy's second go-around for a heart—not a commodity we easily grant second chances for."

He sat back in the chair, his words gone.

"I'm going to schedule you to talk with a social worker."

"About what?"

"I'm concerned about Maddy's care. Is there anyone at home besides you? A wife? Girlfriend? Nanny?" She looked again at her iPad, bringing up the keyboard.

"No, I'm not married. I don't have a girlfriend, and I can't afford a nanny."

"Mmm . . . So it's just you and Maddy at home. And your income? It says you are self-employed."

He was suddenly aware of the fact that he wore a Sammy's T-shirt, a pair of grimy jeans that Jace had grabbed from what he thought might be the clean clothes. Truth was, he needed a shower, a shave, and probably another cup of coffee before he had this conversation.

"I own a bar and grill. And my income is just fine." A lie, but what choice did he have?

She looked up, lips pinched. "You know that's a factor—we need to determine if you have adequate insurance and resources for the aftercare medicines."

"We're fine."

"Really? Because according to our records, our mail came back, returned."

"We moved." He looked away, through the glass doorway.

"And when did you first see signs that Maddy might be rejecting the heart?"

"I . . . I don't know. She started getting sick, and . . ." His voice dropped to a whisper. "She's nine years old. Please don't let her die."

Miss Priestly leaned back, folded her arms over her chest. Sam felt it then—his grip slipping, the sound of a wail stirring deep inside.

"We'll do all we can to help her, but I'll be honest. I'm not sure the board is going to agree to give you a second chance."

The sound grew louder. "What can I do?"

She sighed, and for the first time, he saw real compassion in her eyes. "You might want to consider whether Maddy would be better off in a medical foster home. If you want her to live, you might have to give her up."

"Eden! You're just in time for the game!"

Eden stepped into the room to Grace's greeting, carrying the takeout her family had asked her to pick up on her way over from work. Thanks to her University of Minnesota days, she knew just where to go. Mrs. Chau even remembered her favorite order—house fried rice.

She set the bags on Owen's bedside table, and Grace began to open them. "Take-out Chinese. The one thing Deep Haven can't provide."

"I have no doubt you can cook circles around Mrs. Chau."

"Don't bet on it," Grace said, pulling out the containers.

Her parents sat in chairs pulled close together, leaning against each other. They seemed to have aged a year this week, especially with all the specialists' visits and trying to deal with Owen's panic.

Now, his face still bandaged, he sat up in bed, reluctantly surrendering his gaze to the pregame on the flat screen. The cameras panned the gathering crowd.

"Can you see Casper and Amelia?" Ingrid asked.

"Mom. Are you kidding me?" Eden said, helping open a box of the Chinese food.

"How fun for them to catch the game. I'm just sad Owen isn't back yet."

What, were they all living in some sort of dreamworld? Did they not listen to the doctors? No peripheral vision meant that Owen couldn't track the puck. But Eden said nothing as Grace scooped up some rice for her. She unwrapped her chopsticks and pulled up a chair, watching the announcers.

She could almost smell the crisp breath of the ice, the salty popcorn, the spicy brats. Hear the raucous music ripple through her, feeding her adrenaline.

So maybe she'd miss it a little, but Casper had picked her up in a crazy hug when she arrived this morning with tickets to the game. "You're the best, Sis."

"They're not technically mine," she'd said but accepted the gratitude anyway. She hoped he and Amelia had fun. Besides, it would do her good to sit this one out, let the memory of Russell die a quiet, quick death.

John turned up the volume to hear the two hometown announcers, Reilly and Warkowski. They were talking about Kalen, the new goalie.

"With twenty-five saves last game, he's showing real confidence in the net. He doesn't give up on pucks. He keeps fighting them off. With that kind of determination, he's going to be a real back-bone of the defense."

"Talk about backbone—Jace Jacobsen has the lights on him tonight with the absence of Owen Christiansen. The Blue Ox are a puck-possession team, yet tonight we'll have to watch the chemistry with the newest power forward, Maxwell Sharpe. We were watching in practice—what did you see, Reilly?"

"You know I'm a Blue Ox fan, but LA is a cup-championship franchise," Reilly said. "We need to really work on our power plays, maybe see if J-Hammer can help us out with that."

"No mix-ups in the last game—what's with Jacobsen?"

"No word, although I talked to the trainers this week and they said he's still struggling with migraines. Could have something to do with him playing it easy last game."

Easy? Since when did Jace do anything easy or halfway? And he hadn't mentioned migraines. But maybe that had something to do with his silences, the way he'd suggested leaving hockey.

Eden put her chopsticks down as they played shots of the last game, of Jace backing away from a check, of Owen following it up with a clip. She shot a look at her father, who raised his eyebrow but said nothing.

"The franchise says he has it under control, but who knows. We will see what kind of choices he makes tonight. We're moments away from puck drop. Let's go onto the ice and talk to Jace about tonight's game."

The scene flipped and Eden's mouth nearly opened at the sight of the blonde she'd met at Sammy's—Haylee?—on the ice with Jace, dressed in his Blue Ox uniform, his helmet strap hanging. "So with Owen Christiansen gone tonight, what is your strategy against the former Stanley Cup champions?"

So that's how he knew her. Which gave some explanation as to why he hadn't just pushed her away. Behind him, the music played, nearly drowning his words. "We're just going to play good hockey, try to keep possession of the puck and take as many shots on net as we can. Last game we had thirty-two shots on goal, and we've got to keep the pressure on, get it in the crease."

Even through the television, he had a sort of hypnotic power with those blue eyes, the low rumble of his voice. Tonight, geared up, he looked every inch the beast he became on the ice.

For the first time, Eden could admit that it sent an unauthorized tremor of delight through her.

Oh, boy. She should remember that, most likely, he hadn't given her another thought after dropping her off last night. Probably went back to the bar to cozy up with Haylee.

"Your power-play team was legendary last year. Without Christiansen, do you feel you're at a disadvantage?"

Jace nodded. "You're always at a disadvantage when a player like Owen goes down. But we have a strong team, and everyone is ready to step up. Will we miss him? Yeah. But it's all about team-work. Of course, we're hoping Owen makes it back real soon."

Eden glanced at Owen, hating that he looked like he wanted to cry. Or throw something.

"And what about power plays? Is J-Hammer going to get it done? What are we going to see tonight?"

Jace smiled, and Eden felt a full-on swirl of something sweetly intoxicating.

"Great hockey," he said.

I'd like to get back to the days when I loved to play hockey . . .

He skated away, leaving Haylee to close the segment.

The family sat in silence, Grace staring at her food like she might be examining it for secrets.

Ingrid got up and retrieved a plate of moo shu pork. "Are you going to eat, Owen?"

"I'm not hungry, Mom."

She nodded and took her plate back to her chair.

John cleared his throat. "Owen, I know you probably don't want to hear this, but you have a few choices here. You can blame God for your circumstances, get angry, and turn away, or you can lean into Him and let Him turn this to blessing."

"Really, Dad? That's what you got for me—trust God? Have you noticed that God took away my eye? My life?"

Eden stiffened at Owen's tone.

But John leaned forward, balancing his elbows on his knees. "That's what I got for you, yep. Because here's the truth: life is not without suffering—the Bible tells us that. But the fact is, suffering is part of God's love for us."

Even Eden stared at him now.

"God makes us suffer on purpose?" Grace asked, her tone matching Eden's thoughts.

"He doesn't stop it. And if He has the power to stop it, then you could say that He lets it happen. So the question we have to ask is, if God is love yet God says yes to suffering, how do those two fit together?"

No one answered him.

"We expect God's love to be all nice and neatly packaged. But He'll do what He has to in order to draw us to that place where we need Him. Know Him. Are overwhelmed by His love for us."

He got up, ventured over to the food. Looked in the bag and pulled out a container, which he handed to Owen. "Satan's plan for our suffering is the destruction of our faith. God's plan is for life. For love. You need to make a choice, Owen. Are you going to pray and lean into God? Or are you going to let this take you apart?"

Owen took the food but didn't open it. "Depends on if I get to play hockey again."

"And if you don't?"

"God doesn't love me." Owen met his father's eyes without flinching.

John drew in a breath, let it go.

Eden still held hers.

"Then you've missed the point of your entire hockey experience. God really doesn't care if you play hockey at all, Owen. God's only concern is what you do with the life you've been given."

Owen put the food down and looked away. "My life is over. All I have left is anger."

"That's not true. I get your anger, but don't push away the people trying to help you."

Behind John, the game began. But he continued to look at Owen, even as Owen stared through him to the screen.

Eden wanted to weep. Still, her father's words simmered inside her. *God's only concern is what you do with the life you've been given.*

She set her food down. "I'll be right back."

Going out into the hallway, she quick-walked toward the elevators, then took a right and ventured down the hall to John Doe's room.

His door remained closed, and for a second, Eden's chest tightened. What if he'd died or been moved? Or . . . awakened?

She pushed it open.

He lay in the bed, still quiet, still breathing, the night pressing through the windows. She went over to him and turned on the bedside light.

A nurse had shaved him, and he looked even younger now. Maybe a teenager.

She dug out a Post-it note from her pocket. Thank you, Officer Kyle Hueston. One call to the Deep Haven police, to her high school pal Kyle, and he'd helped her track down the owner of the Jetta at Frogtown Meats and Deli.

"Is your name . . ." She read the paper. "Zachary Ryan?"

She stared at Doe's face for any sign of a response. Not that she expected it, but what if—?

She sighed, put the Post-it back in her pocket. Kyle had also provided her with an address, but she'd googled it and discovered another unsavory location in St. Paul.

One where, she could admit, she'd appreciate Jace's presence if she decided to visit.

But she'd ended any hope of getting Jace to help her last night. And for what?

Her pride. Rightly so, because today at work she'd searched for Jace's name on Twitter and unearthed a picture from last night.

In the photo, Eden sat, mouth hanging open, staring at Jace and Haylee like she'd stumbled into a tryst. She'd studied it so long that Kendra found her. Studied it with her.

J-Hammer ambushed with date. #nicegirlsfinishlast

"Am I the nice girl?" Eden had asked.

Kendra lifted her shoulder. "Guess it depends on you."

She looked like the nice girl. And yes, she did finish last. But what if . . . what if she'd stuck around to fight for him?

Don't push away the people trying to help you.

Maybe she shouldn't have pushed him away quite so quickly. After all, he'd helped her track down the car. And made her a sandwich. She sat down in the darkness. And then, because she'd done it before, turned on the game. Fast-moving and sharp, the Blue Ox stole the puck, taking it down the ice into the opposing team's territory.

Jace passed it to Max, but he missed and chased it, the sound of skates and sticks hitting the ice like shots in the arena.

An LA player slammed Max into the boards and dug out the puck, headed back over the blue line. Jace skated close, reached in with his stick, shot it away.

A defenseman recovered it and brought it toward center ice. He shot the puck to Jace, who brought it up, playing with it.

And then, just as she thought he might pass it off to Max, he looked at the net and . . . took the shot.

It bounced off another player and ricocheted through the knees of the goalie, into the net.

Score! She couldn't help the smile as Jace raised his stick above his head, his players congregating around him with hugs, pounding him on the helmet.

The Blue Ox were on the board.

Eden shut off the television. Stood. Patted Doe's leg. "Tomorrow we're going to find your family. I promise."

Returning to Owen's room, she found Ingrid in the hallway, staring out the window. "Mom?"

She glanced over her shoulder with a smile. But she couldn't hide the stress around her eyes. "Sweetie. Where did you go?"

"Visiting a friend."

"Here in the hospital?"

Eden nodded, not sure if she meant Doe or Jace. Were they friends? Maybe not yet, but . . .

"Well, I wanted to tell you that the doctor is discharging Owen tomorrow morning, and we thought we'd take him home for a few days."

"I think that's a great idea, Mom."

Ingrid touched Eden's arm. "Could you come up this weekend and get him? Maybe you could spend an extra day?"

"I have some vacation time coming, so I could probably get away. Sure. If Casper leaves the keys to the Charger."

"I'll pry them from his hand."

Eden laughed.

"You know, honey, if you want to bring your new *friend* with you, you can."

Eden stilled. "My new friend?"

Too much tease settled on Ingrid's expression. "I believe he plays hockey? With Owen? You two had a date last night?"

Eden's mouth opened. "What—?"

Ingrid laughed. "You're not the only one on Twitter."

"Mom, no, seriously?"

"I'm kidding. Amelia saw it on Owen's feed. Want to elaborate?"

"It's nothing. We're just . . . we're friends, that's all."

Maybe. Sort of.

But for the first time since meeting him, she truly hoped so.

CHAPTER 10

JACE COULD BENCH-PRESS the world today. Especially after scoring twice last night—the last one with four seconds left in the game, another slap shot from center ice. Lucky, but it bounced in past the goalie's body just as the horn sounded.

Then he'd managed three after-game interviews and even got glad-handed from Graham, who ignored Max to talk to Jace.

Like Jace might be the star.

Yeah, he could take on anyone today. And he probably owed a little of it to Eden. He'd heard her voice in his head in the first period, as he worked the puck toward the goal. *You've got a deadly slap shot.*

An impulsive shot, but he'd taken it. And played good, hard hockey. Drank in the applause bouncing off the girders and back onto the ice.

Most of all, he'd gone to bed without a migraine. Sure, the reporters wanted to know why he skated away from at least two potential fights, thanks to a couple nasty, in-the-boards checks, and he'd had to ice his knee, but no fines, no injuries. No reason for a team not to take another look at him at the end of the season.

He might get a contract after all.

It almost made up for the emptiness inside when he thought of Eden and the way she'd walked out of his life, the cold front she'd put up between them. He didn't care or didn't *want* to care.

But being with her, having her around, made him wonder if they could be friends. Or . . . more. Not the kind who just wanted to show up on the front page with him, but the kind who enjoyed eating grilled cheese sandwiches and watching hockey, maybe even the sort of easy company that didn't judge.

Except that didn't sound at all like Owen's nosy big sister. Maybe he hadn't been out with Eden Christiansen but some kind of body double.

I like the fighting. He'd actually confessed that and she hadn't even blinked. As if . . . as if she might understand. Or at least let him admit the very real fear that he *was* a monster. A beast. He had thought of himself that way for nearly his entire professional career . . . thanks to his fight with Boo.

But for a snatch of time, in her eyes he saw someone different. A man apart from hockey—a man who just wanted to share a sandwich with a pretty girl. A girl who might show up to cheer for him, on and off the ice.

Clearly he had forgotten the part at the end where she fled the bar. Even if he had untangled himself from Haylee, the damage was done.

So even though some fragment of Eden's voice remained in his head, he'd have to put her out of his thoughts. She'd never see him as anything but a fighter, a goon.

Jace threw his bag over his shoulder as he exited the building. Still wet from his shower, his hair turned to icy ringlets in the cold breath of January. He'd stuck around long enough after practice today to ice his knee, but he still bore a small limp. He wore his workout clothes—a pair of track pants, tennis shoes, and a team sweatshirt—but he'd left his jacket open, letting the cool air drag down his body temp.

"Jace."

The figure at the end of the tunnel made him slow as his eyes adjusted to the light. White parka, green hat—

And his heart gave a rebellious jump. "Eden? What are you doing here?"

She sort of shrugged, her face betraying hurt at his words. "Hi."

But really, what *was* she doing here? Seeing her, looking cute and a little hopeful, dredged up their dismal, silent ride home, and all his happy feelings died.

He put on a scowl and thundered past her. "I thought we were *very different people.*"

She scrambled behind him. "We are. I mean . . . yes, okay, I did say that. But I . . ."

He could hear her voice fading as he lengthened his strides.

"Jace, listen to me. I found the address of John Doe. At least the registration on his car."

He slowed.

"I . . . I'm sorry. I was hoping you could help me. Just this once."

He turned. Raised an eyebrow as he slung the bag from his shoulder. "Why? Is it in Frogtown?"

"Um. Sorta? It's on the north side—"

"You really don't like St. Paul, do you?"

She lifted a shoulder. Tugged her lip into her mouth. The movement was so adorable and out of character that he stared at her without words.

She came here. For him. To get him. And sure, she needed his protection, but . . .

She came to practice for him.

He shouldn't like that quite so much. He turned toward his car, flicking the Unlock button on his key fob.

"Jace?"

He opened the trunk. Stood there for a moment. In his periphery, he could see her standing there, now a little fear on her face. Like she cared if he turned her down.

"Get in." He dumped his bag inside.

"I'm driving Owen's Charger."

He glanced at her. "Does he know that?"

She smiled, threw the keys up, and caught them. "Nope."

"This could be fun."

She laughed, and it found all his soft, unprotected spaces.

"I'm driving." He held up his hand, and she threw him the keys.

Yes, this could be very fun. He just had to keep it casual, not do anything stupid, like offer to feed her.

He clicked the fob and found the Charger parked down the row. "Ready?"

She shrugged again. "Just don't—"

"Crash it? Drive it into a lake?"

"I was going to say get a speeding ticket, but yes, we need to return it in one piece."

He got into the driver's seat. The thing still emanated the I-am-new fragrance. Eden slid in beside him.

"Where are we going?"

"The Lake Phalen neighborhood."

"Right. Okay." He pulled out and headed north. "So what's his name?" He shot a look at her. She had dabbed on some lipstick, a little mascara, and it only made her eyes look bigger, luminous. He could very well get lost in them.

"Could be Zachary Ryan, but I don't know." She gave a strange, wry laugh. "I went to his room and tried it out on him, but he didn't wake up."

"Sad."

She nodded. He noticed she wasn't holding the handle. "I caught the game last night."

"Yeah?" He tried to keep his voice even.

"Congratulations on your goals."

"If Owen had been there, he would have scored them."

"Maybe. But he wasn't, and you brought in the win."

He smiled at that.

"And no fights. Or penalties."

She noticed that, too?

"Can I ask you something?"

He glanced at her. Nodded.

"Are you thinking of quitting because of the migraines? I listened to the pregame last night, and they were talking about it."

"Who said I was thinking of quitting?" Oh, that didn't come out right, but she didn't flinch. Just kept her eyes on him like a reporter. "Off the record?"

She frowned. "Yes. Of course."

He wanted to believe her—should believe her. So far, she'd

done nothing to betray him to the public. "Okay. Yeah, I get a few headaches, and they've gotten worse with every concussion, but it's nothing to be concerned about."

"Jace, I've read articles about this. Concussions can lead to brain bleeds—"

"I'm fine, Eden."

She sighed, still looking at him. "What is it about you hockey players that you always have to prove something?" Then she touched his shoulder. "You need to forgive yourself. It happened, and it doesn't make you a monster."

Her words had the effect of reaching in, wrapping fingers around his heart, squeezing. He lost his breath.

"Jace."

He shook his head.

"You don't actually believe what the papers write about you, do you?"

He tried to swallow the boulder in his throat.

"Because . . . I don't."

He looked at her then, and she was smiling at him. "I think there's much more to you than that."

Sheesh, now he felt like crying or something stupid. Because, well, had she forgotten that he told her he liked the fighting? And if that didn't make him a monster, what did?

He turned onto Payne Avenue. "What was that address?"

She read off the number. "What if you didn't play hockey anymore? What then? A bar, like Sam's?"

This was easier, and he wanted to kiss her for the segue. "No. I don't know. I don't want to run a bar. Or a restaurant."

"What about coaching?"

"I had an offer last year to teach some clinics. But they wanted me to teach kids to fight. Ten-year-olds punching each other? Um, no." He slowed the car. "We're in the seven hundreds; keep an eye out."

"What about announcing? You know everyone in hockey—"

"I'm dyslexic. I can't read the monitor that fast."

She made a tiny O with her mouth. "That stinks. Owen has a touch of that too. It's more common than people realize."

"Yep. But . . . no, I don't have anything but hockey. Here it is." He tapped the brakes and slowed in front of a two-story Sears, Roebuck house with a tiny front porch, one window overlooking the street. A chain-link fence cordoned off the postage-stamp front yard, and a Christmas wreath hung on the front door as if clinging to the season.

"Maybe he lives with his mother?"

"Stay here," Jace said.

"Hardly. That's why I brought you—so I don't have to stay here."

He glanced at her and found her smiling.

"Kidding."

Right. Sure. But he got out and came around the car, not caring. Actually, relieved. If he was good for something, it might be exactly this.

She eased open the gate and trudged up the icy sidewalk. He nearly slipped twice but made it to the rickety porch as Eden pressed the bell. It buzzed deep inside the house.

Then Eden gave him a tight, small smile. "If this is Doe's house, we'll have to deliver bad news."

He hadn't thought about that part.

The inside door shuddered open, shaking the storm door. A young man in a pair of low-hanging sweatpants and a Coldplay

T-shirt eased open the storm door with his bare foot. He looked as if they'd rousted him out of bed, his hair ratted around his head. "Whatever you're selling—"

"We're not salespeople," Eden said. "We're here because we . . . we're looking for the family of Zachary Ryan."

The man gave her a look that made Jace bristle.

"Funny. What, are you here to serve me or something?"

Eden's mouth opened. "What? No—"

"I'm Zachary Ryan."

Even Jace had no words.

Finally Eden spoke up. "Did you know your car is sitting in the Frogtown Meats and Deli parking lot? It's probably already towed—"

"My car is out on the curb, lady." He nodded past her. "I think you have the wrong person."

He made to close the door, but Jace caught it. "You have a problem, then, because you're listed as the owner of a Jetta—"

"You've got to be kidding me. Still?" He let out a blue word. "I sold that thing two months ago, and the guy still hasn't changed the title."

"You sold it? To whom?" Eden asked. She glanced at Jace, expectancy in her eyes.

"I don't know. Some guy. A friend of a friend. I don't remember his name."

"Can you describe him?"

"I don't know—not a big guy. Blond, I think. That's all I got. Now will you let go of my door?"

"Not until you give me a name," Jace said.

"What is your deal, dude? It's not my car—"

"It is your car until the title is changed. And it's sitting in that lot, racking up all sorts of parking tickets that you're going to have to pay." Jace smiled, this time with teeth.

Another blue word. "Fine. What do you want with this guy?"

"Actually we're trying to help him. He's in the hospital, in a coma, and we're trying to find his family."

This stole a little steam out of Zachary. He considered Eden a moment, then looked again at Jace. "I know you, don't I?"

"Probably not," Jace said quietly.

Zach turned silent. Finally, "Okay. I'll see if I can find his name. I'll contact my buddy and see if he knows him. You have a card or something?"

Eden pulled a Post-it note and a pen from her pocket, scribbled something. "Please call me as soon as you find out."

"Yep," Zachary said.

"I'll make sure the police know where to find you," Jace added, letting go of the door.

"I said I would do it!" Zachary slammed the inside door.

"That was fun," Eden said.

"But we're one step closer." Jace led her back to the car. "I hope your editor likes this story because I have a feeling it's going to be interesting."

She tucked her hands between her knees as he pulled away from the curb. "I have to tell you something. I'm not . . . I'm not really a reporter."

He wasn't sure how to react.

"I write for the obits department at the newspaper. I'm basically a classified-ad taker."

He could admit the fact that she wasn't trying to pry into his life made him breathe better. But—"Why did you say you were a reporter?"

"'Cause . . . I don't know. I've tried for so long to get a real reporter job. An obits rep sounds so . . . inconsequential."

"Not to the family of the deceased. Think about it—you are this person's last chance to leave a mark on the world. You get to help the world figure out what made them special."

She glanced at him. "Exactly. I believe inside every person is something heroic. One thing. I try to find that one thing, something small I can add. Of course, I have to keep it short and sweet, if I can insert it at all. But it makes for a better story."

"No, it makes for a better life. I wish the paper had written that kind of obit for my mother. They hadn't a clue how heroic she was—raising me alone, shuffling me to practice for 5 a.m. ice times. Going into hock to buy my equipment. They only focused on . . . on her mistakes." His throat tightened; he'd never really told anyone that before.

Her voice was soft. "She sounds amazing. You still miss her."

"Of course. She was my mom. She came to every single game and sometimes practices, too."

"What about your dad? Is he still around?"

"No dad." Jace kept his voice even, not quite ready to dive too far into his past. "My parents weren't married, and he wasn't interested. Until, of course, I made the NHL."

"I'm sorry."

"It's all right. I'm used to people only wanting me for my fame." He realized how woe-is-me that sounded. "Not that I minded. For the right people, I'd give it all away. It's just that . . . I guess I thought my life would look different. My fame would feel different. Now I just want normal."

He tightened his grip on the steering wheel, realizing what he'd said.

Silence filled the car as they headed back to the arena. Finally Eden said, "If you want normal, I have an idea. My parents took Owen home today—back to Deep Haven—and they want me to come up this weekend to get him. It's a really pretty place, quiet and relaxing . . . and, well, would you like to come along?"

He turned toward the parking lot, her words wrapping around him, nestling into him. She wanted to spend time with him?

He didn't quite know what to do with the hot spurt of feelings inside. "We do have the All-Star break coming up. I guess it would give me a chance to check in on Owen. Since I am the team captain."

She had the grace not to raise an eyebrow.

"I'll have to see if I can leave Maddy and Sam, but she's stable and just waiting . . ." He sighed as his thoughts touched them for a moment.

Eden slid her hand on his arm. "If you need to stay for them, I understand."

When they stopped at a light and he turned toward her, her pretty eyes caught him with a sweetness.

"I think I can get away."

She smiled. "Good."

And then, because apparently he couldn't stop himself . . . "So do you want to get something to eat?"

Sam couldn't ignore the guilt he felt at leaving the hospital. But he needed a change of clothes—he'd gone through everything Jace had brought him—and a moment of fresh air. Clarity. Some escape from the suffocating reality of Maddy's condition. Of course, he'd waited until she fell asleep, her breathing steady, the Berlin Heart keeping her alive, one beat at a time.

Sam pulled into the bar lot. The place was nearly empty—he'd told Nell to close early on nongame nights. But he didn't want to see anyone, so he grabbed his duffel of dirty clothes, then entered through the back door.

Nell, however, spied him from the bar and raised her hand. He nodded and escaped to his place.

The chill in his apartment crept into his bones—it smelled vacant, the milk that he'd left out five days ago souring on the counter. He flipped the wall switch, and light fell dimly over the threadbare tweed sofa that served as his bed, his blankets still in a heap at the end. Toeing off his shoes, he hung his coat on a freestanding rack, then went to the kitchen, where he capped the milk jug and threw it away. He wet a dishcloth and wiped the counter; crumbs were a good way to attract mice in these old buildings.

Then he went to Maddy's room, stopping in the doorway. He'd shoved her bed into the corner—it took up most of the room, and he'd had to remove the canopy. Her dresser sat in the hallway, but he'd managed to find a place for her Beanie Babies in a basket in her room. They lay scattered around her bed, evidence of Maddy's playtime before everything went south.

Sam emptied the duffel into a hamper in the bathroom, then retrieved clean clothes for the next few days from the closet he used at the end of the hall.

If you want her to live, you might have to give her up. . . .

Sam sank to the floor, leaned his head against the wall. *She's too little to die, Lord. But how can I give her away?*

You have to believe, Sam.

He heard the voice deep inside and thought it might be Mia's. Or maybe just his own desperation talking.

As soon as the transplant coordinator started talking to him, he'd realized he'd failed his daughter—and probably Mia—again. Maddy needed a mother.

He should have dated again, but how could he bring someone into his life? With a child who needed 24-7 care? How would he find anyone who might understand, might willingly walk into this life?

Sam got up, shook away the loneliness. Blew out a breath against the sweat that had formed along his spine. He had to get through, alone.

He filled the duffel with his shaving cream, a razor, some shampoo and soap, a comb. A glance in the mirror made him cringe. If he were the transplant committee, he might turn a hobo like him down. At the least, the social worker would look at his situation and turn in a negative report.

He barely had a home for them to live in, was behind on his mortgage for the bar, and the truth was, he couldn't work and care for his daughter.

He needed help.

But his mother, who'd helped care for Maddy, had passed away two years ago, and his sister had her own children—three of them. She couldn't take Maddy.

Not that he could let her go.

Sam stood in the kitchen, staring down at the parking lot. He'd had plenty of offers for the bar, its location only two blocks from the Xcel Center, a prime spot. And he'd collected enough memorabilia over the years to have a hefty investment.

The bar he could let go of. Not easily, but at least he'd have cash.

And if he had cash, then maybe he wouldn't have to wait—hope, pray—for a heart. He'd done the research. Last time, as Maddy lay in the hospital, gray and slipping from him, he'd gotten desperate. Made some calls. Found a name. Contacts, right here in St. Paul.

He'd found an answer.

Was it really so illegal to pay for an organ? It was an exchange of property, and frankly, the family of the deceased would need the cash. He was doing a service.

It felt like more of a crime to make Maddy suffer. Even die.

If the hospital wouldn't give Maddy a heart . . .

No. They would. They had to.

CHAPTER 11

CLEARLY EDEN HAD LOST HER MIND asking Jace "J-Hammer" Jacobsen, Mr. Charming, America's eligible bachelor, tough guy, and all-around superstar, to her parents' humble lodge in the woods for a long weekend. What had she been thinking taking Monday off, stretching out the three days to four?

He'd said *normal*, and her brain simply clicked over into Eden-will-save-the-day mode. But nothing about Jace Jacobsen resembled *normal*.

Starting with his condo. Eden stood outside the entrance of his building, a twelve-story piece of history with ornate scrolling around the double security doors, a marble entryway, a towering ceiling dripping with a hammered-brass chandelier, and a doorman who announced her even as she waited to be buzzed past the security gates and into the elevators.

No, nothing normal here, especially as she entered the elevator and pressed the button for the penthouse, punching in the code provided by the doorman. The doors opened into a small ante-chamber with a black- and white-checked floor that led to double mahogany doors at the far end.

When she hit the bell, she heard a low drone as if she were entering Dracula's castle. She waited so long she nearly turned to run, and then the door opened.

Jace stood there, looking anything but normal in a pair of sweatpants—*only* sweatpants—his hair freshly wrung out yet still dripping water upon perfect, glistening skin, a towel flung around his neck. He'd shaved, his jaw sharp and smooth, and she had the unsettling urge to press her hand to his cheek, run her thumb over the smoothness of his skin.

She averted her eyes, but not before she caught a glimpse of those sculpted shoulders, a washboard stomach, a scattering of dark hair across his toned chest, biceps bulging in his arms as he hung on to the ends of the towel.

No, not normal. And not the kind of guy she'd ever brought home.

Not like she might be bringing Jace *home*. As in, to *meet the parents*.

Besides, he'd made it clear that he was going for Owen.

"Uh, hi—"

"Sorry, I meant to be ready." He stood aside to let her in, and she walked like prey into the heady scent of freshly showered male.

Oh, boy.

"Practice went a little long today. I'll be ready in a jiff." He pulled the towel back over his head, rubbing it as he took the stairs two at a time.

Who had a stairway in a penthouse? Clearly Jace had to be on the top—very top—of the world.

"No problem. I'll wait." Or flee. Preferably while he ducked back into his bedroom, because what colossally stupid thought had taken possession of her? She blamed it on Jace, luring her with his easy charm and the sense that he actually wanted her company.

A guy with a penthouse apartment overlooking the cupola of the Minnesota State Capitol building hadn't a clue what *normal* meant.

Yes, she should run. Now, as fast as her unathletic legs could carry her.

She pried herself away from the view, noticing the steel-gray pallor of the horizon. She'd hoped to get on the road early, make it to Evergreen Resort in time for a game of Dutch Blitz, but with the sun blotted out by the cloud cover and a hint of blizzard in the air, they wouldn't arrive home until late tonight.

Home. Could she really call it that anymore after nearly ten years away? Or maybe it would always be home because she certainly didn't want to give that label to her shabby apartment on Franklin.

A giant floor lamp arched over the sunken living room with white leather sofas, a black marble fireplace, and white shag carpet. It emanated the sense of a snow cave, the perfect lair for the abominable snowman.

Not a picture hung on the wall or over the mantel. No frames on the marble side table.

In fact—she turned and scanned the room—the place seemed almost austere. No color except for an arrangement of white roses and green zinnias—really, Jace, flowers?—anchored in the center of the glass-topped dining table.

"Hey, Eden!" Jace poked his head out of his room. "Grab a couple vitaminwaters from the fridge, will you? I have a cooler on the counter. There's also a couple of packed dinners in the fridge for us."

Packed dinners? She walked into his kitchen and flicked on the light. It made all the stainless steel and black granite gleam. She opened his Sub-Zero fridge and found the vitaminwaters, along with two white bags labeled with Jace's name. Opening one, she found a bag of grapes, a veggie wrap, and a container of hummus and pita chips.

She'd planned on stopping at McDonald's. What *normal* people did.

He came down the stairs as she was zipping the cooler shut. He'd changed into a royal-blue dress shirt, black jeans, and carried a white sweater and a large duffel bag.

He set it on the floor as he pulled on the sweater. It hugged his body, accentuated his tight waist, and the blue only set his eyes on stun.

Eden wore her old jeans and one of Owen's Deep Haven Huskies hockey hoodies. He'd left it at her house after she'd laundered his clothes, and she decided to borrow it. She'd pulled her hair into a ponytail and couldn't remember if she'd applied makeup—probably, but she'd been in a hurry this morning, and surely it had rubbed off by now.

She should give him the opportunity to bow out. Surely Jace Jacobsen had better things to do than spend the weekend drinking hot cocoa, tucked away in a lodge in the forest. What was she thinking, that he'd join a local pickup game of hockey on the lake or play Sorry! with the family?

Right. She was trying to figure out how to broach the topic when he caught her eyes as he tucked his wallet into his back pocket.

"I can't remember the last time I got away—like, without the press or the team." He smiled at her. "Thanks for inviting me."

Oh. Okay.

"Are you sure you can get away?" She just had to ask, didn't she, and it sounded pitiful and even like . . . like she might not *want* him to go.

But when her breath hung in her chest waiting for his answer, she knew she did.

"It's the NHL All-Star break. I don't have practice until Tuesday." He hiked up the duffel bag. "Although I might have to find a gym in your little town, see if I can work up a sweat."

She had the urge to wipe her brow. "Good. I'm glad."

She couldn't remember having such a hard time choking words out last time she'd chatted with Jace. But he hadn't put his hand on her shoulder before, even if it was to get by her in the kitchen to grab the cooler. "All set?"

"Yeah."

Oh, she would have to conjure up more than one-word sentences if she hoped to enjoy—or even endure—the five-hour trip north. "You have a nice place here."

He flicked off the kitchen light, ignoring the one in the living room. "Yeah. Graham rented it and furnished it. It's a little bare, but I like the view. The sunrises are breathtaking." He picked up his keys and headed down the hallway.

"It's very clean," she said as she followed him out and wanted to snatch the words back. Clean? How pedestrian.

Except, well, maybe he should get used to pedestrian. Normal. Unremarkable. At least for the next four days.

He gave a laugh as they waited for the elevator. "I have a league of housekeepers—they clean the place and stock the fridge."

Of course. Eden wrapped her dirty parka around her and slunk into the lift behind him.

At least she had Owen's Charger. She pulled out the fob and clicked open the doors, unlatched the trunk. Jace loaded his duffel and then slid into the passenger side, dumping the cooler in the backseat.

She had the strangest urge to hand him the keys like she had before. But she knew her way north and was capable of driving Owen's fancy car.

She wasn't *that* ho-hum.

As she pulled out, she glanced at Jace. He appeared sandwiched into his seat, his long legs against the dashboard, his head skimming the roof of the car.

"The seat goes back. You can't sit like that for five hours."

He motored the seat back, reclined it, stretched out his legs. "Better." He'd donned his aviators as if he might be hiding.

Right. Jace hadn't a hope of hiding—not in the car and especially not in her hometown. There was simply so *much* of him. He filled the car with his presence, sitting with one leg pulled up, his hand resting on his giant thigh, the other stretched out, casual, as if he didn't know his own power. His hair hung behind his ears, drying into decadent curls that begged her to twirl her fingers through them.

Oh . . . my. Now where had that thought come from?

They were barely friends, nothing more. She had simply invited him along because he'd needed a break—she would do the same for Owen when he seemed too tightly wound, the game getting into his head.

But one glance at the quirk of a smile, at the sheer size of Jace, and she realized. This wasn't Owen.

Owen was a twenty-year-old kid. Jace was a life-size, devastatingly handsome, even dangerous hockey player. No, not just a hockey player. An enforcer. A tough guy, the kind that made players veer a path around him. The kind that made women line up outside the locker room.

What Eden had just invited into her world was *anything* but normal. In fact, she might as well admit it.

Trouble just sat down next to her for a five-hour drive.

She tightened her hands on the steering wheel, drew in a breath, and it lodged in her chest. It seemed he took up all the available air in the car too. She'd probably need oxygen by the time she arrived in Deep Haven.

"Are you okay? You seem tense."

"I'm fine." Oops, she didn't sound fine. "Great game last night. Another excellent goal."

He nodded. "I kept thinking of what you said."

He did? "What did I say?"

"You said shoot the puck." He smiled and her heart nearly left her chest.

Yeah, oxygen and CPR.

"Sounds like good advice."

"Yep." He reached for the radio. "How about some music?"

He flipped right to the Sinatra station. Michael Bublé's cool tones filled the car.

181

Jace started singing along in a low tenor. "'The night's magic seems to whisper and hush . . .'" Rich and dark, like chocolate syrup sliding through her.

She hadn't a prayer of a normal weekend.

Good thing Jace's purposes in heading north were to help Owen, because clearly he'd read way, way too much into Eden's invitation to her home. For a long, desperate moment, he'd actually talked himself into the idea that they might be friends . . . or even edging toward more.

What had happened to straight-talking, unfazed Eden, the girl who treated him like a regular guy?

The girl who made him *want* to be a regular guy. A guy who coaxed laughter and tease out of her.

Yeah, he wanted *that* Eden back. Not this tightly coiled, pensive driver who could make him leap from a moving—and broiling—car.

Jace longed to turn the heater down. She had it blasting, and he might climb right out of his soggy skin.

It didn't help that the night had begun to bullet them with snow, coming at the windshield like the galaxy in a *Star Wars* jump to hyperspace. He had pulled off his sweater, tried to loosen his shirt, but short of taking it off and hanging his head out the window like a dog, he hadn't a prayer of escaping the sauna in the car.

"I'm turning into beef jerky here," Jace said, hoping for a laugh.

"You're really hot? It's a blizzard outside." She frowned, and he once again tasted the acrid burn in the back of his throat that said she regretted inviting him. "It's just that with all the snow, I want to keep the heat on the windshield. I don't want any buildup."

He wiped his hands on his pants. "I get it. Not the best night for driving." Indeed, they'd already spied a car in the ditch, the tracks spinning off the highway. He should be grateful she kept it below the speed limit, especially in a powerful machine like the Charger. But between the cold shoulder and the iron grip on the steering wheel, he was feeling a little helpless here.

As if, inexplicably, he'd been benched. He was used to controlling the game, the situation, the conversation. The relationship. But he couldn't even figure out what game they might be playing, let alone finagle his way back into it. Eden hadn't spoken a word for twenty miles after they'd picked up hot cocoa at a McDonald's in Hinckley. The gal at the counter turned out to be a hockey fan and gave him a free drink.

Eden had nearly sprinted to the car as if wanting to leave him behind. Weird.

He could only conclude that, the farther they drove into the night, the more she wanted to turn this ship around.

Maybe it was his fault. Maybe she thought he wanted more out of this weekend than . . .

And then he got it. He'd returned home late from practice, shaved in the crazy hope that he might make a good impression on . . . whom? Her parents? He didn't know really, but he'd just climbed out of the shower when he got the call from the doorman. Eden, right on schedule, and he'd barely had time to pull on a pair of sweatpants before she got to the door. At least he hadn't answered in a towel.

He had no doubt he'd be channel surfing in his high-rise if he'd pulled that stunt.

So he'd answered the door half-clothed. Which sent an inadvertent message, apparently. What could he possibly say to fix it? *Eden, don't read anything into that. I'm not interested in you.* Like that wouldn't put a chill into their weekend?

Worse, he'd be lying.

He glanced at her. She still wore her parka, her hat, and even her mittens as she hunched forward. Only the glow of the radio and dash lit her face. And such a pretty face, even in profile—that elegant nose, those high cheekbones, too-alluring lips, now pursed in concentration. Her blonde ponytail hung over her jacket, and he had the strangest urge to run his fingers through it.

It wasn't the first time, either. The moment he'd opened the door, seen her standing there in her faded jeans, the open parka, a hoodie, he'd backtracked in time to his youth, his heart beating at the sight of a cute girl waiting for him after practice.

But not any girl.

Eden Christiansen, *the* girl. The one he'd spent way too much time thinking about over the past week: the way she smelled, sweet and floral, and her laughter, easy and full, finding his chest. The sight of her standing at his door had filled his throat and tasted like a tight and sharp shot on goal.

Like victory.

He'd had to right himself, make a dash out of the room before he did something stupid, like pull her into his arms.

But what if she'd seen it—the desire pooling in his eyes? What if she figured out that she'd somehow gotten inside his skin and that he longed for this weekend more than he had a right to?

"I'm sorry, Eden. I'm just . . . I need air." He cracked the window, and she glanced at him.

"Oh, Jace. I'm so sorry."

"No—it's okay—I . . ." He reached up, pulled his shirt away from his skin.

She turned down the heat. "I guess it is hot in here." She smiled at him before gluing her eyes back to the road.

Yes. Hot. Very hot.

And now he couldn't take his eyes off her, the way she watched the road, their lives in her hands. Solemn. Dedicated.

Eden Christiansen was everything he wanted to be, and she'd invited him into her world.

No wonder he couldn't breathe. He hadn't been this nervous since that first game. The game when he'd cemented his rep with the NHL. With the fans.

The game that destroyed one career and made another.

He refused to destroy this weekend. He had to get his head in the game. Figure out how to get out of this funk and back to that easy place with her, where he didn't feel like he had to prove anything. He could just be himself.

"Nice of Owen to let you drive his car," he said.

"He wasn't happy, but he can't drive with his eye, so . . ." She lifted a shoulder.

"I was thinking . . . he might not be so happy to see me."

"Why not?"

Because Jace might be a reminder of everything he'd lost? And because last night Jace had managed another great game, with a goal and one assist.

Today he made the front page of the sports section. Owen's spot.

Yes, everything about this weekend suddenly screamed *colossally bad idea.*

He should get out at the next rest area, call a taxi, and head back to his chilly apartment in St. Paul. Spend the weekend watching extreme sports, maybe go over to the hospital and share Sam's vigil. Shoot the puck around, kill a few hours in the weight room. Get back into the world he knew.

Jace let out a breath. Slowly. Deliberately. He was blowing the importance of this weekend way out of proportion. It wasn't the Stanley Cup, for crying out loud.

"It's my driving, isn't it?"

"What are you talking about?"

She made a face. "You're so . . . Well, I don't blame you. I was in a car accident when I was sixteen. Was going too fast around a curve and hit a tree. I was fine, but it spooked me. I wasn't comfortable driving for about six months after that. I still don't like driving in the snow."

He still didn't—

"It'll be better north of Duluth. The lake always tames the storm. I promise to keep it on the road."

Oh. She thought he was tense because of his accident. "I trust you, Eden. I know I'm in good hands."

Funny—he meant those words.

She seemed to relax. "I used to love driving home late at night. I'd come home from college and pull up around midnight, and my parents would be waiting for me in the kitchen with hot cocoa or maybe a cold lemonade."

He could see it, Eden as a coed, looking very much like she did now, free of her austere newspaper attire.

"Casper, my younger brother, would usually wake me up early, make me go swimming or snowshoeing or on some kind of adventure with him. Owen would be coming in from practice by the time we got back—he always had early morning ice times. We'd all sit around the table while Mom and Grace cooked us waffles. Sometimes Darek would come over and we'd fight over Tiger."

"Tiger?"

"His son—he's six now. Has us all wrapped around his little finger."

"I just love your family."

Had he said that out loud? He had, because she stiffened, glanced at him. "I mean—it sounds like a family I'd love."

Not much better, but—

"I think they'll love you too, Jace."

Oh.

His chest tightened and he leaned his head against the window, trying not to physically gulp in the cool air.

Then, from Eden: "I . . . I am worried that people will be weird around you."

Huh?

She was watching the road. "I mean, around us. Or . . . like, if we hang out in town. They'll look at you and think . . . well, that we're dating or something. I hadn't really thought about it . . . but . . ."

Ah. No *wonder* she had turned cold and tight-lipped. He hadn't thought about the fact that they might attract attention. "Do you often bring home guys—?"

"No!"

"I didn't mean it that way. Okay, fine, so I appear in town with you. Why would they think that we're dating?"

She swallowed. "You're right. Of course. Why would you be dating a girl like me?"

A girl like . . . ? "Eden, c'mon, don't take it that way. Of course

I would date a girl like you—" Oh, what was his problem that around her he hadn't a lick of charm? "We could date . . ."

Now he *did* want to throw himself from the car. He nearly grabbed the handle. "I just really enjoy your friendship. I've never had a friend who is a girl and . . ."

He had turned into a fumbling high school kid trying to get the girl to like him. Except he couldn't woo her with a few flimsy, slick words and recline the seats. Not Eden.

And he wasn't that guy anymore, anyway. Which made this matter. *Put on your game face, J-Hammer.*

"I think you tell them that we're friends. Right? We are friends? Besides, it's not like we're going to draw any headlines. Who's going to find us in Deep Haven?"

She must've seen the deer the same time he did because his foot slammed into the floorboards just as she jumped. But she didn't hit the brake—just let the animal clear the far side of the road.

"That was clo—"

She sucked in her breath, and he glanced to the near side—their lane.

The lights illuminated a second deer creeping out onto the pavement.

No.

"Hold on!"

Then she gunned it. And screamed. The sound reverberated through him as they surged forward.

The deer jumped into the middle of the lane. Eden kept screaming as she jerked the wheel to the left.

Jace had nothing—no breath, no words, no heartbeat—as they skimmed by the animal.

He thought he saw deer breath on the window.

And then, just like that, Eden righted the car into the lane. Stopped screaming.

For a long moment they simply drove in silence. He pressed a hand over his heart, making sure it restarted.

Finally she tapped the brakes. Slowed to a stop on the side of the road.

They sat there, Jace wondering if his pulse might be audible. Then, slowly, she put out her hand, tucking it in his. The other she used to cover her mouth, as if reliving the moment.

He found his voice, lodged somewhere in his ribs. "Good job, Danica. You've earned pole position."

She hiccuped a moment, then looked at him and . . . laughed. It bubbled out past her hand, delicious and robust and churning free of the horror of what could have been.

He couldn't help but fall into the moment—her sweet, ebullient laughter, the adrenaline rushing out of him as he huddled over, laughing, letting go.

She finally met his eyes, hers glistening. "Sorry. I just saw the deer, and when it looked at me, I thought, *No, this is not a good day to die. For either of us.* I knew if I hit the brakes, we'd spin out, so—"

"So you gunned it."

"And screamed."

"And screamed. I think they heard you down in Tampa. You sure know how to throw a little excitement into a weekend."

She smiled at him, and it unwound all the knots inside.

"Yeah. Maybe this weekend won't be as normal as I promised. But I will give it my best effort not to kill you."

"My team would appreciate that. Besides, maybe normal is totally overrated. How about we have fun?"

He leaned the side of his head against the seat and sighed, the tight knot gone from his chest. The cool air had tempered the heat in the car.

"We are friends, aren't we?" Eden said.

He gave her a soft smile. "I think so. I hope so. I . . . want to be your friend."

The heat flooded back into the car. Or maybe just into Jace. He hadn't felt this naked since they took shirtless shots of him for the entire world to see on the pages of *Hockey Today*.

Her smile faded as she caught his gaze, and for a long, almost-unbearable moment, he nearly put his hand to her face, nearly wiped away the laugh tear tracing down her cheek. Nearly pressed his lips to hers.

He could almost taste the salt of her skin.

But he didn't. Because friends didn't do that. Friends didn't let their mouths grow dry at the sight of her full lips, the bottom now tucked between her teeth. Didn't let the too-heady taste of desire take over.

Friends didn't leave their zone. Friends played their position. "Just friends, I promise." He squeezed her hand.

She swallowed, the slightest play of a smile on her face. "Thanks for coming up this weekend. I'm glad you're here."

He grinned. "Me too. Even with the screaming. But as one friend to another . . . what do you say I drive?"

CHAPTER 12

THE CLEAR BLUE SKIES, the crystalline glitter of a fresh snowfall across the plane of the lake, the shaggy evergreen frosted with powder . . . the magic of the north shore of Minnesota seemed to clear away the shadows of last night's drive.

Eden didn't know how to interpret Jace's weird behavior, except for the obvious—until she'd nearly killed them by almost annihilating the deer, he'd entertained some crazy idea that she'd invited him home because she wanted more from him than friendship.

A thought he clearly wanted to set straight. And had, almost like an edict: *Just friends. I promise.*

They'd practically shaken on it when he'd tightened his hand around hers.

Then she'd relinquished the driver's seat, and he visibly relaxed.

Eden stared at the sloped ceiling of her bedroom, located on the upper floor of the family lodge. Grace had already risen, her twin bed across the room neatly made, a hand-stitched quilt smoothed over the surface. She glanced over to Amelia's bed, expecting to see her huddled under the covers, deep in her Saturday morning slumber. But it also lay empty.

Oh no. Eden could just imagine her taking pictures, posting them on her Facebook page with quippy captions.

Poor Jace. She hung on to the fragile hope that they'd all treat him like family. Nothing special.

Voices from the kitchen drifted up the wooden stairs, down the hallway, along with the irresistible smell of bacon. She listened hard, and her heart thumped when she heard Jace's voice.

Low. Strong. Delicious. Not unlike his singing in the car. Winding through the house and wrapping around her.

Just friends. Yes. Not that she wanted more. More would be . . . absurd. Guys like Jace didn't go for girls like her. He'd even said it—he'd never had a girl who was just a friend before. Which meant he didn't put her in the potential-romance category.

But she hadn't brought Jace Jacobsen to the woods for romance. They'd have a simple, easy, *fun* weekend.

Nothing more.

She heard Casper's laughter and stilled. Last night, he'd waited up with her parents, looking for her headlights in the storm. No cocoa, but her parents had made up the pullout sofa in the study, and she'd winced when Casper offered his bed to Jace instead.

Casper was the last one she expected to go fan crazy on her.

She had to get downstairs and rescue Jace from an invitation to go snowmobiling or snowshoeing or—knowing Casper—play a pickup game of hockey.

She didn't even want to consider what Owen might be doing.

She only hoped he wasn't completely surly to Jace. After all, Jace was still his teammate. For now.

Poor Jace. She hadn't considered what a full-on invasion of her family might do to him. Niceness—the Christiansen family poured it over people until it could suffocate them. He wasn't the kind of guy who needed special sleeping arrangements as if he were royalty.

Eden peeled back her covers, bracing herself for the chill. The frost had scrolled artwork on her window. She checked the floor for Butter before she set her feet down—the dog had followed her upstairs last night, but apparently she'd already escaped.

Eden reached for her bathrobe and pulled it over her pajamas, then padded to the bathroom, relieved to find it empty.

She put her hair in a ponytail, debated, and decided that "just friends" didn't require makeup, then returned to her room and changed into jeans, a tank, and a purple fleece.

She slid on her leather slippers and headed down for a rescue mission.

The sight stopped her on the landing.

Casper sat on a stool at the counter, leaning over a deluxe omelet, while Amelia was curled on the sofa, scrolling through her phone. Grace brandished a spatula over the stove, turning the bacon, while her mother stirred orange juice from concentrate.

Darek, Eden's oldest brother, sat at the table, paging through a newspaper, their dad across from him, wearing his reading glasses as he did Sudoku. No sight of Owen, but there, in the middle of the room, sat Jace, cross-legged on the floor, Tiger propped in the well of his lap. Reading *The Little Engine That Could*. Making noises—whistles and chugging and voices.

Jace wore jeans, a green-and-brown flannel shirt, and a blue ski cap, with his dark hair curling out the back. Had he made a stop at Farm & Fleet on the way up that she'd missed? The man looked like a lumberjack, as if he might belong here. In the woods. In her family.

And no one even glanced at him.

"An omelet for you, Eden?" her mother asked, and she managed a nod even as she caught Jace's glance toward her.

Act normal.

She slid onto a stool next to Casper. "Coffee first, please." From the corner of her eye, she saw Jace return to his book.

Well, if no one was going to make a big deal out of him sitting in their living room on a Saturday morning, she wasn't either. After all, she'd promised him normal.

Although she could admit this felt *too* normal. For pete's sake, Jace "J-Hammer" Jacobsen was in the living room, reading aloud to her nephew. Did no one want to take note of that, turn and gape at him? Besides her, that was?

Her mother poured her a mug, and Eden added sweetener, creamer. Cupping her hands around the mug, she glanced again at Jace. He'd finished the book and was now diving into *Mike Mulligan and His Steam Shovel*. With noises again.

"That's his fifth book," Casper said under his breath. She wanted to hug her brother but didn't move.

"Really?"

"Mmm-hmm. He was awake when I came down, gazing out the sliding-glass door to the lake. I wonder if he slept at all."

How could he, cramped in the sofa bed? But she didn't say that lest Casper suddenly decide to offer him his digs again. Awkward.

"I think it's sweet," Grace said quietly as she slid Eden a plate. "He's not at all who I thought he'd be."

Hmm. She barely tasted her omelet as Jace finished the book, then wrestled with Tiger on the carpet, tickling him before Tiger rolled away, laughing. Jace got up and took a seat at the table. John handed him the sports section without looking at him.

Eden could choke on her breakfast.

"I need someone to pick up some groceries in town," Ingrid said, glancing at Eden. Like it might be a guess whom she wanted to volunteer.

"Uh, I will," she said obediently.

"I'll go with her," Jace added, turning a page. He glanced at Eden, and for a second their eyes met.

She smiled. He smiled back, and everything inside her turned to fire.

Oh, boy. She got up and dumped the rest of her eggs in the sink. "What's on the agenda for today?"

"How about we clear the ice on the lake," Casper said.

Here it came. The so-called impromptu hockey game where Casper invited the entire town to watch the amazing J-Hammer.

"I'd like to do some fishing," Casper added.

Fishing? Ice fishing? What about *hockey*?

"The Blue Monkeys are playing at the VFW tomorrow night. I thought I'd babysit while Darek and Ivy got away," Grace said.

"We can babysit," Jace said, not looking up.

We, as in . . . Eden and Jace? But didn't he want to go out?

Casper glanced at her, and she realized she'd asked out loud.

"I mean, well, maybe we could go see the Blue Monkeys." Her face burned.

"Who are the Blue Monkeys?"

"It's a local band. Darek's best friend plays in it along with his friend's fiancée, Claire." It wasn't that she didn't love Tiger, but—

"Sounds fun."

It did?

"Tiger and I have a big night planned anyway, right, sport?" Grace handed him a piece of bacon, and he grinned at her, his big brown eyes shiny.

"Right!"

"Then it's a date," Darek said. "You and Jace will join Ivy and me at the VFW. And tonight . . . tonight we whip you all in a game of Sorry!"

"Now Sorry! I know. Brace yourself." Jace smiled, and she spied something sweetly diabolical in it. He looked at her, winked, and her heart did another annoying flutter.

Friends. Just friends.

"Are you ready to go to the store?" Eden asked.

See, nothing special here. No hockey, no wild fans, no awkward romance.

Jace rose from his chair, and boy, he did lumberjack in spades, the flannel shirt only accentuating his shoulders, his trim waist.

"You can wear my boots," Casper said, sliding off his stool and retrieving his Sorels. "Your dress shoes are useless here."

"Thanks," Jace said and sat down in the entry, pulling on the boots. He added his leather jacket.

Who was this guy? Eden put on her parka, her hat, and felt dowdy next to his lumberjack glory.

"Do you want the keys to the Caravan?" her mother asked as she handed Eden the list.

"No. I'll take the Charger." Please. She had Jace Jacobsen with her. He couldn't be seen in a Caravan.

Ingrid frowned at her, and she wondered if she'd spoken aloud again.

Jace stood in the drive of the lodge, surveying the destruction on this side of the lake. Beyond the lodge, as far as they could see, wood lay in charred ruin, the snow like a nuclear wasteland. Ash and the deadened remains of the trees evidenced the wildfire that had nearly taken out their property. "You mentioned a forest fire, but I had no idea. No wonder Casper isn't going back to college this semester."

He wasn't? "What are you talking about?"

"He's taking time off to finish a couple of the cabins." Jace gestured to the framed-in shells of five new cabins, Darek's handiwork from the fall.

"I didn't know he was doing that." She climbed into the car, and Jace squeezed himself into the passenger side without a suggestion to drive. Well, it was her town. He was just a guest.

"Yeah. Grace is against it, but having him here would make her feel better about going away to culinary school. She's worried about leaving the family in the lurch."

Grace was going to culinary school? Eden pulled out, glancing at him. Had she slept for a week while he hung out with her family? Why did she not know this?

"Although Amelia is surely in the mood to leave," Jace continued. "She wants to do her first semester overseas. She was looking at Prague. I don't know, though. It feels like she might be getting in over her head. She's only eighteen."

"Okay, who are you? And since when do you know so much about my family?"

"It's not that hard. They're really nice. I just listened. By the way, the local peewee team is having a game this morning, 11 a.m. at the arena. Wanna stop by? I love small-town games."

Really?

They stopped at the Red Rooster, and he grabbed a cart, pushing it behind her like they might be an old married couple. Like he was a regular in her life, in Deep Haven. Indeed, no one even glanced their way as he trailed her through the store, adding green peppers, onions, potatoes, stew meat, and crusty French bread to the cart.

"I hope your mom is making stew," he said. "I love stew."

"It'll probably be Grace, but . . . I read somewhere that you loved sushi."

"Graham's creation. I'm a meat-and-potatoes guy."

She shook her head and stopped in front of the cooler. "My mom suggested ice cream." She reached for the rocky road.

"How about Moose Tracks?" He picked up the carton, waggled it, giving her a smile.

"What, are you ten?" But she couldn't help but smile as she put the container in the cart. "Do I need to spring for a quarter so you can ride the tractor outside?"

"They have a tractor ride? Swell!"

She laughed. Okay, whatever he'd done with cover boy Jace Jacobsen, she liked the lumberjack version too.

A little.

Okay, a lot. Even if he still seemed miles outside her league. Too charming as he unloaded the cart, flirting with the cashier. The girl didn't recognize him—and Eden tried not to acknowledge the strange twinge inside at that.

They headed over to the arena. More of a covered community center built for the curling team, the ice wasn't big enough for a standard rink, so the peewees played outside, a cluster of them in red-and-white jerseys, the other team in teal and black. They chased the puck around the rink, the sound of sticks on ice like firecrackers, dissipating in the cool, crisp air. Cars idled white breath just beyond the wooden fence as parents watched the game.

Jace led her to the rickety wooden stands. "That's cheating, watching the game from the car." He blew into his hands, curling them tight before he warmed them in his coat pockets. "That kid out there, number ten? He's the team enforcer. See how he blocks for the other players or even zeroes in on one? And the coach only puts him out for a couple minutes, just to take out another player."

She watched, her mouth open. "Seriously? I didn't think they did that in peewees."

Jace shook his head. "It's technically not allowed, and they recently banned bodychecking, but they still check. And they don't really call them enforcers. . . . But some coaches just . . . do it. It's part of the game. It only escalates from here."

"Were you an enforcer as a kid?"

"No. I was tough, but I was all talent back then."

All talent. So that's what he'd lost and what he'd gotten back over the last two games. "You still have talent, Jace."

He glanced at her, warmth in his eyes. "Thanks."

Others came to sit next to them in the bleachers, cheering on their team. Not a fan glanced their way, no one interested in the lumberjack in the stands.

Didn't they know hockey? Didn't they recognize something odd about the man sitting beside her? Did all of Deep Haven live in a vacuum?

"When I first started playing, we had an outdoor rink," Jace said quietly. "My mom used to come by after her shift. I'd be playing under the lights, and suddenly she'd appear as if she'd been there all along. I always played better with her in the stands. She even played, you know. For her high school. International Falls has a girls' team, and she was a left wing like me. She used to get out on the ice with me on Saturdays, before work, and help me with my puck-handling skills."

"She sounds like a good mom."

"She was a great mom. A guy couldn't ask for better. When I got my contract with the Wild, she moved to St. Paul. Even went to the practices."

No wonder he had lost himself when she died.

Eden wanted to slip her hand into his, but that would only attract attention. The wind whipped up, chapped her nose, and she scooted closer to him.

"My brothers used to play here at this rink. But when the team got bigger, they had to share the rink with the high school in the next county. We used to drive an hour for practices. I'd bring a book while they played." She tucked her mittens between her knees. "One time, we had a tournament there, a whole-day event. Everyone carpooled, and I had settled myself in the food and game room overlooking the ice."

The red team—the locals—broke away on a power play. A defenseman passed the puck off to a forward, who missed it and chased it into a corner.

"When they packed up, it was chaos, and somehow I got left behind."

Jace was looking at her now, frowning. "By yourself?"

"Yeah. The place went dark, and I realized I was alone. I was about thirteen. I thought they forgot me. Which, of course, they did. It took three hours for someone to come back for me."

"And you sat there in the dark the entire time?"

"Singing 'Jesus Loves Me' and other Sunday school songs to myself, yeah."

"Oh, Eden."

She waved him away. "It's okay. I understood. Hockey came first, and if I didn't start joining in instead of burying my nose in a book, I'd be left behind. So I became head cheerleader."

He was still looking at her, so much confusing emotion in his eyes that she couldn't meet them. Why had she told him that? She gave a wry chuckle. "I'd make the perfect hockey mom."

He sighed. "Yes, actually, you would."

The period whistle blew, and the teams skated into the warming house.

"Are we done here?" Eden asked.

"But we still have one more period left."

"Jace, seriously, you play hockey every day. You want to sit here and watch a bunch of little kids?"

Someone glanced at her at the mention of his name. Jace saw it too, the way people began to nudge their friends, gesture to him. He ducked his head. "Right, okay, let's go."

Now she felt like a jerk. "No—you said you like peewee hockey. We can stay."

"Not if we don't want to draw headlines. But maybe . . . maybe you do." He got up and marched down the stands. They shook with his steps.

Eden followed, the stares of the crowd at her back.

What? Headlines were the last things she wanted.

He wasn't all that bright, but Jace felt just this side of brilliant as he trekked out to Casper's fishing house.

A six-by-six square box of plain plywood on skids, the ice house looked more like an oversize outhouse than a hangout. Casper had attached it to his snowmobile to drag it out to the center of the lake—Jace had watched him as he headed out with a thermos of hot cocoa right after lunch. When Jace finished helping Grace with dishes, he'd left Eden playing Candy Land with Tiger.

Casper seemed the one most likely to confirm what Jace suspected.

As soon as the words about a headline had left his mouth, a light sparked in Jace's head, something that should have been accompanied by the applause of the crowd, maybe a few fireworks. See, despite being clobbered too many times with a hockey stick, he still had some brains.

Eden *wanted* the headlines.

She didn't feel noticed. Or wanted. And somehow, standing at the edge of Owen's—and Jace's—lives, poking her toe into the limelight, made it better.

While that should bother him, he knew—just *knew*—that she probably didn't even realize it. That she hadn't invited him to Deep Haven to exploit him. Not after the way she'd gone white at his words in the stands, silently followed him to the Charger, and apologized for drawing attention to them.

He didn't care. Let the entire town of Deep Haven tweet it out. He could easily explain it away as hanging out with his teammate Owen.

Except that Owen had barely spoken to him at lunch, appearing with his face unbandaged, bruised but healing, dressed in pajama pants and an old T-shirt. He'd eaten his soup, then headed back down to the family room, turning on the television.

The awkward silence went with him, and Jace had to admit he breathed a sigh of relief with the rest of the family. Except for Eden, who had appeared pained at the entire interaction.

So much for trying to help Owen out of his funk. He'd figure out how later. At the moment, Jace was here for Eden.

Because she was his friend.

He knocked on the ice house door, then eased it open. Casper sat on a bench before a foot-wide hole in the ground, his line deep in the chilly abyss. He wore insulated pants and another pair of Sorels—the Christiansens had a plethora of outdoor wear by their front door. He'd hung his jacket on a peg behind him and now wore only a thick sweater, an orange ski hat over his long hair.

Casper looked up as Jace entered. "'Sup?"

"Your mom sent cookies to go with the hot cocoa." Jace handed him a paper bag. "You should be aware of the personal willpower it took not to finish those on my way out. Frankly, I'm not sure I won't fight you for them even now."

"Bring it, J-Hammer," Casper said. "I'll throw down the gloves for my mom's chocolate chip–butterscotch cookies." He took the bag, opened it. "I just wish they would help my luck. Nothing but a couple nibbles so far."

Jace sat on an overturned white bucket. "I don't get the fascination, I admit it. Hours staring into a hole—"

"Think of it as hunting for treasure, but the treasure comes to you." He dunked his cookie in the thermos. The moisture dribbled down his chin. "I can teach you."

"Nope. Actually, I came out here to talk to you about Eden."

Casper raised an eyebrow. "Yeah?"

"She told me this story today about being left at an ice arena as a kid."

"Oh, that's a legendary Christiansen family tale. She was stuck in a book as usual and got left behind. My poor mom didn't even know until the Caravan got back to Deep Haven. They thought she'd gone with someone else. I think Mom broke a few traffic laws getting back to the arena."

"Scary."

"Yeah, Mom was terrified."

"No, for Eden."

Casper frowned. "What? No, Eden was fine. We found her sitting in the entryway, singing. Totally unfazed. But that's Eden. She just rolls, you know."

"Seriously? Imagine you're thirteen and all alone—"

"Dude, I was hunting and fishing by myself by the time I was ten. And trust me, Eden knows how to take care of herself. And others."

"Yeah, she's all about taking care of others, isn't she?"

Casper finished his cookie. "It's what she does. Like Grace— she cooks. And Amelia, she takes photos. Owen plays hockey, and Eden . . . Eden cheers us all on."

"Yes." Jace sighed. "But she's also patient and smart and doesn't pull her punches, yet she knows when to say the right thing."

"You're right about not pulling her punches." Casper picked up his pole. Gave it a tug. "Nope."

"And she loves Sinatra and Michael Bublé."

"Who?"

"And she has a vivid imagination. She believes everyone has a story."

"That's because she writes about them all day long. She's a reporter, after all."

No, actually, she wasn't. But she wanted to be.

Casper hooked his pole into the stand, then leaned back. Considered Jace. "Do you have a thing for my sister?"

"What?" But his voice emerged too high. Jace straightened it out. "No . . . I mean, we're friends, but that's it." Even to his own ears it sounded a little . . . flimsy.

And Casper saw right through him. "Mm-hmm. Okay, listen, not that I'm totally against you liking her, but let's be clear here. Eden has my back. So I have hers. You hurt her, and I don't care who you are, J-Hammer. I'll find you."

The weirdness of the conversation nearly made Jace smile. Except Casper appeared completely serious.

Wow. He hadn't had someone stand up to him, give him a line in the sand, for years. He liked it, liked this family, who didn't treat him as if they might be afraid of him.

"I'm here for Owen."

Casper nodded. "Sure you are. Because you and Owen are spending *so* much time together."

Fair enough. Jace ran his hands over his thighs. "Okay, so yeah, Eden . . . she's special. Really special, which I realize sounds sort of lame, but I like spending time with her. She's not like any other girl I've met."

Casper was watching him.

"She doesn't spook easily, and she . . . she doesn't look at me with a weird sort of fascination. She makes me feel normal, I guess."

"And you like feeling normal?"

"Maybe I just like the fact that someone enjoys my company without having to tweet about it." Or at least, until today, he'd thought she did. No, he still believed that.

Casper's pole bent, and he jumped for it. "I got a bite!" He let it play in his hands a moment, then jerked hard. "Just had to set the hook."

Jace watched as he began to reel in, the pole bending with the fight of the fish. "Wow, that's a doozy."

Casper kept reeling. "The key to fishing is to capture their interest, hook them, and then not let the tension ease up, or they can shake free of the hook and get away."

Jace leaned over the hole, seeing if he could spot the fish.

"Grab the net." Casper gestured behind him.

Jace retrieved the net, lowering it into the water. He spied the white belly of the fish as Casper reeled it closer.

"Easy now . . ."

Jace dipped it deep and came up with the fish, squirming, fighting in the net. He brought it over the ice, and Casper reached in to unhook it and grabbed it by the gills.

Jace got up. "Nice fish."

"Worth the wait," Casper said, winking.

Eden stood at the window, the smell of her mother's cookies twining through her, enjoying Tiger's laugh as he listened to his iPad story through earphones. Jace had trekked outside after Casper as if he liked to fish or something.

"He's a nice man, your Jace."

She glanced at her mother. "He's not *my* Jace. He's here to cheer up Owen."

Ingrid wiped her hands, set the towel on the counter. "Right. Of course. But I did see him watching you over lunch. And you, him."

Eden lifted a shoulder. "It's just because I can't believe that he is actually here, in our home. He's . . . different than I imagined."

"That's what happens when you get to know someone—they turn out to be more than you expect."

"I don't want him here."

Ingrid and Eden both turned at Owen's voice. He had emerged from his hovel in the basement, looking as if he'd slept in his clothes. Apparently his damaged eye affected his ability to bathe. "I don't know why you brought him, Eden, except maybe to shove my face in the fact that I can't play anymore."

Eden saw her mother glance at Tiger. "Owen, he wants to help—"

But he advanced on Eden. "No, he doesn't. Have you seen his games? He thinks he's going to be the star now. He's not here to help me—he's here to make sure that I don't come back."

"Owen!" their mother said.

Owen ignored her. "I want to understand how, after everything, you can switch alliances so easily. I guess any old hockey player will do?"

"Owen!" Eden wasn't sure if she or her mother called his name louder.

He didn't look at their mother, his gaze hot on Eden. His good eye was red, cracked, his lips chapped. He looked thinner, but he hadn't worked out for over a week, so maybe he was losing some of his tone. "No, Mom, it's true. She loves it—hanging around the guys, making sure I stay out of trouble. She just can't wait until I call her to show up and save the day, can you, Sis?"

He turned to Ingrid, hands over his chest. "Or didn't she tell you? How she dragged me out of a bar last week? Maybe she also left out the part where I bring home a different rink bunny after every game—"

"That's enough!" Ingrid glanced at Tiger, who was watching them, his eyes wide. "Eden isn't responsible for your bad behavior. And I'd appreciate it if you would keep your voice down!"

"Then what is she good for? Because the last time I looked, she was still living in a tiny apartment, writing obits, taking the bus to work. Her only life is *my* life. She's no one without me. And now that it's over, she's latched herself to someone else. Some other superstar, just itching to take my place."

The words slid through Eden like a blade.

"Let's see. How many goals did J-Hammer make in the last two games?"

"Three and one assist." The voice came from behind Owen as Jace walked into the room, large and angry, his eyes steel. "That's enough."

"Really, dude?" Owen rounded on him, holding his arms open. "Why are you here, anyway?" As he advanced on Jace, Ingrid whisked Tiger from the room. "What—do you think Eden's some sort of good-luck charm? So what you made a couple goals. It was luck, not talent. *I'm* the talent. You're just the entertainment."

Eden watched Jace. He seemed to be reaching deep not to lash out.

Please don't hit Jace.

The thought stopped her. Made her glance at Owen. She was more worried about Owen's behavior than Jace's.

Still, Jace looked like he might just charge, push Owen into a corner, remind him he was still a punk kid with a stupid mouth.

"Jace," she said softly.

He looked at her, and his gaze softened. "Eden, I got this." He turned back to Owen. "I'm here because your sister invited me, and I came to see if I could . . . I don't know, cheer you up."

"Oh yeah. I'm really cheered watching you steal my career. And even better, drool over my sister? Don't tell me you're not into her."

Jace's mouth twitched. "Eden and I are just friends."

Yes. Of course. Then why did she have the urge to put a hand to her chest, maybe cover what felt like a gaping wound?

"Right," Owen drawled, something awkward and ugly in his broken face. "I know about you and your collection of *friends*. What number is Eden?"

Jace did advance then, grabbing him by his shirt. "You shut your mouth. She's the best thing that ever happened to you, and you're about the most ungrateful piece of—"

"Mr. Jacobsen, could I have a word?"

Eden hadn't realized it, but her father had come into the house, followed by Darek.

John stepped forward and repeated himself. "Just one moment of your time."

Jace bristled, and the look he gave her made Eden want to cry. Like he'd been caught bullying the first graders.

"Dad—"

"It's okay, Eden," John said, putting his hand on Jace's arm.

Darek came around the other side. "Owen, you come with me," he said.

Jace's jaw tightened, but he let Owen go. Stepped away. He kept his voice low. "I'm not trying to take your place, Owen. And you don't need both eyes to see that."

Then he turned and walked out, John behind him.

Owen shot Eden a glare, but Darek grabbed his arm. "Bro, you owe Eden an apology."

Owen shook himself out of his brother's grasp. "Whatever. She's the one who brought him here. Maybe she needs to apologize to me."

CHAPTER 13

JACE WALKED OUT OF THE HOUSE, the fury in his chest alive, ricocheting through him.

He wanted to hit something, hard.

He should probably thank Eden's father for pulling him away, even if it might be to ask him to leave.

John walked him onto the deck, where the sun had begun to settle beyond the trees.

Jace drew in a long breath of cool air. "I'm sorry, sir. You need to know that I wouldn't have hurt—"

"I know."

The snow crunched under his feet as he stalked to the edge of the deck, his hands shoved into his pockets. "I just . . . Owen said some awful things about Eden, and I . . ." He shook his head. "He shouldn't have."

"I know." John brushed snow from the picnic table and climbed onto it, facing the lake. "My son is hurting badly, and frankly, he might be right. Bringing you up here this weekend only pours salt into his wounds."

"I was trying to help." Jace leaned on the deck railing. Across the water, a string of log-framed mansions lined the shore.

"You know most of our place burned down last summer. I would sit here every day, staring across the lake at all that lush, green timber, at the houses still intact, and think . . . why?"

"It's a reasonable question. Why wasn't your place spared?"

"No. Why *was* it spared? See this lodge?"

Jace turned as John gestured behind him.

"It didn't burn. We still had our home. And for the life of me, I couldn't figure out why. Why were we so special? North of here, hundreds of homes burned, but ours was chosen to survive."

"But your land—it's destroyed."

"Yeah. So we get the good with the bad. We have to sort the blessings from the ashes. And that's what Owen must do. Right now he sees only the ashes of his life. We have to give him time to see what remains. Discover what was seeded in the fire."

Jace came over to the table and sat next to John, bracing his elbows on his legs. He stared at his hands, opening, closing. Imagining too easily how it might have felt to put his fist in Owen's face. Make him shut his mouth.

I'm *the talent. You're just the entertainment.* Yeah, well, those words had bounced right off him. It was Owen's insinuation about Eden that dug in, pushed his buttons.

"I don't like it when someone—anyone—speaks like that about a woman." He looked away. "But you were right to step in. I'm sorry. I'll leave today."

"I don't want you to leave, Jace. *You* were right, and Owen probably deserved—even needed—to be confronted. But I can't have a brawl in my living room. And not with my son, who doesn't understand why his life is unraveling."

"I understand. I shouldn't have lost my temper. . . . I guess I just stopped thinking."

John was silent beside him. The wind caught Jace's collar, trickled down his spine.

After a moment, John said, "You don't know me that well, so you don't know that I love football. I am not sure how I ended up with hockey players. I played for the University of Minnesota, defensive end. And wow, I loved tackling. Best day of my life was sixth grade when I started playing tackle football. Just taking my opponent out, right off his feet."

Jace nodded.

"I'll never forget the day in high school when Coach moved me to noseguard. I hadn't a clue what to do at nose and got trampled on. Over and over. I worked up a good ball of steam inside. Then they threw in a play that I knew—it was straight off the snap, a dive at the center's legs. Supposed to slow down the quarterback sneak."

Jace knew just enough football to keep up, but the old man was losing him.

"I dove as hard as I could and took the center down. And that's when I heard the crack. I'd broken both his legs."

Jace's mouth opened, just enough for John to nod.

"I know. I felt sick. I stood over the guy, the stands silent, and I realized something . . . I didn't like tackling because it made me feel powerful, although I'm sure that was part of it. I liked tackling because the fans cheered a good, clean tackle. I liked the applause."

Jace stilled.

"I watched your last game, Jace. You do have talent. Your slap shot could be legendary. Owen is angry, and most of all, he doesn't speak the truth. You're more than entertainment. You're the real deal. Don't let anyone tell you differently."

For some stupid, idiotic reason, Jace's eyes filled. He looked away, blinking.

"Please stay, Jace." John got up, pressed his hand to Jace's shoulder. "My daughter invited you, and you are welcome here. Owen is going to have to get used to that."

Jace couldn't look at John as he walked away. He sat there in the quietness of the late afternoon, listening to the wind shift, letting his eyes dry.

"Jace?"

Eden came around in front of him, dressed in her parka, wearing fat woolen mittens along with her green hat, and handed him his coat. "C'mon. I want to show you something."

He wanted to apologize for Owen's words, but she took his hand, eased him off the table, around the back of the house to a small shed. She opened it and pulled out a long toboggan. "Grab the other end."

He helped her carry it to an older-model F-150 pickup truck with the words *Evergreen Lodge Outfitter and Cabin Rentals* painted on the side. They loaded the toboggan in the back; then Eden got into the driver's seat. It dwarfed her as she worked the gas and fired up the engine. She turned to him, her eyes bright. "Trust me."

Jace got into the passenger seat and hung on as she backed out and took the dirt road toward town.

Silence pulsed between them, and he wanted to ease it, say something, but the fight with Owen seemed like a wedge.

Finally Eden said, "When I was a kid, and the winters grew long, and my mom wanted to kill us, my dad would take us to Honeymoon Bluff. It's a giant sledding hill outside town. He'd sit on the back of the toboggan and line us up in front of him. Then we'd hold on to his legs, and he'd wrap his arms around us—as many as he could—and we'd fly down the hill together."

"All six of you?"

She glanced at him. "We were little. But yeah, he'd pack us all in together. Our fates locked. I remember hiding my face in Darek's jacket—he was always in front—and the snow would get into the collar of my coat, down my back. We'd usually crash at the bottom, and all of us would fly off, eat some snow, laugh until we cried."

He could see her as a little girl, laughing as she sprawled in the snow, her eyelashes glistening.

When they reached town, she pulled into the campground, then drove to the park at the far end, parking next to a well-packed trail into the woods. She got out and reached for the toboggan, but he grabbed it first, setting it on the ground and retrieving the rope.

"Follow me," she said.

Don't lose her. The thought pulsed in his brain.

He followed her into the woods, the arms of the evergreen thick and bushy, snow whisking off in crystalline puffs of fairy dust. They came into a clearing about halfway up a giant hill.

"It's a hike, but it's worth it." Eden started up the hill again.

Jace fell in behind her, his breath forming in the air, the sweet chill of winter nipping his lungs. He should find some skates, see if he could slap a puck around.

"This is my favorite part," she said, standing at the apex of the hill and holding out her arms.

He joined her, turning to the view. Lake Superior stretched out as far as he could see, almost lavender under a sky surrendering to shades of periwinkle and magenta, ice floating near the shore like diamonds on the surface. Snow frosted the rocky shoreline, and the birch shadows stretched fingers across the sledding hill, as if beckoning them to brave it, to fling themselves into the abyss, toward the mysteries pooling at the bottom.

And Eden. Standing in the center of it all, her arms outstretched, eyes closed. Drinking it in.

Yes, this might be his favorite part also.

She opened her eyes, and he looked away before she caught him staring.

"Ready?" she asked.

"Um—"

"C'mon, don't be afraid."

"It's not that. It's just . . . Don't tell Coach or I'll be in big trouble. I'm not supposed to do anything dangerous—"

"Besides play hockey."

"Right."

"Fear not, little prince, I'll protect you," she said.

He gave a laugh, and her green eyes twinkled as she grabbed the sled, positioned it at the top of the hill. "Get on."

Jace climbed onto the back, holding the ropes on the side. Then he made room for Eden, and she tucked herself in front of him, looping her hands around his legs. "You hold on to the toboggan, and I'll hold on to you. Don't let go!"

Never. The word rose inside him, but he shook it away. "Got it."

"Okay!" She pushed them forward, moving her body, and he helped—and then the hill took them.

Slow at first, until the momentum and weight of the sled

combined to rush them down the slope, the wind burning their cheeks, the snow cutting in front of the toboggan, pinging against his skin. Eden screamed, something high and light, and he felt it deep inside his chest.

And then, near the bottom, the slope curved upward, and suddenly they went airborne.

Jace let go of the sled, feeling Eden rise out of the pocket of his legs, and grabbed her around the waist.

Then they landed, and the toboggan bounced out from beneath them. They flew off, Jace still holding Eden to himself, and skidded into the snow.

She landed in his arms, Jace on his back, staring at the sky, adrenaline rippling through his veins.

Then he heard giggling. Bright and delicious. Eden rolled onto her side, facing him. "Are you okay?"

Still lying flat, he glanced at her. "Yeah."

"See? Fun."

Maybe, but better were her smile, her shining eyes, the sparkle of snow on her face.

Oh, she was pretty. The kind of natural pretty that didn't take layers of makeup to achieve. The kind of pretty a guy wouldn't get tired of, that he might want to wake up to every day.

Owen was right. Too right.

Jace's breath caught.

"You ready to go again?"

He closed his eyes. "Maybe we could stay here a moment." Just enough to get his head right. To stop thinking about pulling her down into his arms, then rolling her into the snow and kissing her.

"Sure." She lay back, and the next thing he heard was the sound of her parka brushing the surface of the snow.

He looked over to see her arms and legs moving. "What are you doing?"

"Making a snow angel. C'mon. Make an angel."

"I . . ."

"Don't you know how?"

He did. But his voice had vanished, his throat closed.

"Jace, what's the matter?" She'd sat up and scooted over to him. "Are you hurt?"

Wow. What was it about this day that seemed to find all the embedded shrapnel in his heart? "No. It's just . . . a memory. My mom . . . she liked to make snow angels."

Eden put her mittened hand on his arm.

And that helped somehow, enough for the words to emerge. "When I was about eight years old, she came home from work one night and pulled me right out of bed. Made me throw on my boots and my coat and dragged me outside. It had snowed since I came home from school, and you know how, after a snow, the sky glows orange? It was like a spotlight shone down on us. We lived in this rental house a ways out of town, and it had this little backyard. We tromped out into the middle of it—I remember the snow being nearly up to my knees. And then we just plopped down and made angels."

He could almost feel the snow digging down his frayed parka, hear his mother's laughter. "She had this way of finding the best in life, pulling it out, making it special. I never knew, at the time, what it cost her to keep me in hockey—it's so expensive, you know? She worked double shifts and way too many late nights. But she always showed up for the important stuff. Like games and practices . . ."

"And snow angels."

He nodded. Swallowed hard. "My mom was a cocktail waitress. And . . . well, I don't want to know what else, but the fact is, she wasn't your typical PTA mom."

Eden didn't even flinch. And then he remembered—she'd probably read all that in the newspaper when they scandalized his mother's life right before her death. He wanted to turn away, but Eden had a grip on his arm.

"Your mom sounds like she loved you very much."

Jace sat up, brushed the snow off himself, but she didn't move, so he freed the words lingering inside. Small. Almost broken.

"She told me all the time that I was the best thing that ever happened to her."

"I'm sure you were."

He looked away and gave a rueful chuckle. "Not really. Not until I started playing professional hockey and could get her away from that life."

He started to get up, but Eden grabbed his sleeve. "Seriously, Jace?" She appeared almost angry. "She said it because she meant it. She loved you—it didn't matter if you played hockey or not."

"She gave up a lot for me, Eden. She was going to school to be a nurse when she got pregnant with me. Her parents kicked her out of the house, so she quit school, started working at a bar, and that was our life. She died of lung cancer—didn't smoke a day in her life."

She frowned. "You blame yourself for your mother's choices, how it all turned out."

He lifted a shoulder.

"Jace, you can't carry that. Your mother made her own choices, and she chose you. Because you were worth it. Are worth it. You're an amazing guy."

Her words wove inside him, wrapped around him.

And then, because it felt easier than arguing, easier than putting words to all the emotion roiling through him, he grabbed her scarf and tugged her to him.

Then he kissed her.

Her lips were cold and tasted of snow, but all the feelings bottled in his chest rushed out—anger and regret and appreciation and . . . desire. The idea of holding Eden, of hiding in her embrace, fueled him as he curled a hand behind her neck, pulling her closer.

Except . . . except she wasn't kissing him back.

The realization came to him like a slap, and he pulled away, a coldness sliding through him. Oh . . . no . . .

She stared at him, wide-eyed.

"Eden, I'm so sorry. I—wow. I'm not sure where that came from."

"It's okay, Jace," she said but looked away fast, wiping her mitten across her cheek. "I get it. It's been a crazy day, and of course, I probably came on to you a little. I didn't mean to send you mixed signals."

Mixed signals? If sitting in the snow with him constituted coming on to him . . . yeah, well, he'd had Zamboni drivers who flirted with him more than Eden did.

Which should have been a red-flag alert, a truth he'd bullied right past.

"No—it's not you. I'm sorry, Eden. I guess I'm still learning what 'just friends' means. I totally plowed over that line. I'm calling a penalty on myself." He tried to laugh.

She was getting up, backing away from him, affecting a let's-forget-it smile. "No problem. Hey, so maybe we should get back to the house." She turned away from him, and he closed his eyes.

Every headline, every accusation rushed back at him. She didn't say it, and frankly, his kiss seemed tame compared to his pre-Christian lip-locks, but still, Eden probably thought he'd nearly attacked her.

Maybe he should pack, tonight.

Except then she turned back, extending her hand to him, forgiveness in her eyes, and he was a pitiful sap because he drank it in. Taking her hand, he followed her out of the enchanted forest to the truck.

Just friends. Okay, he could do that.

Really.

"What kind of idiot am I?" Eden lay in bed, staring at the ceiling, warm under her blankets against the chill in the room.

"I don't know; what kind?" Grace said, huddled in her own bed. Amelia also lay under her covers, headphones plugged into her ears, feigning sleep.

Admittedly, it felt as if they'd traveled back in time to high school and late-night conversations about boys, but, well, this qualified. "Jace kissed me this afternoon."

"What?" Grace sat up in bed, a shadow streaming across the ceiling. "He kissed you? Oh, I knew he liked you. The way he was looking at you tonight, a sort of tenderness on his face—"

"That wasn't tenderness. That was horror. Or confusion. Because . . . I didn't kiss him back."

Grace got up and came over to Eden's bed, sat down on the edge. "What do you mean you didn't kiss him back?"

"He grabbed my scarf and pulled me to him and kissed me, and I was so shocked that I just . . . sort of sat there."

"But you didn't push him away."

"Would you?"

Grace smiled. "Hmm . . . Six feet four of pure muscle, tease, and temptation? Nope."

"Grace!"

"I'm just saying, a guy like that kisses you and you don't kiss him back?"

"I was going to—I mean, I think so. But he made such a big deal about us being friends that I couldn't catch up. You should have seen him in the car on the drive up. He practically made me repeat after him, a solemn oath. 'Just friends.'"

"Well, apparently he's not quite as serious about that as you are. As usual."

"What's that supposed to mean?"

"Oh, Eden. You're so . . . well, excuse me for saying this, but tightly wound."

"I just needed a second more to catch up."

"And then what—you would have leaped into his arms and kissed him until the snow melted around you?"

Eden laughed. "You've been reading too many romance novels."

"And you don't read enough of them."

"I do, actually. A stack of them."

"You just don't think they apply to you."

"They are fiction. As in, *not true*."

"You don't think you can get the handsome, hunky alpha male?"

Eden glanced at Amelia.

"She's not a child anymore. Trust me, when her boyfriend kisses her, she doesn't stand there like a board."

"I can hear you." Amelia pulled out one earbud. "Kiss him

back, Eden. He's hot. And nice. He purposely didn't send me back
to start tonight when he had the chance."

"He was too busy taking out Casper," Eden said. "Remind me
to be on Jace's team next time we play Sorry!"

"I can't figure out why you haven't joined yet. Jace is a great
guy—"

"Jace is a superstar. A celebrity. He could have anyone."

Grace took Eden's hand. "And he picked you."

"No. Really. He was just having an emotional moment. He
nearly got in that fight with Owen, and all that unused adrenaline . . . it came out in a kiss. When he realized he was kissing me,
he wanted to run. I saw it in his eyes." She pulled the covers up
to her chin, settling back in bed as Grace rose and returned to her
side of the room.

Except Eden could still feel the smooth, cool touch of Jace's
lips exploring hers, prodding them open. He'd smelled amazing,
all cotton flannel and outdoorsy. Strong. Even breathtaking. And
if it weren't for the shock of the moment, she really would have
let herself kiss him back.

Maybe.

"Next time . . . ," Grace said into the night.

"Just friends," Eden said softly.

"I'd like to be his friend," Amelia said.

Eden threw a pillow at her.

But she let that thought sink into her, trail into her dreams.
The kind of dreams that had her and Jace sliding down Honeymoon Bluff together, tumbling into the snow, laughing. Or her sitting in the stands, cheering him on as he chased the puck around
the ice. Or even sitting next to him at Sammy's, sharing a grilled
cheese sandwich.

The kind that had him pulling her into his arms, his mouth on hers, kissing her with all the delicious passion she felt simmering under the surface of his bigger-than-life persona.

She woke with her heart beating hard as the sun poured into the window. Grace was still in bed, as was Amelia, but Eden slipped on her bathrobe and tiptoed downstairs to make coffee.

She stopped midway, caught by the sight of Jace seated in a leather chair, wearing sweatpants, a T-shirt, a pair of reading glasses low on his nose, a book open on his lap.

A Bible.

He looked up then. Smiled, something slow, even sheepish, and a flood of tenderness coursed through her.

Eden headed for the kitchen, noticing the pot of freshly made coffee. She poured herself a cup, doctored it, and came out to join him.

"I didn't know . . ." She sat down and gestured to his Bible.

"I became a Christian after I nearly died in that accident." His hair was tousled but still curly, and the fragments of her dream nearly prompted her to reach out, run her fingers through it.

No, no, no. Bad Eden. That's the last thing he needed—more mixed signals from her.

His Bible was thick like a study version, with a frayed leather cover as if this wasn't his first time through. Bulletins parted a number of the pages. "What are you reading?"

He met her eyes. "Do you ever feel like you don't really belong in the Kingdom of God? Like you're loved but not liked? Saved but not favored?"

She sipped her coffee, thought for a minute. "I guess sometimes I feel like I'm not necessarily God's favorite. I look at my family and wonder what happened. Everyone else got the talent, and I got . . ."

Obits. She sighed. "I don't know what happened with my life, exactly. I always thought I'd be a great writer, a reporter. But I didn't land the job of my dreams out of college, and since then, I can't seem to find my footing. And yet I don't really have a reason to complain."

"Yeah, that's it. You feel like there should be something more waiting for you, but at the same time, you're grateful for the life you do have."

He seemed so unfamiliar to her, so normal, a man searching, authentic, honest. This wasn't the Jace she'd seen on the glossy pages of *Hockey Today*.

Maybe, just maybe, she'd discovered the real Jace. The one she hoped might be behind all the headlines. "You know what, though? I wonder if most Christians feel this way. I mean, look at Peter. He saw Jesus, who He really was, and told Jesus to get away from him, called himself a sinful man. And Paul . . . he suffered so much that he wanted to die."

"But Paul also said that he considered everything in his life worthless compared to knowing salvation and the wonder of God's love."

"Yeah. And that's the hard part. When we're struggling—when my car doesn't start or when you're injured—"

"Or have a migraine."

She frowned at him but nodded. "Yeah. When life seems to go south, we feel like God doesn't love us. But I keep going back to something my dad said to Owen. Maybe we have to start redefining how we understand God's love. And start hoping. My dad says that hope is one part confidence in God's love for us and one part our delight in Jesus. And that when we start to hope, it changes us, sets us apart. Makes us see life more clearly."

"We look at our own problems, and we say . . . why? Maybe we should look at our *blessings* and ask the same thing."

She took a sip of her coffee. "I think I need to remember that, too. I do have enough. I have this wonderful family, and so what that I'm not a reporter—"

"Yet."

"Yet." She smiled. "This is enough. More than enough." She raised an eyebrow. "However, you *do* have an amazing life."

But his mouth fell into a grim line. "I beat people up for a living. How can God possibly like me? I feel like a cautionary tale—look, kids, don't be like Jace Jacobsen, only skidding into heaven under the pads or, worse, due to a technicality."

Her mouth opened, and he looked away fast as if embarrassed.

He was serious. It was the first time she ever really saw it, the fact that his position as an enforcer dug into him. Made him something he didn't want to be, yes, but also skewed him into believing a lie. The one that called him a monster.

Her voice softened. "For the record, I don't think you like beating people up. I know you said that, but the truth is, it's your job. And you're oversimplifying. But here's the biggest part." She reached for his Bible, turned to 1 John 3, and read, "'See how very much our Father loves us, for he calls us his children.'"

She handed him back the Bible. "Children of God. Beloved by God. Zephaniah 3:17 says, 'He will take delight in you with gladness. . . . He will rejoice over you with joyful songs.' That's what we should be hearing, I think—the delight, the applause of heaven. If we could get that through our heads, it would change everything."

Jace took off his glasses, rubbed his finger and thumb into his eyes. "Did you tell your dad what I said to you? About liking to fight?"

She frowned. "No. Why?"

"No reason." Then he met her gaze. "You know, you're right. It is enough." He smiled. But it didn't reach his eyes, and she wasn't sure why his words sent a fist into her heart.

Eden showered and dressed and didn't blink when Jace joined her family for church, sliding in beside her in the third center row.

She had no doubt he was blocking the view of the screen for those behind him, but she didn't care. Let the world see him, the man behind the headlines, the one lifting his voice in worship. She closed her mouth and let herself listen as he poured it out to the Lord. "Amazing Grace" and "Great Is Thy Faithfulness"—her small-town church loved the old hymns.

A couple regulars recognized Jace, greeting him in the welcome moment. Eden grinned, but as she sat down, Owen's words niggled at her. *She's latched herself to someone else. Some other superstar, just itching to take my place.*

The pastor launched into the sermon, but she couldn't free herself from the grip of Owen's accusation.

What if he was right? That she wanted to be with Jace because he was a star? She wound her hands together on her lap, remembering her behavior yesterday and Jace's words about not wanting to draw headlines.

Maybe you do. Her chest burned. What if Jace thought she only liked him because of his star power? And when she hadn't kissed him back, it added to his wounds. As if she weren't interested in *him*.

No wonder he'd done a full-out backpedal.

When the sermon ended, she slid out of the pew, leaving the

introductions of their resident superstar to Casper and Grace while she escaped to the bathroom.

Eden emerged to find her family gathered in the foyer, a small crowd around Jace, Grace at his elbow. Amelia took a shot with her phone of a couple local hockey players in the congregation posing with him.

Jace looked every inch a celebrity in his dress pants, a gray shirt, a sports jacket. His hair combed back, curly behind his ears, and that intoxicating, half-dimpled J-Hammer smile.

For a second, it blew her off her shoes. What had she been thinking, believing for a second he could do normal? That she might even share the spotlight with him? Not that she'd consciously thought it, but clearly she'd been lying to herself.

As she watched, her family moved en masse toward the exit, greeting the pastor, then heading out the door to their cars.

Eden sighed as she finally followed them out.

CHAPTER 14

JACE HELD THE DOOR OPEN for Grace and Amelia to climb into the back of the Charger, then slid into the passenger side while Casper took the wheel.

Not until Casper had the car in reverse did Jace stop him with a hand on his arm. "Where's Eden?"

Casper glanced behind him as if trying to remember where he'd seen her last. "I don't know. Maybe she's going with Mom and Dad." They had taken two vehicles to church, but Eden rode down with him on the way.

"We can't leave her—"

"We're not leaving her—see, look, Dad's driving up to the entrance. She's coming out. She was probably gabbing with one of her friends."

But as Jace watched her climb into the van, fingers tightened in his chest. No, she'd been standing outside their circle, watching as Amelia—and others—took his picture. And he'd let it happen. So easily slid into a moment of fame and left her behind that he felt ill. No wonder she longed for the spotlight—even the people who loved her pushed her out of it.

No, *cared for*. Not *loved*. The word embedded in his thoughts as they drove away from the tiny Deep Haven Community Church and toward the house. Nice service, decent pastor. It had been a while since Jace sang hymns, and he'd missed them. Mini sermons set to song. Most often he attended the players' service on the road, singing next to Max and Kalen, trying to block their measly voices from his brain. The team chaplain had good sermons, though. The kind that got Jace thinking about his life outside hockey.

A life that had seemed impossible until this weekend. His conversation with Eden wouldn't let him alone. Despite his words to her, no, hockey wasn't enough. Not near enough.

He wanted it all. A family. A home. A wife. Kids.

Like Tiger, climbing into his lap for a story. Jace had nearly folded into a soggy mess yesterday when the kid came up to him holding *Goodnight Moon*. He'd lost himself in what-if as the tyke snuggled in his lap.

It made him call Sam, just to check in on Maddy, who continued to wait for a miracle heart. The sadness in Sam's voice and the camaraderie of the Christiansens only conspired to show him exactly what might be missing from his life. The *more* he longed for.

And then, last night, he'd gone and blown it—big. Kissing Eden like . . . like she wanted the same thing.

He hadn't had a girl stiffen in his arms like that *ever*.

The memory had driven him out of bed, into the early morning sunrise, thirsty for a little hope. He couldn't shake the sense that he lived a mediocre Christian life. Caught in the no-man's-land between God's grace and God's favor. After all, how could God truly delight in a man who had lived Jace's violent life?

Who'd permanently destroyed another's?

That's what we should be hearing . . . the delight, the applause of heaven. Eden's voice, cheering him on as usual. He leaned his head against the rest and closed his eyes, half-listening to Amelia and Grace in the backseat, planning lunch.

He hadn't a clue what the applause of heaven might sound like.

However, Eden should surely hear it. After everything she'd done for others.

"I'd like to do something nice for Eden."

He'd interrupted them, and the car silenced.

"What?" Amelia said.

Jace glanced at her. "I'd like to do something nice for Eden. Something that makes her feel special."

Amelia frowned, and from the driver's seat, Casper added, "It's because he's got a thing for her."

"I knew it!" Grace said. She grinned at Jace, her eyes twinkling. "I heard all about the kiss."

"You kissed her? Dude. I thought we talked about this." Casper gave him a look.

"We didn't—I mean . . . Okay, listen. It was a mistake."

"What, your lips just happened to fall on hers?"

"No, but . . . don't get your shorts in a knot; she didn't kiss me back."

"Yet," Grace said.

Really?

"I'd say give it another go—"

"Grace!" Casper said. "Listen to the man. They're just friends."

"Mmm-hmm," Amelia said, her nose in her phone. Probably tweeting this very conversation.

"Only if he doesn't make another move. Because you know Eden. This is all on him." Grace leaned between the seats. "If you want her, you'll have to try again. Go after her." She peered at him, her face solemn. "Do you want her?"

He stilled. Casper glanced at him. Amelia looked up from her phone. A hand wrapped around his throat.

Then . . . "Yes."

The word came out fast, like a slap shot on goal, and he thought it might have bounced out, so he took a breath, said it again. "Yes. I like your sister."

"More than friends?" Amelia asked.

"Wow, it runs in the family—you guys don't take prisoners, do you?"

Grace grinned and Casper shook his head.

"But what if she thinks I'm too . . . aggressive?"

The car went silent.

"Okay, listen, it's not like I attacked her, so don't start plotting how to leave my body in the woods, but the truth is, I can't shake free of this fear that she'll think I'm coming on too strong."

Grace hung on the seat. "So you make the grand gesture, but you let her decide. And for the record, Casper, it might take something big for Eden to figure it out. Maybe start with something . . . nice, before going in for the kill."

Casper glanced at her in the rearview mirror. "Could you rephrase that for the sake of the brother in the car?"

Grace laughed, and even Jace found a smile.

"What kind of gesture?"

Grace sat back, thinking. Casper took a left onto the road that cut toward Evergreen Resort.

"C'mon, guys. Can't you think of anything she likes?"

"Okay. Uh, let's see. Eden like flowers. And she . . . is into books," Casper said.

"She won a writing contest once, in first grade. Made the paper. Mom cut it out and kept it on the fridge for years," Grace added. "Mom's like that—a keeper of stuff. Drawings and awards. Every time we made the paper, she put it on the fridge. One time I counted, and Darek had five articles, Casper had four, I had some, and Amelia even had a couple photos published. Of course, Owen had like nine articles. Now Mom has an entire separate scrapbook for him. And then there was Eden's article, faded and yellow, still from first grade."

"I remember that," Amelia said. "It finally dried up and fell off the fridge."

"Eden just had the one?"

"Well, she eventually had two. One for the writing contest, and the other was for winning the high school variety show her senior year."

"What's that?"

"Oh, it's part of the senior project. Every senior has to dress up and portray someone from history. It's a competition, and they get graded on it. Eden won that year—I think she played Judy Garland. Sang a song . . . I can't remember, but Darek might know. She was a hit. Stole the show."

They pulled into the resort driveway. Casper turned off the car. "Sorry. I wish we were more help. I guess we don't know Eden as well as we should."

Jace didn't argue with them as they piled out of the car. The

Caravan pulled up next to them. He waited while Eden and the crew got out, then walked with her up to the house, holding the door open for her.

The smile she gave him seemed distant.

Darek was easy to track down after Sunday lunch. Jace left Eden cleaning dishes with her mother as Grace stirred up a batch of monster cookies, Owen returning to his dungeon in the basement. Jace grabbed his jacket and Casper's boots and trudged out into the cold, heading for the sound of a Skilsaw in one of the smaller cabins.

They'd erected five cabins, all two- and three-bedroom shoreline retreats with tiny front porches and empty window boxes. When they finished, and when the forest grew back, the place would be the perfect north shore hideaway.

His sweatshirt covered in sawdust, Darek was busy applying baseboard to the main room of the cabin. The place smelled of pine and fresh paint, the sunlight scouring up jeweled dust particles in its rays.

Darek leaned back on his haunches and nodded to Jace as he came in.

Jace spied John in the bedroom, painting. He smiled at Jace, and the same warm feeling from yesterday licked through him.

He'd never done well around dads. Not the fathers of the few girls he'd actually dated. Especially not his own.

This dad, however, felt different. As if he actually liked Jace. But that was yesterday, when Jace just wanted to be Eden's friend.

"Grab that box of nails, will you?"

Jace handed Darek the nails, and he reloaded.

Darek leaned down, pushing the baseboard against the wall. "Give it a nudge at the end?"

He held the board tight against the wall as Darek nailed it in. "I don't suppose you brought me some of Grace's monster cookies?" Darek asked. "I think I can smell them from here."

"They weren't done yet. I can go back—"

"Nah. I'll get them when I pick up Tiger." He lifted another length of board. "You're good with him, you know."

"He's a cute kid. Got him on skates yet?"

Darek grinned. "Yep. Hey, there are some knee pads in the corner." He nodded toward them, and Jace took the hint. "Just fit the other end of the board to the wall."

Jace grabbed the end. "I have a question for you. Casper said something about Eden winning some contest in high school, maybe as Judy Garland?"

"Oh yeah. She sang 'It Had to Be You.' Eden got it off a recording with her and Bob Hope, had a buddy of hers play Bob Hope's part. Brought down the house, although she won't admit it. First time I ever heard her sing outside church. She was real good, seemed to ham it up, even love the spotlight." He hummed a few bars. "Mom cut out the article, put it on the fridge. I remember seeing Eden reading it a couple times. Okay, hand me the next board."

Jace obeyed. "Did you say you knew the band playing tonight? Is there any way I can get ahold of them?"

Darek glanced at him. "Before tonight?"

Jace felt John's eyes on him from the other room but didn't flinch as he slowly nodded.

Jace took a shower before dinner and came down in a powder-blue dress shirt, a pair of dark pants. Eden sat at the counter wearing jeans and a sweater. "This is Deep Haven," she said, but she disappeared and twenty minutes later reappeared in a floral top, leggings, and tall black boots.

"We're meeting Ivy and Darek there," Jace said. Ingrid and Tiger sat at the table doing a puzzle, and he lifted a hand to them as they left.

Jace stood at the driver's door by the time Eden came out, pulling on her parka. He held out his hand, gesturing for the keys.

"Seriously?"

He raised an eyebrow. "I know my way around town."

"What, did you memorize a map of Deep Haven during your wanderings? Where were you, anyway? I didn't see you all afternoon."

Not yet, Eden. "Being a normal guy. Isn't that what you wanted?"

For a second, he had the crazy hope she would argue. Say that, no, in fact, she'd wanted him to herself.

But her mouth simply tightened around the edges, and he bit back the taste of disappointment.

"Fine." She slapped the keys into his hand and went around to the passenger door. She had to readjust the seat, but he waited until she buckled.

"I just hope Owen doesn't see you driving his car," she said, glancing at the house.

"He hasn't said two words to me since yesterday," he said, backing out. "I thought it was better to stay away from the house today. I don't want any more altercations."

"I'm sorry. I thought he'd like having you here. It'll be a long drive to the Cities tomorrow."

"I can handle Owen if you can," he said.

He hit the radio as they rode into town. Sinatra came on, singing "Cry Me a River."

"'Now you say you love me . . .'"

She frowned at him.

"C'mon, Eden, loosen up. Sing along."

"I don't—"

"I know. You don't get that loose."

He pulled up to the VFW, then went around to help her as she got out, but she beat him to it.

She didn't take his arm as they walked in.

Yeah, well, he had plans to remedy that.

They found an empty side table that seated four, and he moved his chair next to hers. The VFW reminded him of his mother's workplace, complete with the stage, the long bar with local rummies bellied up for beer, the has-beens playing pool, all swagger and story. He'd never liked the Bunny Cocktail Lounge— it always made him want to slink away, especially when he saw men adding tips to his mother's outfit. But she always came home after work, didn't stay after like the other waitresses.

This place was more local hangout than pickup bar. Onstage, the Blue Monkeys twined out their bluesy tune. The lead singer, a pretty brunette with her hair tied back, played bass guitar. Another singer, short-haired, playing an acoustic, stood behind her, harmonizing. Into the mic beside her, a blond man on harmonica added to the bridge, and behind them all, a drummer kept looking at the lead singer as if she belonged to him.

But maybe that's how they all looked at each other in a small town like this. Maybe they considered Eden theirs, and he was walking right into disaster tonight, making the kind of headlines that would send Eden sprinting out of his life.

He was setting up his shot, hoping it didn't go wildly wide.

"What do you feel like?" he asked as a waitress came up to take their order.

"Hey, Kelly, how about a couple lemonades and a basket of curly fries," Eden said. She unwound her scarf, listening to the music, bobbing her head to the beat. As the song ended, she leaned over to Jace. "The gal on the guitar and the guy with the harmonica, they're friends of Darek's . . . Claire and Jensen. The bass guitarist, Emma, is married to the drummer, Kyle Hueston. He's the cop I called to get the license plate info on our John Doe."

Jace knew some of that but just nodded. He glanced around for Darek and his girlfriend but didn't see them. Maybe it was a sign.

Their curly fries came, and he used them to sop up a mixture of mayo, mustard, and ketchup. Eden made a face, shook her head. "Good thing we'll be back to real life tomorrow."

Real life. He sort of hoped not. Maybe a different life, one more real than any in his past ten years.

"I can't believe it—J-Hammer Jacobsen!"

A tall, shapely blonde, well past her college years, held a couple glasses of beer. "I can't believe you're here, in our little town. Did you come with Owen?" She shot her question Eden's direction. "Is he home?"

Eden drew in a breath. "Hey, Bree. Yeah. He's up at the lodge. But he's not going to make it down tonight, and we're leaving in the morning."

"I'm so sorry to hear about his injury. We can't wait until he's back on the ice." She returned her attention to Jace. "You know, me and the girls are big fans."

He slid his arm over the back of Eden's chair. "Thanks."

"We're probably having a party later tonight. You—and Eden, of course—are welcome to stop by." She gave him a grin.

"Thanks, but we've got other plans. . . ." He glanced at Eden and smiled, then looked back to Bree.

Her mouth made a perfect O. "Have fun, Eden."

Eden looked at him once she was gone. "We have other plans?"

He said nothing, just smiled.

"Jace—"

The band ended their song, and he leaned back, clapping, his heart thundering. Especially when Jensen—Darek's buddy—caught his eye.

Jace rose, even as Jensen stepped up to the mic. "We have a great surprise for you tonight. A friend is in town, and he's asked to sing something special. So put your hands together and give a warm Deep Haven welcome to Jace Jacobsen!"

He didn't look at Eden as he went to the front.

His hands had turned slick, his stomach roiling. He needed to get on the ice, warm up, and in about ten minutes he'd be fine. But this wasn't a game, and he had about ten *seconds* to get himself together or fail big.

He took the mic, smiled into the applause. Latched his eyes on Eden. "So I found out that my friend Eden once sang this song, years ago. Apparently she won a contest with it, so I was hoping she might come up here and help me sing it."

Eden sat up in her chair and looked around, behind her. As if he were talking about a different Eden?

The band played the intro, and Jace took a breath, started in. "'Why do I do just as you say . . . ?'"

Eden pressed her hands to her mouth as a few heads turned her direction. A number of others wore grins, some singing along.

Jace gestured to her. "C'mon, Eden."

Her eyes widened, and he sang a few lines to the crowd, then glanced at her again.

"'I wandered around and finally found the somebody who . . .'"

Eden stood. Jace held out his hand to her. "'For nobody else gave me a thrill—'"

Then, without a word, she headed toward the door, pushing past patrons, nearly knocking Bree over.

His throat tightened, his voice turning hollow as he stood onstage. What—? He managed to eke out the last of the lines as the door swung shut behind her.

"'Wonderful you, it had to be you . . .'"

Before the last of the notes died out, nearly before the applause started, Jace was out the door, following his wild shot into the night.

She'd never been more mortified.

Eden didn't stop at the corner, nor at the beach, just headed straight out toward the lighthouse, the breakwater that stretched across the harbor. The last bastion of land before the chilly depths of Lake Superior—where she had writetn her best poetry, where she stared at the stars. Where sometimes she could actually believe that God noticed her.

Not tonight. Clouds blocked the stars, and nothing but the puddle of false light from the tall streetlamps directed her steps.

The wind whipped up, getting under her jacket, chapping her face, and she wiped it with her bare hand, hating that Jace had conned her into wearing leggings and a dress. She had no business trying to look pretty. She'd just freeze.

She heard his voice in the wind and refused to turn around. Maybe she could lose him in the night.

"Eden!"

He was closer now, and she wanted to hate him more for the

fact that he was in shape and could run her down. But then again, that's what he did. Ran over people. Bullied them. Eviscerated them, on the ice and off.

She picked up speed.

She heard him behind her, not even breathing hard. Fine. She slowed, walking through the parking lot of the lighthouse. She didn't have to talk to him, didn't have to show him how—

"Eden!" He caught her arm, and she cried out as he spun her.

He reacted as if he'd hit her, bouncing away, and it felt good for a second to put him in his place. Yeah, he *had* hurt her.

"Eden, what is it? What did I do? I thought . . . I thought you'd like the song. I thought we could sing it together—"

She held up her hand, shook her head, turned away from him. "Just go away, Jace. You're right—I never should have brought you here."

But he didn't leave—in fact, he followed her, stepping in front of her, a wall to stop her cold. "What do you mean I'm right? I never said that—"

"But you were thinking that. That you don't belong here in this backwoods town."

"I like this town."

"Or with my normal, boring family."

"Your family is anything but boring! They're fun and kind and—"

"Fine!" She looked at him then, not caring that he might see her tears. "Then you don't belong with me."

He closed his mouth, his lips a tight line. "What are you talking about?"

Oh, now he was going to act stupid. Or maybe she was the stupid one. "Right. I forgot. We're *just friends*."

She pushed past him, but he caught up again, walking beside her. "I thought you liked that song. I thought you'd enjoy being onstage."

"I don't want to be onstage! Especially with you!"

That shut him up. And hurt him by the way he flinched. It slowed her down just enough for her to hear her heartbeat.

"The fact is, yes, I like that song. A lot. But don't you see, Jace? Next to you, I'm . . . I'm just a shadow." She bit her lip, looking away. "And . . . well, I guess I always thought it would be sung to me by someone who meant it."

His voice softened, so much it hurt. "Eden. What makes you think I didn't mean it?"

She couldn't speak, her voice trapped deep in her burning chest.

He slid his hands over her shoulders. "Okay, I'm going to take another wild slap shot here and say that . . . I like you, Eden. More than friends, and . . . I know I totally crossed the line with you, but—"

"Stop, please." She stepped away from him. "Jace, you and I are worlds apart. I . . . I don't fit into your life. I'm a sidelines girl. I don't want someone—"

"In the spotlight. Right. You said that." He shook his head. "But I don't believe you. I think you're just scared that someone might notice you." He leaned close, his aftershave rich and exotic. "Maybe that I might notice you."

His tenor rumbled through her, and for a second, she was back in the VFW, watching as he took the mic, his blue eyes finding hers. Listening to his voice as he sang, the words landing on her heart, sliding inside.

It had to be you.

No.

She pushed him away. "No, Jace. You don't understand. You've just been swept up in the small-town nostalgia. The minute you get back to St. Paul, you'll see. I'm not . . ."

"Remarkable? You're a girl I might walk right by?"

She closed her eyes.

"Why don't you let me make up my own mind?" He put his hands on her shoulders. Standing in the glow of the parking lot, splashed with light that outlined his shoulders, the wind teasing his hair, the overwhelming beauty of him could chase words from her. "I find you amazingly remarkable. I would totally notice you across a crowded room."

And as she stood there wordless, he cupped her face in his hands and kissed her.

Again.

His five o'clock shadow brushed her chin, her upper lip. He tasted sweet, of lemonade and salt, and his smell rushed over her— masculine, strong, bold.

Jace.

Was kissing her.

And just like before, the force of him in her life turned her . . . afraid.

Yeah, afraid . . . that if she stepped into his embrace, his life, he'd figure out that she shouldn't be there.

He sighed, releasing his hold on her, beginning to move away.

No. No more standing on the sidelines watching everyone else reach for their happily ever after.

Eden curled her hands around his jacket lapels. "Jace," she said softly against his lips, and then, before he could escape, she kissed him back.

He responded like the man she knew, putting those strong

enforcer arms around her and diving in, 100 percent and more. His touch was a little untamed, a groan easing from the back of his throat, all that coiled strength and desire that he showed on the ice pouring into her.

He pulled her closer, deepening his kiss, nudging her lips open for more, a decadent thrill curling inside her. She wrapped her arms around his neck, formed her body to his, swept up by the fact that, in her arms, this amazing man came a little undone.

Yet she also felt everything that lay below the surface—kindness, patience, the tenderness of a man who was so much more than his headlines. The guy who played and fought—and loved, maybe—full-on.

Eden realized she was standing on her tiptoes, maybe even melting a bit, because he finally bent down, picked her up in his amazing arms, and carried her over to a snowy picnic table under a streetlight. He brushed away the snow, then set her on it, angling into her embrace and cupping his hands around her face, meeting her eyes.

She couldn't breathe. Not with the way he was looking at her, his eyes so blue, filled with emotion.

She felt moisture in her own eyes, and it escaped, dripped down her cheek.

He ran his thumb across the tear. "Did I do something wrong?"

She swallowed and shook her head. "The lights are a little bright, I guess. I'm not used to it."

He kissed her nose, her forehead. "You will be, Eden. You will be."

CHAPTER 15

As Sam expected, Maddy had completely charmed everyone in the pediatric transplant ward—doctors, nurses, aides, and fellow patients.

His daughter even had a boyfriend, a ten-year-old named Trey Harrison. Of course she did, because no one could keep from falling head over heels for the nine-year-old with the effervescent smile.

And this afternoon, she and Trey presided over the group of patients, mostly under the age of ten, waiting for kidneys or livers or lungs, as a clown tried to teach them how to tie balloon animals. Only Trey, like Maddy, waited for a heart. Like Maddy, tubes ran from his body to a small cart on four wheels that housed the external ventricular assist device, acting as a heart to pump blood through the body.

Trey's parents huddled at the end of the hall, consulting with their doctor. Word had filtered down the ward that Trey now topped the list in their area, after only thirty-seven days. But he'd already fought one bout of influenza and a respiratory tract infection. Now, according to his concerned parents, his body showed signs of metabolic acidosis and acute peritonitis. He had a ticking clock on his chart.

Sam hated himself for his thoughts. He wanted Trey to get his heart.

He just wanted *Maddy* to be next in line. To live.

The party felt like a Band-Aid, a faint hope to normalize lives, help the children—and their parents—see beyond the hospital walls. Some children could even leave the unit, visit the activity center.

"You know, events like these give parents a chance to escape, grab a cup of coffee, or return home and nap, shower, catch up on work."

Britta, Maddy's transplant nurse. Sam remembered her from Maddy's last stay. He wished he didn't.

"Sam, you didn't leave the hospital all weekend. We have your phone number. We'll call you if anything happens."

He looked away as Maddy showed her new creation to Trey, who had made a crown. Maddy didn't even look toward Sam.

"Here. I'm guessing you didn't have lunch." Britta handed him a Coke.

Sam cracked the tab. "Thanks."

Britta was silent for a long moment. "They wouldn't deny a nine-year-old a heart."

"No—but they can take her away from me, put her in a foster home that can provide the right support."

Britta shook her head. "You're a great dad. You haven't left her side. Not once. I see you. You read to her and sing to her and play games with her—even the social worker sees that."

He took another sip of the Coke, relishing the bite and the way, for a second, it woke him.

"You know, I thought when Maddy got her heart, it was over. I had prayed for so long . . . But the truth is, I'm broke, I have no house help, and I'm barely able to provide for her. If I were looking at my case on paper, I'd agree with the social worker. There is precedent for removing Maddy from a medically untenable situation."

Britta stared at him, her eyes wide.

"If I fight it, it will be worse. The hospital could get the state involved, and I'll lose custody, maybe permanently. But if I sign her over to the hospital, then they can assign her to a medical foster family and she'll go there until my situation changes." He gave a rueful laugh. "Like that will happen. I can't pay the bills I have. How will I pay these? But how can I sign my daughter away? It would be like tearing my heart from my body."

She slipped a hand over his arm.

Sam leaned back against the wall, closed his eyes. He pressed the Coke can to his forehead, relishing the chill against his hot skin.

"Sam, you need a break. Listen, you get out of here. I'll be here to watch her. And you can be back in time to read her a bedtime story."

But he didn't budge. "I can't leave her. You know that."

"Actually, you can. If you don't take care of yourself, you can't possibly take care of Maddy."

That shook him out of his daze and made him reconsider. He looked at Maddy, then back to Britta. "Okay. Just for a little while."

Stopping by Maddy's room, he grabbed his jacket, not sure where to go.

And then, yes, he knew.

He took Washington Avenue to Third. The old depot with the Milwaukee Road sign rose up from the corner, three stories high. He found an empty meter and parked.

The chilly breath of the ice rink saturated the building, the scent of it crisp and sharp. A few skaters were on the ice, but Sam didn't look at them as he headed toward the rental desk.

He laced the skates on with a quick, practiced motion, the feel of the ice beneath his blades beckoning.

He'd forgotten the freedom of it, but it filled him in an instant when he glided over the surface, strong and smooth. He cut hard and crossed over to the left, then skated fast down the length of the arena. On the far side, giant windows pushed back the night, and overhead, girders sparkled against the lights and the glare of the diamond-cut ice.

He rounded the rink again, then stopped, ice spraying. A line of sweat edged his brow, and he bent over, breathing hard, listening to his heart pump. His strong, healthy, reliable heart.

Working out the kinks?

He straightened, trying to shake Mia out of his brain. Trying not to see her dark hair flying out from her stocking cap, the way she turned, skating backward to take his hands.

Why was it when he felt most overwhelmed, she showed up to haunt him? Or to charm him into the past? Sometimes he could still hear her laughter, see the softness, the invitation in her eyes.

Still remember skating up behind her, sliding his hands around her waist, molding her body to his as he taught her to skate. *Follow my movements.*

No one had known him like Mia. No one understood how it felt to hold back fear and hope behind such tightly clenched teeth.

And no one ever would.

You're so beautiful, Mia. He remembered that part too. The smell of her hair. Those doe-brown eyes, her lashes so thick and full that they could mesmerize him. He could almost taste her kiss.

Sam gripped the boards before the memory of holding his wife in his arms took him to his knees.

No. He couldn't think one more minute about Mia or Maddy and how everything had been stolen from them.

Didn't want to believe that God had somehow betrayed him. But maybe he needed to stop relying on a God who didn't seem to care.

But giving up on God seemed so . . . Well, then he'd really be alone, right?

Sam skated off the rink, changed into his shoes, and headed back to the hospital.

The sound of an alarm echoed down the hallway the moment the elevator opened. The code.

Sam took off in a sprint.

No. He wasn't ready—

He heard the commotion, the counting, the orders even before he reached the room. And then a terrible, awful relief swept over him as he clung to the door.

Not Maddy's room.

Trey's.

He stood there holding on to the jamb as he watched the

doctors work on him, the nurses responding to orders, trying to keep his heart pumping. But the child was already blue.

Sam headed to Maddy's room, holding her tight when he heard Trey's mother scream.

Eden didn't need flowers on her desk to put a smile in her day. Jace's voice mail, husky and masculine, asking her out after this afternoon's practice, could fragrance her entire week.

Never mind the stack of obit orders waiting for her or the fact that Kendra had arrived early and seemed to be tracking down another hot lead for the remembrance page. Eden had hunted up the issue from Saturday and spotted a below-the-fold article Kendra had put together, this time about a man who'd helped start a string of restaurants in the Twin Cities, including one that hosted a Saturday dinner for the homeless.

Kendra, becoming a real reporter while Eden hitched herself to one star after another. She tried to shake off her brother's words, tried to lean into Jace's embrace, to tell herself that they could belong together. But the fact was, she still wanted to do something amazing on her own.

She hung her bag over her chair, shucked off her jacket, and sat down, thumbing through the obit orders, the messages.

"Hey! How was your long weekend?" Kendra peered over the top of the cubicle. She had her auburn hair in two long braids today. "Did you do anything fun?"

Eden smiled and lifted a shoulder, tempering her excitement. Wait and see if Jace would still chase her across a crowded room after a week or two. "It was normal. We brought Owen back with us."

"We?"

Ah, shoot. "I might have taken Jace Jacobsen to Deep Haven with me."

Kendra raised an eyebrow. "Seriously?"

"He's Owen's teammate."

"And his bedside nurse? Please."

Owen had still been sprawled on her sofa in surly slumber, so she took his Charger to work. She wanted to suggest he return to his own apartment, but frankly, she didn't know what he might do if she kicked him out. Throw himself from the balcony? Hopefully not, but he'd become a picture of despondency, and she wanted to cry at the sight of him, disheveled, smelly, his hair tangled and unruly. With his bandage removed and the stitches healing, the remnants of the bruises fading from his face, he resembled a meth addict more than a superstar hockey player.

Kendra came around the cubicle and crouched next to her chair, her hazel eyes rich with mischief. "He spent the weekend with you?"

"We didn't really spend the weekend together—"

"You know what I mean." She looked Eden over. "Is that a new dress? What's going on? Are you . . . are you *dating* him?"

"Shh. No. Or . . . I don't know." But she had borrowed a few fresh outfits from Grace, just in case she hadn't dreamed up the entire weekend. She wore a green sweater dress, black leggings, tall black boots. So much color felt flamboyant, but . . . oh, she could nearly burst with the news.

"I kissed him."

"You kissed Jace Jacobsen?"

She pressed her hands to her mouth. Nodded. "I kissed him a lot."

Kendra's mouth opened.

"But you can't tell anyone. Because . . . I mean, really. I don't belong in his world."

"Are you kidding me? Of course you do."

"No. But maybe . . ."

"What?"

"Nothing. I just keep thinking that there is something about him that is . . . normal. He's funny and . . ." Scared. And real and—

"Eden, I hate to tell you this, but there is nothing remotely normal about Jace Jacobsen. Shall we do a Google search and see how un-normal he is?"

"Thanks."

"But that doesn't mean you don't belong together. No one knows hockey like you do. You practically live at the arena."

"I'm not a rink bunny."

"I didn't mean that. I meant you're not wowed by all his star power. You know, because of Owen."

Right. Mmm-hmm.

Kendra lowered her voice. "Is he still searching for that John Doe with you? Because this came in yesterday." She held up a pink message slip. "The caller said his name was Zach. And I quote, although I'm going to have to put on my best nasty voice: 'I tracked down my friend about that guy.'" Kendra looked at her over the top of the note. "Good thing you don't need any specifics." Then, "'He says he doesn't know him, that he just hooked me up with him because he needed wheels. He met him playing pickup basketball at a local community center. Now leave me alone.'"

Eden could nearly hear Zach in her words. "Let me see that."

Indeed, Kendra's scrawls matched her recitation.

"Who is the mysterious unidentified 'him'? Please say John Doe. Please, please."

Eden laughed. "Yes, fine, we're still looking for John Doe—"

"I thought I told you there was no story in that."

Eden winced, glanced up at Charlotte, standing in Kendra's cubicle, peering over the top. She wore a black headband in her hair, too much red on her lips.

"It's just a side project—"

Charlotte shook her head. "Eden, you don't have time for side projects. Not today. You've already taken way too much time off, and frankly, I'm not sure your heart is in this job anymore."

"My heart is in my job! I feel bad for the kid. He doesn't have anyone."

Charlotte considered her, eyes narrowing. Then she walked around the cubicle and held out her hand. Eden gave her the note, and she read it at arm's length, not using her readers. "You'd have to be Bob Woodward to get anything out of this." She handed the message back to Eden. "Has he passed yet?"

"No. I mean, I don't think so. I'm going to the hospital after work, but I hope not."

"Then it's not our department. Kendra, a word, please?"

Kendra made a face behind Charlotte's back as she followed their editor to her office.

Deflated, Eden looked at the slip of paper. Charlotte wasn't wrong—the message was too vague to be of any real help. How many hundreds of kids hung out after school, shooting hoops at any one of the handful of community centers in St. Paul?

And clearly, unless Doe passed away, he wouldn't get a mention in the paper. Maybe not even then. What if he was a runaway or a thief? Maybe he'd committed a crime, and she would just bring unknown pain to his family—if she found them.

Maybe her heart was *too much* in her job.

She folded the note into a tiny square, shoved it into her dress pocket, and reached for her stack of obits. She had enough notices to keep her typing for a week.

Kendra came back but said nothing, disappearing into her cubicle. Eden heard her typing and couldn't help it. She leaned around the edge. "So what did she want?"

"Nothing."

"Kendra—"

"I don't want to tell you."

Now Eden had a fist in her stomach. "What?"

Kendra kept typing, her shoulders rising and falling, as she said, "Charlotte's got vacation time in two weeks, and she's leaving me in charge."

Eden tried to breathe, but a ball of heat caught in her throat. She swallowed past it and found her voice. "That's great, Kendra."

Kendra turned in her chair. "For the record, I didn't ask her for it. I don't even want it. I suggested she ask you, but she told me you were chasing too many rabbit trails—" She winced. "I think what you're doing is amazing."

"No, this was a bad idea. What if he's a criminal or something?" Although something in her gut told her the opposite. But maybe that was wishful thinking. "What if he doesn't even want to be found—if he's hiding? This whole thing was a weak attempt to be something I'm not."

Kendra wore a question in her expression.

"A real reporter. I thought I saw a great story. . . . What if it's just a wild-goose chase?"

"Then it's a wild-goose chase with Jace Jacobsen."

Kendra smiled, but Eden couldn't match it. She wanted it to be more. Needed it to be more.

"I have work to do. Congrats, Kendra. Really." Eden pressed her arm before escaping behind her cubicle wall. She put in her earphones and hit Play on her voice mail, taking dictation.

She avoided Kendra at lunch, eating a stale chicken salad sandwich from the deli, staring at the message from Zach.

When Eden punched out, she debated, then drove toward St. Paul.

What was she doing? Showing up after Jace's practice like a rabid fan? She should turn the car around before he had a chance to break her heart.

But Jace had texted twice since his voice mail, asking again if he might see her after practice, and the sweetness of it, the hope his affection might be real, drew her in.

She pulled into the private section of the lot, sat in her car—no, Owen's car—letting it idle. Finally, when she spied Kalen emerging, his blond hair wet, she got out and walked to the ramp.

Her boots echoed against the cement garage, and she pulled her green pashmina scarf up to her neck—she'd found it and a wool coat in her closet from the early postcollege days when she still went out on interviews.

Kalen gestured toward the entrance. "Owen will be out in a minute. He was talking to Coach. Nice to have him back."

Owen was here? "Uh, thanks, Kalen."

He nodded, and a few other players came out after him, greeted her. She shivered. Maybe she should get back in the car—

"Eden? What are you doing here?" Owen's voice preceded him as he stalked out of the tunnel. "I hope you brought my car."

For a second, she didn't recognize the kid who made her do his laundry, flung an easy arm around any number of the girls who followed him from game to game. This was an older, less reckless version of the boy who'd languished on her sofa just this morning. He wore dress pants, a pullover sweater, a pair of aviator glasses on his head that pushed his hair back, still wet as if he'd showered. He'd even trimmed his beard.

"I came . . . Yeah, I have your car."

"Good. Gimme the keys. I had to catch a ride with Graham today."

That explained it. Graham, his agent, had decided to help Owen straighten out his life. Well, at least he was listening to somebody.

"I don't think you should be driving, Owen. You can't see out of one of your eyes."

"I can see just fine."

Was that what he was telling everyone? She lowered her voice. "Owen, you didn't practice today, did you? You know what the doctor said—"

"I don't care what the doc said. I'm fine. I can see fine. Now give me my car keys." He took a step toward her, something unfamiliar in his eyes.

She closed her hand around them. "No."

"Sis, I'm telling you right now, give me my keys or—"

"Or what, Owen?"

Her breath caught at the sound of Jace's voice, the way it cut, blade-sharp, through the dark corridor. He walked into the light like a Viking warrior, his hair combed back. He carried a bag over his shoulder, his leather jacket open over black jeans and a black pullover.

When his eyes met Eden's, her heart simply stopped. Oh, he was way too handsome for her to think straight.

Owen rounded on him, his voice low. "It's my car, Jace, and I want it."

Jace glanced at Eden.

"The doctor said he can't drive until he's been cleared. He has no peripheral vision."

"Sheesh, Eden. Do you think you could say that louder? I don't think management heard you."

"This isn't a secret, Owen. The entire team knows." She looked at Jace, who had his mouth in a tight line. "Don't they?"

"He showed up for practice today, even though he's on injured reserve. Was on the ice, skating before practice."

"What—?"

"And then your boyfriend here played babysitter and told me to get off the ice. I ended up sitting the bench, thank you oh so much, Captain America."

"Hey, I'm on your side here—"

Owen swore and Eden gasped. He gave her a look of disgust but didn't stop as he unloaded on Jace. "You just don't want me to play. You know that if I play, you're back to being the tough guy. If I come back, you're nobody."

"Owen—"

"It's true. Ask him, Eden." Owen's mouth opened as realization gathered in his eyes. "Wait—you're not here for me, are you? You came to meet *him*." He nodded, holding up his hand. "I was right. You've already changed sides."

"Owen, there's no side—"

"No problem, Sis. I don't need you anyway. I'm going to get

back on my feet, back on the line, and I'm tired of you hovering over me. Please, just give me my keys and stay out of my life."

He snaked out his hand and grabbed the keys, tearing them from her grip. She cried out, and Jace took a step toward Owen.

"What—you want to go at it again, Jace?" Owen snarled.

Again?

But Jace shook his head. "You're a jerk, Owen."

"Learned it all from you, J-Hammer." He threw the keys in the air, caught them. "If you want something, you gotta fight for it, right?" He turned and walked out into the parking lot.

Eden watched him go, not sure if she wanted to cry or slap him.

"You okay?" Jace said.

No. "He's not right, you know. You're not that guy."

"Maybe I am."

She wanted to argue, but he came forward, letting the duffel slip off his shoulder onto the ground. Then he hooked his arm around her waist, pulling her close.

The strength in his movement chased the breath out of her chest, and she steadied herself with her hands on his jacket.

"Hey," he said softly, smiling down at her with a sudden, devastating tenderness. "I'm glad you're here for me." He bent down and gently kissed her. He smelled of soap, with a hint of his hard work at practice still embedded in his skin, and his kiss was so achingly sweet that she felt all the tension from her fight with Owen dissolve into a warm puddle. She pressed her hands against the sculpted muscle of his chest and let him mold her to himself as his other hand wove into her hair, his lips parting hers, deliciously, even dangerously.

If this was the kind of greeting she could expect . . . yeah, she could hang around after practice.

She kissed him back, the emotion of the fight adding a bit more ardor than she knew she possessed. But, well, Jace brought out more of her than she knew she possessed.

He finally leaned back, smiled, warmth in his eyes. But then he winced.

"Are you okay? Did you get hurt in practice? How's your knee?"

"Nothing a little TLC won't fix," he said, winking.

She twined her fingers into his curly hair. Rose up on her toes for another kiss. Okay, being a rink bunny might not be such a terrible thing.

"What do you mean you don't want to look for him anymore?" Jace tried not to let his voice emerge too loud, but he couldn't calculate well with the ringing in his ears. Every word she said—and he said—brought pain, and he just needed to get home, lie down, and drape a cold cloth over his eyes.

The events of today's practice certainly hadn't helped. But he wasn't going to throw down his gloves against a teammate, even if every time he looked at Owen, something nearly exploded inside him. It had taken all his strength—and a couple of the guys watching him—to walk away, let Owen skate it off.

He actually felt pity for the kid, showing up with his gear, a full cage added to his helmet to protect him. Jace knew that getting back on the ice and playing hard exorcised demons. Helped a guy work out his frustrations.

So, yeah, after the tussle with Owen, Jace had practiced hard and worked up an aching sweat, his shots on goal like lightning.

He probably should have expected to walk out of practice with the niggling of a migraine, but he'd gone nearly a week without a headache and thought he could shake it away with a cool shower, a nice dinner with Eden.

However, as he drove them to his condo, the pain moved to the front of his brain, starting to pulse. But he'd been looking forward to seeing Eden all day and wasn't going to let a headache keep him from showing her that they could make this work. Have a normal relationship.

He tried to focus on her words, the explanation she offered for wanting to quit their search for John Doe. He didn't know why, but the suggestion put a rock in his gut.

"I didn't say that, Jace. We've just hit a dead end. Zach came back with some lame, vague information about a community center, and I think that's all we're getting from him."

"I could go back and see if he might be more helpful," Jace said, trying not to wince.

She put a hand on his arm. "No, it's okay."

He glanced at her, tried a smile, but he felt pretty sure it looked more like a grimace.

"Are you sure you're okay?"

He nodded, and wow, his brain slammed against his skull.

Just get home. Rest. He could still have a nice evening with Eden.

"Besides, my editor is angry that I'm working on this—so mad that she even put Kendra, my coworker, in charge when she goes on vacation. I can't believe it—I've been there about four years longer than she has, and she gets—really, Jace, you look pale."

"I just need food." He downshifted, then hit the brakes as traffic piled up, and pain exploded through his head. He wanted to cry as he sucked in a breath.

"Listen, we don't have to—"

"I already ordered!"

Shoot, that came out louder, sharper than he meant. "Sorry."

She gave him a feeble smile, but he'd hurt her. He put his hand out and caught hers even as he pulled into his underground garage. The shadows made him blink. He touched his brakes and fought to focus. The garish underground lights strobed in his eyes, and his headache pulsed in reply.

He pulled into his space and got out. Eden hung her bag over her shoulder and followed him to the elevator.

"I don't think we should give up, Eden. What if he needs us?" He reached for her hand, found it, and held on, bracing his other hand on the wall.

"You don't look so good."

"I have a little headache. I just need to lie down."

The doors opened and he gathered himself, managing to stumble inside. He leaned against the elevator wall, letting go of her hand, then slouching down, his head in his hands.

"Now you're scaring me."

"Just put in my code. I'll be fine." He gave it to her and felt the elevator rise. He fought the urge to curl into a fetal position right there on the floor but opted to get on all fours and crawl off when it opened into his hallway. Eden shuffled beside him and took his hand, helping him up. It was a little like a first grader helping him off the floor, but he took it and even allowed her to put her arm around his waist, ease the key fob out of his hand, and open the door.

He had the presence of mind to disable the alarm, then dropped his bag on the floor and stumbled to the living room, where he collapsed onto the sofa, pressing a pillow over his face.

"What can I do?" Her voice seemed to ricochet in his head.

"Cold cloth. And painkillers—in the cabinet."

"I'm on it."

He heard her in the kitchen, but the migraine had seeped through his brain, flooding every cranny. Everything hurt, and he just had to breathe through it, calm down. He thought he heard himself moaning.

Suddenly a cool cloth draped over his face. Her hands pressed his cheeks. "You're sweating."

Just thinking about forming words hurt. He moaned again, and she disappeared.

He could hear her voice in the distance as if she was talking to someone—maybe the doorman bringing up his dinner order, the one he'd placed this morning in anticipation of tonight.

Food hadn't a prayer of staying in his stomach.

And then Eden was back, replacing the cloth. "I found the pain reliever, but I don't think that's going to cut it. Here." She gave him the medicine and held a glass of tepid water to his mouth.

"Holy Tea," he whispered. "That helps."

She was gone again, and he wanted to call her name, bring her back. Make her put her cool hand on his face again. Yeah, that had felt good.

Maybe he'd conjured her up with his powers because she reappeared.

This time she had a cup of something hot. She moved her hand behind his neck, but it only added claws to the pain.

"Jace, you're really scaring me."

He couldn't remember it being this bad before, where it felt as if his brain might be bleeding out of his ears. A thousand needles laced his body, and he wanted to roll into a ball and cry. But that would hurt too, and now—oh no, his stomach began to lurch.

He pushed her away, rolled off the sofa onto his knees, and retched all over his white carpet. Then he collapsed on the floor, put his hands over his face, and the sounds that came out of his mouth sounded very much like weeping.

But he'd stopped caring.

"In here. He's in here."

Eden directed the EMTs into Jace's living room, where he lay curled up on the floor, groaning, almost incoherent. "He hasn't responded to anything I've said in twenty minutes. I think he's having a stroke or . . . I don't know."

It took both EMTs to get him to stop writhing, and she watched, hands over her mouth, as he tried to push them away. But he was clearly over the edge because he kept asking for Sam, sometimes her, but mostly just crying.

That was the worst part of all. His moans sliced through her, cutting into her chest, and she nearly started weeping herself.

They finally gave him a shot of painkiller, along with a sedative, although he grabbed at the bigger of the two men and pushed him away with a half growl, half groan.

Then they somehow maneuvered him onto a stretcher and wheeled him out. She should have requested firefighters, big burly men, for that.

Eden followed them in Jace's car. She'd called the team trainer, and he'd sent her to the university hospital, where Owen had his surgery. She guessed there must be specialists on staff who worked with the team. The ambulance turned on the lights but not the siren, parting traffic all the same.

She parked in the lot and raced through the building, finally finding Jace in the ER, an IV strapped to his arm, a slew of doctors huddled around him.

"He has a migraine—or it started that way," she said before a nurse ushered her out, past the doors into the waiting room.

And then there she was, standing just outside his life, watching. This time not family but relegated to the vinyl chairs of the waiting room. She sat down, leaned her head back.

What if he needs us? The last thing Jace said to her, really, before the migraine took him.

Us. It rattled her how easily that pronoun seemed to slip from Jace. As if they truly belonged together. As if he meant it.

Us.

She picked up a magazine. Paged through it without reading an article. Put it down. Paced. Bought a Hot Pocket and a Coke. Called Owen and didn't leave a message. Considered John Doe.

Tried to get a peek inside the ER.

Read through all the Facebook messages on Owen's wall.

Tried to forget the way her brother had changed into a person she didn't know. Wondered if it might be her fault.

Change your name or change your ways. What if she'd started it all? What if her words had caused him to go out hunting for a fight that night?

What if she'd inadvertently cost him his career?

"Miss Christiansen?" A nurse appeared through the double doors, wearing pink scrub pants, a floral top, her red hair pulled into a messy ponytail. "He's asking for you."

Eden could hug the woman for not using Jace's name but instead nodded and followed her down the hall.

Jace was most certainly a little high on a vibrant cocktail of migraine drugs. And none too happy about it, either. She could hear him down the hall, his voice loud, saying her name.

He brightened when she appeared beyond the curtain.

"Hey, Jace, I'm right here."

He gave her a sloppy smile. "I thought I lost you."

"Of course not." She ran her fingers down his arm, caught his hand. "You scared me."

"I'm fine." He rolled his head toward the IV bag, then back to her.

"You're not fine. I'm just hoping you didn't have a brain bleed or something."

He closed his eyes as if in pain. "You called Adam."

"You were throwing up. And crying. I didn't know what else to do."

"I wasn't crying."

Of course not. "No. Not crying. Just very pained moaning. With tears."

One side of his mouth tugged up. "Adam's worried I can't play."

"More than worried. Hey, Eden. Sorry it took us so long to get here." Adam Moe, the team trainer, came in, followed by the team doctor, Robert Wilson. "You did the right thing, bringing him in. Jace is too stubborn to take care of himself."

"I was fine." Only he winced at the end of his slurred words.

"You weren't fine and you know it. You just didn't want me to know," Wilson said.

"Know what?" Eden asked.

Adam and Wilson exchanged a glance.

Jace looked at her with sad, glassy eyes. "They're worried I'm going to blow up my brain."

They weren't the only ones.

Adam crossed his arms over his ski jacket. "He's had too many concussions, and this is the effect. Migraines. They could lead to a stroke or brain bleeds. A coma."

They didn't say it, but the word *death* parked at the end of that sentence. Eden turned to Jace, and she didn't know if he avoided her eyes out of shame or morphine. But she had to reach out, sit down. Run her hands over her face.

No wonder he wanted to help John Doe, coma boy. The whole thing hit too close to home.

"I knew he had migraines, but . . . I didn't realize it was this bad. Why is he still playing?" She turned to Adam, Doc Wilson, and gave them her best I-want-answers face.

"Aside from the fact that, with Owen gone, we need him?" Adam said.

Jace had his eyes closed.

"And that he's been migraine-free for the past two games," Wilson added.

"I would point out that he hasn't gotten in a brawl during the past two games," Eden said.

"Agreed," Wilson said. He looked at Jace. "You want to talk about what happened in practice today?"

She stilled. "What happened?"

"Your brother didn't tell you?" This from Adam.

Oh no. "I only know he showed up at practice. And clearly Jace isn't talking, either. So spill it."

Adam blew out a breath. "Fine. Owen showed up today wanting to practice. He said if he wore his helmet and a visor, he'd be fine. I thought it would be good for him to get back on the ice, some light practice, see what he could do." He sighed. "Probably not a great idea because it was clear as soon as he got on the ice that he was missing passes and a little unsteady on his feet."

"The optical surgeon said he'd have some vertigo issues."

"We just have to get him up to speed, make him game ready—"

She stared at Adam. "You can't be serious. Owen isn't ready to play—the doctor said he might not ever play again."

Adam looked away.

She shook her head. "I want him to play as much as you do, but the fact is, he can barely see out of his left eye! His peripheral vision is shot, and he's going to get killed out there. What's going to happen when some defenseman comes at him on his blind side? He won't be able to brace himself for the check. He'll get smashed."

"Probably why Jace told him to get off the ice."

She looked at Jace, back to Adam. "Just a guess, but Owen didn't handle it well."

"He went after Jace and angled him into the boards from about five feet away. Max and Kalen rounded Owen up, talked him off the ice. Coach benched him."

"And it never occurred to you to take a look at Jace?"

"This is hockey," Wilson said. "Players take hits all the time."

"Yeah, and each one adds up a little more until you land in the ER with a brain bleed!" She didn't know when she'd found her feet, started shouting, but a couple nurses glanced her direction, and it occurred to her that maybe Wilson had sent him here for the privacy. "Sorry."

"I'd like the news to not get a whiff of this. But yeah, I'm not sure it's wise for Jace to keep playing. We might need to put him on the injured reserve list—"

"No." This from Jace, who winced as he said it. "I'll be fine."

"Jace!"

"I'm *fine*." He even made to get up, pushing the covers off. They'd put him in a gown, and he appeared a little silly, all that muscle and bare body trying to climb out of bed. She averted her eyes because it didn't seem that he cared much for modesty.

Adam pushed him back into bed. "Not so fast, pal. You're spending the night. We'll talk about Thursday's game in the morning."

And Eden would talk to him about any game at all tonight.

Jace glared at Adam, but the drugs made him pliable and he collapsed into the bed, leaning his head back.

"He needs sleep." Wilson reached for Eden as if to walk her out.

"I'm sure he does. But if you think I'm leaving so he can walk out of here after we're gone—and I can guarantee that is exactly what he's going to do—then apparently you haven't been paying attention. I'm not a fan. I'm not a rink bunny. I'm *family*."

Jace gave the smallest smile as he drifted into the morphine.

Eden moved with him when they took him to the third floor. She'd spent the night in a chair before and had no problem doing it again. When they got him settled in the room, she pulled up next to his bedside to watch him sleep.

In repose, he had such a beautiful warrior's face. She had the urge to trace the scar over his eye, then move to his strong jaw. The wan bedside light picked up the flecks of gold and red in his whiskers, and his long lashes lay against his cheeks.

She'd hardly ever seen him quiet, and a wave of compassion washed over her. Oh, Jace. She laid her head on his bed, closed her eyes.

Eden awoke with a hand on her shoulder, her neck aching. A nurse stood in the glow of the hallway light streaming into the room.

"Would you like a blanket? We don't usually allow visitors, but . . . it's so nice of you to visit again."

Eden frowned at the woman even as she accepted the blanket. She looked familiar—sturdy, with white hair like a halo around her head, wearing a scrub top with tiny hockey players and Band-Aids printed on it. And a pin that read, *Be nice to nurses. We keep doctors from accidentally killing you.* Eden tracked to her name tag: Becky Norman.

It came to her. "You take care of John Doe."

The nurse nodded. "And you visit him. Or did."

"I was out of town." She stood, extended her hand. "I'm Eden Christiansen. How is he?" *Please, please still be alive.*

"He doesn't have an infection, and he still has brain activity, so we're not sure why he hasn't woken up." Becky walked over to Jace, checked his IV bag, took his pulse. He didn't stir.

"Has anyone else been in to claim him?"

She closed the curtain that divided. "Just you, honey. And J-Hammer here. You're all he has." She checked her watch. "Get some sleep. I'll be just down the hall if you need me."

"Thank you."

Becky stopped at the door. Smiled. "We all need someone to watch over us, don't we?"

CHAPTER 16

WHAT JACE HAD DONE to deserve waking with Eden asleep next to him, her head on her folded arms, he didn't know.

He still couldn't believe she'd fought for him—her exchange with his trainer and the team doc last night hadn't escaped him, despite the drug-induced fog. And the fact that she'd stayed all night . . .

She deserved better than him, a guy who'd spent most of his life trying to figure out how to hurt people. And enjoying it—or . . .

John Christiansen's story rose inside him. So maybe Jace hadn't enjoyed the fights, but rather the adrenaline he got from the applause, the approval sliding in and filling all his empty places.

He still thirsted for it.

Maybe he'd never slake his thirst, but Eden seemed to temper it—just having her here, as the sun slid over the room, the rose gold of morning hueing her pretty face, balmed all the jagged, bruised places inside.

He put his hand on her head, her hair silky between his fingers, and an unfamiliar fullness swept through him, thick and sweet and tasting of something he'd forgotten.

Love.

Oh . . . no. He swallowed, but the feeling didn't dissipate, only grew and pulsed inside him. Yeah, maybe.

He loved Eden Christiansen. The kind of love that made him long for her smile, her belief in him. The kind of love that made him want to know her. Want her to know *him*.

The thought caught him up, took his breath. Because what if she did?

What if she knew exactly the kind of man he truly was? The things he tried to bury in his heart?

And that made it all the worse because Jace realized with brutal clarity that he *didn't* deserve her. Not this woman who so easily gave up herself for others, who saw him—oh, how he hoped—as the man he wanted to be instead of the man in the headlines.

His touch roused her and she opened her eyes, blinked. Then she looked at him, her hair tousled, so much worry in her expression that it could steal words from him. "Good morning, tough guy. How are you?"

He swallowed, not sure of his answer.

"Is your migraine gone?"

"Yes." He ran his hand over her cheek. "You didn't have to stay. . . ."

Her smile dimmed.

"But I'm glad you did."

"Oh." She sat up, out of his reach, and tried to smooth her hair. "I must look like Medusa."

"I think you're beautiful."

That seemed to rattle her, but he didn't temper it with anything but a smile, trying to put into his eyes exactly what it meant to him to have her spend the night at his bedside.

Which made him the most selfish man on the planet. "You're missing work."

She shook her head. "It's all good. I called in, and I'll take the later shift. Kendra's covering for me." She scrubbed her hands over her face. "Not that it matters. I'm like a factory worker, typing in death notices. They could get a robot to do my job."

"Eden—"

"No, it's okay." She smiled at him, something fake and shallow. "Let's talk about you instead. Like the fact that when you said you suffered from a few headaches, that might have been the understatement of the world? Excuse me, but you could *die* if you get into another fight." And now her smile vanished, her expression angry.

"I think that's oversimplifying—"

"I talked with Doc and Adam. They told me exactly how simple it is. I can't believe you are still playing—"

"Eden, it's part of the job. It's who I am."

"There are plenty of hockey players who don't get into fights."

"It's not just that—it's a violent sport. And hitting and checking and crashes are part of the game." He reached out for her. "Owen was trying to remind everyone he still has the . . . chops . . . for the game."

"No. Owen was angry and trying to get back at you. Don't defend him."

"He wants to play—I don't blame him."

"You don't blame him? At what cost? His vision? Your *life*?" Her voice rose, and he glanced past her to the door. Thankfully, it remained closed, but how long could they hide out here before the press found them?

"Listen, Eden. I'm a hockey player. Don't ask me to be someone different." He couldn't read her expression and maybe didn't want to. "I'm hungry. Are you?"

She narrowed her eyes. "This conversation isn't over."

"I know. But not here. Please?"

"I could force down a cup of coffee, I suppose. But you're not leaving—"

"I am leaving. Before the press gets wind of me."

She opened her mouth, but he held up his hand. "I promise to talk to Doc Wilson. But I'm starving and I don't want hospital food."

"Probably because you left your lunch on your pristine white carpet?"

"Ugh—"

"Don't worry; I cleaned it up."

And now he felt worse. "Eden, you're not my housekeeper."

She made a face as if his words stung.

He caught her hand. "But thank you." He ran his thumb over her hand. "The last thing I remember is you telling me you ran into a dead end with John Doe. But I know you can find him. Don't tell yourself what you can't do but what you *will* do."

"Are you my coach now?"

"If I have to be. Be glad I'm not making you skate lines."

She laughed, and it turned his day golden.

"C'mon—let's sneak out of here. I have an idea."

She made a great accomplice as she found his clothes, then watched the door from the hallway while he dressed and they made their escape. No one stopped them as they got on the elevator and Jace hit a button.

"What are we doing?"

"Checking on John Doe." He took her hand and walked her to Doe's room, easing the door open into the quietness of the morning, the dim light, the sound of the monitor analyzing his vitals. He seemed so peaceful, but Jace knew if the guy was still in there, he longed to break free of the dark mesh that held him prisoner.

He knew it because he feared it. Experienced it. Last night, as the drugs took him, his body had moved as if through gravy, the world blurry, tilted on its axis. Not unlike the moment he'd plunged into Gray's Bay in Lake Minnetonka, into the darkness that had sucked him under.

"Are you okay? You're pale. Is your headache coming back?" Eden looked at him, worry in her eyes.

"We can't leave him trapped like this." He stood over Doe. "Every time I see him, I think about going into the lake. I was totally wasted, but it was like slamming into the boards with no padding. Just a hard slap and then darkness sucking me under. If a couple of high school guys coming home after a late game hadn't seen me, I would have died down there. They dove into the water—risked their own lives—and pulled me out."

She nodded.

"I suppose you read about it."

"Owen was all over it. He idolized you, and it shook him. It shook us all."

"It was my birthday—and two days after my mom died. Did you know that?"

"No."

"I know what it's like to be alone. Trapped. And to wish you could break free, start over. Afraid that you've gone so far down, you'll never find the light."

"There's always light, Jace. God's love is too bright for the darkness to win." She turned to Doe, wrapped her hand around his. "We'll find your people; I promise."

So this was what love felt like. Only this wasn't the deep tenderness he'd had for his mother. No, this felt more like explosions in his chest, the sense of going under.

Jace turned away before he couldn't breathe.

He felt Eden's hand on his arm.

"While you were sleeping, I googled the area and found an address for a community center in Frogtown. It's not far from the deli. Would you go with me?"

Then she laced her hand in his, and he would have followed her anywhere.

They trailed a plow into the Frogtown area as fat flakes drifted onto the windshield. Jace turned on the wipers, the rhythm pulsing in time with the lingering pain in the front of his head.

Shovels had already dug out the lot of the Hope Community Center, but a thin layer of powder lay upon an old Suburban. Jace pulled in next to it, glanced toward a flooded lot beside the center. A makeshift ice rink.

Eden climbed out of the car, holding on to her Caribou coffee as if it were a hand grenade, for protection. And yes, in this neighborhood, for once he wished she were wearing her long, puffy parka and UGGs. Although he wouldn't argue at the sight of her in leggings tucked into those long, slender boots.

Jace slid his eyes off her and opened the door, the heat blasting in the entryway.

A half basketball court on one end, carpet and a tutoring center on the other, the place looked like the neighborhood hangout, with old furniture around an ancient television set. Pictures of work teams and kids playing sports hung in cheap metal frames on the wall. Along the far end, a mural of the community suggested the diversity of the area. A verse marked the top of the mural. *1 John 3:18. "Dear children, let's not merely say that we love each other; let us show the truth by our actions."*

A man wearing a sweatshirt that said *Hope is alive*, his dark hair cut short and graying around the edges, emerged from an office near the door, his hand outstretched. "Matt Conners. I'm the director here. How can I help you?"

Jace took his hand. "Jace Jacobsen. This is my friend Eden. She works for the paper."

Matt was nodding. "You play for the Blue Ox, right? Great couple games—what, three goals? You have an away game tomorrow, right?"

He wasn't sure why the man's words warmed him. "A quick game against Chicago; then they follow us home for a rematch."

"Good luck. How can I help you?"

Jace launched into the story about John Doe. He caught Eden's hand as he talked. Life just felt better with her next to him.

"So we're trying to figure out who this kid is. He looks about twenty, blond . . . plays basketball. It's a long shot."

Matt had gone quiet. "Hudson. It sounds like Hudson Peterson. He was a regular around here until a couple weeks ago. Just . . . vanished one night. He was out delivering some sandwiches to a bunch of homeless kids, and well, he never came back."

"You didn't report him to the police?"

"We called, but we didn't know where he lived—he just showed up about six months ago and started helping out with the youth. And the homeless shelter down on Sixth. And we'd see him at church sometimes. I thought he might be a college kid from the area. Maybe Bethel or Northwestern."

Eden spoke up. "Peterson's a pretty common last name, especially for Minnesota. Is there anything else you can help us with?"

Matt turned to stare at the pictures on the wall as if trying to pick him out. "I think he ran track. He was talking about starting up a track club when spring came around. Mentioned a sprinters team. Maybe he ran track for a local school."

"Okay. Thanks." Jace held out his hand.

Matt took it but didn't let him go right away. "Have you ever thought about coaching? It's all volunteer, but that's part of the problem." He motioned to a set of pictures, a collection of motley seven-year-olds with broken gear raising their sticks in triumph. Jace recognized himself as a kid in the too-fresh, eager faces. "We could use some help."

"He'd love to coach," Eden said next to him, and he shot her a look. She was grinning, something of mischief in her eyes.

"I'll think about it," Jace said. He gave Matt his number. "Let us know if Hudson turns up, will you?"

He pulled Eden outside, into the cold.

"What?" She climbed into the car as he went around, slid into the seat. "Jace?"

With Matt's words, a darkness had climbed inside his chest, settling like dust. "I'm not coaching a bunch of kids, okay? I have nothing to teach them."

"What are you talking about?"

"I'm talking about the fact that no one should be taking any lessons from me." He reached for the ignition, but she stopped him.

"What's going on?"

"You seem to be missing something here. People will always see me as J-Hammer Jacobsen, goon. They don't want me teaching their kids."

"The only one who sees you as a goon, really, is you. I think you'd be a great coach."

"No. Trust me, I wouldn't." He moved to put the key in the ignition again, but she took it from him. "Eden, c'mon—"

"Why do you keep saying that? Okay, yeah, I can admit that I thought you were a jerk, a womanizer, even a brawler. But then I got a good look at the real Jace Jacobsen, and I see this kind, tender, compassionate man—"

"I nearly killed someone, okay?" He didn't mean for his voice to bounce out so hard, so angry. "There, see? I'm not the guy you think I am."

Only then did he notice that she hadn't flinched. "I know about Boo. It's hockey. It was an accident."

But she didn't understand. "I wish it were just Boo." He ran his hands down his face. Shoot. He hadn't wanted to go here. But maybe he'd get it all out, like ripping off a Band-Aid, and then she could walk away before she really got into his heart and destroyed him. "I didn't tell you everything about . . . about my dad. What you don't know is that I nearly killed him. Beat him within an inch of his life."

There, he'd said it. And it sounded as horrible as it was. He closed his eyes and hated that the moment rushed at him, just as full and loud and brutal as the day his father had shown up that last time.

"I'm sure it wasn't as bad—"

He ignored her because really, she hadn't a clue. "I wish I could say I was young and impressionable. That I didn't know what I was doing, but I did." He ran his hand over his mouth, took a breath. "I'd only met him once before, briefly, after a high school game. My mom didn't know he was there, and the minute he came up to me, she intercepted us. I remembered him as a big man, soft hands, thick around the middle. We had the same hair, the same eyes, and it unnerved me. I was so angry that Mom had never let me meet him . . . but later, he showed up again. It was right after I signed my contract with the Blue Ox. It was generous, and of course, it made the news. I came out of the tunnel after the press conference, and there he was. I'm not sure how he got into the private lot—probably used the same slick skills he did to lure my mother into dating him.

"I recognized him immediately. And like a little kid, I even felt happy. Like this man I'd never known might care about me. Maybe he'd come to the press conference to tell me he'd been watching. That he was proud of me."

His chest tightened, and he put his hands on the steering wheel. A chill had settled in the car and was now traveling up his legs. He gave a rueful laugh. "Yeah, he'd been following me, all right. Following the money. I stood there listening to him tell me about this business deal he wanted to make, and my entire body turned to ash. I turned him down, probably a little more vehemently than I should have, and he got in my grill about it."

Jace didn't want to go on, didn't want her to hear the rest, but she put a hand on his arm. "You hit him."

"No. I walked away." And he should have kept walking. Just walking. Then he wouldn't have the darkness eating at him every day, wouldn't feel as if he could never escape the moment when he saw exactly who he was.

When he turned into a monster.

"I was almost to my car when he made a slur about my mom."

He let the silence fill the car. Let her imagine the rest and then had to say it aloud, just in case she didn't get it. "I took him down. I . . . I was beyond anger. I was livid. I destroyed his nose with the first punch—there was blood spurting everywhere—and then I put everything I felt about him and the life he forced my mother to live into my fists. I kept seeing all those jerks she had to smile at and smelling the cigarettes on her skin, and I exploded."

He shook his head, hearing his fists crunch bone, the cries of the man who had sired him. "My teammates came out and wrestled me off him. I think one of them drove him to the hospital, dumped him there. My guess is that they suggested they'd finish the job if he ever mentioned it because, while I lived in mortal fear of the cops showing up, nothing happened. Just the memory, digging around inside me."

He looked at her then, found her eyes, because he really wanted her to get it. "And I'd do it again, Eden. I would do it again."

Her breath rose and fell in her chest, her gaze unwavering. "Me too."

Huh?

"I would too, Jace. I'm not saying that what you did was right, but it was human, and the only one blaming you is yourself."

"And God."

She blinked at him. "What?"

"Oh, sure, God forgave me, but He can't really like me. Because this is the way I am. And frankly, it's a little cruel, because He made me this way."

"Oh, Jace—"

He looked away. See, this was way too much information to give her. So much for her believing in him. Loving—

"Jace." She moved then, dropping the keys on the mat, getting up on her knees on her seat, and taking his face in her hands. "You are God's child, and that means He's crazy about you. And that doesn't change because you do something stupid—or even do something terrible. God's love simply is. We can't sin it away—our only option is to accept or reject it. But He isn't cruel. And He does like you. That isn't dependent on whether you deserve it but because you are His child."

He stared at her, longing to believe her words. "No, Eden. Because God also says that a man who has hate in his heart murders his brother, and there is no eternal life for him." He steeled the truth into her eyes. "I hate my father."

Her eyes filled, and he gave her a small, sad smile. They sat there in the quiet of the car, and he wanted to cry too.

Because she was finally figuring out she'd been right about him all along.

He gently pushed her back into her seat, reached past her, and picked up his keys.

His cell phone buzzed in his pocket and he pulled it out. Read the text. "That's Graham. I gotta get to practice."

She looked at him, her expression stricken. "Jace—no. Your head . . . please—"

"Eden." He touched her face, ran his thumb down her cheek. "This is who I am. It's all I have."

Then, although he expected it, his heart broke a little when she didn't argue.

If Sam hoped to give Maddy a new life, he had to do it now, before his courage failed him.

He still shook, residue of watching the nightmare of Trey's death two days ago. Sure, he'd only known the kid for a week, but he and Maddy had hit it off, and the ten-year-old seemed to be on his way to victory.

A new heart.

He'd liked Tony Hawk video games and the Avengers movies, played a mean game of Dominion, and slept with a plush football his dad gave him. As if believing in someday.

Sam couldn't erase the scene of Alyssa's and Mike's lives unraveling. Blood covered the floor of the room, the tubing ripping from Trey's body as the doctors attempted to reconnect the device before racing him to surgery.

An autopsy would tell the full story about what had gone wrong, but Sam knew the truth.

Only he could save his daughter. It had just taken him a couple of days to work out the details.

His old suitcase, the one he used to take on the road when he traveled with the team, lay on the sofa. He'd already filled it with a few of Maddy's things—shirts, her favorite jeans, a few of the Beanie Babies, a picture of Mia pregnant, her hands over her belly, smiling into the camera as if they'd all live happily ever after.

He was trying. Oh, he was trying. He just needed a little help.

Only two days ago, it had seemed that God might be on his side. Or at least not trying to destroy him. Then Trey died, and he couldn't deny the fear that had snuck into his bones.

God just might let Maddy die.

The light washed over the other suitcase, the one crammed with cash. It had taken him longer to liquidate his remaining assets than he'd thought, and finally a loan shark had traded him cash for the bar. Sam grabbed the passports—he'd had one made for Maddy a year ago, when he thought of taking her to Canada to visit Mia's parents. With the new border laws, it seemed only prudent.

He opened the page, ran a thumb over her smiling face, the shine in her eyes.

Downstairs, the bar had closed for the night. Nell had left a slew of receipts, notes, and orders on his desk, but he couldn't look at them.

He'd stood in the hallway for a long moment as he came in, before escaping upstairs, watching the lights from the street skim over the smooth wooden floor he'd refinished, the memorabilia collected from years in hockey, pictures and sweaters and posters and . . . The breadth of all he left in his wake could crumple him. But he'd surrender it all for Maddy.

Anything, even his life, for Maddy.

"Sam! I saw the light on and thought someone might be robbing you."

Sam jerked around and found Jace in his doorway. He'd left it open in his rush, because at midnight, who would find him packing? Except Jace, of course, who kept rock-star hours. The man wore his leather jacket and workout gear, and when he walked into the room, Sam didn't know whether to run or to collapse in relief.

Jace would understand. He'd help, too. After all, he was as worried as Sam, even calling him while he was on vacation up north.

But he also might stand in his way, try to talk some sense into him.

To Sam's thinking, this was the only thing that *made* sense.

He kept his voice cool, light. "So, of course, you decided to come up, surprise the robbers, and what, make a citizen's arrest?"

Jace didn't smile. "I saw your car in the lot. What are you doing? It's midnight."

"Maddy's sleeping. I had to get away, and this was the only time."

Jace nodded. "Right. How is she?"

Sam forced a smile, his hands around the passports. "Hanging in there." Even he could hear the faux hope in his voice. "What are you doing up so late?"

"Had a meeting with Graham. Then stayed to work on my slap shot."

Jace's attention grazed the open suitcase of money, then came back to Sam. He stepped into the apartment and shut the door. "What's going on?" he said quietly.

Sam took a breath, walked over to the case, zipped it. "Nothing."

"Sam. That's a lot of money. And you're packed."

"You should go, Jace."

"I'm not going anywhere." Jace put his hand on the suitcase, met Sam's eyes.

Fine. "I'm getting Maddy a heart."

Jace just stared at him, and for the first time, Sam stepped outside the panic in his brain and registered his words. But he couldn't go there, couldn't think it through from the outside anymore.

He was all in.

"You don't get it, Jace. Maddy is going to die if we don't find one soon. And I don't even know that she'll be approved for the transplant list. I'm afraid, after everything they find out, it's not going to go my way—"

"Sam. Stop. First, they're not going to deny Maddy a heart."

Sam shook his head. "I don't have time. A little boy who had her same condition died a couple nights ago. She's alive because a machine is pumping blood through her. And any day she could form a clot or get an infection or the machine could malfunction—"

"Sam, breathe. Think about this. What are you talking about—checking Maddy out of the hospital, getting on a plane—for where, Mexico? She's on a Berlin Heart—have you thought at all about that? Because this is crazy talk."

Sam stared at him, Jace's words finding his bones. Then he sank onto the sofa. "I don't know. Maddy is my whole life. Wouldn't you do anything for your child? You better than anyone understand doing the unthinkable for someone you love. Look at what your mom did for you. Or . . . what you did to your dad."

Jace's face went taut. "That was different."

"Not much."

"She could die and you could go to jail. Have you lost your mind?"

Sam pressed the heels of his hands into his eyes. "I don't know. Maybe. But I have to do something. I can't just sit by her bedside, helpless. Praying to a God who clearly isn't listening." He shook his head. "Why is this happening, Jace? I'm trying hard here to hold on to something, anything. But . . ." Sam looked at his friend, his voice tinny. "If I don't take care of her, who will?"

"Dude." Jace sat on one of Sam's ratty chairs. "I'm going to give you the same speech you gave to me that morning I woke up in the hospital, nearly drowned. God has not forsaken you. He cares. He weeps. He loves you. And I don't understand why you were the one chosen to go through this with Maddy, but you are. I know you're tired, but you're not alone. However, you will be if you walk away from God. And I can't think of a more terrifying place to be. God will bring you through this if you let Him."

Sam considered him. "You still believe that? That God loves you? That there is a plan in all this?"

Jace drew in a breath. "With everything inside me, I'm trying to." He stood. "C'mon. Let's go back to the hospital. I'll sit with Maddy so you can get some sleep."

"You're just trying to babysit me."

"That I am."

CHAPTER 17

"I HOPE YOU'RE READY to cheer, Hudson, because I'm expecting a win tonight."

Eden set the single-serving pizza on his bedside table and pulled up a chair. He seemed unchanged since yesterday, when she'd stopped in with Jace. Still caught just below the veil of consciousness. She touched his hand. "We're getting closer. Don't give up."

Not a twitch. But she had to believe that inside—deep inside—it nudged something. Maybe that's what it took to awaken someone to life. Seeing who they truly were, telling them they weren't forgotten.

She sat in the chair and used the remote to find the channel for the Blue Ox away game. The announcers chatted in the pregame, and she tried to spot Jace warming up on the ice behind them.

It's all I have.

His words still thrummed inside her, so painfully spoken in

the car. She'd wanted to reach out, to grab him by the lapels and say, *Me. You have me.*

But that sounded so eager and desperate.

She should have said it anyway. Because the moment he dropped her off at work, kissing her good-bye with such a lingering sadness in his touch, she knew . . .

She loved him.

Sitting there in the car, listening to Jace pour out his gut-wrenching story, watching his face tense, seeing the scene behind his tortured eyes, she'd wanted to cry with the flood of pity that filled her chest. She felt his frustration, his hopes, so brutally dashed.

She was with him in that dank parking garage, pummeling the man who had stolen so much from him.

And the emotion scared her.

Yes, she loved him. Not the crazy, unrealistic kind of fan love but the kind that wanted to stand beside him and fight his battles. The kind of love that saw the man he wanted to be, the compassion, the honor.

Not normal at all. But maybe she didn't want normal. No, she wanted amazing.

Which meant that maybe she did belong in his world. And sure, he might believe he only had hockey, but he was just afraid of throwing everything into his dreams and having them implode.

Weren't they all, really?

She turned up the volume on the television as the Blue Ox took the ice. The camera flashed on Jace, and he raised his stick, smiled. Warmth swirled down, right to her belly, pricked only by the slightest edging of fear.

Please, God, keep him safe.

She noticed Owen's absence from the lineup, as did the

announcers, who segued into an update of his injuries. She guessed the team trainer still had him on injured reserve tonight.

She reached for a piece of pizza and ran through the events of the day, just to keep them straight for her conversation with Jace after the game.

The fact that Hudson might have run track had hung in her mind since leaving the community center, so much so that she'd spent last night googling his name.

Nothing popped.

She'd needed the newspaper's access to state high school rosters and track meet results, so at lunch, she did a search for Hudson Peterson and came up empty. Expanded it to the nation and still found nothing under his name.

"Whatcha doing?" Kendra had said, setting her coffee down beside the computer as she started her late shift.

"Trying to find a kid named Hudson Peterson, who may have run track."

"Really?"

"Except I've googled him and run his name through the paper's files and nothing is coming up."

"Peterson is a pretty common Minnesota name." Kendra retrieved her chair and brought it around the cubicle.

"You're telling me. There are forty-seven Petersons in the track-and-field meets from the past ten years. I narrowed it to the past five, and there are seventeen Petersons."

"None of them named Hudson."

"Nope. But I was thinking, when I was going to school, we had a number of kids who used their middle names. Like this one girl, her middle name was Watson—like a family name—so that's what we called her. Watson. Sorta like Sherlock Holmes. . . ."

Kendra ran her finger down the screen. "Niles, Jacob, Drake, Myron—"

"That's it. It's gotta be. Who would want a name like Myron?" Eden googled his name.

She scanned the first few hits for a Myron Peterson. One on Match.com, one located in Iowa, and the third listed as a runner on a track team from St. Cloud in an article filed in the *St. Cloud Dispatch*.

Eden clicked on the link to the article and saw that it included a team photo. The world slowed to a crawl as the picture loaded. She stared at the screen, trying to confirm his identity.

Myron Hudson Peterson stood with three other guys, holding a baton, wearing the green and white colors of his high school team.

"Is it him?"

"I don't know. Could be. He's wearing a bandage over his head now, and his face is gaunt . . . but yeah, maybe."

Young, blond, and handsome, Myron filled out his track uniform, wearing a smile, the kind that someone full of life, of hope, might possess. She read his name, just to confirm. "He's a junior in this picture."

"Which would make him around nineteen now. Does he look nineteen?"

"Could be. I'll google his name as a senior runner." Nothing popped up. "Funny that he didn't race as a senior."

"Maybe he didn't place. Can you find an address?"

She searched but found nothing for St. Cloud, Minneapolis, or St. Paul. She pulled up the white pages for St. Cloud and did a quick search.

"There are 137 Petersons listed in the St. Cloud phone book."

Kendra picked up the headset. Handed it to Eden. "I know what you're doing after your shift."

Except what if she got the wrong Peterson? Yeah, that would be a fun conversation. Maybe she'd save the part where he lay near death until she really needed it.

"I think I'll start with the school. Certainly they'll help the Minneapolis *Star Tribune* track down a John Doe."

"Spoken like a real reporter," Kendra said.

Eden stayed after her shift ended and spent the last hour of the day convincing the principal of the St. Cloud Saints to hand over Myron Peterson's phone number. Yes, he knew Myron—or Hudson, as he preferred to be called. No, he hadn't raced as a senior, but the principal wouldn't reveal why. He'd finally given her the number when she told him the story.

"Apparently obits has sway after all," she said to Hudson now. "So I called. And I called. And not even a machine. So I'm thinking I should head up there. Deliver the news in person." With Jace.

Yes, Jace deserved to have a taste of this moment. She glanced at Hudson as the game played. "You were a handsome guy, Hudson. I'm so sorry for what has happened to you. But we're going to find your family, and you're going to wake up and be just fine."

The television erupted with a siren, cheering, and she saw Jace circle the ice, his hands high.

A cadre of Blue Ox players descended on him, thumping his helmet.

She leaned back, toed off her shoes, and set her feet on the bed. *It's all I have.*

Not anymore. And tomorrow, when his plane landed, she planned on meeting him with the truth.

I love you, Jace.

Sam hated this room. With the happy animals painted on the walls, the bright-colored furniture—all a facade to hide the truth.

In this room, children died.

And with them, parents died.

Until then, like the cheery animals on the walls, parents had to plaster on fake smiles. Pretend as if their world wasn't imploding a little more with every beat of the heart monitor.

"One more chapter, Daddy. Please?" Maddy looked up from where she was playing with a pile of Beanie Babies. Apparently the penguin was the teacher, trying to teach the other animals to fly.

One more chapter of *The Farthest-Away Mountain.* The book Mia had left for her daughter, an heirloom copy. Sam had read it so many times that he could quote it.

"One more chapter, honey; then you sleep." He managed it in a voice that didn't break, didn't betray that tomorrow morning he would no longer be her daddy.

At least on paper, temporarily.

She plopped the animals in the middle of the bed and leaned back, closing her eyes as he opened the book, reading the scene about Dakin's tears bringing the brass ogre to life.

He felt like the ogre, except his life, his heart, were slowly hardening. Jace had done the right thing in stopping him from his crazy behavior. But with everything inside Sam, he longed to pull Maddy into his arms, steal her from this hospital, and simply drive.

Leave it all behind as if she'd never gotten sick, never needed a new heart to replace the one God gave her, so much like Mia's.

He finished the chapter, then kissed her forehead, pulling the covers to her chin before he moved to the recliner. Green and red lights from the monitor played on the ceiling like lasers. He reached out for Maddy's hand, found it, and held on.

Oh, he didn't want to let go.

When the woman walked into his dream, the ethereal place just below consciousness, at first he thought she was Mia. Long black hair, doe-brown eyes. She wore pink scrubs, however, and that threw him, along with the necklace, a dangling gold cross.

Not Mia, but not frightening, either. She wore a smile, something of peace in her expression as she walked toward him.

He tried to rise, feeling himself awaken . . . but perhaps not, because he couldn't move, his arms pinned to the chair.

She sat on Maddy's bed, gazed at her with such compassion that the fear drained from him, leaving only warmth.

"You are not alone," she said when she turned to Sam, but it seemed he felt her words more than heard them. She got up, leaned down, and kissed his forehead. Then she stood over him, her lips unmoving.

"And I will give them singleness of heart and put a new spirit within them. I will take away their stony, stubborn heart and give them a tender, responsive heart." The verse thrummed deep inside him.

Mia's verse.

He woke with his hand to his head, his heart thumping into the darkness. Maddy's machines kept hissing, the lights still glaring on the mirror across the room, like eyes.

He let go of Maddy's hand. Then, slipping to the floor in front of the recliner, he bowed his head. Heard Jace's words again.

I know you're tired, but you're not alone. However, you will be if you let go of God's hand. And I can't think of a more terrifying place to be.

"Oh, God, I don't want to give up on You. On the belief that

You love me, that You love Maddy. But I'm so tired. And I feel so alone." He pressed his hands to his eyes, the tremor in his voice scaring him.

"I want to believe. Help me to believe, Lord. Give me the strength for whatever lies ahead."

Above him, from Maddy's monitor, the beeping turned to a siren, filling the room with the sounds of his daughter's heart crashing.

Jace had barely slept with the press interviews stretching long into the night, but he could also blame the heady taste of adrenaline, so reminiscent of his rookie days. Except this time he hadn't made any headlines but the ones he longed for.

A hat trick. Three goals in one game. Jace could feel the wind in his teeth on that last one too, the way he took the puck down the ice, faked, and bulleted the shot between the pads of the Chicago goalie.

Not a hint of a migraine, either, which told him that winning was the cure. Winning and the sound of the crowd. He'd let himself take another lap around the ice as the Blue Ox fans in attendance threw their hats in celebration.

He'd gone back to the hotel with the team, but then Graham picked him up and they'd gone out with Haylee and a number of other sports reporters, delivering interviews into the wee hours.

No wonder he slept hard once he got back to the room, right through three phone calls—one from Eden, the others from Sam.

Sam wasn't picking up, and that had Jace's gut in a knot as he showered and caught up with his team at brunch.

"Dude!" Max slapped him a high five over the table, nearly upsetting his eggs Benedict. At another table, Graham sat with Adam and gestured Jace over.

Jace pulled out the chair opposite Graham. The dining room had cleared out, mostly just players at tables around the room. A few sported licks from last night's game—tomorrow's would be a rematch with some heat.

Bring it. Jace couldn't wait to get back on the ice, a new taste of competition sluicing through him after last night. He just might end this season with a fat new contract.

The kind of contract that could foot Maddy's hospital bills. That could help Sam afford a nanny. He'd texted him on his way down in the elevator, but it looked as if it hadn't sent. Jace pocketed the phone, still sick at their last conversation; watching Sam's faith unravel had shaken him more than he wanted to admit.

He depended on Sam to remind him that God was on his team, even when life took a cheap shot. He felt almost guilty that lately it seemed God had begun to smile on him.

After all, Eden hadn't made a run for the door when he told her about his past, his father. Sure, she hadn't exactly declared her undying devotion, but she'd kissed him like she meant it when he dropped her off at work.

And today she'd called. He'd find a quiet place at the airport and see if he could talk her into coming to tomorrow's game. Not that she wouldn't, but with Owen sidelined . . .

Maybe she'd be there for Jace. The thought strummed a warmth deep inside, an anticipation he could taste.

Graham slapped a folded sheet of paper onto his empty plate. "Someone is onto you, Jace, and if this gets out, all your recent games could be for nothing."

"What are you talking about?" Jace unfolded the paper, stared at it, the blood draining from his chest.

"The last thing the franchise needs is news of you being hospitalized for your migraines."

Adam leaned forward. "We'll be in big trouble with the NHL if they find out we let you play so soon after a migraine. You trying to get me and Doc fired?"

Jace set the paper down, his breaths shallow. "How did this get out?"

Graham shook his head. "You tell us, Jace. Who else was there? Who else knew about your episode besides Adam and Doc?"

Eden. Jace's throat burned with the name. But . . . how . . . ?

It's a great—even front-page—story. The kind of story I've waited for.

Her words stung him, and he studied the paper—a printout of an online article—again. He felt a silly relief when he saw it had come from the Yahoo! sports page.

Still. Eden had been the only one in the room with him. A darkness pooled deep inside, started to gurgle, worked up to his chest.

She couldn't have done this. Please.

"Well, you'd better figure out who leaked it and make sure it doesn't happen again, because . . ." Graham glanced at Adam, and a smile emerged. "I got a new contract offer for you. Came in last night."

Jace tried to change gears, but his mind still circled around the article. Maybe that's why Eden tried to call, to give him a heads-up.

Or maybe . . . to get more dirt on him.

"What are the deal points?"

"Three year, one-way, $4.5 million. Sign before the season ends."

He swallowed. Reached for his water.

"I think I can get you more, but we'll have to wait for the season to end, and—"

"I'll take it." The words rushed out too quick. He took a breath, finding a smile. "I mean, I'll think about it, but it sounds like a good idea."

Adam raised an eyebrow, but Graham grinned. Nodded. "I agree. It's a good contract." He raised his glass to Jace. "I should have trusted you. You're right. You can outskate Owen Christiansen."

Owen. The sick feeling continued to climb up from his gut to his throat.

He shouldn't care that Owen's career was tanking. Owen didn't deserve for him to care, not with the way he'd treated Jace and especially Eden.

And maybe not with the way Eden had treated Jace. He picked up the article again. Read it through.

Details, like Adam's suggestion that they needed him, and his and Eden's fight about him playing again, the summary something only Eden would know. And then a detail about him leaving the hospital without checking out.

Who else would know that?

He folded the article and slipped it into his athletic bag. Yeah, it made the franchise look bad. What was Eden trying to do, get him canned?

A waitress came over. "Something to eat?"

"Coffee, please."

She smiled at him, something of invitation in it. He smiled back, the J-Hammer grin.

He texted Sam again as the bus drove the team to the airport. His call went to voice mail in the moments before their plane took off. "Sam, we gotta talk. I have good news."

As the clouds parted for them, Jace stared out the window, the article's words burning a hole inside him.

The kind of story I've waited for. He closed his eyes, leaned his head against the cool pane of the window.

"Hey there, Jace. You okay?"

He opened his eyes. Haylee had slid into the seat next to him. She wore team gear today, looking more like a fan than a reporter. He remembered interviewing with her last night, but their conversation blurred into every other.

Now she smiled, a little mischief in her eyes. "Great game last night."

"Thanks."

"I was thinking, maybe after we land, we could sneak away. You've been promising me an exclusive all year—and I'm calling in my chip."

He frowned. "Haylee, I don't think—"

"Aw, you're not getting rid of me that easily." She leaned over and gave him a kiss on the cheek before she returned to her seat.

Maybe his migraines weren't quite over.

He pulled out the article and read it one more time, searching for clues, denial.

But it all came back to Eden.

They landed and a cadre of reporters lined up for a quick press conference. Jace filed out with his team and waited with Graham as Coach took the podium. He checked his phone, but Sam hadn't called back.

He did, however, see one missed call from Eden.

And then, as he looked into the crowd, the reporters firing questions at the team, he spotted her. Lingering in the back, yes, but wearing a press badge as if she belonged there, her blonde hair tied up, messenger bag over her shoulder.

She even carried a digital recorder.

And he realized that he'd been played. Not the entire time, maybe, but definitely the last few days as he'd opened up his soul and let her inside. He couldn't imagine the copious notes she might've been taking, dissecting his life, tracking down the facts.

Did she think he was a fool? That he wouldn't figure it out? A girl like Eden wasn't interested in a guy—a goon—like him.

He wanted to hit something, hard, for being so stupid.

"J-Hammer! Your hat trick last night puts you in the footsteps of Gretzky and Lemieux. Are we looking at a future Hall of Famer?"

He stepped up to the mic and pasted on his smile, the public one. He kept his eyes off Eden, found a cute blonde in the audience. "Don't you know I've always been a Hall of Famer?"

If she wanted to see the true J-Hammer in action, he'd give it to her.

He should have listened to his instincts and stayed far away from her. "I've just upped my game. Everyone thinks I'm all power, but I have talent, too. That hole that Owen left—yeah, we're sad to let him go, but we'll be okay. I can promise that."

He smiled again, this time through the tightening of his throat. He glanced at Eden, then away.

She had turned a little white, her mouth open.

"So you're saying Owen Christiansen is out of the game?"

Coach stepped to the mic again. "We're not sure what Owen's future will hold, but we're thankful that Jace—and the rest of the team—have stepped in to fill the gap."

The rest of the team. Right. Jace let a sardonic expression fill his face.

"What about your migraines, Jace? Any comment about today's article?"

He looked right at Eden then, his eyes cold. "Rumors. Vicious rumors. I'm in perfect shape." And then, just in case Eden might think his actions were a game, think he wasn't onto her, he stepped out of the lineup and gestured to Haylee. She came up to him, working her way through the crowd.

A few eyes turned his direction.

"Ready for that exclusive, honey?"

Haylee raised an eyebrow. Then grinned, nodded.

So he levered his arm over her shoulders and pulled her against him, sauntering out of the press conference, a hundred flashbulbs lighting his way.

Leaving in his wake a whole new Twitter stream of headlines about J-Hammer, the team bad boy.

CHAPTER 18

EDEN CREPT BACK into the newspaper office without Charlotte popping her head out, taking her to task for her overlong lunch break. What a fool she'd been to sneak in with the press corps, thinking Jace would be glad to see her, that his eyes might light up.

If anything, he'd looked downright furious that she'd invaded his world. Like she didn't belong there.

Which she didn't. Clearly.

And clearly she'd been fooling herself about Jace and everything she'd supposedly seen under that playboy exterior.

Give him a taste of success and he turned into exactly the man she'd originally thought he was.

She felt soiled, the redolence of bus exhaust on her clothing, and scoured by pitying eyes that had watched her misery as she climbed aboard public transportation and tried to hide her chapped face.

She'd taken a taxi to the airport, thinking maybe Jace would drive her home. See, that's what happened when a girl assumed.

When a girl stepped off the sidelines.

She should have known that, somehow, Jace would make her a spectacle for ridicule.

"Hey, where'd you take off to?" Kendra moved over to her cubicle as Eden hung her coat over her chair, tried to focus on the screen. "Charlotte was looking for you. Said to tell you to come into her office when you returned."

Eden blinked, wishing she could shake Jace's smug smile, the way he'd tucked Haylee close to him as if she belonged there, from her brain. "I had to . . . run an errand. The bus was late coming back."

"Are you okay?"

Eden pressed her hands to her face. Her skin still felt hot, and maybe she should have composed herself more. But she couldn't stand there as the rest of the team took the microphone, players who would recognize her. Who would know that, with Owen off the traveling roster, she'd shown up for one purpose.

"What happened?" Kendra, beside her now, frowning. "You've been crying. Did you get bad news? Is Owen okay?"

"Owen is just fine without me." In fact, they all were, weren't they? Without her butting into their lives. "You were right when you said Owen was taking up all the available space in my life. That I was obsessed. I need to get my own life."

"Huh?"

She drew in another long breath. "I never should have involved Jace Jacobsen in my search for John Doe—a search that is probably a bust anyway. I can't get ahold of anyone at that number, and it's probably not even his family. My imagination is my downfall. I thought maybe I could help him . . . help myself . . ."

Kendra gave her a sad, tired look.

She might have given herself the same weary expression. This was what happened when a person tried too hard to find significance. To change her life. She should probably admit that obits was where she belonged.

But Kendra was shaking her head. "Your imagination is what makes you good at this job, Eden. You're the one who taught me to look beyond the facts to find the real story. You see the potential inside everyone—that's your gift."

Kendra's phone rang, and she disappeared behind her cubicle wall.

Her words, however, curled around Eden, soaked in.

She stared at the story blinking on her screen. She'd interviewed the funeral director, discovered that the deceased had the same mail route for thirty years. A small detail, but it deserved notice. She could wrap an entire world around the idea of a mailman showing up, rain or shine, every day for thirty years.

Yeah. Maybe she did see the potential . . . or duped herself into believing it.

"Eden!"

She turned to see Charlotte headed her way and got up. "I'm sorry I was late—"

"I need you on a story."

Oh?

Charlotte handed her a pink telephone slip. "Russell Hays asked for you by name. It's some retired state senator, and his family wants a full story on the remembrance page. But I think there's more here, and Hal says you're always looking for a great story. So head over there and interview them. I'm holding a slot open for Saturday's edition if you can get it in tonight."

Eden took the note.

The editor paused. "The truth is, I'm not sure what to make of you, Eden. Despite the fact that you don't seem to want this job, you're rather good at it."

She looked at Charlotte.

"Eden, there's a call on line two for you," Kendra said.

Eden picked it up, hating that her heart fell when a woman's voice answered.

"Eden, this is Becky Norman, over at the hospital. We met a few times when you were in John Doe's room?"

"I remember."

"I know this is unorthodox, but I thought you should know that his brain activity is starting to diminish. I think you may be running out of time to find his family."

No.

No, they weren't. God couldn't do this to her, not today.

"Please go into his room, Becky, and tell Hudson that I'm on my way to find his family."

Charlotte frowned at her as she hung up. "Eden—"

"No, Charlotte. Don't you get it? I don't want to be good at this job—I'm supposed to be a reporter." She shoved the note back at her editor. "This is not my life!"

No. Her life was more. Bigger. Her life had more significance than chasing the shadows of dead people. Or cheering on people who discarded her at the taste of success. "I quit."

Charlotte took the slip, her mouth a tight knot of disappointment. "Fine. Go." She handed the slip to Kendra without a word, then headed back to her office.

And Eden tried to ignore the terrible roaring in her heart.

She *didn't* want this job, did she?

The sun was just dipping into the western skyline when Eden disembarked from the bus at her stop. The tow truck met her there, and although the old Taurus fought to surrender its repose, it finally shivered to life.

"You need a new battery," the mechanic suggested. Yeah, well, maybe she needed a lot of new things.

Hobbies. Friends. Goals. Career. Life.

She wiped her cheek as she merged onto 94, heading northwest for St. Cloud.

The GPS on her phone directed her to a small farmhouse outside the city, where the pastureland lay rumpled under a fragile layer of snow. She drove up the dirt driveway and parked in front of a white two-story home that needed some Tom Sawyer attention. Under the glowing outside light, she noticed paint flecking off the clapboards, and an old entryway listed to one side as if hoping to make a run for it. A rusty blue Buick sat in front of a large, empty barn, the scent of livery and hay drifting from the open door, haunting the air.

Eden wrapped her coat around her and stepped up to the front door, stomping through the snow of the unshoveled walk, glad she'd changed into her standard UGGs and parka.

No need to be fancy anymore.

The bell echoed, deep and bold, as if it might have been holding its breath, waiting for release after years of dormancy.

Eden shivered as the wind picked up snow and ghosted it into the darkness.

Footsteps, then a woman appeared. Maybe in her early forties, her dark hair caught up in a messy ponytail, she wore what looked like a pair of pink scrubs, a gold cross around her neck. She held open the storm door. "Can I help you?"

"Hi. My name is Eden Christiansen, and I'm with the Minneapolis *Star Tribune* . . ." She took a breath. "No, actually, I'm just here as a private citizen, looking for the family of Myron Hudson Peterson."

She tried to read the woman's face, not sure.

"That's my son."

The words had the power to shake Eden even as she pulled out her phone. "I hate to ask in this manner, but . . . this is all I have for identification." She brought up a picture she'd snapped at the hospital and showed it to the woman. "Is this him?"

She saw the answer in the woman's expression, the way she pressed a hand to her mouth. "Is he . . . is he dead?"

"No, he's still alive. He's in a coma, though."

"Where is he?"

"The University of Minnesota hospital."

A pause, then, "Come in, please." Her hands were shaking, and Eden could barely suppress the urge to take them in her own.

She held the door for Eden, then walked past her toward the kitchen. Eden stood in the family room, stalled by the cascading sense of time. She'd walked into the seventies—dark paneling encasing the room, with a threadbare blue floral sofa and a couple gold velvet rocking chairs centered around a redbrick fireplace. History lined up on the mantel in a collection of framed photographs. She picked up one, recognized a younger version of the woman in shorts and a T-shirt, her arm over a younger version of John Doe, smiling, holding a medal strung around his neck.

"Sophomore year. Hudson and his four-by-one-hundred team

went to state, got fifth place." She was holding the phone to her ear, and as she turned away, Eden heard her talking to someone, calling in sick.

Eden felt a little sick for her.

She put the photograph back and picked up another, this one with Hudson and an older man dressed in overalls and a gimme cap.

The woman walked through the room, rubbing her bare arms. The place collected the chill of the hour. "That's his grandfather. He was so proud of Hudson. I'm so grateful he didn't see his dark years." She opened the closet in the hallway.

"His dark years?"

She pulled out a coat, her hands still shaking. "Oh, he had so much potential, our Hudson. He was a gifted runner, and we just knew he'd get a number of scholarship offers when he graduated. But it all fell apart. And then this—" Her voice trembled. "Just when he put it all back together." She stood there for a moment as if trying to figure out what to do. "I need to go."

"Of course."

Eden fought the urge to press her for more of the story. She followed the woman outside and got in her car, strangely unsettled. She'd done it—found Doe's family—and yet . . .

The Taurus didn't even cough. An hour of driving and the battery still couldn't muster the strength to start?

She got out as the woman climbed into her own car.

"Do you need a ride?"

Eden nodded.

"Get in," she said, and Eden settled into the plush, aged velvet of the old Buick. The car, like the house, needed work, but the entire place seemed well-loved.

"Olivia," the woman said as she backed around Eden's clunker. "I'm Olivia Peterson."

"Nice to meet you." Eden would have to call AAA, but for some reason, sitting here beside Olivia felt almost . . .

Complete. As if she were meant to accompany this woman back to her son.

They pulled onto the highway, the moon starting to rise in front of them. A sprinkling of stars winked against the plane of night.

"Can you tell me what happened?" Olivia asked.

"I don't know exactly. I found him in the hospital almost two weeks ago, and they had him listed as John Doe or you would have been notified earlier. He was found in Frogtown about a week before; I suspect he was mugged."

"He's been alone all this time?"

Eden wanted to deny it, but she nodded. "Sorry."

"No—I'm just so glad someone tried to find out who he was. Did you say you were with the paper?"

She smiled. "No. I'm just a friend."

Olivia said nothing. Then, "I was trying not to worry. He seemed like he was better, and I didn't want to hover. I've done that enough."

She looked at Eden as if for absolution, but Eden had nothing. "Tell me about him. Hudson. He ran track?"

"Yeah. He was amazing. I went to all his track meets—embarrassed him terribly by running the length of the bleachers during one of his races, like I would somehow help him win."

She gave a sad laugh, caught in the memory. But it ended in a trembling sigh. "He's my only son. His daddy died in the military. We got married straight out of high school. Young, I know, but we were so much in love. I was still pregnant with Hudson when he died. I named him Myron after his father—something I'm not sure he appreciated."

"And Hudson? Is that a family name?"

The conversation seemed to bring her out of her panic. "No, that's after Hudson Taylor, the missionary. His dad and I planned on being missionaries someday, but . . ." She lifted a shoulder. "I went home to live with my parents, and Hud and I never left. He grew up hauling hay and feeding cattle and running a tractor, and he was my entire life. I loved him. Too much, really."

"How can you love a child too much?"

Olivia glanced at her, her eyes glistening. "When you don't let go. When you can't bear for them to make mistakes, so you hang on to their wings, and when they leave the nest, they fall instead of fly."

She passed a car, stayed in the fast lane. "He just had so much going for him—and I couldn't bear for him to destroy it." She set her cruise control. "In the end, that wasn't my decision."

"What happened?"

"A stupid mistake." The silence stretched between them as she seemed to consider how to frame her words. "It was junior year, the state meet qualifier. He and his four-by-one-hundred team had trained for years for that moment. Not just because it was for state, but because the rest of his teammates were seniors. They had all forgone the one-hundred-meter-dash event to save their stamina for this one race. He was the first leg, the fastest sprinter on the team. I remember standing there in the grass, just outside the track, lined up with his block, holding my breath as he took his mark. And then . . . I don't know what happened, but for the first time in his sprinting career, he flinched. Just a slight movement off the blocks. It's called a scratch, and according to state high school rules, he was immediately disqualified."

"You're kidding. No second tries?"

"Nope. His entire team had to come in off the track. He crumpled right there in the grass. I'll never forget it, the sight of my boy weeping in the middle of the field. And I wasn't the only parent crying. It was terrible. His teammates came around him, and they were so kind. But Hudson never forgave himself. And it made it worse when one of the seniors on his team joined the military. He hadn't landed a college scholarship like he hoped, so he joined up, went to Afghanistan, and was killed in a roadside bombing."

"Oh no."

"Hudson unraveled. He blamed himself. I tried to tell him that his friend made his own decision, but Hudson couldn't hear it. He dropped out of high school, and suddenly my boy with so much potential vanished. Instead he became this man who hated life. Violent, angry. He started drinking and fighting, and too many times I picked him up from a bar or at the police station. I thought he was going to kill someone . . . or himself."

She merged onto 694 as they approached the city.

"What did you do?"

"I didn't know what to do. At first I kept hovering. Making his breakfast, doing his laundry . . . being his mother. My father had died or maybe he would have figured it out, but . . . well, it took Hudson coming home wasted one night and throwing a lamp across the room for me to realize the truth."

"What?"

"I had to let him go. It didn't mean I stopped praying, but I did have to be willing to let him fail."

She ran her fingers under one eye. "I told him that I would

always love him. That he'd always have a home with me, but that he had to start respecting himself—and me—if he wanted to live there. Three days later, he left. It was the hardest thing I ever did—watching him tear out of the driveway, knowing I might never see him again. With everything inside me, I wanted to run after him. But I had to let him walk alone so he'd stop leaning on me and start leaning on God."

Eden wrapped her arms around her waist, wishing Olivia would turn up the heat.

"And it wasn't just for him, either. I'd let him give my life meaning. But that wasn't his place. I, too, needed to learn to put my hope in God and let Him fill those empty places. And as I did, I discovered that I stopped being afraid, started seeing how much God loved me—and my son."

Olivia turned off 694 onto 94. "I prayed he'd be a missionary, but I forgot that in order to do that, he had to have his own encounter with God. And I had to remember that God loved my son as much—more—than I did. The best thing I could ever do was let him fail, stop being his savior, and let Jesus do that work."

She went under the Minneapolis tunnel, then merged toward the hospital. "And then the most amazing thing happened. He found Jesus. And everything changed. He came back to me. Just showed up at the farm one day, whole, healthy . . . redeemed. He'd started working with some inner-city kids and a homeless shelter, and for the first time I saw what Myron and I had prayed for. A man with a heart after God."

She focused on the road for a moment, then said, "Can I ask you something?"

Eden nodded.

"What made you want to look for my boy's family? What made you want to find me?"

The memory of Hudson lying on the bed, peaceful yet alone, flooded back at her. Pity? Compassion? No . . . hope.

"I think God nudged me off the sidelines and into his life."

Olivia nodded as she pulled into the parking garage. She found a space and turned off the car. Sat in the darkness for a moment. "I'd really like it if you came with me, Eden."

Eden reached out and found her hand. "It would be my privilege."

Jace couldn't erase the look on Eden's face from his memory, no matter how long he talked to Haylee. They'd headed back to Sammy's, in case he might find his friend there, but Nell hadn't seen him in days. Just to make sure, Jace had gone up to his apartment.

It remained how Sam had left it two days ago.

When Sam had talked crazy, nearly done something to derail his life. Not unlike Jace, who'd let his anger drill a hole clear through his brain. His heart.

He still couldn't bear to talk to her, but she hadn't called him either. And why would she? Especially after he let Haylee take a picture with him and post it online with a "J-Hammer Tells All" promo for her ESPN blog post.

He should have talked to Eden before jumping to conclusions. Just like he had with his dad. He was impulsive, and . . . why did he immediately assume that Eden would betray him?

Jace took out his phone, scrolling down to her number. Hovered his thumb over it. And what, exactly, would he say? The shame made him put the phone away. Even if she had written the story, she didn't deserve his behavior. He *felt* like a bully.

Instead, he'd track down Sam. And maybe, on his way, check on John Doe. He wasn't sure if it had all been a game to Eden, but if she didn't show up at his bedside, Doe would be alone.

The image of her at Jace's own bedside in the ER, angry and fierce, rushed back at him. What had she said? She wasn't a fan; she was *family*.

He leaned against the cool steel wall of the hospital elevator and closed his eyes, feeling that word seep into his chest. *Family.*

Eden was family—his family. Or he'd wanted her to be. The woman he woke up to every morning. He could almost see her hauling hockey gear from her van, him holding the sticks as they ran after their towheaded sons. And a daughter. He'd like one, like Eden, feisty and smart. So smart.

The image seemed so real that he didn't realize the elevator doors had opened until an orderly on the other side alerted him.

Jace stepped out of the elevator, shaken from the vision.

Hungry for it.

Betrayed by it.

He heard voices from the end of the hall, turned the corner, and slowed, puzzled by the crowd gathered outside Doe's room. Young people sat on the floor or leaned against the walls. Some of them praying, others chatting. A few texting.

"What's going on?"

A kid with long, stringy hair under a wool cap peered at him. "Are you here for the prayer meeting?"

Huh? Jace frowned at him, then turned to enter the room. The door was open, people standing in the entrance, some sitting on the empty second bed. He excused himself as he moved through the crowd.

And then he spied Matt Conners. Parked on the other side of John Doe, his Bible open, reading the Psalms. He looked up as he saw Jace.

"What's this?" Jace noticed a woman in scrubs—probably a nurse—holding Doe's hand.

"Hey, Jace," Matt said. "Nice to see you again. We're here to pray for healing. Wanna join us?"

He had no words.

"Jace Jacobsen? Are you the one who helped find Hudson?" This from the woman standing beside the bed. She was petite, with dark hair pulled into a messy ponytail, her eyes tired. But she smiled at him, warmth in her expression.

"Yes—who are you?"

"I'm Olivia Peterson. Hudson's mom." She held out her hand, taking his in a firm grip. "I had no idea he was hurt or I would have been here. Every day." She turned to the boy in the bed, and it tugged on Jace, an old, familiar memory.

Hudson hadn't moved, his eyes closed, his vitals still monitored on a screen behind the bed.

"How did you find out?"

"Eden Christiansen found me. She drove out to St. Cloud tonight, just as I was leaving for my shift at the nursing home. She told me what you did."

Eden. A bloom of renegade warmth filled him at the thought of her finishing their search. But he couldn't wrap his mind around it.

Unless . . . "Did you know she works for the paper?"

"Oh yes. But she mentioned that she was there as a private citizen."

He drew in a breath. "Is she still here?" He looked around in case he'd missed her. But he couldn't imagine walking into a room and not spotting her.

"No. She said something about a story she had to write."

A story. Yes, see?

"Apparently she pieced together what happened," Matt said.

Jace noticed how Olivia turned back to her son, ran her hand down Hudson's face.

Matt looked at Hudson too. "I remember when he first came to us. He showed up for the basketball program. Hung around for the Bible study and the food. I think he was taking classes at a local Bible college, but he hung out at the community center a lot."

Olivia just kept holding his hand, such a look of love on her face that it could undo Jace.

"One night, I found him in the gym. Just . . . running. He'd get to the line, crouch as if he might be on a starting block, and then leap forward." Matt held the Bible to his chest. "I never figured that out."

"He was practicing his starts," Olivia said quietly. "He spent way too much time hating his mistakes, even hating himself. I suppose sometimes they came back to haunt him."

She said nothing more, and finally Matt continued. "He eventually collapsed on the floor, hot and sweaty, and I couldn't help it—I had to ask. He said that every race is a new one, and he was making sure he started right."

"Matt mentioned he was interested in track," Jace said.

"He was one of the best hundred-meter sprinters," Olivia said. "But he never had a chance to be a champion. Not until he lost everything he dreamed about." She kissed his forehead the way she might have when he was a young boy. "And then he became the champion God wanted him to be. He finally stopped caring about winning—or losing—and learned to surrender."

The words wheedled inside Jace.

"Hudson decided that he could start every day and be the man he wanted to be. One day at a time." She pressed his hand to her chest. "He finally, finally understood grace."

Jace glanced around him, noticed the room had gone silent. A couple of the girls were crying, a few of the guys examining their shoes. "Do you all know him?"

Nods.

"He tutored me in algebra," one girl said.

"He shot hoops with me after school," a young man said.

Olivia was smiling at them, her eyes shining.

"I'm so sorry this happened, Olivia," Jace said.

She reached out and took his hand. The gesture startled Jace, and for a second, he didn't know what to do.

"You know, Hudson was one of your biggest fans. He'd be honored to know that you had watched over him."

Jace's throat thickened. He swallowed past the burr in it, looked away.

"It's a mother's greatest privilege to give birth, to raise a child. But a woman's greatest honor is to look at her son with pride and know that she's helped him become a man."

She sank down on the chair next to the bed. "They say he has no brain function. I can't believe this is it. He had so much life left in him."

Her words reached inside Jace, took hold, and the question spilled from his mouth before he realized it. "Olivia, I apologize for even asking this, but . . . is Hudson an organ donor?"

She stared at him a long moment, pain, even shock on her face. "I . . . I don't know. I don't think so."

Jace felt Matt's eyes on him. Oh, he shouldn't have asked that—

But then she looked at him, something of desperation in her eyes, and he took a chance. He reached for the other chair and sat down. "Can I tell you about my friend Maddy Newton?"

CHAPTER 19

Eden could hear music pulsing out from under Owen's apartment door—loud metal, his workout playlist.

She stood in the hallway for a moment, holding a pizza, her courage dissolving. What if he slammed the door in her face, told her she had invaded his life enough?

Because she had—she knew it. She wasn't sure when she had gone from cheering to being so invested in his wins, his decisions, that they wove into the fabric of her own.

But she had to let him go.

She took a breath and knocked, then hit the button when he didn't respond.

Owen opened the door, shirtless, wearing a pair of baggy

workout shorts, a towel over his head, his skin glistening. She offered a smile and held up the pizza. "Can we talk?"

His eyes narrowed, but after a beat, he held open the door.

She'd helped him find the two-story loft, helped him pick out the gray paint, buy the glass-topped buffet, the black leather furniture. She would have preferred more color and perhaps a Monet rather than the mural of the Blue Ox logo painted on the wall. But it wasn't her apartment.

He walked to his stereo system, turned the ruckus down. A P90X DVD was frozen on the screen. He turned it off, then went to the fridge and pulled out a Powerade, opened it, and downed half of it in one gulp. He wiped his chin with his arm. "I suppose you're here to pick sides."

"Nope. I brought you a pizza," she said. Then took a breath. "An apology pizza."

He shook his head. "It's about time."

Eden slid the pizza onto his granite counter. "Owen, don't be a jerk. I never picked sides against you. But what I did do is hold on to you too tight."

He frowned.

"I can be a little bossy."

His expression relaxed, the slightest smile tweaking his face. "A little bossy?"

"Okay, I can be a lot bossy. And overprotective. But that's over now. I'm walking away."

"What does that mean? I thought you said you weren't picking sides. Are you not coming to my games?" For the first time, probably ever, he appeared to care.

In many ways, he was still that teenage kid who wanted his family in the stands. Or maybe he'd never give that up.

Maybe everyone wanted fans in the stands—was that so terrible?

"Of course I am. I know I'm not Mom, but I've been your number one—okay, maybe number two fan for as long as I can remember." And she could remember a lot. Broken fingers, tears, frozen toes, even that small scar on his chin, parting his beard. "But somehow in the mix, I sort of started equating your successes with mine—"

He moved as if to agree, but she held up her hand. "And your failures with mine."

His mouth tightened.

"I have ached with you over your injury, Owen. I know what it means to you to give up hockey."

"I'm not giving up hockey," he said. "Hey—you're not talking about that press conference today, right? You know Jacobsen is just being a big shot after his hat trick. I can get a hat trick—"

Don't react. Don't argue. She just listened to him as he reminded her of his stats and everything he hoped to accomplish.

Finally she said, "I know you're going to be a great success, Owen. Because I'm on your side. And so is God."

After a moment, his expression changed. "Okay. You might have had a good reason to be bossy," he said, his words quiet. "I've been . . . not handling things well."

Oh? But she said nothing, just pulled out a stool.

"Even before the accident, I sort of thought . . . this is it. I finally did it—became a hockey star, landed a stellar contract. I felt invincible . . . and that made me stupid. The more I dove into the life my buddies said I should have, the more it felt ugly and wrong. And . . . the more I couldn't face you."

Couldn't face her?

He toweled the sweat off his head, threw the towel on the floor by the bathroom. She didn't pick it up.

"I knew I'd disappointed you, and I hated that feeling. Fought it."

"You only disappointed me because I knew you'd worked so hard and have so much potential. And I want you to hold on to it. But I'm going to stop trying to hold on to it for you."

He considered her with an athlete's eye as if sizing her up. "No more dragging me out of bars?"

"No more cleaning out your car."

"No more telling me what women I can date?"

"No more crashing on my sofa."

He nodded. "Deal."

"Deal."

Owen pulled the pizza over, opened the box. "Of course it's Canadian bacon."

"And green peppers and pineapple."

He looked away then. Blinking. "Eden, you are more than a big sister to me. You're my closest friend." His gaze, when he returned it, seemed embarrassed, his smile lopsided. "If it weren't for you, I don't know where I'd be."

"Still looking for your skate guards?"

He laughed. "Maybe." He handed her a plate of pizza. "I'm watching game tape tonight. Wanna join me?"

She took the pizza, picked off the pineapple. Fought back the urge to ask why. To throw in cautions about him playing.

To remind him that he'd lost his mind, because with one hit . . .

The best thing I could ever do was let him fail, stop being his savior, and let Jesus do that work.

"Stop looking at me like that," he said, going over to the sofa.

Sitting down with his pizza, his Powerade. She refused to mention how the grease would be impossible to clean off the leather.

"I didn't say anything."

"Good, because then I don't have to bring up Jace Jacobsen and how I think he has the hots for you."

She swallowed. "No, he doesn't."

"Sheesh, Sis, are you totally blind? He's into you—I saw it last weekend." He picked up one of his slices. "Just watch yourself. He's got a reputation."

"I know. He's trouble." She smiled, wishing she didn't have to believe her words. She needed to not care, to be disgusted by him. Clearing her throat, she found the words she really meant. "Fear not, Bro. We're barely friends." Hopefully he didn't hear the tremble in her voice. But maybe if she said it enough, she could erase the memory of when she'd thought they might be more.

She clearly had to let Jace go too. Because Olivia was right— the more she hung on to Owen or Jace, the more she used them to fill the emptiness inside.

"You'll be at the game tomorrow, right?" Owen said, angling the pizza into his mouth.

"Have I ever missed one of your games?" But they wouldn't let him play, would they?

Owen grinned, folding the rest of the slice into his mouth. "Nope."

She picked up the remote. "One period."

"Sam?"

The room looked like a dungeon, curtains drawn, only the monitor lending enough light for Jace to make out his friend.

Sam sat against the wall, on the floor, his head in his hands.

Jace slid down next to him, not sure his friend had heard him. "I'm sorry it took me so long to get here. I called and texted—"

"My phone died. I left my charger at home. I couldn't . . ." He sounded hollow, his voice echoing out of him. "It doesn't matter. Maddy has an infection. She's not going to last long enough to get a heart."

"Then she's at the top of the list, right?" Jace found the words from deep inside, past the knot of panic. "And I have good news, buddy. The Blue Ox offered me a new contract. It's a good one, and it's enough—"

"No."

The word wasn't sharp but blunt and defeated. "What?"

"It's over."

"Sam, you can't talk like that. Maddy's going to get her heart. I know it."

"I let her go, Jace. I signed my daughter over to strangers so that she could get on the transplant list. I actually have no legal right to be here, but the nurses took pity on me—"

"What are you talking about?"

Sam lifted his head, and the look on his face made Jace wince. Maybe he had said that too loudly. "What do you mean?"

"They termed our situation medically unsustainable. Accused me of neglect. Told me they'd take me to court—"

"They can't—"

"They can, Jace. And . . ." Sam swallowed. Sleeplessness hung under his eyes. "And it's for the best. I know that."

"How can it be for the best for Maddy not to live with you?"

"Because Maddy will live."

He had no words for that. But now, yes, he understood Sam's tone. *Please, God, let him be right.*

"We'll get her back, Sam." He had the strangest urge to leap from the floor, pull Maddy into his arms, run from the room at top speed.

And that urge silenced him. No wonder Sam had gone a little crazy.

"The thing is, I realized something." Across the room, the monitor beeped, steady, the oxygen a soft rush in the night. "All this time I thought it was up to me to make sure Maddy got a heart, kept her heart. And yes, she's my child. But it was right there, all the time. The answer."

Jace stayed quiet beside him.

"'And I will give them singleness of heart and put a new spirit within them. I will take away their stony, stubborn heart and give them a tender, responsive heart.' It's a verse in Ezekiel. Mia read it to me right before she died. She told me that God had already given her a new heart and that I had to let her go. I had a dream last night, before Maddy went into arrest . . . and I heard that verse again. And I knew . . ." He looked at Jace. "I had to let go."

Jace frowned.

"I've been trying so hard to hold on through all of this. But I think I'm supposed to let go—and ask God to hold on to me. To pick me up like I do Maddy and carry me. I can't do it anymore. I've been angry and stubborn and . . . and I need a new heart as badly as Maddy does. I'm tired of trying to fix it. I can't do it, and I don't think I'm supposed to." He closed his eyes, leaned his head back. "So I'm sitting here, letting go. Putting my daughter into the hands of the Lord. Believing His plans are greater than mine, and that He loves me and Maddy more than we can imagine. I'm letting Him carry me where He wants. And praising Him with every beep of that heart monitor."

Jace ran his thumbs under his eyes, wiping away the moisture.

Maybe he needed a new heart too. One not full of anger and stubbornness and . . . hatred.

He heard Eden's voice, closed his eyes to let it soak through him. *My dad says that hope is one part confidence in God's love for us and one part our delight in Jesus. And that when we start to hope, it changes us.*

Maybe that's what it meant to have singleness of heart. To trust in God's love, to not be divided in that belief by your own fears, failures, doubts. To delight in Jesus. He hadn't spent any time delighting in Jesus, too afraid Jesus might not delight in him. But if he had, if he truly knew Jesus, Jace might have more confidence in His love.

Or maybe he'd see more fully what a wretch he truly was. *I hate my father.* He still winced when he heard those words replay in his head.

But then Olivia was there, smiling at her son, so much tenderness in her eyes it could make Jace soggy. *Hudson decided that he could start every day and be the man he wanted to be. . . . He finally, finally understood grace.*

Jace didn't truly understand grace. Maybe that's what made him feel like he had to keep checking, keep finding the limelight. Because he couldn't get his head around the fact that he already had it. A fresh start, in God's eyes, every day.

That's what grace was. The chance to start over, to be used for glory instead of destruction.

The chance to forgive himself because God already had.

Maybe, in fact, he could be undeserving *and* favored by God at the same time.

Jace leaned forward, hung his head. Closed his eyes. Listened to his heartbeat.

And then, in the quiet, he heard her voice.

God's love simply is. We can't sin it away—our only option is to accept or reject it.

Accept it.

"Maybe I could sit here and let go with you for a little while," Jace said quietly.

CHAPTER 20

ONCE UPON A TIME, Jace had loved game day. Had woken with a stir inside, a coiled anxiety in his gut that he couldn't wait to unwind on the ice. But somehow that had vanished years ago.

Now, mostly he dreaded it. He still loved the taste of adrenaline, the crisp smell of the ice, the sound of skates and sticks echoing off the girders. He loved fighting for the puck, the wind in his ears, the sound of a shot on goal, slapped in from the blue line.

But he hated the coal in his chest, burning at the fact that to win the crowd, he'd have to drop his gloves, land his fists on someone's face.

A woman's greatest honor is to look at her son with pride and know that she's helped him become a man.

Olivia's words had dogged Jace all night. Mostly because of the dark, jagged fear that no, he hadn't grown into the kind of man who deserved his mother's pride.

His mother had sacrificed everything she had for his dream. And he deserved none of it.

Worse, he kept seeing Eden's stricken expression as he'd wrapped his arm around Haylee. Someone who betrayed him shouldn't be that surprised . . . unless . . .

Unless she hadn't been the one to write the article. The thought had made him twist his sheets into a tight knot, made him wake early and turn on his computer. Then type in Haylee's blog address to check out his exclusive.

In the recent posts, however, he found the article about his injury, word for word. It looked as if Yahoo! had picked it up from Haylee's site and reposted it. But how could she know about his hospital visit? On the side, she had a number of pictures from recent events. He recognized one of the brunette and redhead from his birthday party.

Jace stared at the redhead. He'd seen her somewhere else, just couldn't place her.

And then, he did. At the hospital. The ER. After they'd filled him with morphine, she'd gone to bring in Eden.

Or maybe his mind was playing games with him and his wish for some other truth.

He somehow had to get out of this funk and prepare for tonight's game, so he headed to the arena to work out, then got a massage and took a long shower. But when he came home for lunch, he stood at his window, staring out at the skyline, Eden's face still lingering in the back of his head.

He wanted to see her. Tonight. Before the game. Or maybe just hear her voice.

Jace leaned his head against the cold window. Whether or not she'd written the article, he'd proven to her that he was exactly the guy she'd once believed him to be.

After making himself a protein shake, he sat down in his austere living room. The carpet still reeked of cleanser.

On the dining room table, his phone buzzed, and he went to get it, catching the face as he answered. "Max."

"Dude. You gotta get down here. Owen's here and he's planning on suiting up tonight."

"What?"

"He came in about an hour ago with Adam, who's duking it out with Coach. But Owen's on the ice, warming up. I think he's going to play."

And Jace's surly press conference yesterday, almost egging him on, hadn't helped.

"I thought he was still on injured reserve."

"They took him off this morning."

Jace hung up the phone, grabbed his gear, headed for the door.

Having Owen sidelined had given him a chance to truly play again. To be the guy who slapped it in, saved the day.

But he didn't want that at Owen's expense. Jace had pushed himself back on the ice while injured too many times, and he knew exactly what propelled Owen to sharpen his blades and strap on his helmet.

Because like Jace, Owen couldn't imagine being anything else. But what if . . . what if there was more? What if there was a life outside hockey, with Eden, or—?

Or whatever God decided. He might even use Jace for His glory if Jace actually let Him be in charge.

Jace pulled into the parking area, then jogged down the cement corridor into the building, through the tunnels to the basement locker room area. The place swam with the odors of athletes—sweat, Bengay, cotton towels—the steam from the showers turning the room humid and soggy. Teammates, half-dressed in their breezers, pads, and socks, walked around the room. Others sat on the benches, wrapping fingers, stretching.

Jace dumped his bag on the bench near his locker and headed back to Adam's office.

He found it empty, so he headed out to the ice in his street clothes.

In the sounds of blades slicing ice, the rocket shot of a puck against the boards, Jace recognized Owen trying to prove something. He climbed up next to Adam on the bench, watching Owen's smooth strokes, the way he handled the puck.

"One hit and he could destroy that eye," Jace said. "I can't believe he's off injured reserve."

Graham stood on the other side of Adam. "We want him in for a minute, maybe two. Not long enough to get hurt, just enough to remind the fans, stir up some excitement. Keep his name in the headlines."

He'd make headlines, all right, if he got checked and all that fancy stitching opened up. A bloody rink would embed in the minds of the fans forever.

"I don't think this is a good idea."

Graham stepped down from the bench, walked by Jace. "Maybe it's time you got back to playing the position you were hired for."

Enforcer? Jace narrowed his eyes, but he kept his hands in his pockets. His gaze turned to Owen, and for a second, he was back in the bar, watching Owen grapple on the floor the night of Jace's birthday, Eden marching up to him.

You're the team captain. Who else is supposed to watch Owen's back?

Yes. It was time to start playing the position he'd been given.

Eden could no more stay away from the game than she could stop breathing.

But she went late. Not enough that she might miss the puck drop, but late enough that she didn't have to watch Jace—or Owen—warm up. Make eye contact, wave.

Worry.

Still, the taste of dread crawled up her throat and settled in the back of it as she watched the team skate out.

Owen had dressed. She noticed he wore a full grid face mask. It might protect him from injury, but it wouldn't repair his vision.

How they'd gotten him off injured reserve, she didn't know. But it wasn't her business. Not anymore.

She blew out a breath, clapping as the players lined up for the national anthem.

When it was over, Cora greeted her with a side hug. "It was fun to meet Amelia. And Casper. He's quite the clown."

"He keeps us guessing," Eden said, sitting down, her eyes on Owen. Maybe he was just there for show. Indeed, he didn't take the ice with the first line.

Jace, however, took his position at left wing, looking big and fierce and indestructible.

He played his part well, if not honestly.

The puck dropped, the Blue Ox came up with it, and the game took off, fast and hard, a Chicago forward hot for the net as he stole the puck from Max and brought it down to face Kalen. The goalie blocked a number of shots, then fell on the puck as a couple Chicago players crashed the net, piling up in a mess.

Jace skated away, unscathed, and went to the bench as the second line came out. No Owen still, and for three long minutes, Eden could breathe.

Until one of the opposing defensemen took a shot, clipping one of the Blue Ox forwards with his stick and landing in the box for a two-minute penalty.

Owen Christiansen skated onto the ice to the thunderous roar of eighteen thousand fans.

Eden wanted to cover her eyes. Owen skated fast, picking up the puck, charging down the ice. He took a wrist shot at the goal, through traffic, but the goalie mitted it, dropped it back out, and the period ended scoreless.

"Want a hot dog or cocoa?" Cora asked as she scooted past Eden.

"Nope." Mostly because her stomach couldn't bear it.

After the break, the team emerged from the tunnel, and Owen took the bench. Max lined up and received an easy pass from center ice, shooting it to Jace as they brought the puck into Chicago territory. He played with it, firing off a quick wrist shot. The goalie snapped up the puck, dropped it to his defender, who shot it back out to the neutral zone.

Max intercepted it and brought it around—another shot. It bounced off the goalie's pads, and Max and an opposing forward scrabbled for it near the crease. The puck popped out and a Chicago player streaked down the ice with it, one-on-one with Jace, who fought him into the boards.

The puck bounced out, but not the player, who slammed Jace into the corner before catching up to the puck.

Jace seemed unfazed.

But the ref called boarding, giving Chicago another two-minute penalty.

Owen came off the bench, back on the ice, and Eden figured it out. If he could only go out on the power play, when the Blue Ox were up a man, maybe he wouldn't get hurt.

Jace stayed on the ice and shot the puck to Owen.

And then everything happened in slow motion. Owen took the puck, racing down the ice toward the goal. Fast and hard and unaware of the big Chicago enforcer barreling toward him.

On his left side. His blind side.

He didn't see it coming, couldn't brace himself. In her mind's eye, Eden watched Owen crash into the boards, his helmet screwing off, his face hitting the ice. Saw his injury explode, his eye destroyed.

She rose to her feet. "Owen!"

And then, even as his name sputtered out of her mouth, Jace appeared. As if he, too, saw the future. He had streaked down the ice and lunged at the Chicago player, intercepting him.

Putting his body between Owen and the hit.

Jace slammed into the wall with the force of a locomotive.

Eden watched, a scream in her lungs as his head hit the boards. Watched as he crumpled.

She missed, completely, Owen's spectacular wrist shot for a goal. The siren sounded, the stands erupting.

And Jace lay sprawled on the ice, unmoving.

CHAPTER 21

THE IMMENSITY OF THE BLACKNESS poured through Jace, so dark that he couldn't see his hands before his face and so complete that it could choke him like smoke in his lungs. Still, the scent of the ice rose up around him, seeping into his sweater, his skin. And in the distance he heard a thunderous roar, until it faded out.

Then he was alone. With just a singular voice in his head.

Jace.

He tried to see where it was coming from, but the darkness refused to relent. So he stopped clawing at it and settled back to listen.

Jace.

Mom? He turned his head, tried to find her seated in the stands, to hear her more clearly.

But even her voice faded away, and then he had nothing.

Except for the touch. Soft, caressing his hand, sending ripples of warmth through him. His entire body shivered, but the heat on his hand centered him. The ruckus in his chest began to slow.

Then, peace. It swept over him like a blanket, through him like a fragrance.

And he slept.

"Mr. Jacobsen." Light flashed across his eyes. Jace recoiled, flinching. Again, the light, and he moaned. He must have reached for something because his hand closed around fabric. He groaned against the thudding of pain in the back of his head, then receded again into the night.

It finally became shadow, and he opened his eyes, blinking into the dim light.

Pain in his hand radiated up his arm, a burning river under his skin. The smells pinched his nose, watered his eyes.

"Welcome back."

His attention went to the voice, and he blinked, his eyes focusing on a doctor leaning over him. He wore a surgeon's cap, a stethoscope around his neck. He held up a finger. "Can you follow my finger, Jace?"

He squinted but followed it—left, right, up, down. "What's going on?" His voice emerged across a washboard, parched. And his throat ached.

"You had a brain bleed from that fall you took on the ice. We had to go in and relieve some of the pressure."

"You nearly bought it, dude."

The doctor glanced up, and Jace followed his gaze, words leaving him when he saw Owen standing on the other side of the bed. He wore a leather jacket, looked as if he'd come right from the game.

The game. "Did we win?"

Owen shook his head. "Two to one, Chicago."

"We'll get 'em next time." But he winced as he said it.

"Let's take one day at a time," the doc said. "You need to rest, recover from surgery."

"Surgery?"

Owen made a face.

"You were lucky." The doc patted him on the shoulder. "But you had a lot of people pulling for you. Get some rest, and I'll be back later."

As he left, Owen pulled up a chair. He looked like a wreck, his eyes bloodshot, his hair tucked under a baseball cap.

"Did you sleep here?" That felt weird, Owen sitting by his bedside.

"Nah. I'm not in love with you, Hammer."

"What's that supposed to mean?"

Owen lifted a shoulder. "I'm not my sister. I'm not going to go all gooey over you, cry at your bedside."

"Eden was here?" The question hung, desperate and weak, in the air, but he didn't care.

"Yeah. She stayed here and held your hand all night. You woke up about an hour ago—don't you remember?"

"No."

"She took off after that. Said you probably didn't want to see her."

Oh, Eden. He closed his hand, still feeling the warmth. "I want to see her."

Owen stood, hands in his pockets. Considered him. "I have to ask you something. I've been trying to sort this out, and there's this team rumor . . . Was Max the one who hit me?"

Oh no. "Why does it matter?"

"It matters."

"Let it go, Owen."

"Would you let it go?"

Owen's words hung between them, his expression fierce. In that moment, Jace saw himself, the man he'd been. The man he refused to be anymore.

Yes, he would let it go—now.

But Owen cut off his answer. "Listen, I saw the game tape. You took the check for me, Hammer. I guess I owe you. So this is me saying thanks." He started to move away.

"Owen—wait. Don't make my mistakes and let anger turn you into a guy you don't want to be."

Owen shook his head. "It's over. Adam is taking heat for clearing me to play. I think he's going to get fined, maybe suspended. And apparently I'm done in the NHL, at least until I get my eyesight back." Owen met his gaze, darkness in his eyes, something Jace recognized. "Hockey was all I had."

Jace watched the way Owen drew in a breath, the hard set of his jaw. He was serious. "I'm sorry, man."

"Yeah, well, here's the deal. I know you have a thing for my sister. And I'm pretty sure she has it for you too. And you're not the total jerk I thought you were. So you're going to keep an eye on her, promise not to break her heart, or I'm going to come back and find you and break something essential."

"Dude, Eden and I—"

"If you say you're just friends, I'm going to have to rip out your IV and strangle you with it."

Oh, why not. He had nothing else to lose. "Yeah, okay. I'm in love with her. She's amazing. She can find the good in anyone. I can't imagine my life without her."

"Yeah, I get that." Owen pulled his keys from his pocket, looked at them for a moment. "I'm sorry for what I said at my folks' place—the things I accused you of. I think I was jealous. She'd spent my whole life taking care of me, and suddenly there you were. Taking my place."

"I could never take—"

"Dude."

Jace smiled.

Owen didn't smile back. "I need you to give these to Eden." He dropped the keys on Jace's bedside table.

"What are you doing?"

He started for the door.

"Owen! I know you're angry and upset, but you can't just walk away. You gotta tell her—tell your family—where you're going."

Turning, Owen tugged something out of his back pocket. A notebook, bent in the center. He slapped it onto the table. "She left this too—I saw her writing in it, and when the doctor came in, she snuck away. I think she forgot it."

"Owen."

The kid paused once more. "If it weren't for Eden, I wouldn't have had any of this. I love her, Hammer. Really, don't break her heart."

Then he was gone, and Jace was tied to the stupid bed, his head bandaged, wearing a hospital gown. He couldn't exactly chase Owen down the hall.

Although he debated it.

Jace picked up the notebook. Eden had been the one holding

his hand, and the thought of her sitting beside his bed while he fought the darkness . . .

He didn't deserve her. But oh, how he loved her.

She made him feel favored. Blessed.

He opened the notebook, ran his hand over the writing inside. Names and stories, tidbits of information.

What was this?

He kept turning pages, found snippets of stories, short stories, more descriptions of places, a number of strange interviews.

And toward the back, a freshly inked essay. One about a boy named Myron. And when he read it, Jace began to sob.

Eden quick-walked down the hallway, her heart thundering.

Jace would live. She didn't care if he saw her, if he said her name, if he even noticed that she'd spent the night at his bedside, praying and holding his hand. Yeah, she'd planted herself right there beside him, and not even Adam had the courage to move her. She didn't care that she might not belong in his world. She would happily stay on the sidelines of his life if he would just . . . live.

She couldn't bear the fact that once upon a time she'd called him a monster. A troublemaker. A jerk.

He'd nearly gotten himself killed to protect her brother.

And they'd shaved his hair. All of that long, dark, beautiful hair. She wanted to weep, seeing him like Samson, his strength sapped in the hospital bed.

But he would live, and now she'd learn to watch him on television, or read about him in the paper, and be thankful for the two weeks they'd been friends.

Thankful, really, for Hudson Peterson and how he'd brought them together. She took the elevator to his floor, got off, and looked for Becky at the nurses' station but didn't see her.

She headed down the hall to his room, trying to brace herself for the somber disappointment of seeing him still in a coma, Olivia by his bed, holding his hand, the same as when she'd left them.

Or maybe he'd woken up. She prayed the sound of his mother's voice had tugged him free from the grip of unconsciousness, brought him back to the land of the living.

She longed to see his eyes, his smile, the boy she'd found grinning at her in the online photos, the pictures in Olivia's house.

The door was closed, and Eden knocked before entering. No answer, but the day was early—perhaps she shouldn't be disrupting . . .

She eased the door open. Sunlight streamed in through the window, rose-gold light that dappled the sheets of the empty bed.

Empty. For a second she stood there, a hand of dread reaching up to strangle her. Then she walked into the room, ran her hand along the bed, remembering Hudson's frail body under the cotton sheets.

What if they'd moved him? She held on to the thought, turning, intending to go down the hall to ask.

Behind her, an orderly came into the room carrying an armful of sheets. She looked about twenty-five, her brown hair pulled back in a ponytail. "Oh, hello. Can I help you?"

"I was looking for Hudson Peterson—they originally had him listed as John Doe. Where did they move him?"

"Um . . ." She appeared stricken for a moment. "Mr. Peterson passed in the night."

Passed . . . oh . . . The hand around her neck began to cut off her air.

"We're making up the room for a new patient."

"What? No. I mean—wait. You can't—" Eden closed her mouth, shook her head. They couldn't just . . . just replace him. Just fill his bed. "This is his room."

She sank down on the opposite bed, staring at the sunlight folding into the sheets like rivulets of gold. "I thought this would work. I thought if I . . . if I found his family . . ." Her eyes filled. "How could he die? He wasn't supposed to die. He was supposed to wake up. To live." She took a shaky breath. "That was the deal. I find his family, and he wakes up."

"I'm so sorry." The orderly set down the pile of sheets. "I can leave you alone for a few moments."

"No. That's okay. I barely knew him, really. I just . . . thought I could help him. But I guess I was dreaming. As usual."

"You did help him."

She turned at the voice and found Becky standing at the door. Once again wearing her printed hockey scrubs, a stethoscope around her neck.

"What?"

"You did help him." Becky shooed the orderly away, then turned back to Eden. "I think he was holding on until you found his family. You let him die in peace."

"But . . ." She pressed her fingers to her eyes. "I know this sounds crazy, but he wasn't supposed to die. I thought if I found him, if we discovered his story, God would see him—and spare him."

Becky's hand touched her arm. "But God did see him. He

sent you, Eden. You were God's plan to show Hudson that he was loved. Because you cared, Hudson was not forgotten."

Eden walked over to his bed, rested her hand on the covers. This wasn't right. Wasn't fair.

"It doesn't matter how much I care. It doesn't change anything. John Doe is still replaced with one change of the sheets, his life forgotten." She turned and walked out of the room.

Sam ran his hands over his still-drying hair. Somehow standing in the shower had sloughed away the fear, at least for the moment. The hot water cleared his mind, banished the cobwebs of the past week.

Helped him hold on to the fragile reality, the feeble hope.

Maddy was getting a heart. He could hardly believe it this morning when the doctor woke him from where he lay curled on the sofa and informed him of the sudden availability of a heart. They'd prepped her and taken her away before he had a chance to get his bearings.

Before he could wallow in the good-byes, the what-ifs.

He couldn't let himself linger on the idea that a family had lost their child to give him his. Instead, he prayed over Maddy again, then kissed her and breathed out any last grip he had on his daughter.

She was safer in God's hands.

He needed a shave, but at least he didn't resemble a derelict now. Didn't offend himself with his own smell. He leaned back on the vinyl waiting room sofa, shooting a glance at the television, turned to subtitles to honor the hush in the room.

Across from him, a couple waited in quiet worry, the husband pacing. Sam couldn't watch, the movements stirring up his own restlessness.

"Coffee?"

He looked up, first at the cup, then at the woman holding it. He stayed for a moment on her beautiful brown eyes. Doe brown. Her long, dark hair was pulled back, and she wore pink scrubs with a gold cross necklace.

"You," he said with a quick intake of his breath.

She pulled back. Frowned.

"Nothing," he said quickly, reaching for the coffee. "Is this for me?"

"It's black, but there are fixin's at the bar. You looked like you needed something to occupy your hands."

He hadn't noticed how he'd been fisting them over and over. "Black is perfect." He wrapped his hands around the cup, let it warm him.

The woman gestured to the chair next to him. "May I?"

He nodded and she sat beside him, leaning back to release her ponytail, run her fingers through her hair.

"Waiting is the hardest part," he said. "It's one thing to wait and hope for a heart, another completely to know your child is on the table, her life about to change."

"Your daughter is getting a heart?"

He nodded. Gave a ghost of a smile.

"Have you been waiting a long time?"

"This time around, no. Two weeks. But the first time, eight months."

"Oh, my. This is your second heart transplant? How old is your daughter?"

"Nine."

She considered him a moment, then looked away, leaning her head back against the wall.

"How old is your child?"

"He's nineteen."

"So much of his life ahead of him. Heart? Lung?"

"Everything. Heart, lungs, liver, corneas . . ."

Sam stared at her, stricken. "How—?"

"My son isn't receiving a transplant. He's a donor." She had a smile despite her words.

His breath stilled, his body taut with the sudden urge to run. Or maybe to pull this woman into his embrace and weep with her. Only she hadn't dissolved into a tangle of grief, just spoken it as if her son might be competing in a sporting event. "I'm so sorry."

She folded her hands then, the first sign of her pain. "Thank you. The funny thing is, I have this strange, breathtaking feeling of pride. I raised a son who not only filled my life with joy but will now give it to others. It's as if the grief I know I feel is being replaced by this almost-divine sense of triumph.

"I'm more proud of my son today than I was when he was a track star." A tear dropped on her cheek, but she smiled. "I hadn't thought about doing this until someone told me how it could save lives. His heart is going to a college student in Chicago. A musician. Hudson always did want to play an instrument. And his eyes to a woman in Seattle, a nurse. His liver is flying all the way to Boston to help an international patient with a rare disease. His lungs are staying in Minneapolis; his pancreas is headed to Arizona to help a father of three. And his kidneys are flying to California. One to LA, the other to Anaheim." She drew in a long breath. "I'm just waiting until it's over; they promised me I could see him one last time, say good-bye."

Sam had the strangest urge to hold her hand.

"Did I mention he was a track star? I have this crazy image of him running in heaven. Lining up, practicing his starts." She looked at him. "Of course, they're perfect."

Her smile freed him to nod. "Spectacular."

She said nothing then, just met his eyes, her own glistening.

"Sam Newton," he said quietly.

"Olivia Peterson."

He wasn't sure why he reached out, took her hand. Or where the words came from, but they felt solid and right. "You're not alone."

She startled, then wrapped her fingers around his grip. "Neither are you, Sam Newton."

CHAPTER 22

Methodically, over the course of the week, Eden had slowly turned her apartment over. Searching in the bedroom—and while she was at it, cleaning out her closet of all Owen's old hockey gear, the skates and workout wear and pads and gloves. Then she'd moved to the living room, unearthed a stack of hockey magazines along with a few *Greatest Hockey Moments* DVDs. He'd also left his water bottle under the coffee table.

In the kitchen, she emptied out the protein shake containers, gathered all the powdered drink packets. These she put together in a box, along with a knee brace, an Ace bandage, and a gnarled tube of Bengay she found in the bathroom.

She'd called Owen three times, but he hadn't answered. The last time she saw him, he'd been standing guard in the hallway outside Jace's room, a ten-year-old-boy expression on his face. Like he knew he'd been caught. A sort of sad desperation that made her want to drive over to his apartment, pound on his door.

But no. Because she had to let him go. Had to let both of them go. Owen. Jace. She couldn't show up in their lives like a fan anymore.

If they wanted her, maybe they would show up on *her* doorstep. For now, she could watch their highlights on channel 9. Or occasionally catch the games live, although maybe she'd give those tickets away too.

Because why bother? Nothing she did would really change lives. Really matter. Including those stories locked in her notebook. So what that it was lost? She kept trying to tell herself not to care, not to upend the apartment in search of it.

Or maybe her search had more to do with the fact that she had no idea what she might do from here. With the space before her that echoed with the sound of defeat. Maybe it was time to go home, start rebuilding the resort with Casper and Darek.

Still, the inexplicable urge to find her notebook drove her to empty even the coat closet, her last hope. Maybe she'd dropped it out of her messenger bag. She had the closet torn apart, her parka, her wool coat, her summer slicker, her trench coat, her ski jacket— all lying on the floor in her living room. And beside them, her tall black boots, her UGGs, her hiking boots, her running shoes, her cowboy boots—when was the last time she'd worn those?

She stared at the empty closet, at the pile of coats.

Then, suddenly, she picked up her grimy white parka. Grabbing her keys, she marched outside to the Dumpster and threw the parka in. Dropped the top, watched it shudder. Stood there shivering, tears burning her eyes. Stupid coat, stupid hope . . .

The UGGs would go next. After the snow melted.

She was turning to head back inside when her gaze fell on the man standing by her security entrance. Tall, with a lazy grin. He wore a leather jacket, dress pants. And he looked at her with one eyebrow raised, as if humored.

Jace.

Just seeing him hurt. From his black stocking cap, to that now-close-clipped beard, to his broad shoulders, strong legs, dress shoes—it all sent a spear of pain through her.

No matter what had possessed him to land on her doorstep, she refused to crumble. She could play through the pain. Owen had taught her that.

She still had her dignity if nothing else.

"You look like a Russian thug in that hat." She paused at the door, her arms curling around herself against the cold. "What are you doing here?"

His smile seemed undaunted. "We need to talk."

"Fine. Talk."

He looked sheepish now, telling her that her tone had stung him. "You didn't write an article about my migraines, did you?"

"What? No. Of course not."

"I'm such a jerk."

"Yeah, actually, you are." She pushed past him, toward the door, but he stuck out his hand to stop her. "Move."

"Not yet. Please let me apologize, tell you how sorry I am for hurting you."

His words prickled the back of her throat. "I forgive you. Now please move."

He shook his head. "No. We have someplace to be, and I don't want to be late."

"Listen, if you want to be friends or something, sure. Whatever. But I'm not going anywhere with you."

He stepped in front of her when she tried to move, and she ran into a wall of muscle. Wow, and he still smelled good. Unfair. "Aren't you supposed to be at home resting?"

"You're so bossy."

"And you're in my way." She refused to look up, into those hypnotic blue eyes, or she just might be lost. "Please—"

His voice softened. "I'm not moving, Eden. Call me a goon or a bully—"

"I'm not calling you any of those things, Jace. I just need you to move and let me walk out of your life. Let me go back to the sidelines. I'm good there. I'm even happy there. I don't mind, I promise."

"Oh, Eden. When will you figure out that it's my turn to cheer for you?" He lifted his hand as if to touch her, then let it fall. "Open the door, get changed, and please, come with me."

It was how he said it, how he stepped aside, a vulnerability in his expression, that furrowed her heart, made her let him into her building, her apartment.

"What happened in here?" he asked at the tumble of clothing, the boxes of Owen's hockey gear.

"I lost something." She walked over to a stack of books, moved them off the sofa to the floor. "Here. You can sit here, and don't move."

He lowered himself to the sofa, moving a bit gingerly. She wanted to help him, but her heart simply couldn't manage it.

"I'll wait here while you change clothes."

Apparently he was serious.

"What am I wearing?"

"A black dress. And your black boots. Something somber."

What? She swallowed, locked her bedroom door, and found a knit black dress in the back of her closet. She added leggings and came out with her hair up, a bit of makeup on. Not that she was trying or anything, but—

Jace made an appreciative sound, and her heart did stupid, crazy things.

"I still don't know why you're here, Jace." She used her annoyed voice, but it didn't seem to faze him as he walked over to her.

"Now the boots. And grab a jacket. There seems to be a collection here on the floor to choose from."

She slipped into the boots and grabbed her wool coat, a scarf. "I don't understand."

"You will." He held open the door, and she followed him downstairs, outside, and to his GT-R. The car smelled freshly cleaned. They pulled out and down to Hennepin Avenue.

She rode with her hands on her lap. Clasped. "Isn't the team on the road this week?"

"Mmm-hmm. A ten-day stretch—six games, three cities."

No wonder Owen hadn't called. She'd left a few messages, but she didn't want him to think she was holding on too tight. And she'd even congratulated herself for missing the last game. See, she could let go.

"What do you mean you can let go?"

Oh, she hadn't meant to say that out loud. "Just that . . . I'm not going to watch his games. I can't bear to see Owen on the ice, knowing he could get hurt."

He went strangely quiet beside her. Then he slipped his hand over hers. She stared at his hand, so strong, tender, and had the strangest urge to cry. "What don't I know, Jace? Is it Owen?"

He nodded.

Oh, shoot. She didn't want to care, didn't—

"He's not on the team anymore, Eden. He left town. I thought . . . I thought he'd call you."

"What are you talking about? He didn't leave town. He would have called—"

"He left, Eden. Or at least he said he was going to. He told me to give you these." He dug into his jacket pocket and pulled out Owen's Charger keys. Then he dropped them in her open palm.

She stared at the keys.

"He left?" Silly, stupid tears edged her eyes. That explained why he hadn't answered his cell. She glanced at Jace, and he met her eyes ever so briefly. The compassion in them could tear her asunder, so she looked away.

"Why would he do that?" But she already knew. Because he had to figure out on his own that God was his Savior. Not hockey. Not his family. Not even Eden.

She closed her hand around the keys. "Where are we going?"

They'd turned onto the highway toward St. Paul. "To visit a friend."

For a Saturday in February, the sky was a bright, glorious blue, the cirrus clouds sparse in the sunshine. "How are you feeling?"

"Good. No memory loss."

Oh. She didn't want to ask if he remembered her sitting at his bedside.

He reached down, turned on the radio. Michael Bublé hummed over the speakers.

Jace started to sing quietly. "'You think you've seen the sun, but you ain't seen it shine.'"

He pulled off, toward Frogtown, and she recognized the

neighborhood even before he stopped in front of a church. The lot was packed. She got out, watching young people file in. On a Saturday?

He came around the car and extended his arm.

Okay, she'd play along. Maybe it was some sort of Saturday worship.

But when she spied the picture in the foyer, she got it. She stood in front of the poster-size print, taken in by the smile, the twinkle in the eyes of Myron Hudson Peterson. Track star, evangelist. Beloved son and friend. Handsome, with dark-blond hair, he leaned into his picture like he was leaning into life.

Or eternity.

Eden pressed a hand against her mouth, the pain fresh in her chest. "I still can't believe he didn't make it."

"He did make it, Eden. He made it all the way to heaven," Jace said quietly. He put his hand on her back and ushered her inside. They found a place near the back, since the church was packed. She recognized Matt Conners when he got up to lead the first hymn, "Amazing Grace."

Jace stood, his voice ringing out, something new in it she didn't recognize. Stronger. Or maybe just truer.

When they sat, he ran his arm along the back of the pew, tucking her close to him.

She didn't move away. Apparently, in this moment, they belonged together.

Matt shared some thoughts from the pulpit, but Eden barely heard them. Friends rose, gave accounts of Hudson, who he was. A friend who'd been in track with him told the story of his buddy who ran every race as if it might be the last.

And then Olivia.

She wore a black dress, white pearls, beautiful in their simplicity, her hair pulled back, her face stoic.

Jace took Eden's hand, wove his fingers through hers. She let him and even hung on.

Olivia looked out across the crowd. "We wouldn't be here today if it weren't for two kind souls who decided that they couldn't let my son die alone."

Jace squeezed her hand.

"One of them penned an amazing story about my son. I'd like to read it for you today."

Eden froze. She glanced at Jace, and he leaned down to her ear. "I added just a couple details."

Olivia pulled out the notebook—Eden's notebook—and began to read.

"It takes courage to stop, to see. To make the invisible visible. But that is what Hudson Peterson did one frozen January night.

"He saw the unseen, and because he did, he saved a life.

"Alena Tippen disembarked from the bus at midnight, weary after her shift at a nearby diner. She didn't see the man behind her, didn't realize he'd invaded her shadow until he looped an arm around her neck. He dragged her to a nearby alley, and it might have ended right there for her had Hudson not heard her cries, muffled by the snow falling on that icy night.

"Hudson wasn't big or even particularly strong, but he was fast. Champion fast. And that night, he was out delivering blankets and sandwiches to the homeless in

Frogtown, St. Paul, something he did often for Hope Community Center.

"He heard Alena's screams and started running. His arrival was enough to stop the attack, and her assailant fled. But he still had her purse, and Hudson had his speed. He took off after the attacker, and the details from there turned dark.

"Four hours later, a caller reported a John Doe, bleeding, unconscious, and hypothermic in a nearby park.

"Hudson, the man who saw the invisible, had become invisible.

"Some might wonder how Hudson became such a hero. To the average eye, his past might be considered unremarkable. The kind of life easily forgotten.

"Myron Hudson Peterson was born to Olivia and Myron Peterson in March of 1994. A soldier who perished while in service, Myron Peterson never saw his son, but he left a legacy of honor that Hudson strove to live up to. Named for his father and for Hudson Taylor, because his parents prayed for a child with a heart for evangelism, at an early age Hudson proved this hope by working in youth outreach at his local church. As a high schooler, he had the heart of a champion, excelling as a sprinter and helping lead his team to fifth place in the state track meet as a sophomore. He continued to live the legacy of his father as he volunteered at Hope Community Center, tutoring and assisting with the after-school athletic program. Matt Conners, the director of the community center, said that Hudson had aspirations to begin a track program and instill in other young people the heart of a champion.

"His favorite Scripture, according to his mother, was Philippians 3:14: 'I press on to reach the end of the race and receive the heavenly prize for which God, through Christ Jesus, is calling us.' Hudson pressed forward all the way to the finish line, a true champion of the faith.

"Is it possible to have a remarkable life by simply caring for someone else? To be a champion by losing everything? To become a hero by becoming invisible?

"Hudson taught us that the answer is yes.

"See, we pass them every day. They sit on a ratty piece of cardboard, wrapped in bags, fraying woolen hats, matted and dirty hair in tangles down their backs, wearing old Army surplus jackets.

"They hold out their hands, and we avert our eyes as we drop a quarter, maybe a dollar.

"Why? Because they scare us. They are different, broken, weary, forgotten, and we try not to notice them because they frighten us. They are monsters to us, and if we saw them as any different, we might have to connect, to care.

"It might cost us something.

"We all judge each other. We see what we want, what we believe based on stereotypes, on rumor, and even on our own fears. We put people into categories and assign behaviors to them, and it isn't until we take the time, until we commit to the cost, that we see beyond those stereotypes.

"We see beyond someone who frightens us with their

reputation to a person God loves. We see beyond a person the world might call a monster to a man of compassion and honor. A man who might not even see himself that way anymore but with the slightest nudging could become a hero.

"Hudson knew that, to these forgotten, these unseen, God says, 'I see you, and My heart breaks for you. I long to heal you. To comfort you. For you to rise up and know you are Mine. I am proud to be your daddy.'

"Hudson knew that to live a remarkable life, it started with seeing just one person and reminding them of God's love."

Olivia looked up, smiled at the audience, and didn't bother wiping the tear from her chin. "I believe God handpicked you, Eden, to walk into that room and find my son. It had to be you who told his story because only you understood how to give him a voice. Thank you for caring for the forgotten and believing in a hero."

She took a breath. "My son, Myron Hudson Peterson, passed away peacefully last Saturday surrounded by the love of friends and family. And what you don't know is that after he saved Alena's life, even after his death, he went on to change the lives of seven other individuals by donating his lungs, his kidneys, his liver, his pancreas, his eyes, and his heart." She closed the notebook, rested her hand on the cover. "I love you, Son. I'm so very proud."

She descended, and Matt led the congregation in a chorus of "It Is Well with My Soul." But Eden couldn't breathe. She slipped out, past Jace, desperate for fresh air.

He followed her, catching her on the sidewalk. "What, Eden? What's wrong?"

She couldn't speak, her hand over her mouth. *One story. One great story.*

"I just wanted you to see that you have a gift. A way of seeing people. Of bringing out the best in a person for the world to see."

She met his eyes. "I think God has been trying to tell me something for four years. I'm . . . I'm *supposed* to be in obits."

Jace nodded.

"In fact, being on the sidelines, making sure people aren't forgotten, giving them a final voice, is exactly what I love doing. I just . . . I didn't want to believe it. Charlotte was right . . . I do write about life."

"Yes. And you find the remarkable in the so-called ordinary." He touched her hand. "Here's what you need to see. God put you in exactly this place to stumble into Hudson's room, to find him. Because only you could see beyond Hudson's tragedy to the hero inside. And because of that, because you found his mother, you helped save seven people." His eyes filled. "You don't even realize the impact you make on the world by simply caring about one person. Like Hudson. Like me. You made me see the man I could be—"

"The man you are, Jace." She couldn't help the words—they spilled out. "You're a wonderful man, with the heart of a protector. I should have never called you a bully. Or a monster."

"And I shouldn't have made you feel like you didn't belong in my world. Like you were anything but the sunlight in it. I love you, Eden Christiansen. And I would chase you down; I would fight for you; I would find you. You are the face I look for in the stands. The only face I look for. No one has ever made me feel more like the man I want to be. Please say you forgive me."

She couldn't move, couldn't breathe. Just stared at him. Then, somehow, nodded.

She'd saved lives. And Jace might be saving hers back.

"Do I have to wear a sweater with your name on the back?"

He laughed. "I wouldn't mind."

Then she hooked her hands around his neck, pulling his head down to hers. Holding on to this amazing man as he bent down to kiss her.

And Jace Jacobsen, hockey star, the man in the limelight of her heart, never did anything halfway.

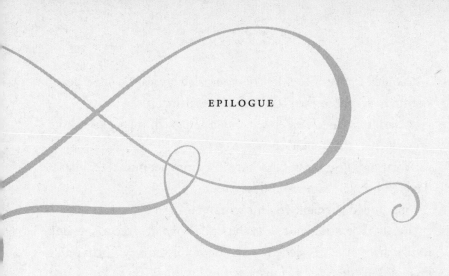

EPILOGUE

THE SCENT OF SPRING—of buds on the lilac trees, the greening grass—and a hint of anticipation hung in the air as Eden slammed the door to the Charger, then dashed across the street to the newspaper offices.

She still had Charlotte's voice mail message on her phone, not wanting to erase it, just in case . . .

But she shouldn't put so much into this meeting. Especially after the way she'd walked out on her job.

Charlotte didn't owe her anything.

She got a visitor's pass, then took the elevator to her old digs. Frannie greeted her, then called Charlotte. "You can go back," she told Eden.

A quick glance at Kendra's desk revealed it vacant—she'd heard she'd transferred to the social media department.

Charlotte's door was closed. Eden knocked, then pushed the door open at the invitation.

Wearing a knit dress, Charlotte rose from her desk. Her glasses dangled from a chain around her neck.

She smiled. "Thank you for sending it to me."

Really? Eden tried not to let the smile flood her face as she sank into a chair. "I felt I needed to apologize for the way I behaved. I know I don't deserve my job back, but I wanted you to know that I understand now, and you were right. You do write about life, and it's a privilege to give people their final moment. I'm sorry I didn't see that—and for the way I treated my job."

Charlotte came around the desk, leaned against it. Considered her. Then she gave a small smile. "Apology accepted." She reached behind her and picked up a sheaf of papers. "*Memoirs of Lives Well Lived: Reflections of an Obituary Writer.*" She handed Eden the pages. "When did you have time to write it?"

Eden took the manuscript, running her hands over the smooth paper. "I've been writing it for years, really. Collecting stories—"

"Of life."

Eden found herself nodding. "Yes. Tidbits and details of the remarkable lives of the people who pass through our department. I found that when I interviewed their loved ones, there was so much more to them that their obits couldn't contain. One by one, they touched lives. Maybe just one life, but it was enough."

"Do you have a publisher yet?"

"I sent it to a few agents. We'll see."

"You once said that you didn't want to be good at obits. Why not?"

Eden raised a shoulder. "Because I thought I was supposed to be more. But then I realized God had already put me where I could shine. I belong in obits."

Charlotte wore a warmth in her expression Eden didn't recognize. "It took you long enough." She got up, went back around her desk. "Because I have a little house in Florida I just bought, and I've been waiting four years for you to be ready to take my place."

She winked at Eden, and Eden had no words.

"You start training for obits editor tomorrow. Now get out of my office."

She'd probably missed the first period, but she left her spring coat in the Charger and pulled the hockey jersey from her bag, tugging it on over her shirt. It looked a little ridiculous with her short black skirt and black leather boots, but Jace liked it when she wore his colors.

The white and red of the Hope Community Center Polar Bears.

The bullet shots of the puck on the ice, the cheers of the crowd swelling as the tykes fought the battle, made her hustle. She caught a glimpse of the time clock and winced. Third period? Already? At least the Bears were up by one.

She ducked her head as she scampered into the stands.

"Eden! Over here!"

The voice rose over the din, and she spied Sam waving. He wore a stocking cap, a red Polar Bears sweatshirt, and gestured for her to sit beside them.

Next to him, Olivia had Maddy on her lap, her arms clasped around the girl. Maddy grinned at Eden as she slid onto the bench.

"You're late," Maddy said, her cheeks a healthy pink. They had her dressed a little on the warm side, but Eden didn't blame Sam for overprotecting his miracle.

In fact, Olivia and Sam's relationship seemed like a miracle too. Eden didn't exactly know how they had ended up together, but maybe those mysteries she'd leave in the Lord's hands.

"How's it going?"

"Jace is in rare form tonight. Hasn't yelled at the refs once," Olivia said.

Yeah, well, he'd tamed since quitting the league. Just a little. She found him easily—standing behind the bench, hands on his hips, shouting to his kids as they fought for the puck. She watched him gesture, those strong hands coming to rest on the shoulders of one of his players as he gave instructions, then sent him onto the ice. Another player came in, and Jace patted him on the head.

The Bears shot the puck into the goal, and the siren sounded. The crowd rose to its feet, cheering.

"Burgers at Sammy's after the game?" Eden asked as they sat down.

Sam nodded. "But I can't stay long. I still have boxes to move, and Maddy needs to get to bed early."

Olivia clasped his hand in hers, and Eden wanted to weep at the sight of her joy. According to Jace, Sam had rented a house with a backyard, and the hospital had allowed him provisional custody.

With Jace managing the restaurant, Sam mostly stayed home to care for his daughter. And Eden suspected there might be a new mommy in Maddy's future.

The game buzzer sounded, and the team emptied onto the ice. The audience found its feet, clapping for the win, and Eden gathered up her bag. "I'd better find Jace and pretend I didn't miss most of the game."

Sam wore a strange smile.

She walked through the crowd to the box, rapped on the Plexi-glas. Jace turned, and his smile could still make her heart stop, still strike her with a sort of disbelief that he'd chosen her. "I'll be right back," he said, winking.

She'd wait right here on the sidelines for him—forever, if it took that long.

He wore a suit jacket over a Polar Bears T-shirt and jeans. She missed his long hair, but after three months it was finally grow-ing back. Now he sported a respectable curly mop, short enough for the parents to see him as a real coach instead of a part-time volunteer.

But who wouldn't trust Jace Jacobsen with their ten-year-old? Especially when he took the ice and they piled on top of him.

He laughed and wrestled free.

And then he pointed at Eden. The boys skated toward her, calling her out on the ice. She climbed over the wall. "I don't have skates," she yelled to Jace, but he shook his head, just motioned her to join him.

It didn't help that his fleet of tiny henchmen half dragged, half pushed her to the center line. She nearly fell, but Jace caught her.

"What?" she said, laughing.

He smiled at her, so much mischief in his eyes that she stopped laughing.

Her stomach did a strange, almost-wary flip.

Then the lights went out, turning the entire arena dark. "Jace?"

He found her hand as a bright light shone down from the stands, puddling them in the middle.

Only Eden and Jace. And, well, twenty young boys standing around the darkened perimeter.

"What's going on?"

He still wore that crazy grin, and now he knelt in front of her. "Jace—"

"Shh. Stop being so bossy," Jace said softly. He reached for her other hand. "Eden," he said in a voice that seemed roughened, "I know I don't deserve you, and every day I'm amazed that you love me. You are a compassionate, beautiful, breathtaking woman, and more than anything, I'd like to share the rest of my life with you. You are the only woman for me, and I've been waiting for you my entire life. Will you marry me?"

Eden stared at him, words flushing out of her. She opened her mouth. Closed it.

"Eden? I . . . um . . . Well, you don't have to answer—"

"Yes." The word came out softly, too softly, so she said it again. "Yes, Jace Jacobsen, I will marry you."

The crowd around her erupted. Jace stood and caught her in his arms, twirling her around in the spotlight.

And then the houselights came on, full and bright and blinding her for a second as Jace set her back on the ice.

It was then that she saw them, gathered in the box, cheering. Her mother, wearing a wool headband in her hair, and her father, his blue eyes warm as he winked at her. Casper, grinning like he'd just won something, and Grace, clapping her mittens together. Amelia was holding up her phone, snapping a shot, and beside her, Darek held Tiger on his hip, his fiancée, Ivy, next to him wiping her cheeks.

Only Owen was missing, and his absence sent a sliver of sadness through her.

"How did you get them all down here?"

"Are you kidding me?" Jace grinned and hooked her around the waist. "They wanted rink-side seats for the big event."

She saw it in his eyes—the man he'd been, the man he would be. The champion, the husband. The father.

As he kissed her to the cheers of the crowd, it was just a little bit untamed, a little bit wild, heating up the ice around her.

And to Eden, it was exactly perfect.

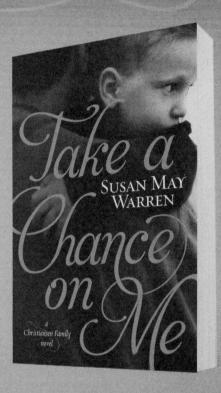

CHAPTER I

IVY MADISON would do just about anything to stay in the secluded, beautiful, innocent town of Deep Haven.

Even if she had to buy a man.

A bachelor, to be exact, although maybe not the one currently standing on the stage of the Deep Haven Emergency Services annual charity auction. He looked like a redneck from the woolly woods of northern Minnesota, with curly dark-blond hair, a skim of whiskers on his face, and a black T-shirt that read, *Hug a logger—you'll never go back to trees*. Sure, he filled out his shirt and looked the part in a pair of ripped jeans and boots, but he wore just a little too much "Come and get me, girls," in his smile.

The auctioneer on stage knew how to work his audience. He regularly called out names from the crowd to entice them to bid.

And apparently the town of Deep Haven loved their firefighters, EMTs, and cops because the tiny VFW was packed, the waitresses running out orders of bacon cheeseburgers and hot wings to the bidding crowd.

After the show was over, a local band would take the stage. The auction was part of the summer solstice festival—the first of many summer celebrations Deep Haven hosted. Frankly it felt like the village dreamed up events to lure tourists, but Ivy counted it as her welcoming party.

Oh, how she loved this town. And she'd only lived here for roughly a day. Imagine how she'd love it by the end of the summer, after she'd spent three months learning the names of locals, investing herself in this lakeside hamlet.

Her days of hitching her measly worldly possessions—four hand-me-down suitcases; a loose cardboard box of pictures; a garbage bag containing *The Elements of Legal Style*, *How to Argue and Win Every Time*, and *To Kill a Mockingbird*; and most of all, her green vintage beach bike—onto the back of her red Nissan Pathfinder were over.

Time to put down roots. Make friends.

Okay, *buying* a friend didn't exactly qualify, but the fact that her money would go to help the local emergency services seemed like a good cause. And if Ivy had learned anything growing up in foster care, it was that a person had to work the system to get what she wanted.

She should be unpacking; she started work in the morning. But how long would it take, really, to settle into the tiny, furnished efficiency apartment over the garage behind the Footstep of Heaven Bookstore? And with her new job as assistant county attorney, she expected to have plenty of free time. So when the twilight hues of evening had lured her into the romance of a walk along the shore-line of the Deep Haven harbor, she couldn't stop herself.

She couldn't remember the last time she'd taken a lazy walk, stopping at storefronts, reading the real estate ads pasted to the window of a local office.

Cute, two-bedroom log cabin on Poplar Lake. She could imagine the evergreen smell nudging her awake every morning, the twit-ter of cardinals and sparrows as she took her cup of coffee on the front porch.

Except she loved the bustle of the Deep Haven hamlet. Nestled on the north shore of Minnesota, two hours from the nearest hint of civilization, the fishing village–turned–tourist hideaway had enough charm to sweet-talk Ivy out of her Minneapolis duplex and make her dream big.

Dream of home, really. A place. Friends. Maybe even a dog. And here, in a town where everyone belonged, she would too.

She had wandered past the fudge and gift shop, past the walk-up window of World's Best Donuts, where the smell of cake donuts nearly made her follow her sweet tooth inside. At the corner, the music drew her near to the VFW. Ford F-150s, Jeeps, and a hand-ful of SUVs jammed the postage-stamp-size dirt parking lot.

She'd stopped at the entrance, read the poster for today's activi-ties, then peered in through the windows. Beyond a wood-paneled bar and a host of long rectangular tables, a man stood on the stage, holding up a fishing pole.

And that's when Deep Haven reached out and hooked her.

"Are you going in?"

She'd turned toward the voice and seen a tall, solidly built middle-aged man with dark hair, wearing a jean jacket. A blonde woman knit her hand into his.

"I . . ."

"C'mon in," the woman said. "We promise not to bite. Well, except for Eli here. I make no promises with him." She had smiled, winked, and Ivy could feel her heart gulp it whole. Oh, why had she never learned to tamp down her expectations? Life had taught her better.

Eli shook his head, gave the woman a fake growl. Turned to Ivy. "Listen, it's for a good cause. Our fire department could use a new engine, and the EMS squad needs more training for their staff, what few there are. You don't have to buy anything, but you might help drive up the bids." He winked. "Don't tell anyone I told you that, though."

She laughed. "I'm Ivy Madison," she said, too much enthusiasm in her voice. "Assistant county attorney."

"Of course you are. I should have guessed. Eli and Noelle Hueston." Noelle stuck out her hand. "Eli's the former sheriff. Hence the fact that we've come with our checkbook. C'mon, I'll tell you who to bid on."

Who to bid on?

Ivy had followed them inside, taking a look around the crowded room. Pictures of soldiers hung in metal frames, along with listings of member names illuminated by neon bar signs. The smells of deep-fried buffalo wings, beer, and war camaraderie were embedded in the dark-paneled walls.

A line formed around the pool table near the back of the room—what looked like former glory-day athletes lined up with their beers or colas parked on the round tables. Two men threw darts into an electronic board.

Then her gaze hiccuped on a man sitting alone near the jukebox, sending a jolt of familiarity through her.

Jensen Atwood.

For a moment, she considered talking to him—not that he'd know her, but maybe she'd introduce herself, tell him, *I'm the one who put together your amazing plea agreement.* Yes, that had been a hot little bit of legalese. The kind that had eventually landed her right here, in her dream job, dream town.

But Noelle glanced back and nodded for Ivy to follow, so she trailed behind them to an open table.

"Every year, on the last night of the solstice festival, we have a charity auction. It's gotten to be quite an event," Noelle said, gesturing to a waitress. She came over and Eli ordered a basket of wings, a couple chocolate malts. Ivy asked for a Coke.

"What do they auction?"

"Oh, fishing gear. Boats. Snowblowers. Sometimes vacation time-shares in Cancún. Whatever people want to put up for charity. But this year, they have something special on the agenda." Noelle leaned close, her eyes twinkling. Ivy already liked her. And the way Eli had her hand wrapped in his. What might it be like to be in love like that? That kind of love . . . well, Ivy had only so many wishes, and she'd flung them all at living here, in Deep Haven.

"What?" Ivy asked.

"They're auctioning off the local bachelors."

And as if on cue, that's when the lumberjack bachelor had taken the stage.

Ivy sipped her Coke, watching the frenzy.

"So are you going to bid?" Noelle asked.

Ivy raised a shoulder.

The lumberjack went for two hundred dollars—too rich for Ivy's blood—to a woman wearing a moose-antler headband. He flexed for her as he walked off stage, and the crowd erupted.

A clean-cut, handsome young man took the stage next, to the whoops of the younger crowd down front. "That's my son," Noelle said, clearly enjoying the spectacle. He seemed about nineteen or twenty, tall and wearing a University of Minnesota, Duluth, T-shirt. He was built like an athlete and had a swagger to match.

"He plays basketball for the UMD Bulldogs," Noelle said. She placed the first bid and got a glare from the young man on stage.

A war started between factions in the front row. "Should I bid?" Ivy asked. Not that she would know what to do with a bachelor ten years younger than her. Maybe she could get him to mow her lawn.

"No. Save your money for Owen Christiansen."

Probably another lumberjack from the woods, with a flannel shirt and the manners of a grizzly. Ivy affected a sort of smile.

"Maybe you've heard of him? He plays hockey for the NHL."

"No, sorry."

"He's something of a local celebrity. Played for our hometown team and then got picked up by the Minnesota Wild right after high school."

"I'm not much of a hockey fan."

"Honey, you can't live in Deep Haven and not be a hockey fan." Noelle grinned, turning away as the wings arrived.

Ivy ignored the way the words found tender space and stabbed her in the chest. But see, she wanted to live in Deep Haven . . .

Noelle offered her a wing, but Ivy turned it down. "Owen's parents, John and Ingrid Christiansen, run a resort about five miles out of town. It's one of the legacy resorts—his great-grandfather settled here in the early nineteen hundreds and set up a logging camp. It eventually turned into one of the hot recreation spots on the north shore, although in today's economy, they're probably struggling along with the rest of the Deep Haven resorts. I'm sure Owen's appearance on the program is a bid for some free publicity. Owen is the youngest son of the clan, one of six children. I'm sure you'll meet them—all but two still live in Deep Haven."

A redhead won the bachelor on stage and ran up to claim her purchase. Ivy escaped to the ladies' room.

What if she did bid on Owen? Truly, the last thing she needed in her life was a real bachelor. Someone she might fall for, someone who could so easily break her heart.

Maybe she could ask said bachelor to show her around Deep Haven. Teach her about hockey. Certainly it might give her a little social clout to be seen with the town celebrity.

She could faintly hear the announcer stirring up the fervor for the next contestant, then a trickle of applause for the main attraction as he took the stage. She walked out, standing by the bar to survey this hometown hero.

They grew them big up here in the north woods. Indeed, he looked like a hockey champion, with those wide shoulders, muscular arms stretching the sleeves of his deep-green shirt that read *Evergreen Resort—memories that live forever.* He stood at ease like one might do in the military, wearing jeans that hugged his legs all the way down to the work boots on his feet. The man looked like an impenetrable fortress, not a hint of marketing in his face. So much for winning the audience.

In fact, to use the only hockey term she knew, he looked like he'd just been checked hard into the boards and come up with some sort of permanent scowl, none too happy to be standing in the middle of the stage of the local VFW as the main attraction.

"C'mon, everyone, who will start the bidding for our Deep Haven bachelor tonight?"

Ivy looked around the room. It had hushed to a pin-drop silence, something not quite right simmering in the air. She glanced over to where Jensen Atwood had been sitting and found his seat vacant.

On stage, the man swallowed. Shifted. Pursed his lips. Oh, poor Owen. Her heart knocked her hard in the chest. She knew exactly what it felt like not to be wanted.

"One hundred dollars? Who has it tonight for our local hero?"

She scanned the room, saw patrons looking away as if embarrassed. Even Eli and Noelle had taken a sudden interest in their dinner.

Owen sighed and shook his head.

And right then, the pain of the moment squeezed the words from Ivy's chest. "Five hundred dollars!"

Every eye turned toward her, and for a moment, she had the crazy but horribly predictable urge to flee. But the words were out, so she took a step forward, toward the stage. "I bid five hundred dollars," she said again, fighting the wobble in her voice.

Ivy shot a look at Noelle, expecting approval. But Noelle wore an expression of what she could only pinpoint as panic. Wasn't she the one who'd suggested Ivy buy the man?

And then from the stage, she heard, "Well, that's good enough for me! Sold, to the pretty lady in the white jacket. Miss, come up to the stage and claim your prize."

Still, no one said a word—not a cheer, not a gasp, nothing. Ivy swallowed and met the eyes of the man on stage. "I'll meet him by the bar," she said, her voice small.

Owen looked as relieved as she was that they didn't have to create some public spectacle. He moved off the stage and the auctioneer mercifully introduced the band. The men in back resumed their pool playing.

Ivy couldn't help it. She edged over to Noelle. "What's the matter? I know he looks a little rough around the edges, but—"

"That's not Owen," Noelle said, wiping her fingers with a napkin. She shot a glance past Ivy, possibly at the stranger she'd just purchased.

"What?"

"Owen couldn't make it. That's Darek Christiansen. His big brother."

Ivy turned now, found her man weaving his way through the crowd. He didn't stop to glad-hand anyone or even slap friends on the back.

In fact, it seemed she'd purchased the pariah of Deep Haven.

Noelle confirmed it. "Brace yourself, honey. You've just purchased the most ineligible eligible bachelor in town."

A NOTE FROM THE AUTHOR

I AM IN A SEASON OF LETTING GO. First, my oldest son trotted off to college; then my beautiful daughter had the nerve to leave me. And just this year, my third child packed up his car and drove away.

I can admit the recent leaving might have been the most difficult. Oh, I cried buckets of tears over the first two, but with the college-going of my middle son also went the evenings of sitting in the football stands, watching him score touchdowns. I've logged thousands of hours in the car and in bleachers, back and forth to football and basketball games and to track meets. More than that, I gave my heart to my athlete, helping him through injury, defeats, and even victories. I've earned the title of jock mom. Thankfully, I still have one football player at home to root for.

Letting go has caused me to wonder, however, *How much of my identity have I put into my children's successes? Their losses?*

I am the first to admit that my darlings have made mistakes. Not life-altering ones, but serious enough that I've had to choose whether to get involved or to stand back and let life deal with them. Consequences are always powerful enforcers . . . but how far should you let your children fail? In sports, you learn you can't score the touchdowns for your kids or make baskets for them. But I admit I've been known to run down the bleachers, trying to keep up with my track star as he crosses the finish line, just to urge him on.

It pains me to see my children make mistakes. But without mistakes, they won't learn. And some of my best lessons have come from the mistakes I've made.

As I settled in to write this story, I was in a season of struggling to find the balance between stepping in and letting go—letting them fail. And I realized that their failures were neither my fault nor my responsibility to fix. If I truly wanted to support my kids, I needed to guide them toward their heavenly Father, so He could meet their needs.

Frankly, in letting go, I'm learning that God can meet my needs, too.

As I took a look at failure and letting go, I also began to wonder about the other side of it. A life redeemed. Can God take failure and turn it to victory? The Bible shows us over and over that He can and He does. And when He does, we find ourselves uniquely equipped for the next season in our lives. If we start seeing failure not as an end, but as a part of the journey, then suddenly our lives become not about regret, but about gratitude.

In fact, the story idea for *It Had to Be You* was birthed by this concept: what if God could take your regrets and redeem them? Hudson Peterson's track meet story actually happened. I was at a track meet, standing on the sideline watching this poor young man crumble as he realized his failures. The memory haunted me and I wondered, *What if? What if it destroyed him? How could he come back?*

Grace. We come back by reaching out to Jesus. By letting Him redeem our failures.

I am letting go. But I'm also holding on to my heavenly Father, who is at the helm of my children's lives—and my own. And thankfully He will never let go.

Thank you for reading *It Had to Be You*! I hope you are enjoying the Christiansen family as much as I am. Stay tuned for Grace Christiansen's story in *When I Fall in Love*. Here's a hint: you'll see our friend Max Sharpe again!

In His grace,
Susan May Warren

ABOUT THE AUTHOR

SUSAN MAY WARREN is the bestselling, Christy and RITA Award–winning author of more than forty novels whose compelling plots and unforgettable characters have won acclaim with readers and reviewers alike. She served with her husband and four children as a missionary in Russia for eight years before she and her family returned home to the States. She now writes full-time as her husband runs a resort on Lake Superior in northern Minnesota, where many of her books are set.

Susan holds a BA in mass communications from the University of Minnesota. Several of her critically acclaimed novels have been ECPA and CBA bestsellers, were chosen as Top Picks by *Romantic Times*, and have won the RWA's Inspirational Reader's Choice contest and the American Christian Fiction Writers' prestigious Carol Award. Her novel *You Don't Know Me* won the 2013 Christy Award, and five of her other books have also been finalists. In addition to her writing, Susan loves to teach and speak at women's events about God's amazing grace in our lives.

For exciting updates on her new releases, previous books, and more, visit her website at www.susanmaywarren.com.

DISCUSSION QUESTIONS

1. In her letter, Ingrid remembers that Eden has been a storyteller all her life. Do you think Eden recognizes that trait in herself? Why or why not?

2. Ingrid tells her daughter, "My prayer for you is that you would believe God has a good story for you, too." Have you ever struggled to believe that for yourself? If so, why?

3. Eden fears that she doesn't measure up to her talented siblings, that her only value is in being the family cheerleader. How would you describe the role you play in your family or the role you played while growing up? Do you think others would see it the same way?

4. Jace has lost some of his passion for hockey and knows that continuing to play poses serious risks, but he feels unable to do anything else. How would you have advised him in this situation? When you have faced a crossroads in your own life—whether in a career, a relationship, etc.—how did you decide what to do?

5. Despite warnings that she's too invested in Owen, Eden feels responsible for her brother, believing it's her duty to watch his back. How much responsibility should family members have for one another? Where do you think Eden goes too far?

6. Jace struggles with his role as an enforcer for the Blue Ox, wondering if the violence of his position makes him a monster—especially because he admits to sometimes enjoying the fights. John Christiansen suggests that Jace might like the applause and approval he receives better than the fighting. Do you think he's right? What makes fans cheer for the violence in sports?

7. Max Sharpe, one of Owen's teammates, worries he was the one who caused Owen's injury. Jace tells Max to keep this news from Owen. Do you think that is wise advice? What do you imagine would've happened if Max had confessed to Owen?

8. In chapter 9, after Owen is injured, his father talks with him about the role of suffering in our lives. Do you agree with John's perspective? In times of pain or difficulty, do you tend to get angry with God, as Owen does, or lean into Him?

9. As Maddy gets sicker, Sam has to consider whether he can provide for her in the way she needs or whether she would be better off in a medical foster home. What would you do in his situation?

10. During his visit to Deep Haven, Jace concludes that despite all she says, Eden *wants* headlines, wants to be part of Owen's and Jace's limelight. Yet when Jace gives her the

chance to share the spotlight with him, Eden runs. Why do you think she reacts this way?

11. Eden denies her feelings for Jace, insisting she wants a "normal" man. Why does Eden believe herself unworthy of a man like Jace? Have you ever felt undeserving of someone's love or affection? What words of wisdom would you give to Eden as she struggles between what she wants and what she believes she deserves?

12. While Jace knows he's been saved, he doesn't believe God could favor or even like him. Similarly, Eden feels as though she's "not necessarily God's favorite." Do you think God favors some people over others? What does it take for Jace and Eden to feel liked or favored by God? Have you ever struggled with similar questions about how God feels toward you?

13. Sam nearly makes a desperate, illegal decision out of his fear that God will let Maddy die. Has there been a time when you were tempted to take matters into your own hands on behalf of someone you love? What was the result?

14. When he sees an article about his migraines, Jace jumps to the conclusion that Eden is involved, damaging their relationship. Has a misunderstanding or snap judgment ever hurt one of your relationships? What does that relationship look like today?

15. Eden, Jace, and Sam all have to learn lessons about holding on too tightly. How does each character act on the realization that he or she needs to let go? Have you had to learn a similar lesson in your own life? Describe that time.

16. Eden feels that her attempt to help Hudson failed, but nurse Becky tells her, "You were God's plan to show Hudson that he was loved." Olivia and Jace also echo the idea that Eden was handpicked to find Hudson, connect him to his family, and tell his story. Do you think they're right? Have you ever felt that you were singled out by God for a particular task? What was it?

17. In her story about Hudson, Eden asks, "Is it possible to have a remarkable life by simply caring for someone else?" In your opinion, what makes someone heroic? How is heroism achieved? Through a person's actions, the way he or she lives, one's character?

18. By the end of *It Had to Be You*, both Eden and Jace have made decisions about the future of their careers. Were you surprised by their choices? Why or why not?

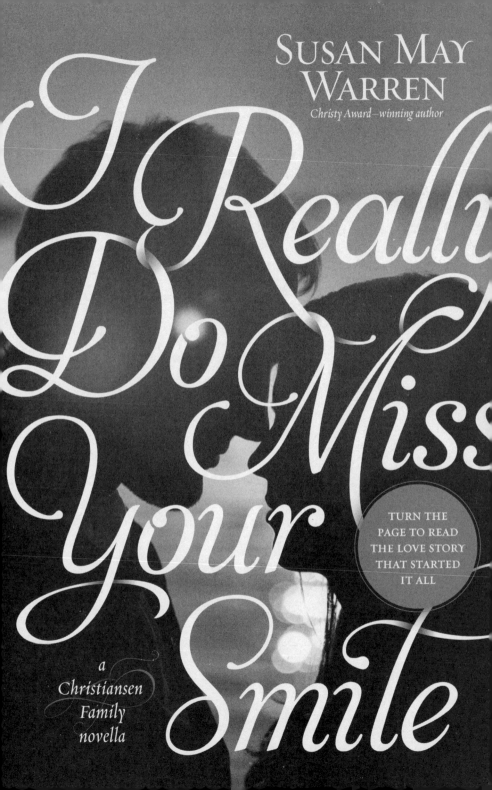

SUSAN MAY
WARREN

Christy Award–winning author

I Really
Do Miss
Your
Smile

TURN THE
PAGE TO READ
THE LOVE STORY
THAT STARTED
IT ALL

a
Christiansen
Family
novella

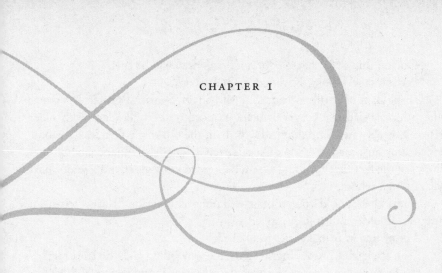

CHAPTER I

1976

Ingrid hadn't spent two years waiting for tonight to let her sister's threats scare her away.

Kari stood in the bathroom at the tiny mirror, spraying another layer of shellac on the long Farrah flick she'd taken an hour to craft. "I swear, if you embarrass me, I'm ditching you."

Of course she looked like a younger version of Farrah Fawcett, with that long blonde hair parted in the middle, finely plucked brows, the perfect pout to her glistening lips. The Deep Haven boys wouldn't be able to tear their eyes off her.

All except one. Hopefully.

Ingrid met her reflection in the mirror. "I won't embarrass you."

Kari narrowed her eyes, her gaze burning through Ingrid. "Fine. But not a word to Mom and Dad, or this is the last time you'll go anywhere with me."

Not a word to Mom and Dad about what? She didn't want to ask, to sound naive.

Kari studied her. "You need more blue eye shadow if you want to make an impression." She grabbed the powder. "Close your eyes."

Ingrid obeyed, feeling Kari's hands rough on her face as she painted her. Kari had already plowed through her suitcase, finally unearthing a pair of jeans and a plaid shirt, knotted at the waist over a tube top that her parents wouldn't see until after she left the house. She'd dressed Ingrid in a T-shirt and a pair of overalls.

"Do you think . . . that . . . John Christiansen will be there?"

"Perfect, take a look," Kari said, stepping back.

Ingrid glanced in the mirror. She wished she'd at least gotten her bangs cut. Still, she hadn't a prayer of being noticed next to her glamorous older sister. Not with her limp, long straight hair, the too many freckles. The blue eye shadow just made her look like a CoverGirl model wannabe. She put her hopes in the fact that Kari knew best, being two years older and a senior next year in high school.

"And I already told you, you have to unhook one side." Kari reached for Ingrid's shoulder, but Ingrid yanked away.

"I don't like it. It makes me feel naked."

"Don't be such a prude, Ingrid. Trust me, guys like a girl who tries a little."

The hair, the eye shadow, the overalls—this was Ingrid trying. "I don't like feeling undressed."

Kari rolled her eyes. "Johnny Christiansen won't notice you, anyway." She painted on another layer of lipstick. Popped her lips. "You need to get over your crush." She picked up her new woven purse. "Whatever you do, don't ask him to dance."

Don't ask him to dance? But she'd rehearsed it for the last six months. Saw herself walking up to John, her voice casual even as her heart hammered through her ribs, smiling up into his devastating blue eyes, his long, dark Robby Benson hair brushing the collar of his jean jacket as he leaned against the brick wall of the Ben Franklin, and . . . well, for the first time, he would see her.

He'd take her hand, lead her into the street, under the diamond starlight of the sky over Deep Haven, casting magic into the night as the band rolled out covers from the Doobie Brothers or Styx. The wind would carry enough tang of summer, the breeze off the lake fresh and mysterious. And as he put his hands at her waist, as she looped her arms around his neck, he would realize . . . Ingrid Young had grown up.

Yes, tonight, John would take his eyes off Kari and finally notice the girl from cabin 12.

Ingrid grabbed her bag, flung it over her shoulder, and raced after Kari as she headed down the gravel path toward the parking lot of Evergreen Resort. Kari made a point of standing on the gravel walkway and calling out to their parents, reading on Adirondack chairs by the lake. The canoes for guests lay on the beach like walleye, the water a tin gray, a streak of red parting the waves as twilight cascaded through the trees.

"Home by midnight!" their mother yelled back, waving. Their father looked up from the book on his lap—Ingrid recognized it as his Bible. He gave Kari a look, something of warning in it.

Ingrid's insides tightened a little. But this was Deep Haven, not Minneapolis. How much trouble could Kari get into, really?

Ingrid didn't glance at the lodge as she climbed into their father's red Pontiac. She knew the Christiansen family lived upstairs, knew that the new red-and-white Chevy pickup in the dirt lot belonged to John. He'd pulled it onto the grass this morning, and she'd seen him out with a bucket and suds on her way to town. He'd stopped Kari when they returned, offering to take her for a ride, a jar of Turtle Wax in his hand.

Ingrid could have strangled Kari for the way she lifted her nose, shook her head.

Take me for a ride. She'd tried to cover up for Kari's rudeness by complimenting the truck, but he just ducked his head, went back to polishing.

Maybe he'd finally figured out that Kari didn't like small-town boys. Even if they did have a summer tan and a nice set of football biceps, a smile that could make a girl forget that she wasn't the beautiful, long-legged cheerleader of the family.

"Remember, don't embarrass me," Kari said as she rolled down the window and tugged a pack of Benson & Hedges from her bag. Ingrid's eyes widened as her sister lit up and blew smoke out the window.

She looked away. Bit her lip.

Kari ejected the Pat Boone album and shoved in an 8-track of the Steve Miller Band.

"Where did you get that?"

Kari shrugged. "Contraband. You'll learn."

Ingrid had no doubt she'd learn a lot tonight.

The music lured them in as Kari parked the car off Main Street, then led Ingrid to the festivities. The town barricaded off all four blocks of Main, the street edging the harbor where the lake slid over the rocks in rhythm to the beat. A perfect night for the annual Fisherman's Picnic street dance. Kari slung her purse over her shoulder and added a swing to her hips as she forayed into the crowd. Mostly teenagers, some adults, groups of locals intermixed with the congregation of tourists who claimed Deep Haven during the summer. Like her parents, who'd rented the same cabin at Evergreen Resort for the last twenty years.

In a way, Ingrid had grown up with John, watched him go from annoying kid who pushed her off the dock to hunky football player who could sweep her breath from her lungs with a single blue-eyed look. Last year, during the precious hour her parents allowed her to attend the festival, Ingrid perched herself on the steps of the State Bank and glued her gaze on John, watching as he hung out with his pals, leaning against their trucks, flirting with girls like Kari.

This year, he'd flirt with her.

Kari walked right into a crowd of friends. Ingrid recognized some of them from past years—it seemed the same resort crowd trekked into town the same week every year. A couple faces she recognized from their school, down in Wayzata, a suburb of Minneapolis.

Ingrid stood at the outskirts, shooting her gaze in and through the crowds. The band started playing the first few bars of the new England Dan and John Ford Coley song.

"Wanna dance?" The words brought her back, but their aim was focused on Kari, who giggled and surrendered to the attentions of a letter-jacketed senior from Minneapolis. Craig. Brown hair, brown eyes, nothing spectacular, except that Kari put her arms around his neck, her body close.

Ingrid looked away, searching, and her heart stuttered in her chest when John parted the crowd and strode into a wash of streetlight, a rock star. He wore a jean jacket, a white T-shirt tucked into his jeans, a pair of tennis shoes, and when the wind raked his long, beautiful brown hair from his face, she couldn't breathe.

Now. She'd ask him now before her courage died. Besides, he was already heading toward the clump of dancers. She dashed out into the street, nearly knocked over a couple girls, and caught his arm.

"John?"

He turned as if startled and, for a second, seemed not to recognize her.

And why not? With her makeup and hair, she didn't resemble at all the tomboy fifteen-year-old he'd seen landing a fish off the dock this morning.

Thank you, Kari.

"Uh . . . hi, Ingrid." He had a low voice, and she could feel it touch her bones.

"Would you . . . would you dance with me?"

There. The words were out and she added a smile, tremulous at the edges. He frowned, looked at the dancers. Then at her. He smiled. "Sure."

She could barely walk as he took her hand and wove them through the crowd. She noticed how he planted her next to Kari, and Ingrid wound her arms around his neck.

They swayed to the music, his hands on her hips. She settled her cheek on his jacket. He smelled good—woodsy, with a touch of cologne, like he'd tried. She locked her fingers behind his neck.

"There's a warm wind blowing, the stars are out, and I'd really love to see you tonight."

She hummed to the song, then smiled at him.

He was looking over her shoulder, his gaze glued to someone behind him, his jaw tight. She glanced over her shoulder and spied Kari nestled up against Craig.

"I like your new truck."

He glanced at her. "Thanks." He smiled again, but up close, she realized it didn't touch his eyes.

She swallowed her heart back into her chest, let it burn there. He held his hands loosely on her waist even as she pressed her body close to him.

He sighed.

Then suddenly he moved his hands to his neck and grabbed her wrists. "I gotta go."

He unlatched her arms and pushed past her.

As she turned, she saw Kari leaving the dance floor, Craig in tow. And behind them, pressing through the gap in the crowd, John, hot on their trail.

Ingrid wrapped her arms around her waist, listening to the last of the song die into the night.

Whatever Kari Young saw in Mr. Letter Jacket, he had nothin' on John Christiansen. John just had to help her see it.

He hadn't spent the last day washing and waxing his new Chevy C10 to lose her in the arms of a guy from the city. He'd waited for this night an entire year, saving every dime, working after practice at the fish house, then snowplowing and even trapping on the property north of his place until he could pay cash for the truck.

He deserved Kari's attention tonight. So he was a year younger than her—he'd made varsity defensive end last year and had a flock of girls who chased him around the school.

And one look at her last Sunday as her family pulled into the resort told him she'd been worth the wait. She even smiled at him as he'd helped unload her father's Pontiac, brought their bags to the cabin. She leaned against the railing to the deck in those short shorts, her blonde hair long and feathered away from her face, and asked him if he planned on attending the Saturday night dance.

If that didn't sound like an invitation, what did?

He would have asked her to dance if it weren't for her pesky kid sister. Sure,

Ingrid wasn't a dog—not with that long silky blonde hair, but she had braces and was only fifteen, for pete's sake. Still, what was he going to do—brush her off and let it get back to his dad? Ingrid was a guest, after all.

He left the crowd, following Kari and Craig to the beach. Craig sat on the big rock jutting from the middle of the beach and reached for Kari, who giggled and settled her arms around his neck. Craig stuck his hands in her back pockets.

The sight turned John hot, and he probably lost a little of his mind when he closed in on them. "Hey, Craig, did you bring your wheels with you this year?"

Craig looked up, frowning, and Kari glanced over her shoulder. An enigmatic smile played on her beautiful lips, and he could nearly smell her sweet fragrance in the breeze.

"Yeah, so?"

"A bunch of us are going to the gravel pit. Not that you'd be interested." He hooked his thumbs in his pockets, casual. Like he couldn't care.

His heart thudded against his ribs.

"Yeah, sure, whatever." Craig reached for Kari's hand, but she broke away and turned to John.

"Was that your truck you were washing today?"

He nodded.

She pressed a hand to his shoulder. "It's pretty."

He managed to shrug, keeping it casual, not at all like his heart was nearly leaping from his body.

He scoped out the crowd for Nate and found him talking to a couple out-of-town girls, evidenced by their fancy hairdos and designer jeans. Lean and wiry and dressed in his cross-country letterman's jacket, Nate looked like he might score based on the grins the gals were giving him, but church-boy Nate wouldn't have a clue what to do with a couple city girls.

Not that John did, but he planned on figuring it out, should he get the chance. He motioned to Nate as he walked past, and his best pal jogged up to him. "What?"

"We're going to the gravel pit."

Nate raised an eyebrow but nodded, following him to the truck. He climbed into the cab, and a couple of John's football buddies landed in the bed, slapping the roof of the cab as John tore out of town and headed up Gunflint Trail toward the gravel pit.

A string of cars lined up in his rearview mirror: Craig in his fancy red Jeep,

Kari riding shotgun, her sister behind her—hair wild in the wind—another car full of resort kids . . . probably Nate's chicks somewhere in the mix.

Last year, Bradley and his Camaro challenged Craig to a drag race along Country Road 44.

Craig edged up beside John on the narrow road, then punched it hard and flew past him, spitting up rocks onto John's new paint job.

"Think again, jerk!" John floored it and moved out into the left lane.

"Dude, it's dark—I'd rather not die tonight," Nate said.

"Hey! Everything's copacetic. Chill." John gripped the wheel and whooped out the window as he passed the Jeep. Kari sat with her pretty feet up on Craig's dash. Behind her, Ingrid held onto the roll bar with a death grip. John laughed as he flew past them, his headlight slicing through the darkness. "Bam! That's right—in your face!"

He hit the brakes and skidded into the entrance of the gravel pit, letting his truck spin up dirt as it stopped. The Jeep rolled in behind him, screaming Zeppelin, followed by two more cars. His football pals jumped over the bed, high-fived him.

Kari climbed out of Craig's Jeep, but John noticed that she stood slightly apart from him, her arms akimbo. She wore the kind of smile that could make John do crazy things.

Like, "Can your pansy-rich-boy Jeep climb to the top of that?" He pointed to the gravel hill, some thirty feet high.

For the first time, Craig's expression slacked, a little muster falling away. *Yeah, that's right, cheese head.* This was north woods, real-man stuff.

"No problem. Let's rock it."

Craig climbed back into the Jeep, cranked up his radio.

Ingrid had joined her sister, and Kari looked at her, frowning, then lifted her fist. "C'mon Craig!"

That stung, but she'd change sides before the night was over.

Craig shifted into gear and gunned it toward the gravel pit, the headlights shining against the gray metal of the gravel. His wheels dug in and he churned up the side, grinding his way ten feet high, maybe more.

Then the night burned with the sickly sound of the car coughing, spitting up gravel, the wheels clogged. The Jeep ground to a halt, beaten.

Cursing. Craig put it into reverse and backed it down. Got out, folded his hands across his chest. Glared. "Your turn."

"Catch ya on the flip side." As John got into his truck, he glanced at Kari. She looked at Craig, then back to him.

Suddenly she stepped up to him, hanging on his open window. "Can you really do this?"

"Of course, babe."

She wore mischief in her eyes. "Far out."

He gave Nate a thumbs-up and gunned it. The truck hit the wall too hard, but the force gave it enough momentum to charge up the gravel. He passed Craig's sinkhole, slowing but still climbing. Higher, past halfway.

And that's when the ground started to give out. He felt the truck rock over to the driver's side, and he made the mistake of gunning it.

The left wheels stopped turning, the right churning up pellets with the force.

Then the truck flipped, right onto its side. The momentum pushed him over, and then again, rolling down the hill, faster, like a log.

John braced himself, slamming against the door, the far window, pain flashing through him.

The sickening crunch of metal filled his ears as his world turned black.

He slipped in and out of the shadows against a blur of sounds, his face wet, his head on fire. Somewhere in the background he made out Nate's voice, but he couldn't be sure what he said.

Again, darkness.

"Johnny boy, wake up."

The voice drew him out of the cottony grip of unconsciousness, and he blinked against the harsh lights overhead. He felt fuzzy around the edges, gray pressing into his peripherals.

Nate stood above him, blood on his letter jacket, his eyes dark, even angry. "Man, Johnny. You could've gotten killed."

The Deep Haven ER. John recognized the desk, the array of medical condiments on the painted cart, the smells of regret. And was that Nate's mom at the trauma desk? Oh no.

Which meant his dad would find out. "My truck. Don't tell me—"

"It's pretty wrecked."

He groaned. "That's just aces."

"And you knocked yourself out. Got about ten stitches in your head there where you hit the glass. Broke out your side window."

John just wanted to close his eyes, sink back into the darkness.

Nate folded his arms over his chest. "You did manage to make a friend, though. She kept the pressure on your cut all the way to the hospital. I think she likes you, man." Nate winked.

A friend? Kari—

The voice came into the room before her, sweet and kind, and for a second, he had no words for the blonde who came to his bedside. "I found him some water. Oh, you're awake."

He hadn't exactly seen her before, not really, and for a second he took a good look at her freckles, the long blonde hair parted in the middle, a little too much makeup on her—okay, yes—sorta pretty face. She wore a pair of overalls and smiled down at him, so much concern in her eyes that he felt like a first-class jerk.

"Hi," she said. "I'm glad you're okay. You scared us a little."

He smiled back at her, reached for the glass. "Thanks, Ingrid."

CHAPTER 2

1977

John Christiansen had no right to ignore her. Not after she'd held pressure to his wound, fetched him water, and even helped him lie to his parents about the accident.

Ingrid had spent the year remembering that moment when she'd pushed back the hospital curtain, holding the glass of water, and he'd looked up at her, surprise on his face. Sure, it faded in a second, and then, after a moment, he'd loosened up, and they'd collaborated on a story to tell his parents.

Not that she liked lying, but . . . well, maybe it showed him that she could be trusted. That they could be friends.

She'd spent a year preparing for this week in Deep Haven, losing a few pounds, scouting through Kari's wardrobe to find the right attire. She'd even purchased some contraband *Cosmopolitan* magazines to teach her how to apply makeup.

She deserved notice this year. Especially since Kari boycotted the trip north. Without her beautiful big sister to distract him, John would see Ingrid and realize that he missed her, even if just a little.

But ever since her arrival, he'd dodged her. Like when she went to the outfitter's shack to offer to help him pack up supplies for a group of adventurers. He'd barely acknowledged her presence as he filled Duluth Packs with camping equipment and homemade granola.

And then later, when he'd hung out at the dock, she'd worn her new red bathing suit, the one-piece that tied behind her neck and showed off her curves.

He'd barely looked at her, even when she dove off the dock, swam out to the floating platform.

Finally, last night at the campfire, she'd watched him through the flames, sitting across from her, laughing at one of his sister's jokes. "Your marshmallow's about to burn," she said, one second before it torched.

He'd jumped up, shaken it, and didn't even look at her. As if it were her fault it turned to ash.

Now Ingrid stared at her choices, laid out on the bed. She'd planned on wearing a jumpsuit, one of her sister's discards, with a red scarf at her neck. Instead, she reached for the jeans, a halter top, a jean jacket.

If he was going to ignore her, then she'd ignore him, too. She pulled on the jeans, the top, then parted her hair in the middle and gathered it into two long ponytails.

She should stop trying to be Kari. John Christiansen simply wasn't going to notice her, and she had to stop dreaming.

"Back by ten," her father said as he handed her the keys to the Pontiac. She refused to search for John, to glance at the basketball court or maybe the grilling deck as she left the resort.

But his battered truck, which now looked a little like crinkled newspaper, wasn't in the lot.

The summer sun warmed her arm as she hung it out the window, heading toward town. The sultry smell of campfires lingered in the air; the lazy sound of a band seasoned the festivities as she pulled into town and found a spot next to the drive-in ice cream parlor.

Sawhorses cordoned off the four blocks where vendors hawked fish cakes, popcorn, and cotton candy. Down the street, she heard the whine of a chain saw and spied, on a stage, two contestants sawing apart a log. Wood chips flew from the power; dust feathered the air.

On the beach, tourists lounged on picnic blankets while children threw rocks into the waves of Lake Superior, indigo blue under the clear skies.

The whirring stopped, and she turned back, saw one of the contestants pounding his fist into the air.

The announcer introduced the next contestants. Her breath caught in her chest when she heard John's name.

He mounted the platform, and she just stared. He wore a black T-shirt, a pair of faded flared-bottom jeans, and work boots. His shaggy dark hair stuck out of a mesh gimme cap, and he appeared bigger, stronger, his body chiseled from those hours as a football player. She'd heard from her parents' conversation with Mr. and Mrs. Christiansen that he'd made varsity defense last year.

He ripped the chain saw's cord, holding the machine as if it were a toy. It roared to life, and he gunned it.

Then the starter pistol cracked, and he set the saw onto the log, about the size of a tire, chewing through it, first down, then back up, shearing off a chunk of wood five inches deep. It fell like a saucer onto the pile of sawdust, and he lifted the saw above his head. They announced his time, and she didn't care how he did.

Clearly she hadn't a hope of ignoring John Christiansen.

Ingrid stayed in the crowd, standing just far enough away to watch him as he jumped off the platform, glad-handed his football pals, local boys who'd emerged from the woods for the festival. Most of them worked as trail guides or loggers during the summer months.

The tourists—big-city kids—mingled in their own cadre of camaraderie, smoking and eyeing the local girls, who'd dolled up for the weekend festival. John made it to the final two, fighting it out against a Paul Bunyan the size of an ox. The crowd went wild when the hometown boy won the match.

Ingrid tried not to be pitiful as she lingered behind John and his friends. She wasn't spying, just . . .

"Hey, John, sign up for the fish toss! Let's see if you can win that, too!"

She watched as they stopped in front of the booth, his buddies scribbling their names to register. She recognized Nathan, John's friend from the hospital. He'd filled out this past year, his hair long, to his shoulders. He wore a cast on his arm.

John shook his head. "And who am I going to toss with, dude?" He gave Nathan a push and grinned.

"But you have a title to defend."

"Yeah, our title. If you hadn't decided to go dirt-biking—"

"I'll do it with you."

The words issued from her mouth before she could stop them, and they had the effect of parting the crowd. John turned, looked at her, and for a second, time stopped, her heart lodging in her ribs.

His blue eyes darkened and he frowned, took a breath.

"Hey, yeah. I remember you. Ingrid, right?" This from Nathan, who stepped past John and drew his arm around her shoulders. "You were there last year, after the accident."

"Nate—" John started, warning in his tone. But Nathan directed her toward the booth.

"You're a guest at Evergreen Resort, right?"

She nodded as he shoved a pencil in her hand.

"See, John. She'll help you defend your honor."

But John didn't move. "I don't need help defending anything."

She wrote down her name, then turned and handed him the pencil.

He stared at her. The first time in a week, he looked at her.

He was angry with her. She read it in his pursed lips, the way he sighed. And the look of annoyance in his eyes.

Like maybe she knew too much. Like maybe he didn't want her remembering his mistakes. No, he hadn't just been ignoring her. He'd been trying to erase her.

She bit her lip, turned back to the sheet, and began to scratch out her name.

"Fine. Yeah. Let's toss a fish."

Her eyes burned, and she blinked back moisture. "No, forget it."

"I said yes, okay?" He came up behind her and nearly grabbed the pencil from her grip. "Yes."

"No, I don't want to—"

"Ingrid."

She looked away from him, but he leaned down, found her eyes. And made a face. "I'm sorry. It's cool. C'mon, for Evergreen?" Then he gave her a one-sided, chagrined smile.

She couldn't speak, but she didn't stop him from penciling in his name next to hers.

His hand on her arm burned as he led her away to the ice chest to choose a slimy northern pike to toss.

She stared at the fish, stiff and clammy. "You don't have to do this."

"Yeah, actually, I do." He leaned down, picked up a fish. "Really, I'm sorry I'm such a jerk."

She stared at the fish—the gray-black skin shiny, the eye bulging out of its long, lean head almost as if it might be in shock. "What do I do with it?"

"We stand apart and toss it. You gotta catch it, or we're out. Then we take a step back and repeat. The last team to catch the fish wins."

She held out her hands, and he dumped the fish into it. It smelled, and slimy goo slipped off its body onto her skin.

John laughed and she looked at him. "What?"

"Your expression. It's priceless."

"This is gross."

"Mmm-hmm," he said. He reached out and pulled one of her ponytails. "I have to admit, Ingrid, you're nothing like Kari."

He shook his head, walking away, and she wasn't sure that was a compliment.

She wouldn't last the first round. John watched Ingrid's nose wrinkle as she handled the fish, trying to find a grip along its slimy body, and he just barely stopped himself from shaking his head in defeat.

He should have simply walked away. The second she piped up from where she'd been shadowing him, he should have pretended not to hear her. But then Nate had to go and rope her in and . . .

Right then, the image of her standing in the hospital a year ago, looking so worried, so compassionate, blood staining her overalls, rushed at him, and he just froze.

It wasn't her fault that Kari left the gravel pit with Craig, that John's parents—when they discovered his lie—had grounded him for six months. That his truck resembled a crushed can of Tab. Seeing her this week brought it all back, along with the searing prick of humiliation, and he'd done his best to dodge her.

Until now.

What he'd seen in her blue eyes, something raw and desperate . . . he'd recognized it. He'd stared at his own desperation in the mirror more times than he could remember this year, longing to yank back his stupid challenge to Craig.

Clearly Ingrid hadn't gotten over her crush on him. He wasn't stupid—he saw how she followed him, how she'd tried to get his attention by diving off the dock, making a big deal about swimming out to the floating platform. And at the campfire, her invasive gaze kept him from paying attention. He'd nearly lit the forest on fire with his marshmallow.

All the same, as she stood there in front of his friends, in front of Deep Haven, he just couldn't hurt her.

Besides, if his father found out he'd turned down a longtime guest at the resort . . . well, he might just be grounded for another six months.

So he'd toss her the fish, she'd drop it, and they'd all go home happy.

"Let's practice," he said and gave her a grin his father would be proud of.

She stepped back, grabbing the fish behind the gills with both hands. "It's really slippery."

He laughed. "It's a fish. Have you ever caught a football before?"

She shook her head. "But I play volleyball and softball."

Really? He didn't know that. Which accounted for the way she swam out to the floating dock, the strength with which she pulled herself out of the water. And yes, he'd noticed her curves as she wrung out her hair. He was a red-blooded male after all.

"You want to hold the fish with two hands underneath it." He took the fish, showing her how to grip it behind its gills with one hand, the other around the small of its body, right before the tail. "You'll sort of launch the fish at me, keeping the head up, so it lands in my hands the same way."

He tossed the fish at her, and to his shock, she caught it.

So maybe they'd last the first round.

"If you have to, get your body into it. You can pin it to yourself, hug it to keep it from sliding away."

"Gross."

He laughed, but his smile vanished as they practiced.

Wow. Nothing like Kari at all. In fact, he couldn't even imagine Kari touching the fish, let alone cradling it in her arms. "Just keep a tight hold on it, and don't let it wiggle away."

She looked at him, her eyes big, and nodded.

She had pretty eyes. Blue with flecks of green around the edges. Like the lake on a sultry summer day. He hadn't really noticed that before.

The announcer called for them to line up, and he took a spot next to Eli Hueston, a running back a couple years younger than himself. "You're going down, Hueston."

Eli grinned at him. "You're throwing with a girl."

He had John there. John held out his hands. "Okay, don't overthrow—"

She swung it toward him, stronger than he'd expected, and he caught it with both hands, just above his shoulder.

"Sorry!"

So maybe she had the arm strength to get them to round two.

Eli had also caught his fish, along with the string of other locals. Only a couple tourists at the end had dropped their catch. The entire line backed up.

"Ready?"

She nodded and crouched as if she might be ready to field a grounder, and he had to grin at the determination on her face. He flung the fish, and she bit her bottom lip as she held out her hands, catching it like a pro.

Her face lit up, bright and sweet. "Got it!"

Two more contestants went down, and they backed up.

"Northern pike comin' your way!" She flung it hard, and he took a step back catching it away from his body. The fish had begun to dry; it made it easier to hold.

Which was probably why she caught the next pass, twirling in a circle with the momentum. She held the fish above her head to the roar of the crowd.

He looked down the row, saw that only Eli, himself, and two others remained.

Ingrid grinned at him, bent low, warmed up with a swing, and then let the fish fly.

He caught it, but it slipped and he bobbled it. Finally he wrapped his arms around it and hugged it to his body, the head near his own.

"Getting friendly with the marine life, Johnny boy?" Nate called. John made a face at him but grinned when two more contestants went down.

He and Eli remained. John blew out a breath.

Eli went first, and John watched the fish soar through the air toward Clay Nelson. He held his breath as Clay bobbled it, and then the pike dropped with a smack onto the pavement.

A groan released from the crowd. John glanced at Ingrid, and she had him in her gaze, something solid and calm in her expression. She smiled, and strangely, he felt it slide over him, through him, and touch his bones.

He nodded, took a step, and flung the fish.

He tossed it poorly. Short and high, like a pop fly, and he groaned.

But she moved like a softball player, getting under it, her eyes following it down as she held out her arms, angling for the right catch.

It smacked into her embrace, and she curled it into her body.

The crowd roared as she turned to John. Then she held the fish high like a trophy, slime covering her tank top, grinning as if she'd won the World Series.

He came toward her as she dropped the fish. Without thinking, he swept her up in a hug. More instinct than intent, it just felt right to pull her to himself, swing her around. Her arms went around his neck, and her body molded to his, small, strong, as if they fit.

It jolted him, this sudden closeness, and heat zapped through him, a surprising rush of warmth.

Appreciation. Respect—that's what he'd call it. He put her down, and she looked up at him, drinking him in with those way-too-pretty eyes.

And he realized if he didn't watch himself, he'd be in big trouble. Because no, Ingrid was nothing at all like her sister.

CHAPTER 3

1978

This summer, Ingrid would end it in John Christiansen's arms. Not just because she'd been dreaming of this night for more than three years, and not just because it just might be their last opportunity, but because she'd seen it in his eyes.

Last summer, as the band played the Bee Gees's "How Deep Is Your Love," he'd started across the street toward her, the interest in his gaze telling her that maybe, in the course of one evening, he'd stopped seeing her as Kari's kid sister and instead considered her something more. Or different.

If it weren't for some pretty local girl intercepting him, it would have been Ingrid with her arms laced around his neck, breathing in the smell of sawdust and woods on his skin.

And then, to make curfew, she'd had to leave the dance, the stars still sprinkling romance on the evening. She'd waited up on the deck of the cabin, though, relieved when his truck lights skimmed across the trees before midnight.

As her father said, nothing good ever happened after midnight. Not that John was that type of guy. One reason her family kept returning to Evergreen Resort was Sunday church service by the lake. Her dad liked the way John's father, Chester, preached in his moccasins. John was one of the good ones, and this year, she just knew he'd give her his heart.

She hoped he liked her hair. Bangs, and she'd spent an hour curling the ends. Kari would be proud of her, although who knew when she'd ever see it—her sister hadn't returned home from her trip to California after she graduated from high school. One year and only sporadic calls. John should be grateful Kari hadn't broken his heart, too.

Ingrid pulled on an orange sundress, then slipped her feet into a pair of flip-flops. She didn't know when she'd felt so pretty.

"Midnight?" she asked her father, who sat on the deck reading a newspaper in the lamplight.

He swatted away a mosquito. "Eleven."

"Daddy, I'm not Kari."

He looked up at her, his lips pursed.

"Please?"

"Midnight, not a second later."

She popped a kiss on his check and grabbed the keys to the new Ford Country Squire wagon.

Air Supply's new album played on the 8-track, and she hummed along as she drove to Deep Haven. She'd hardly seen John this week—he'd taken a group out to the Boundary Waters for a canoe trip and returned only last night. She'd watched him this morning as he dove off the pier, swam out to the floating dock and back. Then he'd taken his canoe out onto the lake and spent the rest of the morning fishing.

Probably working on his summer tan. He'd filled out over the year; she'd read in an old copy of the Deep Haven newspaper that John made all-conference in football, had accepted a scholarship to the University of Minnesota.

Which meant that he'd forget about her unless she made an impression.

If she could find him, that was. As the band played on the stage, she wandered through the crowds, teenagers smoking in groups on the sidewalks, youngsters throwing rocks into the lake, couples dancing in the street. A thumbnail moon hung over the dark water as if smiling. Approving.

She leaned against a park bench, rubbing her arms as the wind came up, prickling her skin. Certainly he wouldn't miss the Saturday night dance.

"Ingrid? Did you come alone?" She turned and smiled at Nathan, John's friend. He wore a pair of dark-red polyester pants, a wide-collared print shirt, looking every inch the future college boy.

"No . . . well, yes. I was looking for John."

"He's here somewhere." He held out his hand. "But you look so pretty, you should be dancing."

She smiled again and took his hand. It was smooth and warm. He led her to the street, wound his arms around her waist.

She kept herself apart, her arms loose across his shoulders. "So where are you going to college next year?"

He shook his head. "I'm not. I had a scholarship at Winona State, but . . ." He lifted a shoulder. "I'm just going to stick around here for a while." His eyes had gone dark, hooded, but she didn't press.

She propped her chin on his shoulder, and as he turned her, she saw him. John, wearing a plaid shirt, jeans, and a canvas jacket, leaning against a streetlamp.

He stared at her without a smile, his gaze fixed. She stilled for a moment, and Nathan released her. "Are you okay?"

She nodded, forced a smile. Glanced past his shoulder. John hadn't moved from his perch under the glow.

Nathan followed her gaze. "Oh," he said, then gave her a wry smile. "Thanks for the dance."

She knew she should finish the dance, but John had the power to make her forget anyone else. She walked toward him as he pushed away from the lamp. "Hey," he said.

"Hi."

Football had sculpted him, his muscles chiseled, his shoulders broad. He'd cut his dark hair, but it still hung over his face. The wind combed it back, revealing his too-blue eyes. "You look nice," he said quietly. "Real pretty."

She bit her lip, hiding a smile.

He looked her up and down. "Let's get out of here."

She didn't resist when he took her hand, pulling her down the street. He motioned to a motorcycle.

"This is yours?"

"Yep. Traded in the truck." He strapped a helmet below her chin, his hands brushing her skin. He met her eyes then, and his expression softened. "I was hoping I'd see you tonight."

Oh. Any lingering worry left her and she climbed onto the back of his bike, wrapped her arms around his body. He was solid and warm despite the wind teasing her dress. He drove her through town, then down to the rec park. He slowed and took the bike off-road, onto the trail back to Honeymoon Bluff.

She'd heard of the place, the bald hill that overlooked the lake. Kari's stories tripped through her head.

A shiver threaded through her, but she hung on as he gunned it up the hill. They stopped at the apex, and he put his foot down, moved the bike back onto the kickstand.

"Wow," she said as she stared out over the inky lake. The moon teased a finger of light across the surface, and in the distance out on the water, a freighter's lights winked in the darkness.

"Yeah," he said, but when she turned, his gaze wasn't on the water. He helped her off the bike, held her hand, and found a place in the grass for them to sit.

She sat next to him, smoothing her skirt. The wind raked up gooseflesh and she shivered again. John shucked off his jacket and settled it over her shoulders. A gentleman, John was, despite his quiet mood. Maybe he was nervous, too.

"You were gone all week," she said and then realized it sounded as if she might be desperate, might have been pining for him.

"I know." He picked up a long blade of grass and slipped his fingernail into it, splitting it down the middle. "I saw you, though. This morning. I was going to say hi but . . ." He put the grass to his lips, blew, and whistled into the night.

"But?"

He blew out a breath, tossed the grass away. "But I'm going away in a couple weeks, and . . . I wasn't sure it was such a great idea."

"What are you talking about?"

"I'm going to the university to play football."

"I know," she said softly.

He turned to her then, something she couldn't read in his eyes. He reached out and touched her hair, twirling his finger through her curls. "I like your hair tonight. It reminds me of Kari's."

Oh. She tried not to let that bother her.

He let her hair slip from his touch. "I just don't want you to get hurt."

"Why would I get hurt?"

He met her eyes then. Touched her face, drawing his fingertips down her cheekbone. "I probably won't be back. So I was thinking that tonight is our last night together."

Maybe. Or not. She leaned into his hand, kept her eyes on his.

He moved his hand behind her neck, leaned forward, and kissed her.

She'd never been kissed before, wasn't sure exactly how to react. Should she stay still or maybe move her lips like he did? She opted to leave them pliable and soft, to drink in the taste of him and let him nudge her mouth open, to deepen his kiss. It sent a thrill through her, sparks that touched her stomach, and she didn't stop him when he moved closer, winding his hand around her waist and leaning her back onto the grass.

He kissed her neck, leaving a trail of heat prickling her skin, and she trembled.

"John?"

He held her in the crook of his arm and raised his head. "Yeah?"

"Do you love me?"

He stilled, frowned. Then shrugged. "Yeah. I love you." He bent to kiss her again.

But with his words, something shifted, a darkness pooling in her gut, an acid climbing up her throat. He kissed her neck, then her lips. His hand moved northward, off her waist.

She shook her head, wriggling away from him. "No."

He looked up, frowning. "What? I thought this is what you wanted."

She turned away from him, her eyes burning, horrified when a cold tear dropped on her lips, still on fire with his touch. "I thought so, too. I don't know what's wrong with me."

She wrapped her arms around herself, wishing she hadn't left his jacket in the grass.

He scooted closer to her. "I thought . . . I mean . . . You agreed that this was our last night together."

She glanced at him over her shoulder. "But I didn't mean . . . Well, I'm not Kari."

"Obviously." His mouth formed a tight line.

She turned away. Hated the pleading in her voice. "Maybe we could . . . we could write to each other."

"Yeah, sure." He got up, held out his hand. "C'mon, I'll take you back to the dance."

She stared at his outstretched hand, more tears forming. "But . . . couldn't we just sit here for a while?"

"It's called Honeymoon Bluff for a reason, honey."

She stood then, meeting his eyes. "You're going to do just fine at the university." Then she brushed past him, nearly running back down the hill toward town.

Maybe it was a good thing she'd never see John Christiansen again.

He wasn't sure what had happened, but this night hadn't turned out remotely like he'd planned. Or hoped.

He'd spent the better part of a year plotting this evening, how he'd wipe any lingering doubt from Ingrid's mind that he might not be as exciting as a city guy—cool, aloof, the kind of guy a girl might find irresistible.

"Ingrid, c'mon, get on." He revved the bike near her, not wanting to scare her, wishing he could roll back the night and restart it. He'd tell her how he'd raced to town tonight, hoping she'd be around and how his heart felt a little black when he'd spied her dancing with Nate. How that orange dress, her hair long and curled, had made him forget last year's smell of fish, the way she used to drive him crazy, and how all that changed somehow until he just wanted to take her into his arms.

And then his brain stopped working. The feel of her in his arms, soft and smelling so good—flowers, maybe—and the sense of anticipation on her lips.

He'd lost himself a little.

No, a lot.

When she'd pushed him away, he'd been embarrassed. Now it seemed he couldn't fix it.

"I'm not going anywhere with you, John. You're not the boy I thought you were."

He winced at that, trying not to let her words sear his chest. But she was right—for a moment there he hadn't recognized himself, either.

He could still feel her in his arms, feel her hair between his fingers, taste her on his lips.

He'd kissed a few girls before, but no one like Ingrid. No one with such innocence, such wonder in her touch.

Yeah, he didn't deserve her. But she had no right to treat him like he'd . . . like he'd attacked her.

"I know I screwed up. Just—please, let me explain!"

She stopped so abruptly, the motorcycle whizzed past her. He had to stop, pull it up on its kickstand, then climb off and race back to her.

She stood under a tall oak, the shadows pooling around her. The music from the street reached out as if to reel them in. The lights of the town sparkled, fireworks against the murky water.

She folded her arms across her chest, her face tight. "I'm listening."

He swallowed and reached for her, but she backed away. "Okay, yeah, I know maybe I went a little too far. It's just . . . I wanted to impress you."

"By being rude to me?" She shook her head, started to brush by him, but he stepped in front of her.

"I'm not always going to be small-town," he said. "You have to know that."

She frowned. "But being small-town is what I like about you."

"But I don't want you to. I'm headed for big things. I'm going to play professional football . . . and well, I might never come back here."

She frowned at him. "Of course you will."

He shook his head. "Don't you get it? I have to leave, or I'll be stuck here forever. Running the resort like my dad. I don't want that."

"I get it," she said softly, so much sadness in her eyes, he realized that no, she didn't get it. Not at all.

She brushed past him then, and he let her go. He could find a dozen girls at the dance who might want to watch the stars with him on Honeymoon Bluff.

He parked the bike and headed over to a group of girls. He knew one of them, a regular from the rental cabins down the shore. A short blonde, she smoked a cigarette, and he reached for it, took a drag, then handed it back to her. She smiled at him, so he pulled her onto the dance floor.

He danced with each of her friends, watching for Ingrid to return. When she did, her face looked chapped under the streetlights, as if she'd been crying. He turned away, smiled at the girl he was dancing with, and gave her a long kiss.

She tasted of an ashtray. She tried to pull him to the beach, but he shook his head and disentangled himself.

He spied Ingrid talking to Nate. She was rubbing her arms, and Nate slipped off his jean jacket and put it around her shoulders. John's gut tightened.

Why did he care so much about this stupid girl? Sure, she was a babe, and yeah, she'd kissed him like he meant something to her. But he didn't have time for a girlfriend, not with football camp starting in a week.

Maybe we could write. Yeah. Like he would remember her name in a year.

Still, he sat on a rock, settled in the shadows, watching as she let Nate buy her cotton candy. She laughed, but he decided it could only be fake.

To his relief, she left early, long before the band stopped playing. He got on his motorcycle and followed her home at a distance, just to make sure. He turned off his lights, and after she'd parked and found her way to her cabin, he pulled in, parking the bike behind the house, and headed out to the end of the dock.

He couldn't swallow away the lump lodged in his throat as he sat and leaned back on his hands, staring at the stars. He'd destroyed something tonight, and it bugged him that he even cared.

He'd just been trying to have some fun like every other guy down at the festival.

He didn't see his father's shadow until it loomed over him, until the scent of his Old Spice seasoned the breeze. He glanced over his shoulder, saw his pop standing behind him, wearing a flannel shirt, an old cap, hands in his jean pockets.

"What are you doing out here?" John said.

"I thought I'd take the canoe out, see if I couldn't get a better look at the stars."

John frowned at him but shrugged and got up, following his father to shore to help put their canoe in the water. They'd spent the better part of the last four years building the wooden canoe from scratch. They'd found and cut the wood, molded the pieces to fit, from the ash gunwales and the cherry decks to the caned seats and even the cedar strips that comprised the body. His father had carved their names into the smooth maple yoke and kept the canoe protected from the guests.

Now, they toted it to the water, letting it slide into the dark, murky surface of the lake, the moonlight icing the waves with a soft gleam. His father climbed into the bow, picking up a paddle on the way, and John took the stern.

They slipped out onto the lake, quiet, soundless. A loon mourned over the surface of the water. His father kept paddling until they reached the center, then set the paddle across the bow to drift.

John brought his paddle to his knees. The exertion of paddling had eased the knot from his chest, but something inside him still ached.

"Seeing the sky spilled out like this brings a hymn to mind." His father began to hum, and John heard the words in his head. *"O Lord my God! When I in awesome wonder consider all the worlds Thy hands have made . . ."*

He didn't join in, just listened to his father hum, consumed with the terrible urge to tell him about tonight. But despite their hours together, working the resort, building the canoe, he'd never quite found the right time—or the courage—to tell him the truth.

John took a breath. "I'm not coming back, Dad."

His father stopped humming, but he didn't turn.

"If you're expecting me to take over the resort . . . I'm planning on playing football."

He saw the old man's profile as he nodded. "I know."

John hadn't expected that. Nor the way his father went back to humming as if he didn't care that John was throwing away his legacy. Their legacy.

"Isn't it interesting that, against the darkness, God provided light for us to find our way home?"

"So you'll have to find someone else to run this place. Because it's not what I want."

His dad nodded again, still humming.

"I was made for bigger things."

"I have no doubt you'll be a success at whatever you do," his father said quietly, unruffled. He picked up his paddle, began to move them through the water.

John had expected something more—protests, anger—from his father. A cool whoosh of relief inside at releasing the truth.

Nothing. Fine. If his father wanted to live in denial, then that was his problem. John dug in, paddling hard. But he *would* be someone—and he'd do it without Evergreen Resort, without Deep Haven. Without Ingrid Young. Really, he'd already forgotten her.

"Son, you'd better ease up or we'll ram the shore."

"It's cool, Dad." John maneuvered them past the dock, toward shore. Above, the moon dipped behind a cloud, turning the shoreline dark.

"To the left, John!" His dad put out his paddle, steering them hard, but not quite fast enough. The canoe slid over a boulder under the water just a foot offshore, and John heard the sickening crunch of wood, then splintering as the rock tore at the shell of the boat.

His dad jumped out, picking up the bow of the canoe to rescue it, but as John clambered out, he saw water filling the boat.

He muttered a curse that soured the air. His father said nothing as he towed the canoe through the water to shore.

John helped him turn it upside down, then ran his hand over the wound. They'd have to tear off the cedar strip, remake it, refasten it, reseal it—hours upon hours of work.

His father sighed deep and long. Then, "I guess we'll have to repair it."

"No, it's not worth it." John dropped the paddle onshore. "Just turn it into firewood."

He heard his father pulling the canoe farther onto shore, out of the way, but he couldn't bear to watch. Maybe it was for the best. Nothing to draw him back to this achingly small town, their backwoods resort.

His gaze drifted over to cabin 12, where a thin light burned on the deck. He thought he heard a screen door whine, thought he saw a shadow cross the light.

Yes, he'd leave this place and these memories and finally be the man he was meant to be.

CHAPTER 4

1979

"Aren't you going to town tonight?"

Ingrid looked up from where she sat on the Adirondack chair, her feet propped up on the wide arm, and stuck a thumb in her book while she answered her father's question. "Nope."

The sun had ducked behind the trees on the far side of the lake, the buzz of moths flirting with the deck light a hum behind the slurp of the lake on the shore, the far-off cry of a loon across the water.

She'd miss Evergreen Resort next year—she could admit it, despite the memories that dogged her as she'd driven north, the air cooling. Along with her resolve to face John.

And tell him what?

Something. Anything to prove that she wasn't the love-struck teenager from last summer—no, every summer. She'd spent the year sorting out the churning emotions wrought from last year's train wreck of an evening. She might have overreacted.

After all, John hadn't treated her like she owed him something, not like Michael did at this year's pre-prom date.

In fact, compared to Michael, John might be considered gallant. Especially the way he'd followed her home that evening as if making sure she returned to Evergreen Resort safely. And she'd seen him watching her as she tried to lose herself in Nathan's easy friendship. But she'd failed miserably, and it hadn't helped that John seemed to dance with half the girls in Deep Haven.

But he'd taught her a valuable lesson, and she'd realized that Kari was right—boys only wanted one thing. Well, they wouldn't get it from her, and frankly, the thought helped her scrape John from her heart.

She was so over John Christiansen. So over being naive and stupid.

"Are you sure, honey? I know how you love the street dance."

"I'm fine here, Daddy." Ingrid opened her book, finding her place, reading the sentence three times before he walked away. Or not. Her dad pulled up another chair and perched it front of her.

"What?"

"You could talk to him, you know."

"What—? Who?"

Her father frowned. He'd aged more than the two years since Kari left, since she returned home and dismantled their lives with her drug abuse, her anger, her string of live-in boyfriends. How they could grow up in the same family and turn out so differently confused Ingrid. Still, the age, the worry, only deepened his frown.

"I'm not blind. You've been pining for John Christiansen since the first day you saw him, swinging into the lake from the rope on that big oak."

"I wasn't pining. Just . . . just wishing he saw me and not Kari." In fact, she had a terrible nagging suspicion that's exactly who he might have been hold-ing in his arms last year. At least in his mind. "But those days are behind me."

"You know he's here, right? Showed up yesterday, leg brace and all."

She lifted her book, her shoulder.

"He might never play football again with an injury like that. He could use a friend."

Then he could choose from any of the girls he'd danced with last year. She wasn't wowed, not anymore. "We're not friends, Dad."

Again he frowned. "Funny. That's not what you said three years ago, when you covered for him after his accident."

"I was a stupid girl, with stupid dreams." Like the idea that a guy like John might see her, plain Ingrid, instead of flashy Kari.

Oh, see, just the mention of his name stirred up old hurts. She stared at her book, the lines blurry.

"Of my children, Ingrid, you are not the stupid one." He leaned forward, met her eyes. "But you are the compassionate one." He patted her knee and got up. Turned to glance at the lodge.

In the glow of the light cascading over the lodge porch, she saw John sitting on the picnic table, his crutches leaning against it, his hands clasped, head bowed. Defeated.

Shoot.

She put her bare feet into the cool grass, let the blades find her toes. Became again the girl holding John's wounded head as Nathan drove him to the ER.

No, not that girl. Because she was over John Christiansen. And all men for that matter, at least for now. But her dad was right; maybe he needed a friend.

And because she was over him, she could be that.

She tucked the book under her arm and headed down the grass to the lodge. The night was cool on her skin, her tan rich after working as a lifeguard all summer. She wore her cutoff jeans, her red staff shirt. Down at the fire pit, she spied John's mother, Eva, and his dad, Chester, building a campfire. Her parents would spend the evening roasting marshmallows, their own Saturday night tradition.

John didn't look up as she stepped onto the deck, stood at the edge. She tried not to stare, not to wince, but his knee seemed three times its normal size, inflamed and red, evidence of the hyperextension injury. If possible, he'd filled out even more this year, his body thick and strong, proof of a year of conditioning. He wore a pair of maroon football shorts, a white gopher-emblazoned T-shirt, his hair shorter than she ever remembered, just over his ears. It still fell in a long, tempting lock over his eyes.

"John?"

He looked away, and the pain on his face speared her heart. She came over to sit beside him on the picnic table. "I heard about the accident." She didn't add that, in fact, she'd followed his first year at the University of Minnesota, knew he'd gotten into a couple games near the end of the season.

"How'd it happen?"

He still hadn't looked at her. Now he shook his head. "Stupid accident. My spikes got caught in the wet grass, and I was slow coming off the ball. The center dove low, for my knees, and I just felt it pop. And then I was down."

"Did it hurt?"

His mouth tightened in a grim line. "It hurts more to know I might not get another chance to show what I have to offer. That it's over before it even began."

"You went in a couple times last season—"

He shot her a look, his eyes wide, and oh no, she hadn't wanted to give that away. But she forced a smile, shrugged. "My father follows Gophers football."

He nodded like that made sense.

"But why is it over? Can't you come back? After surgery, after you heal?"

"I'll be away from the game for a whole season. What if I can't come back?" He closed his eyes as he spoke, too much vulnerability in his words.

"Really, John? This from the guy who tried to pound all the dents out of his truck after he rolled it. And convinced me to catch a slimy trout—"

"Northern, and as I remember, that was your idea." But she'd coaxed the slightest smile from him.

Oh, she'd forgotten how much she'd missed it.

"And what about the chain saw competition? That guy doesn't give up."

He said nothing. Then, "And what about the guy who totally blew it last summer?" He met her gaze, serious now, his eyes so blue it could take her breath away. "I'm really sorry, Ingrid. I thought . . . Well, it doesn't matter. I shouldn't have assumed."

Her throat thickened, and she looked away. So maybe she had pined a little for this version of John Christiansen, the one she knew was locked inside all that small-town swagger.

But she wasn't stupid, so she found a just-friends smile. "It's okay, John. I probably overreacted. We were both just kids." Translation: young, immature, and not going back there.

She stared out at the lake, at the cracking fire, the sparks vanishing into the sky.

"Are you going to college?"

"Peace Corps. Peru or maybe Ecuador. And then I don't know. Maybe I'll be a teacher. Or a missionary."

He frowned at that.

"What?"

"I just thought . . ." He lifted a shoulder. "For some reason I thought you would move to Deep Haven." He shook his head. "I'm not sure why. It's silly—I mean, everyone is trying to get out of here, right?"

Not right. "I'd love to live in Deep Haven someday. I love the simplicity, the way everyone knows each other like a family. I love the beauty of the north shore, the blue of the lake against the cloud-streaked sky, the smell of campfires, the crunch of pine needles under my shoes. It's a life I want. I've always dreamed of living here. I can't understand why you're so desperate to leave."

He opened his mouth, closed it. Then rubbed his hands together. "All my life, I've been trapped here while tourists roll through the resort, bringing with them the life in the city. New cars, movies—stuff we don't have up here. Deep Haven is caught in a time warp, Ingrid. Nothing exciting ever happens here."

"That's good, isn't it? That's why people come here—"

"And that's why people leave. I want more than Deep Haven, than this resort. I want a bigger life. A better life."

"I guess we have different definitions of what is better," she said softly.

The silence shifted between them, and in it she felt his gaze on her. She refused to turn, to let him see the sadness in her expression.

"Ingrid, I gotta know. Did I wreck it so much that . . . that I can't come back? That I can't fix things between us?"

The question startled her, and she stared at him, wide-eyed. Her throat filled, her words gone.

She had no choice but to get up, glare at him, and flee.

So much for not being stupid.

He'd made her run away. Again. John watched Ingrid stride off the porch into the darkness, and he wanted to shout with frustration.

Come back.

In fact, he'd wanted to shout that all year. *Come back.* Or maybe he just wanted to reel back time to the night when things felt simpler, easy.

When he'd believed in himself. When he stood at the crest of his future and longed to dive in.

He ran his hand down his leg to where the swelling started, pressed it with his thumb and fingers, feeling the fluid, wincing.

He hadn't wanted to return to Evergreen, but he was short on options after his injury. The docs in the Cities said that maybe it would heal on its own, but after three weeks, he thought he heard the word *surgery* muttered in the doctor's quiet words to his coach.

Surgery, rehabilitation, and maybe, someday, football.

He might end up in Deep Haven after all. A life almost lived.

Down by the lake, the campfire spit into the night, tiny red embers snuffed out by the darkness. Laughter lifted from the night, his parents, and a few of the guests in their Saturday night ritual. He couldn't remember the last time he'd missed the Saturday street dance. If ever.

He stared after Ingrid. She'd missed it, too. Why had she stayed home tonight?

The thought stirred a fading hope and he got up, reaching for his crutches, and headed out into the darkness after her. He didn't remember the path being this rocky and nearly fell twice, but he made it to cabin 12. The light over the deck pressed out over the lawn, the empty Adirondack chairs. He'd started for the stairs when he saw the figure just inside the glow of light, down by the shoreline.

She had her knees up, her arms clasped over them, her head buried in her arms like she might . . . be crying?

His chest thickened for a moment, but he couldn't bear to leave her there, even if he'd caused her tears, so he limped toward her.

She didn't even lift her head. "Go away, John."

"Please, Ingrid—"

She looked up at him, her expression in the wan light incredulous. "Seriously?"

"I know I blew it—I . . . Maybe we could just be friends?"

Her gaze, in the glow of the porch light, looked right through him, and he nearly turned around. Then she sighed, long, painful, and turned back to the lake.

She hadn't said no. Which gave him the courage to sit next to her, stifling a groan as he went down.

"Friends, huh?"

"We could write."

She let out a burst of laughter, short and harsh. But her expression softened and the knot in his chest loosened. "Listen, John, just so you know, I'm not interested in dating. Anyone."

"Ever?"

She looked away.

"Why are you crying?"

She blew out another breath. "Because I don't want to be stupid. Again."

Because of him. Because of the way he'd treated her. "I'm so sorry—"

"It's not just you, John." She picked up a rock, threw it into the water. It splashed, unseen, in the distance. "It's . . . guys. I should have listened to Kari."

"What did Kari say?" He had a feeling he knew, though, and his throat tightened.

When she looked at him, he knew he'd guessed right.

"Ingrid—"

"Stop, John. I know you're sorry. I forgive you, okay?"

"How can I make it better?"

She shook her head. "You can't. It's just . . . I'm a silly, stupid girl."

He didn't like how that sounded, and his voice lowered, the timbre of dread in it when he asked, "What happened?"

She went quiet then, and he felt the silence string around him, banding his chest. "Ingrid—"

"I didn't go to prom."

Huh?

"I mean, I was asked, but . . . my date wanted to go out before prom to 'get to know each other.'" She finger-quoted the words. "Which meant, well, getting to know each other."

He stilled. "Please, don't tell me—"

"Nothing happened. I mean, something happened, but not enough for Michael."

He couldn't deny the crazy relief that flooded through him.

She swallowed. "He canceled a week before the dance and asked someone else. A girl from another school. Someone prettier."

He had this terrible urge to track down the guy and take him out at the knees.

"I still have the dress. My mother made it for me, spent weeks finding the right pattern, the right material, getting it just right, preparing for the perfect night." She shook her head again. "See, I'm a silly, stupid girl."

He felt sick. "No, you're not, Ingrid. Not every guy is like that." Oh, he wanted to mean that.

She met his eyes then, her wounds in her gaze. "I wish I could believe you."

He had no words, his shame thickening his throat.

"I just want a man who wants what I want. A home, family. Small town, yes, but a man of honor, who wants me, not Kari and not . . . Well, I want someone who is willing to wait for me."

Her words stirred something inside him. "Please give me another chance, Ingrid."

She considered him, and in the space of time, he felt his heart bang against his ribs. Then, "Were you serious about writing to me?"

He was nodding even before the words crested her lips. "Every day."

Her gaze was in his, testing. She was so close, if he simply leaned forward, he could kiss her. Just brush her lips with his like a whisper. He could hardly breathe with the desire for it, the taste of her suddenly real and bold and unquenchable.

But he didn't. He just stilled and watched her, holding his breath until . . .

Until she nodded. "But only if you promise to get back in the game." She pointed to his leg. "I want to see you play football, John Christiansen."

He smiled. "I'll send you tickets to my first game." He held out his hand. "Friends?"

She hesitated a moment, then took it. "Friends."

Maybe he could start over after all.

CHAPTER 5

1980

Dear John,

Thanks for the news clipping of your spring scrimmage with the Gophers. I knew you'd make it back on the team! And yes, I'll take you up on your offer for tickets next fall. I can't wait to see you play. I can imagine how much hard work it took to get back into shape, but that's who you are, so I'm not surprised.

We finally finished the roof on the school. It's a shiny tin that's already turning to rust in the rain and sunshine of the mountains. Sometimes I sit on the back porch before English classes start, drinking a cup of tea and watching the mist lay low over the Andes mountains. There's a smell here, a ripeness in the air stirred up by the wet breezes of the rain forest. Humid and almost moldy, so different from the pine of Minnesota, but I've learned to love it. There's a parrot that's taken roost near my dormitory—it wakes me up every morning with a squawk, like it's warning me not to miss the day. I long for the loon call across the lake.

Ecuador is colder than you'd think, especially here in the mountains. I love the U of MN sweatshirt you sent me for Christmas—even if I got it in March!

It's been harder than I thought to go away for a year. I thought I'd love the Peace Corps. I used to think, when I watched slide shows from missionaries in our church, that I wanted to be a humanitarian aid worker. I didn't realize how much of that time would be digging wells

433

and giving TB shots. I've discovered, however, that people here want the same things we want—safety, health, family . . . love. It's made me realize, too, that I probably don't have to leave home to do something that changes lives.

You'd be proud of me—I learned how to drive a clutch! Phil Samson taught me (although I thought he might kill me before I got it). Now I'm driving the Jeep for the team, transporting people to Quito and back. The new team flies in a few weeks before our annual retreat to Evergreen—I hope to make the trip with my family again this year. I don't know your plans, but I'd really love to see you.

Ingrid

John could see her sitting cross-legged on the ground, her notebook in her lap, her lip caught in her teeth as she wrote to him. Her long blonde hair would be caught by the cool Ecuadorian wind, her skin a deep brown, her arms shaped with muscle. When he'd read about her learning to drive the Jeep, a crazy, unbidden tightness grabbed him around the chest. He couldn't bear the thought of her laughing with this Phil guy.

John should have been the one teaching her how to drive a clutch.

Maybe he'd take her out on his motorcycle tonight, lean over her shoulder as he taught her how to shift gears, put his hands on her hips. She wouldn't even notice as he'd breathe in her smell, let her soft, silky hair slip through his fingers.

Maybe he could even hide how he'd started to thirst for her letters this year. How he longed, as his physical therapy bore down on him, to jump on a plane and escape his so-called dreams and find new ones.

With Ingrid.

But she'd be back tonight, and because of that, he'd returned to the resort for the summer, guiding fishing trips and preparing Duluth Packs and repairing cabins and cutting firewood and hoping, waiting for her to return.

Holding his breath for their Saturday night.

When her parents arrived a week ago—alone—he could admit to a layer of panic. So much that he'd managed to casually ask, one night by the campfire, if she might be coming home. The fact that she would drive up when her flight came in set a swirl of heat in his gut, one he couldn't seem to douse.

He rinsed his razor in the sudsy water, then scraped another layer of whiskers off his cheek. He'd never seen the guy in the mirror quite so well groomed. In fact, he hadn't seen so much of his face in years, but he liked the shorter cut, especially since it hid the fact that he'd begun losing his hair. And it revealed the rather-gnarly scar above his eye.

He'd probably end up like his grandfather, bald at thirty. But maybe Ingrid wouldn't notice his lack of hair. He rinsed his face, dried it, then dressed in a clean pair of jeans, a gold T-shirt. He'd grown another inch this past year and put on fifteen pounds of muscle.

She might even be impressed. He hoped she'd see more than the guy from last year, ready to throw himself into the lake, or the kid in his foolish high school years who'd actually thought Ingrid Young might be forgettable.

Right. With every letter, Ingrid lodged further in his brain, his heart, until she dogged him at practice, stalked him in the library, edged into his dreams. Her belief that she could change the world irked him until he realized she'd changed him, made him long to be the person she saw.

He kept every piece of mail, found himself responding on notebook pages, hastily scribbling his thoughts—who knew what he really wrote—and shoving them into an envelope before fear turned his letter into a crumpled wad.

Ingrid Young was about as forgettable as the sunrise.

John glanced out his window and saw a new car in the lot, an old Dart parked beside the Youngs' station wagon.

He experimented with some cologne, then grabbed his jacket and headed downstairs.

His mother took a batch of cookies out of the oven and let them rest on the cutting board on the counter. He swiped one.

She stopped him with a touch to his arm and pointed to her cheek. He obliged with a kiss and headed outside.

For a moment, before he hopped on the bike, he debated walking down to her cabin, knocking on her door, asking if she might want a ride. But . . . but tradition created magic. He wanted to spy her at the dance across the crowded street, make his way to her, see the anticipation in her smile.

He found Nate at the Deep Haven Realty booth handing out brochures.

"How's your mom?" John asked, taking a brochure. Nate's picture on the back evidenced his friend's hard work this past year—and his future.

"In remission. We're hoping she's licked the cancer." Nate glad-handed a tourist couple, turned his attention to them. "Are you looking to buy land in Deep Haven?"

John purchased a fish burger from the Lions Club booth, keeping a casual eye out for Ingrid as twilight slid over the harbor in shades of lavender and rose. Behind him, the smells of the remnant summer, grilled hamburgers, cotton candy, and the sweet tang of ice cream hung in the air. The street band, set up on a stage in the park, began to warm up.

He was watching a family of towheaded boys losing a war with their ice cream cones when he spotted her, wearing a pair of jeans, a sleeveless shirt, her back to him. A little thinner than he remembered, but that's what overseas living did. She stood with a cadre of longtime guests from Evergreen, laughing. He caught her profile briefly as he headed toward her, tasting his heart.

"Ingrid?"

She turned, and for a moment, everything stopped. The sounds of the band leaning into the first few bars of Blondie's "Call Me," the cheers of an enthusiastic, eager audience, the stir of the summer wind, his pulse.

Not Ingrid. Kari. She had a hint of a burn on her nose, her face clean and tanned, looking every inch the beauty he knew she'd be. And in the way her eyes lit up, the smallest memory of her invading his dreams revived.

He whispered her name almost involuntarily, and she laughed.

"Really? You're that surprised to see me?"

"I thought . . . Well, is Ingrid here?"

Kari stepped close to him, blew out a ring of smoke. Only now did he notice her T-shirt, the neck ripped down to reveal too much untanned flesh. How could he have ever confused her for Ingrid? "Ingrid didn't come home."

He frowned. "But . . ." He swallowed his words, fought against the tenor of disappointment. "What happened?"

"I don't know. She just said she was staying. Who knows why Ingrid does what she does."

He knew why. Because Ingrid cared about people more than fun. If she didn't come home, she had a good reason. Like the new team hadn't shown up, or they needed help at another village, or maybe even that she couldn't bear to leave the youngsters she'd invested a year in.

He moved away from Kari, but she caught his arm. "John. Really. Ingrid? Listen." She moved herself against him, her hand around his neck. "Once upon a time, you chased me through Deep Haven, remember?"

He wished he didn't. He unlaced her arm from his neck. "That memory faded long ago."

She pouted, something false and dangerous. "Let me remind you."

But he stepped back, shaking his head. "Tell Ingrid, if you write to her, that I'll be here next year."

She rolled her eyes, but he headed to his bike, lifting a hand to Nathan. His friend frowned, but John didn't look back as he drove toward Honeymoon Bluff.

If there were any memories he longed to stir, it was the ones of holding Ingrid in his arms. And the strange, lingering hope that he might again.

They hadn't made promises to each other. In fact, if Ingrid could recall their last face-to-face interaction, she'd reminded him that they would be friends, just friends.

She'd even sealed it with a handshake.

Apparently those words sank in, found fertile soil.

So she shouldn't have thought, despite the warmth in his letters, that over the year they'd tacitly agreed to be more.

She tucked her knees up into her sweatshirt, now fraying around the cuffs, and rested her chin on her knees while her fingers creased the edges of Kari's letter to a razor-sharp edge.

To the east, sunlight began to spill into the valley, ribbons of light dropping into the tangled green forest, thick with spires of bamboo. From where she sat, two giant steps would plummet her into a gulley a thousand feet deep.

Times like this, she liked to sit at the edge.

Even if John hadn't felt a shift in their correspondence, that didn't mean he shouldn't have told her about his night with Kari. Lies by omission still counted as lies.

The wind chased up the hill, tugged at the letter. She nearly let it go but then gripped it tight, crumpling it in her hand.

She might have to read it a dozen more times before she believed it, before Kari's descriptions touched her bones.

I saw John Christiansen. You're right; I'm not sure why I never really noticed him before. Wide, sculpted shoulders, he's tall now and every inch a linebacker. He came down for the street dance, and the moment he saw me, I saw it—that subtle shift in his eyes that told me he remembered me. Of course he remembered me. He'd been pining for me for years.

He mentioned you, so apparently he considers you friends. It's nice you two can stay in contact for now.

I probably shouldn't kiss and tell, Ings, but the truth is, he was worth the wait. He took me to Artist's Point, and we watched the waves roll in all the way to dawn. I hope you don't mind, but I figure with you off digging wells and giving TB shots, you had more important things to worry about.

I hope to see you at Christmas!

Love,
Kari

Worth the wait. Ingrid closed her eyes, felt the moisture burn her cheek, wiped it away before it fell. Yes, indeed, he would have been. She could see him as Kari described him. Tall, his hair cut shorter—he'd mentioned how he liked it out of his face, although honestly, she'd miss the forelock of dark hair—muscles stretching the sleeves of his maroon University of Minnesota T-shirt.

He would look at her with his too-handsome smile she missed and ask her to go for a ride on his motorcycle.

She'd dreamed of it for months actually.

And he hadn't helped, not with the suggestions he'd made in his last letter that she might mean more to him. She'd received it two weeks before she intended to leave Ecuador, two weeks before the torrential rain that cut off all communication. She'd barely been able to get a telegram to her parents.

> *I decided to move home this summer, help my dad with the resort. I know I keep saying I don't want to come back but . . . but I was thinking that maybe you'd be home, and I was thinking that if the night was warm and the stars were out, we could take a ride on my bike.*
> *I'd really love to see you.*

I'd really love to see you. That didn't speak of a man easily wooed into rendezvousing with her sister.

But maybe she'd simply seen the John Christiansen she drew in her dreams instead of the man he kept claiming to be.

She should pay attention.

Behind her rose the smells of the open kitchen, sausage frying with fresh eggs, the whine of hungry dogs rising, the early morning attention of a rooster.

She missed the soft lap of the lake on the fir-padded shore.

"Ingrid, you okay?"

She looked up to see Phil, dressed in a pair of cutoff green Army pants, a Hawaiian shirt, and Birkenstocks, leaning over her, his shadow blocking the sun. He wore a tan and a gentle smile, the sun bleaching his blond hair.

He reminded her a lot of Nathan, John's best friend. Quiet. Understanding.

She looked at him, tried a smile, and he plunked down next to her. Pointed to the letter. "News from home?"

She folded it in half. "My sister. Telling me about the summer vacation in Deep Haven. My family goes every year, and this year, well . . ."

"Bummer. I know you wanted to leave, but with the rains—"

"It's fine. Worst was, I couldn't get word out until it was too late and . . ." She lifted a shoulder. "It's no big deal."

"You could go home for Christmas. With the road rebuilt, they'll have another team of recruits ready to replace us."

She nodded. Sighed.

"You miss home."

"I miss . . . Deep Haven."

"Or someone in Deep Haven."

She glanced at him, and he lifted his own shoulder. "You talk about him every time you get a letter. John had surgery. John made it off his crutches. John made varsity. John, John, John—"

"I'm sorry."

"I get it. Or did, until I see that look on your face."

She bit her lip, turned away. "I guess I just thought we were . . . we were meant to be. I've loved him since I was thirteen—"

"Loved?"

His question settled between them, and she rolled it around in her head. It sank into her like the heat of the sun.

Yes, loved. Maybe an adolescent crush at first, but over the past year, she'd seen a different side of John. Fragile. Searching. Hopeful. Courageous.

The man she knew he'd become if she gave him time.

The man who'd been worth the wait. At least for Kari.

She nodded. "Loved. But maybe that's over." She tucked the letter into her shirt pocket. "I'm thinking of staying."

"Re-up for another year?" A new warmth rose in Phil's coffee-brown eyes. His voice softened. "I'd like that."

Then he reached over and wove his fingers with hers. Sweet—the kind of intimacy that didn't scare her, didn't flood over her, didn't bring with it a breathlessness that made her ache for more, despite the warnings in her head.

But maybe sometime it would.

"Can I show you something?"

She nodded, and he helped her up, then held her hand as he led her away from camp, toward a path that wove up a hill, through the forest. They walked in silence, their feet whispering on the worn path. They reached the apex of the hill, and he directed her across the top, pointing out roots and fallen bamboo, parting leaves bigger than her face. They finally emerged into a tiny, worn clearing.

"Look down, over there."

She followed his gesture, and there, through the trees, dropping two hundred feet down and spilling into the dawn with jeweled spray, a waterfall. The fresh breath from the fall of water rose into the air and brushed her skin with moisture, soft and cool.

Her skin prickled.

"The locals call this Angel Falls. You stand here and close your eyes, and you feel like the angels are breathing on you."

She closed her eyes.

The mist feathered over her, Phil's hand wove into hers, not letting go, and Ingrid wished she felt angels instead of the weeping of her heart.

CHAPTER 6

1981

This should be the happiest day of her life. With the sun cascading through the trees, jeweled fingers of light reaching out to embrace her, the smell of marshmallows roasting over a campfire, the chorus of the lake, the north shore wind in the trees . . . yes, she should be over the moon.

After all, not every day did the man of her dreams propose to her. Okay, so he might not have officially proposed yet, but Ingrid could read through Phil's flimsy attempts to hide the fact he'd chased her father down alone yesterday. After nine months of dating, she could figure out why.

Besides, they'd talked about it so many times, it felt like the next logical step in their relationship.

Yes, she should be celebrating. Not casting glances over to the lodge, seeing if she could spy John's motorcycle in the dirt lot. Not wishing for a glimpse of him over the week they'd spent here; probably her last. Not hating herself for the shards of disappointment that pierced the blanket of joy that should be hers.

She should hate John Christiansen for skulking around her heart. And he hadn't picked up the hint in real life, either. Despite the obvious cooling in her letters and then her eventual silent treatment, he continued to write. As if he hadn't betrayed her, hadn't broken her heart.

And she could blame herself, yes, just a little, for not telling him how his actions with Kari eviscerated her. But she had no claim on him, not really, so what would she say?

"Are you okay, darling?" Phil handed her a golden-to-perfection marsh-mallow, swelling between two crisp graham crackers, a slice of Hershey's chocolate dissolving into the mess. "You seem far away."

She found a smile for him. He'd cut his hair since Ecuador, something his substitute teaching position at the elementary school in suburban Minneapolis demanded, and looked preppy in his oxford shirt and khakis, even if he still wore his trademark Birkenstocks.

"Yum, thank you." She took the s'more, tried to maneuver it into her mouth. Marshmallow goo landed on her chin, and she laughed as she tried to lick it off.

"Phil tells me you're thinking of applying to college, maybe getting a degree in education," her father said. He wore a strange, enigmatic look. The kind that said he knew her, wasn't buying her false cheer.

Which made it only worse because no, it wasn't false.

Phil was the right man. Her brain told her that after watching him embrace his classroom of fourth graders, after he'd spent Christmas with her family, playing monopoly and attending Christmas Eve service. After encouraging her to apply to college to get her degree. Phil hadn't an unfaithful bone in his body, wanted a family, a home. Might even consider moving to Deep Haven someday.

"I have the application but I haven't filled it out yet."

Phil glanced at her. "But she will."

"Why don't you two kiddos head down to town for the street dance?" her mother said, adding another marshmallow to her stick.

Oh, Mom. And then what? Fight another slough of memories? Joining her parents for their annual vacation now seemed a colossally bad decision.

"A street dance? Sounds fun," Phil said, a gleam in his eye.

Oh no. He wouldn't propose during . . . She took a breath. "I wouldn't mind staying here."

"No, let's go," Phil said, standing.

She couldn't help it—she glanced at the lodge again. But John hadn't shown up all week; she should stop kidding herself. He wouldn't suddenly appear on the sidewalk, see her dancing with Phil.

And what if he did?

Oh, see, her heart had decided to simply draw a wall around her feelings for John, let them simmer, while every other part of her fell in love with Phil.

She hoped it was enough. It had to be enough. Because John Christiansen didn't belong in her heart, not anymore.

Ingrid changed into jeans, flip-flops, a white sleeveless shirt, grabbing a

jean jacket before climbing into Phil's VW Beetle. From the highway lead-
ing down the hill, Deep Haven spread out before her, lights twinkling like a
Christmas package, the lake dark and mysterious. She gathered her long hair
in her hand, trapping it to keep the wind from blowing it into tangles.

"Such a beautiful little town," Phil said. "I can see why you vacation here
every summer. So many childhood memories."

She smiled, nodded. Looked out the window. Remembered the feel of
the wind on her face as she'd wrapped her arms around John. Shook the
memory away and reached for Phil's hand. He gave it a squeeze right before
he downshifted.

They parked at the new ice cream parlor, Licks and Stuff, then got out
and wandered toward the music. The band played "Endless Love," and Phil
roped his arm around her, pulled her to his side. His body radiated warmth
against the cool evening, and she leaned against him as they stopped next to
a streetlamp, watching the crowd.

Sawdust littered the street from the annual chain saw competition—she
didn't want to consider who won this year. At the harbor, children skipped
stones across the water, counting the sound of splashes until they faded.

She spotted Nathan in a short-sleeved oxford, dancing with a slender
blonde sporting the smile Ingrid should be wearing.

Phil nestled his arms around her, pulling her against his chest, her back to
him. "I'm not sure it has the magic of Angel Falls, but I can see the charm."
He pressed a kiss to her head. "Want some cotton candy?"

She looked up at him and nodded. "Sure. Thanks."

"I'll be right back." He disappeared into the crowd, her man, fetching her
a treat.

The song changed—Air Supply's "The One That You Love"—and she
wrapped her arms around her waist, began to sway. Hum.

A voice behind her filled in the words. "'Hold me in your arms for just
another day.'"

She stilled, the tenor strumming through her body. Oh . . .

No. She turned, and her mouth opened at the sight of John standing
behind her, grinning like a man proud of himself, holding a secret.

"What are you doing here?" She didn't mean for it to emerge quite like
that, quick and sharp, and his smile faded a little.

"I skipped practice and drove five hours to get here. It's our Saturday
night." His blue eyes clouded. "I thought . . . I miss you, Ingrid. And I hoped
you'd be here. Aren't you glad to see me?"

A fist had grabbed her chest, started to squeeze, yet despite the suffocating loss of breath, she couldn't stop herself from nodding.

Oh yes, she was painfully, terribly, ecstatically glad to see him.

Shoot.

He smiled then, and her world dropped from around her. Such blue eyes, they simmered under the glow of the lights. He wore faded jeans, a hooded sweatshirt under a jean jacket, his dark hair shorter, thinning almost, but it only gave his gaze that much more power to undo her. And Kari didn't lie about his linebacker build.

Ingrid tightened her jaw against the sudden burn in her chest, her eyes, at the memory of Kari's words. No, no—she turned away, not wanting him to see her stupid reaction to the memory of his betrayal.

"Ingrid, what's the matter?"

"Nothing. I'm—yeah, I'm glad to see you." She ran her fingers over her eyes. Silly girl—he should not have this much power over her. Especially since she was practically engaged to another man.

She searched the crowd for Phil but didn't see him. Then it didn't matter because John stepped in front of her. "Ingrid, please help me understand what's going on here. I don't understand why you stopped writing me. Or why you suddenly . . . I don't know. I'm not a very emotional guy, but it felt as if . . . Are you angry with me?"

She closed her eyes. Opened them and looked away, toward the harbor, where a thousand stars fell into the water. "It doesn't matter anymore."

"It does matter—to me. I . . . I came here last year, looking for you—"

"And found Kari, I know." Sarcasm. Anger. She heard it in her tone, the feelings as fresh as they'd been last year.

"Yeah. I saw her, too. But I realized something. I didn't care about Kari. I . . . Gee, Ingrid. I missed you. Your smile. Your laughter. I wanted to see you."

"Funny. Did you figure that out before or after you two had your fling?"

He just stood there, not moving, and she finally looked up at him. He seemed stricken, shaken by her words. And a cold, brutal realization stole through her as he said, "I don't know what you're talking about, but I barely spoke two words to Kari last year."

Oh no.

The hand in her chest returned, pressing against her sternum.

"Clearly we have to talk." He curled his hand around her arm, and she let him lead her away, off the street, to a nearby alley.

She didn't have a thought to resist him.

Kari had lied to her. All this time . . .

Ingrid couldn't breathe. He released her when they reached the shadows of the alley, and she turned, braced one hand against the brick wall, her other hand over her eyes.

"Are you okay?" His voice fell so achingly tender over her. And away from the smells of the festival, she could smell the scent of soap, the remnant of his afternoon practice on his skin.

She couldn't look at him, or she'd be undone. "Kari wrote me a letter and told me that you two . . ." She couldn't say it. "She said—"

"I can figure it out," he growled. "And you believed her?"

It was the hurt in his voice that made Ingrid look at him. The raw emotion on his face nearly stole her words. "I remember . . . You've always had a thing for her, and Kari is awfully hard to ignore."

"I haven't thought of Kari in years," he said quietly, his hand reaching up to touch her face. It lay large and warm on her skin, and when he brushed his thumb across her cheek, she thought she might cry. "You're the one I can't forget."

John. This couldn't be happening. Not now.

And what about Phil? He'd be looking for her. She had to get back to him, just simply walk away from John. Now.

She put her hand to his, intending to pull it away, but he misinterpreted her meaning. Or maybe not because he cupped her face with his other hand and searched her eyes, and she didn't move away.

How could she when he looked at her with a hunger, a need that stripped the moisture from her mouth.

She opened her mouth to protest but didn't even try to stop him when he leaned down to kiss her.

He delivered the kind of kiss she'd dreamed about for too many years. Not the arrogant, sloppy kiss of his youth, but purposed, deliberate. The kind of kiss that spoke of patience and longing.

The kind of kiss worth waiting for. He tasted of salt, as if he'd eaten french fries on the road, and the brisk tang of Coke, and as his mouth moved against hers, the world blurred around her.

John.

He made a sound in the back of his throat, something deep, as if he'd had a tight fist over his emotions and they'd begun to spill out. Or maybe that was her sound because he lifted his head, and in the silence she could hear her heart pounding, filling her ears.

Then, in a whisper, "I love you, Ingrid. It scares me a little how much I love you."

Her eyes widened, but she had no words as he bent his head and kissed her again, this time wrapping one arm around her waist. He braced his other arm on the building behind her, pulling her up against the solid, hard planes of his football physique.

And despite the warning screaming in the back of her head, her arms went around his neck, and she simply surrendered. Surrendered to the rub of his five o'clock shadow against her skin, the softness of his mouth as he nudged her lips open, the rhythm of his heart against hers . . .

John. Finally John.

He shouldn't have panicked. Shouldn't have let what-ifs stir in his brain until he skipped practice and jumped on his motorcycle, driving like a man on the verge of losing his last chance.

Or maybe he did exactly the right thing, because holding Ingrid in his arms as she molded her body to his, every doubt, every hour reading and rereading her letters trying to decipher why she'd turned cold to him, simply slipped away.

Only her sweet surrender in his embrace remained. She tasted like marshmallow and chocolate, sweetly dangerous, and the way the smells of the north shore embedded her hair, her skin, it felt like coming home. *She* felt like coming home.

Honestly, he'd dreamed of kissing her like this, like they belonged together—as though finally, finally, he could free the tight hold he had on his heart—for two years, ever since he'd asked her if they could start over.

Since she'd agreed to let him into her life.

And now she had her arms locked around his neck, the night humming around them, the caress of the waves on the shore, the music drawing them into a quiet dance as he slowed his kiss, lingered at her mouth, then pressed his lips to her cheekbones, the well of her eye, down to her neck.

He could inhale her, she tasted so good, but he didn't want to scare her. He refused to repeat the fumbling stupidity of his youth. So he closed his eyes and just put his head down and curled her closer.

"I was worried," he said into her neck. He lifted his head. Found her beautiful eyes. "I was worried that . . . that maybe you'd found someone else. That you . . ." He swallowed. "I know we said just friends, but I was starting to think, over the past few months, that you really meant it."

She looked away, her lower lip caught in her teeth, and for a second, the fear returned, quick, like a sliver in this perfect night.

He leaned back, trying to search her face, to reassure himself.

"We're okay, right? I didn't totally screw this up? Because I was thinking that maybe you were right. Maybe if you wanted to, I could come back to Deep Haven—"

"John—"

He had her attention now, by the shock on her face.

"I know I always said I wanted to play NFL football, but—" he tried a smile—"I keep thinking about what you said about always wanting to live here—"

"But you don't want to live here. Football is your dream. And you had an amazing year."

She started to untangle herself from his arms, and her words, her light tone didn't seem to make sense. Didn't she want this?

"I know, but . . . the NFL is . . . That's a pipe dream, right? That's not really going to happen."

Now she was really freaking him out because she was backing away, breathing fast, rubbing her hands on her arms as if cold. He took a step toward her, wanting to fix it, but—

"No, John. Listen. You can't give up your dreams for me. You have to play football. It's what you've wanted your whole life."

He stared at her, nonplussed. Was it? "I don't understand."

"I . . . Oh, John . . ."

She wore a stricken look, not at all the response he'd expected. And the sliver inside swelled, wove its way deeper.

"What's going on, Ingrid?" he said, his voice low, containing an edge he hadn't heard for a year, maybe more. Back when he had to prove himself, back when he felt like he wasn't enough.

"I thought I'd misread you . . ." She was shaking her head, backing into the street, taking his heart with her when suddenly he heard her name, distant, above the crowd.

She winced.

And just like that, he knew. A terrible knot twisted in his chest, and he actually had to put out a hand to brace himself on the wall.

Ingrid came toward him. "John, I . . . You . . . I thought you had chosen my sister! I was hurt and angry, and it just happened."

He held up his hand, wanting to stop her from talking, the words tearing through him. "Who is he?" he managed.

"Phil. I met him last year in Ecuador."

He tightened his lips, nodded. "I remember. He taught you how to drive a Jeep."

She went a little white then. "Yeah."

He straightened, his balance back, but pressed a hand to his chest, willing himself not to cry in front of her. Shoot, he might be having a heart attack.

Her name again, and she stepped out of the alley, waved.

John had the strangest urge to run. But not alone—to reach out and grab her and just flee. Jump on his bike and head anywhere but here.

Because even as she smiled, even as the owner of the voice appeared, worried, holding a stick of cotton candy, John knew Deep Haven had no place for him without Ingrid.

But he didn't run. Didn't reach out for her, didn't land an uppercut to the man who landed a kiss on the woman he loved. He just stood there, the world opening up beneath him as this tourist came right up to Ingrid as if she belonged to him. "Where'd you go? I was worried."

Clean-cut blond hair, an oxford shirt, a pair of khakis—a city boy, a wannabe roughneck with Birkenstocks. Of course. She'd only pretended to want a Deep Haven boy. Just like Kari.

"I was catching up with an old friend," she said to Phil, her voice lacking a bit of her usual shine.

John just shook his head. But he wasn't the guy who, once upon a time, might have behaved badly, so he stuck out his hand. "John Christiansen. My family runs Evergreen Resort."

"John. Sure, Ingrid has mentioned you." Phil's voice was cool but carried the finest edge of warning that made John glance at Ingrid. She held her cotton candy and stared at it as if it held the secrets of the universe.

"Really."

"I haven't seen you around this week," Phil said. "What brings you to Deep Haven?"

John heard the dare in it, but Ingrid appeared as if she might shatter, on the verge of tears, and he couldn't bear that, despite the roaring inside.

"I just came up for the night. But I'm headed back to the Cities. I have practice on Monday."

"You're not attending services tomorrow? I hear your dad is a great preacher. My future father-in-law says that he preaches the gospel in moccasins."

Father-in-law? He closed his mouth, his jaw tighter than he intended, but Ingrid only looked at Phil, her eyes big, as if he'd leaked a secret.

Phil wore a smug, confident smile.

"Congratulations, Ingrid," John said quietly.

"John, we—"

He held out his hand to Phil. Shook it. "Take care of her, then."

"Good luck next season. Maybe we'll come to a game." He slipped his arm around Ingrid. She was staring at John, a look he couldn't read on her face. He avoided it.

"I'll make sure you get tickets," John said, then glanced at Ingrid one last time. She'd wiped all pretense from her face, the emotion on it raw, desperate. Like she hadn't wanted to hurt him, like maybe, their friendship—or more—had been real.

As if, for the briefest of moments back in the alley, she had belonged to him.

That made it all the worse. Somehow he found his voice. "I always did want you to see a game."

Then he turned and headed back down the alley, forcing himself not to run, not to howl, and vowing, even as he got his bike, never to return to Deep Haven again.

CHAPTER 7

1982

Rain spit from the sky, tears upon the windowpane, the trickling of a river outside the cabin evidence of the rainiest week they'd had in seven years at the resort. Ingrid's father lit the furnace at the far end of the two-room cabin, and it glowed hot enough to temper the chill of the misty day. Still, Ingrid sat on the sofa, curled in a homemade knit afghan, trying to focus on her novel.

She read a sentence three times before putting the book down on the arm of the sofa. Kari looked up from where she was playing a game of cards with her husband, Bradley. Their son, Matthew, sat on the floor, gumming the ear of his stuffed bear. "Aren't you going to town? They're moving the dance into the community center—I heard about it in town today." She peered out the window as a roll of thunder fractured the air.

"No. It's my last night here. I'll spend it with the family."

Kari shook her head, picked a card from her hand. "Gin."

Bradley made a face, and Kari giggled. "You know you can't beat me." How her sister had managed to land true love while Ingrid still couldn't pry herself away from her broken heart seemed colossally unfair. Especially since . . .

Ingrid took a breath. No. They'd already had the fight; Kari had already confessed the truth—that she'd seen John's expression when she told him Ingrid hadn't come home and that jealousy had burned inside her. Especially since, *he belonged to me first.*

Ingrid didn't argue, didn't want to remind her that John belonged to no one. He made that perfectly clear from the beginning. Not Kari, not Ingrid, not Deep Haven.

And that had never been clearer than when Ingrid chased him down at a football game, some nine months ago.

Like a love-struck fan, she'd waited for him, maneuvering down to the sidelines after the game, praying he'd see her, that her presence might shock him out of the silent treatment long enough for her to explain.

To tell him that she and Phil had called it quits.

After all, she couldn't give her heart to one man when it belonged to another.

But clearly John didn't share her problem. That day at the football field could still send a shudder through her, still cause her to unravel with regret.

John had run off the field, helmet in his hand, his dark hair glistening with sweat, looking fierce and amazing in his football pads after a win. The crowd pressed around her, but she'd called out his name.

For a second, his gaze turned, caught hers. And in the sudden darkening of his eyes, so abrupt after the energy of the win, she saw the truth.

He didn't want her. Maybe even hated her, or something like it, because his jaw tightened, his eyes narrowed, and a shiver went through her.

This John, maybe she didn't know.

But she wouldn't have let it deter her. Wouldn't have let his anger push her away. Because she owned the truth, and he needed to know—

Then, from the opposite sideline, a shapely blonde in a Gophers cheer-leader outfit launched herself at him, arms around his neck.

And John wrapped one of his strong arms around her, picked her up, and twirled her around, kissing her hard on the mouth.

He didn't look Ingrid's direction when he put the girl down, just draped an arm over her and headed into the locker room.

Ingrid signed up for a trip to Uganda not long after that. Nine months later, she had her ESL certificate, and the sooner her flight left next week, the better.

She hadn't planned on joining her parents at Evergreen this week, but with Kari happily married and little Matty delighting their days, she couldn't deny them this last family outing.

Thankfully, and like she'd suspected, John hadn't returned home.

Ingrid got up, draping the afghan over her shoulders, and headed into the back bedroom. Her Bible lay on her bed, open to what she'd read this morning in Ecclesiastes. *"Cast your bread upon the waters, for after many days you will find it again."*

Her letter to John, creased and dirty, lay in the folds of the Bible, a place-holder. She took it out and closed the Bible. She should probably throw this away. After all, she'd mailed it three times, and each time he'd sent it back.

Message received.

She pocketed it in her jeans, then lay down in the quiet of her room to read. An hour later, creases in her cheek from the bedspread, she woke up to the quiet hush of an abandoned cabin. Rising, she walked out into the living room and discovered the rain had stopped, a watery twilight flooding the lake in reds and purples. She spied Kari and Bradley outside on the shore, her father reading on a chair outside.

"I've made cookies for the campfire tonight," her mother said from the tiny kitchen. "Would you be willing to take some over to the lodge? Poor Chester is still weak from his treatments, and I don't want Eva to think she has to cook for anyone."

Ingrid took the plate covered in tinfoil. "What's wrong with Chester?"

"Cancer." Her mother said it softly. "But they think they got it all, and with the chemo . . ." She folded her hands and sighed. "We never know, though, do we?"

Ingrid shook her head and slipped on her flip-flops.

The path to the lodge was edged with mud, the grass glistening, the sky still mottled with anger. She spied a figure sitting on a chair, blanket wrapped around his shoulders, and for a moment, her heart leaped into the past. To John, wounded and angry, right before he'd begged her to start over.

How she longed to snatch back that moment, or a thousand others, and rewrite their story. But they would have no more fresh starts. And tomorrow she'd leave Deep Haven and never look back.

She climbed the stairs to the deck, and Chester looked over at her. The cancer sucked the life from his face, leaving it gaunt and tired. He wore a flannel shirt and jeans, but he swam in them, the veins on his hand purple and thick as he reached for the cookies. "Your mother is a gem."

"She is. I agree." Ingrid stood there a moment, not sure what to say.

"I don't suppose you'd sit with me for a bit."

She slid onto the picnic table, right where she'd tried to cheer up John so many years ago.

"Your parents tell me you're headed to Africa." His hand snuck in under the tinfoil and emerged with a cookie. He offered it to her, but she shook her head.

"I'm teaching ESL; it's a five-year contract."

"Five years. That's a long time."

She raised a shoulder.

He took a bite of the cookie. He said nothing then, leaning back and closing his eyes. "I'm really going to miss this place."

She frowned. "Where are you going?"

He smiled. "Heaven."

"Oh, Mr. Christiansen—"

"Sweetie. I know it, even if no one else does. And frankly, I'm not sure I'll tell them."

"You mean John doesn't know how sick you are?"

Chester shook his head. "If he finds out, he'll only come home. And that's the last thing he wants right now."

"But he belongs here."

She wasn't sure where that came from, but she felt it, her words as natural as the pine scent scoured up by the rain.

"I mean, I know he wants to play football, but he should be here with you."

"But he has to figure that out for himself. I can't make him love this resort. I can't make him love Deep Haven."

"But he does love Deep Haven; I just know it."

Chester looked at her, a warmth in his eyes that she recognized. "You're right, Ingrid. And when he realizes this . . ." He took a breath. "Well, I was hoping you might be here."

Her mouth opened a little, but she closed it fast. "I don't know what you mean—"

"I mean I'm asking you for the impossible. I'm asking you not to go to Africa. To stay in America and wait for him."

"Mr. Christiansen—"

"I'm going to die, Ingrid. And when I do, he'll need you."

"He doesn't need me. He has that cute blonde—" She winced. "Sorry."

"He doesn't have anyone. He didn't make the draft, so he's playing arena ball in Iowa. Andrea didn't stick around."

Oh. "But he could come back, get on a team, right?"

"Maybe. And the fact that you still believe in him tells me that you still care for him."

She reached for the plate of cookies. "It doesn't matter. I hurt him, and he doesn't want me."

A low chuckle emitted from Chester. "He wants you. And you're right; he wants Deep Haven. And this resort. It's in him, and when he needs it, he'll realize that." He turned to her. "And he'll need you."

She found a cookie, tasted it. The chocolate swam in her taste buds. Savory. Familiar. "I wish that were true, but I don't think so. And I can't wait for a man who is never going to show up."

Chester turned back to the lake. The rain had washed a canoe out into the water. It rode the waves, bobbing closer as they rippled toward shore.

"Cast your bread upon the waters, for after many days you will find it again."

Right. She handed the plate back to Chester. "I'll be praying for you, Mr. Christiansen." She caught his hand, felt the bones, frail and brittle, but he squeezed her hand back, strength in his grip.

"And I will be praying for you. We're really going to miss your smile around here."

She landed a kiss on his cheek before heading back to her cabin. A loon mourned over the water, and she couldn't blame the rain for the wetness against her cheeks.

His father decided to die four minutes into the third quarter. Not soon enough for John to ditch the game at halftime and catch a plane for northern Minnesota, but with him still on the field, lining up to blitz the quarterback.

He didn't get off the line of scrimmage, the running back breezing by him. He should have stayed on the ground, the taste of frustration locked in his teeth.

That felt better than facing the emptiness of Evergreen Resort without Chester Christiansen.

John retrieved the floral arrangement, a big one sent by the Lions Club, and brought it to the house. "I'll be back to get the box of casserole dishes in a minute," he said to his mother, struggling to climb out of his truck. He should have taken his father's old Buick to the cemetery, but he couldn't find the keys. He longed for his motorcycle, but he'd sold that a year ago, tired of the memories, the what-ifs.

He set the arrangement on the Formica countertop and paused, the view of the lake just beyond his parents' sliding-glass doors strangely calling to him. Pristine blue water, lapping against the dilapidated dock, shaggy evergreens waving in the wind. Cirrus clouds dragged across the sky, reluctant travelers.

"He never fixed the dock," John said.

"He left it for the new owner." Eva dropped her purse on the bench by the door.

John tried to shrug off her words. After three generations, the legacy of the Evergreen family resort would pass to different—and unfamiliar—hands.

Funny, he'd always considered that but had never truly felt those words until now.

What if they took down the rope swing by the big oak? Or decided to do something stupid, like upgrade with television sets in the cabins?

He retrieved the casseroles. "How long before the resort changes hands?"

His mother's lined face—aged a decade in the last year—put a knife in his chest. Dad owed them all an explanation, including Mom. He'd told her that he was in remission—and hadn't even mentioned his cancer to John.

But a man didn't survive in the north woods of Minnesota without a Norwegian stubborn streak. Still, his father could have prepared them all, allowed John to pick up the pieces.

Given him a reason to come home. Maybe . . . even to go after Ingrid, beg her forgiveness. Tell her he'd been a fool instead of letting her fly off to Africa.

A stubborn fool who didn't deserve her. She was right to leave him, probably.

"Soon," Eva said in answer to his question. "I made arrangements to go live with my sister in Minneapolis. Maybe I can watch one of your games."

Or maybe it was time for him to face the truth. He hadn't made the NFL, and arena ball only bandaged the wounds, didn't heal them.

"Nathan is coming over later with some paperwork." His mother put enough casseroles in the freezer to outfit them for a year. But that's the kind of town he lived in—no one starved in Deep Haven. "You know, he's making a real name for himself in the real estate business now that his mother is over her cancer."

Not a flicker of resentment from his mother that maybe, just maybe, God might have spared her husband, too.

"I still can't believe he stuck around. He had that cross-country scholarship—"

"Some people simply belong in Deep Haven, honey." Eva patted him on the arm. "By the way, the sink is leaking. Could you take a look?"

He climbed under the sink, found the soggy wood from where the pipe leaked. "How long has it been like this?"

"A year or so."

Of course. Judging by the state of the entire resort, his father had abandoned any repairs long ago. As if he'd already resigned them to the next owner.

Instead of asking his son for help.

Their last real father-to-son conversation had happened when he was eighteen, when he hadn't the wisdom to listen. Now he longed for the old man's quiet voice against the lap of the lake, telling him what to do with his life.

"I need tools."

"Look in the garage." Eva ducked into her bedroom to change out of her mourning dress.

He headed outside past the potholed basketball court to the garage.

Flicking on the light, John paused for a moment. The redolence of grease soaked into the dirt floor, a century of oil and gasoline embedded in the walls. The ancient twin-track snow machine sat dormant, hibernating. He headed toward the tools scattered along the far workbench and squeezed around a long, tarped object propped on sawhorses.

No. He paused for a moment before he flung off the tarp.

The canoe. He stared at it, wordless. Last he saw it, the boulder had gashed a hole in it larger than his fist. He'd told his father to turn it to firewood. He ran his hand over the keel, expecting to rut against the gash. Instead, smooth, fresh wood met his touch.

"He spent all last spring on it. His last project." His mother stood in the door, her eyes glistening. "Take it out."

Take it out. Maybe one last time.

John hoisted the canoe up by the portage pads and carried it out to the lake. A summer wind skimmed the surface as he flipped it, lowered it onto the water. It parted the surface without a sound.

Paddles lodged in the gunwales, and he climbed in the back, retrieved one. The canoe slipped like a prayer through the pristine waters.

And then he saw it. His name, etched in the crossbar next to his father's. The sun warmed it, and he couldn't help but reach out, run his fingers into the grooves. His eyes burned. "Why didn't you tell me?"

A loon answered, a mourning across the water. He paddled the length of the lake, the sun hot on his shoulders, the scent of the pine in the air.

You'll have to find someone else to run this place. Because it's not what I want. In the quiet of the hour, his voice echoed back.

But maybe he did want it. The thought gathered beneath him, sluiced adrenaline through his chest.

How long had he been dodging it? This truth? He belonged here on Evergreen Lake, in Deep Haven. This life, this faith, this legacy. Sure, he'd made a name for himself in the Cities but . . . but maybe not the name he wanted.

Not the life he wanted.

He leaned forward, closed his eyes. The sobs came from deep in his chest, soft until they rushed over him. He put both hands over his head and let them take him, consume him. Wring him out.

He wasn't ready to say good-bye.

I have no doubt you'll be a success at whatever you do.

He'd thought he'd had to leave to become someone, a man. A success.

Maybe he didn't have to. The thought trickled into his grief, parted it.

In fact, maybe that was why Dad fixed the canoe—and nothing else. Maybe he knew.

John leaned back, listening to the lap of the water against the canoe. So much beauty here. Pine trees, shaggy and full amid the white paper birch. The blue of the lake against the aqua sky. He heard the song deep inside and let himself hum it. *"O Lord my God! When I in awesome wonder consider all the worlds Thy hands have made . . ."*

Yes. Maybe his father hadn't called him back because he'd wanted John to discover the beauty on his own. He wiped his eyes.

I'm sorry, Lord. I'm sorry that I despised the legacy my father gave me. The legacy You gave me. It's time for me to come home. Please, help me.

He didn't have to leave. Nathan could help him figure this out, help him withdraw the sale.

Yes, he could stay. Build his own legacy. Raise his own family . . .

Then, as if still drifting across the barren, gray lake, he heard the past, something his father said too long ago. *Isn't it interesting that, against the darkness, God provided light for us to find our way home?*

Light. Like Ingrid's smile, cutting through the darkness of his anger, his stubbornness, his frustration.

He sat up, pressed a hand to his chest.

Wow, he missed her. So much that the ache felt like something he'd never escape. He still remembered the sickness that spread through him as he saw her standing on the sidelines a moment before Andrea landed in his arms.

It irked him the rest of the season, enough that he asked his parents about her last summer when he'd called, just to see if she was there. Enough that he discovered she hadn't married Phil.

Which meant that day in the stands, he'd hurt her as much as she'd wounded him.

Probably she was better off in Africa. But maybe one day she'd come back. On their Saturday night. Maybe he'd even write to her and invite her.

Tell her how he'd really love to see her. How he so desperately missed her smile.

He'd build a home for her and wait.

The waves had nudged the canoe toward shore, so he picked up his paddle and headed in, the sun low in the trees, the golden rays turning the lake to butter.

As he drew near, he saw a woman standing on the dock, a white sundress fluttering in the wind. He put his hand over his eyes to shade his view, and his breath stopped in his chest.

Ingrid raised her hand and smiled.

Even from here, she could undo him, her blonde hair long and straight, pulled back in a hair clip. She was tan and thin, probably from her work in Africa.

He pulled up to the dock, his heart large in his chest. "What are you doing here?" Oh, he didn't mean it like that. He wanted to leap out, to crush her to himself, to touch her hair, run his hands down her arms. But . . .

But what if she returned only to say good-bye?

She reached down for the canoe, wrapping the rope around the dock pegs. "I . . . I was worried."

He climbed out, grabbing the paddle. "Worried?"

She straightened, her eyes just as beautiful as he remembered. "How are you?"

He must be wearing his grief on his face. Still, he shrugged. "I'm okay. I guess. It's hard. He didn't tell anyone and . . . I thought you were in Africa. Um, you didn't fly home for . . . Well, I mean . . ." Oh, boy, he was as eloquent now as he was at seventeen.

"Don't you want me here?" She wrapped her arms around her waist, and he couldn't bear it.

He dropped the paddle. "No. Of course I want you here. I . . ." Shoot, he was tired of holding back, of denying the layer of truth that simmered deep inside. "I missed you, Ingrid. Wow, it hurts how much I missed you, and the fact is, I'm staying. And not because you want me to, but because . . . it's where I belong. I know that. And I also know you have this other life now, but—"

"I didn't go to Africa."

She gave him a smile then, and the power of it rushed over him. Nearly took him out at the knees.

"You didn't?" He no longer cared that he sounded desperate, foolish.

She shook her head. "Your father asked me to wait. He told me that you'd be back and that this time, you'd stay."

"How could he know that?"

"John, really? He was your father. He knew you."

He did, didn't he? The thought washed over him, through him. His dad had done this—given him a home, a future. Ingrid. "I can't believe you . . . you waited for me . . ."

"I've been waiting for you since I was thirteen years old. I don't know how *not* to wait for you, John."

She lifted an envelope from her pocket. Took his hand and pressed it into the palm.

He stared at it. "Your letter."

"You don't ever have to open it. But it says that I'm sorry I didn't believe in you. And that it will never happen again."

He looked up at her, at her incredible blue eyes, glistening in his, at the way the wind teased her hair, at the way she smiled at him, nothing of guile in it.

The way she'd always smiled at him, as if he were her whole world.

"I love you, Ingrid."

"I know." She stepped up and caught his face in her hands. "You've always loved me. It just took you a while to realize it."

Then she drew his head down and kissed him. He couldn't move—not at first. But he wrapped his arms around her and caught up, drawing her into his embrace, his world.

The world they called home.

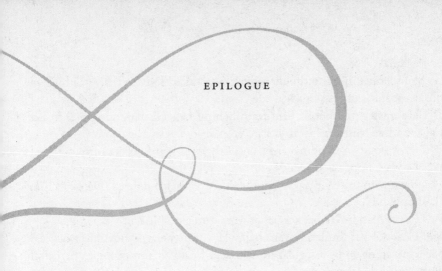

EPILOGUE

1987

Sometimes, she still stood at the edge of the curb, her breath caught, hoping he'd see her across the crowded street. She wore a pretty white dress tonight, her arms and legs tan from the summer working outside, tending the garden, caring for guests. John had rebuilt the basketball court, added a swing set to the yard for the guests' children. His latest project was attaching a rope to the old oak over the lake, at the far end, by the Gibsons' place.

She spotted him through the crowd, talking to Nathan, but didn't raise her hand, didn't try for his attention.

Just stayed there, listening to the band belt out Starship's "Nothing's Gonna Stop Us Now," her hands over her secret, the one still hers alone.

Overhead, seagulls cried out, and the smell of hot dogs sizzling on a nearby grill lingered in the cool summer air. Earlier, the blue-skied day, heavy with marshmallow cumulus clouds had suggested the perfect summer evening. The kind of evening where she and John would sit on the shore, throwing rocks into the lake.

But not tonight.

She wrapped her arms around her waist, swaying, watching. He needed a cut, but she couldn't bear to cut the curls from his dark-blond hair. And those blue eyes—they had the power to hold her captive.

She couldn't take her eyes from him.

Then, as if he heard her, he turned. His smile could steal her breath from her chest. She lifted her hand to wave but didn't have to because he ran toward her, through the crowd.

"Mama!"

She scooped him up, holding his tiny toddler body to her, breathing in the sweet smell of his skin.

"He missed you," John said from behind her. His hand dropped to her waist, and he landed a kiss to her neck.

"I saw you two standing there, and I thought you'd never notice me."

"I always notice you."

"Mmm-hmm," she said, wiping ice cream from baby Darek's chin. "Contraband."

"I can't help it. He has special powers. You gave birth to a charmer."

"I know." She tousled Darek's hair. "Have you been getting into trouble?"

"He's going to be a regular lumberjack. I caught him trying to make off with one of the chain saws."

"Right. And he's also Superman."

"I'm just saying, we have our hands full."

"His father's son." She laughed.

He curled his arm over her shoulder. "I was hoping I'd see you here tonight. Are you feeling better?"

"Must have been something I ate." She kissed the little boy and handed him back to John. He propped Darek on his hip.

"You missed the fish-throwing contest."

"Oh, for sad."

He laughed. Then his voice turned low, husky, the sound of missing her in his tenor. "Will you dance with me?"

She pressed her hand to his whiskered cheek. He smelled of sawdust, the benefits of maintaining his reign as the Deep Haven chain saw champion.

The band strummed an oldie, an England Dan and John Ford Coley song that stirred memories of that first summer, of hope and young love, the promise of so many tomorrows.

"I thought you'd never ask."

Don't miss more great

DEEP HAVEN NOVELS

Romance and adventure on
Minnesota's north shore . . .